Thought Soldier
The Infinite Parallel

DSW SHAW

ISBN:978-1-3999-6471-5

Prologue

AfterSting

I'm alone in the world, but I'm not alone in the dark.

I have raced to my last breath across my poor, dying world in a desperate bid for more days, hours, minutes but, like all my kind, I have reached the finish line only to be confronted by a ravenous bear. With an erection.

It's over for all of us, now. The race is wasted and, as I await the end; this.

Trapped, compressed, pinned on every side, feeling buried alive, the very membranes of my eyes ache from the pressure as I strain to see into absolute blackness, with helplessness my hated companion but joined by the flesh of others in my prison. The tangy reek of their sweat mixes with rotten tooth breath and other, far more cloying bodily stenches that hint at the horrors they might yet inflict on me.

Yes; trapped, but not alone. Never again to be alone. Pressed into this last small space we are all equally embedded in the darkness and all equally doomed.

Yet they are not vulnerable as I am. Despite all that my powers once promised, I am left exposed, naked in my clothes as the warm, moist male flesh presses close and threatens a final horror to precede my pre-booked death. My powers have forsaken me and I am just a woman, now. How easily they might overcome me and use me disposably, for no better reason than a distraction from the nightmare closing inexorably in upon us.

Such distraction is a better reason than I could raise in objection.

And I can hardly play the victim when the devastation all around us is my fault; every life claimed already and the last few still to die press weight against the choking throat of my conscience.

For all the belly-scolding dread of what I might suffer here in the dark, there is nowhere left but this cell because, just outside, there creeps something so much more hideous than human lust, more final than the misery of violation, more unimaginably cold and eternally emptying than such suffering, that I wouldn't even consider it.

It will steal us wholesale and consume our thoughts, our dreams, our hopes, the final beat of the heart and finally the meat from our bones.

I have spent cold, trembling months fleeing death across the dying Earth. I have beaten and been beaten, have gouged eyes and clawed at testicles to save myself for this lonely, pathetic end. I have fed others to the stalking mindless maw out there. We all have. Throw a fellow survivor into its path and win a free day; maybe only an hour. And all the while, that semen-drooling dog called 'hope' has clung tight to my leg and pumped me ever onward, despite the unrelenting misery of my fear.

And now this. Nowhere left to run to. Just waiting. Waiting to be... *consumed*.

But for all my fear of the pain, of the very fact of dying itself, I am, deep within me in a quiet dark place, relieved that there is nothing left now but the end.

I am, finally, done.

I shuffle uncomfortably on the rough and tired velour of the seat beneath me, trying to wedge myself into it, or onto it, but it is unyielding and the worn springs creak as they jab up against my flesh, trapped as they are just beneath the rough cloth, exhausted by the pressure of my body. The dry aroma of dust and ancient farts escapes the seat fabric and mingles with the tangy, throat-clogging rancid stench of musky, unwashed human meat.

The sick irony is that finally, as the end closes in on me, I must face the horrible irony that, for a short time just before all this, I had actually started building a life that was worth fighting for. I'm not even lying to myself this time. A life I had built from nothing. It was a small life, but it was *mine*. It's so fucking unfair. That warm untainted time, finally finding love in those last days and then, of course, Armageddon on final approach, ladies and gentlemen — trays in the upright position, please, as the fan gets brownwashed.

The cold black is closing in, now, and all too soon the last of us, the very last smears of humankind, will be sucked in, gulped down and *digested* as the delusion of reality is torn down around us like old, dry wallpaper.

Everything I thought I had was a squirt of piss in a big ocean of shit. And now the shit's rising up over my chin.

Fuck.

I need to breathe in again, but when I do I'll get to breathe more of this rank air, a stink I must endure just to live on a little longer, robbing the monster roaming my darkening world of its next victim; at least until it reaches here and takes me without ever once seeking my consent.

I am ready to die. But I still want to live. Just for minutes. Maybe only seconds.

All my fault.

I could have been the source of victory in this war, or at least, I could have driven him back. The Enemy.

I wonder, in my terror, how bad it is going to hurt when his hideous avatar overtakes me, seizes me in its grasp, shreds my still-living meat.

I start at a slight movement beside me. It is a man. I smell him. His sweat. His maleness. It has been a long time since I allowed that rank, manly stink so close to me. I can't say I ever much cared for the smell of the male, not even in my brief liaison with... No. That small flower of momentary joy, with *him*, has long-since shrivelled in a desert of misery as dry as the scorched, dead bones of the man with whom I shared it.

Our moment, and not much consolation now, that's for fucking sure.

This nearer male is not the only one in here with me. Stinking in the dark with me, drenched in sweat and fear. Not alone.

There is a sound.

Unexpected in the roaring silence, it is brief.

A soft click.

Greasy yellow light suddenly smears away the worst of the darkness and I glimpse a hairy male hand as it is lowered away from the courtesy light in the ceiling. Two fishy eyes peer out of a sagging, stubble-spattered face that has turned to look back at us in the small pool of grim light, a loose chin draping onto the hairy skin of a shoulder that is bare but for a thin, greyish-white band of vest material. This male is the source of most of the foulness in this place. Although he is the further away of the two, the stench of his rancid flesh is unbearable and I have to swallow hard to keep the chunky bile down below throat level.

"It's gonna cost you," the cabbie burbles, his arm draped across the back of the driver's seat as he eyes us up. Well, Me. He eyes *me* up. In a world where money no longer has any value...

The male beside me stirs in his seat. "We will pay."

There is cold aggression in his voice. A threat. He is being protective.

That's nice.

Pointless, but nice.

The man in the front twists still further to look at us, releasing a tangy waft of armpit stink as he does so. "Fuck am I gonna do with *money!*"

His gaze visits me below the waist and lingers. He belches, as if I might need further convincing that his body, his fluids, were somehow not the tasty treat I had been dreaming of.

The man beside me, my smelly but loyal companion, glances out of the window, where the darkness is far deeper than any night we have ever seen, before leaning forward sharply toward the cabbie.

Shit. I have seen him kill more than once and it's always brutal and ugly. He looks like a man, but he isn't, and his horribly inhuman strength is matched by a total willingness to twist off bodyparts, to extract organs.

"Drive," he states flatly. "I will not ask you again."

The man in the front gives a shrug and a huff, then turns in his seat. "Sake."

A moment later the car vibrates as the engine fires up, and then I am hurled against the seat back. I bounce and my hair clings to the tacky headrest that a million lice have called home during the lifetime of this mouldy old shitheap of a taxi. I shuffle and clumsily right myself, casting an embarrassed glance at the man beside me as I do so.

He is looking at me. At me, not my body, and in an age where the few remaining men still alive have forgotten the difference between consideration and rape, this is a rare thing and something to be savoured.

I let myself gaze back at him. In another life... but he has had another life; this one was never really his. Borrowed, stolen, enrobed in false flesh; he and I were never meant to be together, let alone together here, at the funeral of all existence.

The car swerves and a stunningly bright stripe of fierce white light slices across my vision. Lightning. It casts my companion's strong angular face in flash shadows and then is gone, leaving a scolding after-image burnt into my eyes.

The lightning is a bad sign. It isn't really lightning, but a symptom of the death-throes. We are tiny tadpoles in a vast pond. When the pond is being drained, do tadpoles realise that their universe is ending?

It's coming.

There is the sound of a wet fart, probably a shart, as the terrified cabbie wrenches the wheel round and the car lurches and throws me around on the seat to bump my forehead on the side window. He makes a weak, high noise as he wrestles the wheel to get us on a straight path again, away from the bleak hunter. Even this fetid old creep has forgotten his plans for 'payment' now, with the enemy seeking us through the dusty ruins outside. His fate is tied to ours.

I stare out into the once-again impenetrable blackness and with nothing to do but fear or remember, I find myself thinking of the terrible things I have had to do, have had to sacrifice, just to live this long. Terrible things, done solely for the chance to live on, to persist a little while longer in this pointless shell of a life. I have become cold and cruel, have done bad things and allowed by companion to enact far worse things. Yet *not* through choice. I have seen for myself that there is no milk left in the tit of human kindness.

Two things happen at once.

Lightning bursts into life and whites out the world.

The cabbie squeals like a pig and stomps the brake and I hear myself emit a similar squeal as my world lurches around me.

In the white flare the maw lurches toward us, inexorable, a vast impenetrable blackness sucking earth and grass and glass and concrete into itself.

My cry is joined by the naked animal shrieks of my companions. I smell shit and don't know if it is mine of theirs.

We have been reduced to the primal fear of the prey beast.

The maw is an absence of everything, a sentient black hole, yet from the core of it something is emerging, spewing forth even as our reality is sucked in and consumed – perhaps some new and emerging reality destined to replace our universe once we are gone. Chaos from form, ruin from matter. Who knows. All I am sure of is this simple truth: I am going to die now.

I lunge forward and grab the cabby's shoulder and shake at it violently.

"Drive, you cunt!" I shriek at him. *"For fuck's sake, drive!!!"*

The shoulder collapses beneath my hand, the skin a mere veil of dust that puffs free of him and exposes bone beneath his vest strap as his meat crumbles like ancient cheese and his head rolls around toward me.

I am faced with the milky, drying eyes and twisted, folding face of a relic. He has been reduced to fungal dust and powder by the mere approach of that void. Its sharp-knifed castration of the physical laws has reached out to touch and destroy him.

But I know his mind will be alive in there, screaming out in impotent silence.

His head folds down into his chest, and his chest crumbles into his vest.

I turn to my companion and see the same hopeless sorrow in his gaze as there must be in my own. "We're too close. It's over."

He takes my hand in his great paw as he sits back into his seat. Acceptance will drive away the last vestiges of fear.

We are in the middle of an atrophy zone.

It's over.

Resignation breeds hopeless relief. Our battle, our journey, is done.

The relentless march of the maw sounds like a grossly oversized heart thudding away, or a death factory labouring on, pounding matter to oblivion out there in the darkness, swallowing great chunks of it, until all too soon the car around us will suddenly shred and the light will wink abruptly out.

"Laura," my companion murmurs.

I close my eyes, hearing my name spoken for the last time, and grip his hand tight.

His hand is gone. I open my eyes and glimpse, just for a moment, the composite alien form beneath his human façade, but then that, too, is gone and I am alone to await my fate.

My greatest enemy. My last and only friend.

Loneliness kicks me in the belly and fear returns like a freight train packed with scolding adrenaline.

Biting down to control my mortal dread, I close my eyes. Draw a breath. There is nothing to do but await the moment when my own flesh will fall prey to the brutal, primal force of un-creation. Wait for that cold, hideous touch.

The fate of the universe was in my hands. Such great power had been entrusted to me, yet for all my arrogant presumption I failed.

Hot bitter tears squeeze out to wet my closed lashes; tears of self-pity for the girl I was, for the woman I should have become, for the opportunities I missed.

I feel a pull against my flesh, gasp with the realisation of the arriving moment and then I am wrenched outward in all directions at once. Pinching pain becomes clawing pain very quickly as I feel my skin stretch and split in raw red rips. I shriek as my right shoulder opens, my left breast is torn in two and, utterly cripplingly mortally terrified I feel my skin break free.

There is raw pain like an extracted tooth, with that same sensation of cold air touching internal things, but all over me. My skinned breasts, my flayed belly, my eyelids peeled to expose watering eyeballs and then a flash and darkness as my corneas are pinched off like onion skins.

I want, I need to scream but that which made my voice is gone and, as my muscle turns into pie crust and breaks up, the physical pain ends. The nerve endings in my dying meat have finally shorted out and the fear of pain ends to leave only the fear of death itself.

There is a distant, raw ache, like that extracted tooth on the second day.

Pieces of me flutter away like the dusty corpse remnants of a huge moth squashed by a slipper. I know it is happening but I don't know how, because my senses are all but gone.

Blind now, deaf, without even the sensation of air blowing over my dusty crumbled skin, I am dimly aware as the last of my meat flees my bones to be chewed up in the maw.

Freshly cut free, I feel my mind exposed, the last of me, so that I know my body has died. All that remains is my mine, winking out more slowly in the abyss, this once-mighty weapon in my arsenal, now a drifting remnant screaming a formless protest against death, voiceless yet shrieking uselessly into the void in a last act of desperate protest as everything that ever existed of me finishes to be lost and forgotten.

My final cry exists only in a mind that is closing and it echoes, momentarily, in a last slice of existence until, all too suddenly it, too, is consumed and there is no me.

-1-

I hadn't been sleeping well for a while. A good few years, in truth, but I hated doctors in general and mine in particular (fucker always mentioned my weight), so rather than face up to it, I'd fallen into the habit of staying up with a nip of something (maybe two), usually watching some trash TV until I got myself deadweight tired.

Whisky worked best, although my one close friend had very subtly hinted that I should give it up; at least when we were out together. She was subtle about it, too. Her exact words were, as I recall, 'You look like a fuckin' geezer, Laur, get a girl's drink for fuck's sake.'

By which, of course, she meant that by proxy, because she was out with me, I made her look gay and hence less likely to harpoon herself a live-specimen 'fit' male willing to harpoon her right back before sprawling asleep across her tits.

My pal Jen. Bless her. Champion penis eater.

Still, it was advice well-ignored and, as usual, by Late O'clock on this, as any, warm summer's night, the whisky had done its job nicely and I killed the TV as I felt a cosy haze of fatigue cuddle up around me.

I trudged heavily up the stairs of the old family home, the moon-blue light from the landing window washing across the ghastly floral wallpaper, as my bare feet pressed into the rough hessian threads of the stair carpet and took me to my room.

The bed was more welcoming than it had been in a long while as I nudged Basil the Bear off my pillow and, with a yawn, pressed my feet between the cool sheets, slid down and sank into the fresh doughy chill of my pillow.

Halfway between dream and reality already, I imagined my hair billowing out on that pillowy whiteness like a girl from one of those romantic films.

Yes, yes. I know you're thinking it. Soppy bitch; but in that moment I was a perfect fit for that romantic movie moment. OK, so most movie actresses these days don't have backsides that the kindest of their friends would call 'ample', but come on; give a girl her delusions.

Besides, it was late and I was more than a little bit tweatybirds, what with the whisky, so cut me some fucking slack here.

I tucked the top of the sheet under my breasts, lifted my behind to uncrumple my bedshirt and drew my eyelids down hopefully.

Opened my eyes again with a sigh.

A cool breath caressed my throat and puckered my nipples as a light summer breeze sighed at the window, transforming the net curtain into an ephemeral ghost that danced in the moonlight streaming in from outside. I lay, lightly dazed by booze and fatigue, and waited for sleep to claim me. Faintly I heard my alarm clock ticking and wondered if I had remembered to set it, prevented by the alcoholic haze from bothering to sit up and check.

I was nagged by the ingrained certainty that it was wrong not to care about being late for work. It's odd how, when life is safe, being first into the office on a Monday morning can seem like the most important thing in the whole of Creation.

A light seemed to be glowing on the headboard above me. Startled, I tilted my head back to look, worried it might be a spider caught in the moonlight, but as I moved my head I saw that my headboard was

Gone.

Whoa.

"Fuck meh–!" I uttered as I lurched into what should have been a sitting position, but which actually sent me staggering as my feet slammed down hard onto a cold, rough surface and a cutting wintry chill sent jagged micro-cramps into my foot arches and pulled my toes into curled claws.

It was not just my headboard that was gone, it was my entire bedroom.

I looked up gain. Where my headboard had been, I now saw an ancient and very worn iron streetlamp, from which a rheumy yellow glow rebuked my doubt, while far above that streetlamp hung a night sky. A much darker night sky than the one that had been outside my bedroom window, this one bereft of stars or moon and radiating a merciless chill.

A *winter* sky.

Its utter blackness seemed ominous in a way that the real night sky never did, as though it were the sky of some sinister alien place that I should never have to visit.

My head spun a little, reminding me that I'd been drunk before this happened. Was I dreaming? I didn't remember falling asleep, but...

My vision swam as I looked around myself. I was outdoors. Standing outdoors, impossibly, beside the archaic iron streetlamp, my bare feet pressed onto freezing cold concrete, in an alleyway overgrown on one side by skeletal bushes and bordered by a rough stone wall. Tall black iron fence bars curved up from the stone wall, provoking a really creepy sense of familiarity that gave me a shiver.

I wavered now, tottering on my feet. A chill of wintry wind fluttered my nightshirt and sliced into my thighs, my belly and my rapidly-crinkling nipples. I glanced down at the numbing cold sensation at the lowest end of me and saw my bare feet pressed onto that icy cold pavement. I could feel cramp coming. I didn't have long.

Shit.

I clapped my arms around myself reflexively as my body began to shiver violently, from this shocking icy gloom, the searing coldness that lanced the bottoms of my feet evoking a predictable yet gruesome cramping that caused my toes to curl violently.

"Fu-uck!"

The word fled on a pillow of cloudy breath, but I regretted it as it filled the silence and alerted anyone lurking out there to my helpless semi-naked presence.

My nipples were puckered so tight, I was in danger of having my tits turn inside out, and as my only saleable asset I really didn't want that, so I clasped my arms tighter around myself, trying in vain to retain some bodyheat.

It was a killing cold. Real. This was no dream.

I had fallen into this place halfway along the narrow length of a grey-concrete alleyway that curved out of sight in both directions, bordered on both sides by stone walls, wintry bushes to one side and, weirdly, pervaded by a faint smell of burning toast.

I sniffed.

Yep. Definitely toast, but the weak aroma so lost that it was as though it were a smell from somewhere else that had lost its way and become trapped here along with me.

The street lamp above me was one of three on this stretch of the alleyway, each casting a weak ivory oasis in an otherwise oppressively dark place. To escape, I'd have to venture out into the darkness.

What the fuck was going on?

And yet, I was struck by a realisation...

This place was not as alien to me as it should have been. Somehow, I sensed that I had been in this place before, maybe in another... dream?

The wind's icy fingers lashed my belly once again, a sensation too shockingly vivid to be a part of any dream. This was real, impossibly, and I was in real trouble.

When you're up to your neck in shit you can either start swimming or start swallowing – and despite what may have been written on the wall of a school toilet long ago, I had never been one to swallow.

I drew a deep breath, tried to ignore the pounding of my heart, the thuds hard enough to rock my body, and strode off in the direction I'd been facing since I arrived.

Ow, ow; fucking co-old! Bare feet on icy concrete. I had to move; it hurt, but I had to. But it *fucking* hurt.

As soon as I moved off the spot where I had landed, I noticed a sound, building up from somewhere off in the distance but getting closer. At first I thought it might be the blood pounding in my head, but as it grew louder it became industrial, a throbbing whump like the workings of a distant factory, or a giant mechanised heartbeat. Definitely getting closer.

Despite the cramping in the arches of my feet, I stepped up the pace in the hope that I could just walk out of this insanity as quickly as I had plopped into it.

The noise built rapidly and seemed more melodic, more organic, much more like a great giant heart, now, pumping existence into this impossible place.

I ran, then.

Ran like a fucker, panic creating a wild, mindless, stumbling tumble, my crinkled nipples rubbed raw against my rough tee-shirt, my toes and heels shedding skin and blood onto the freezing concrete, but not caring as that noise built to a crescendo, became the ravenous panting of some vast pursuing beast.

At my shoulder. About to pounce.

My legs declared *Independence* and I pitched headlong at the concrete. I managed to get a hand out, scraping it horribly but breaking my fall enough that I could roll onto my back and then, exhausted, my lungs scolded by each gulp of icy air, was able to clamber clumsily into a sprawled sitting position.

I was glad in that moment that I always wore bedpants. The indignity of the fall was only slightly relieved by its lack of gynaecology, but still, the relief was faintly there.

Silence.

I sat, cold and trembling, on the cold pavement.

The noise was gone. I seemed to be alone.

I started to clamber up and cried out as my aching calves failed and spat shards of pain into me. I bit my lip and forced my legs under me, hands grabbing at the unforgiving stone wall beside me as I straightened up.

I was stunned into forgetting my pain by the realisation that there was a man watching me.

He was in shadow, just beyond the halo of the nearest streetlamp.

I made a noise halfway between the word 'oh' and a dry gulp. Then, composing myself, I tried again.

"Hello?"

Nothing. The figure did not move, not even slightly.

"Erm, hi?"

Silence, and no sign of life.

"Erm, I don't suppose there's any way you *didn't* just see my bum, is there?"

A hopeless attempt at levity. The figure seemed unmoved.

I went to speak again.

The figure lumbered two paces closer.

"No, really," I gabbled, real fear welling up at the realisation that I was completely alone with this someone. Alone, exposed and in a cold and lonely place.

The figure lumbered forward another step and passed into the pale cream pool of the streetlight.

And now, a spray of acid burst loose in my belly.

All fear of the human horrors I might face were buried in the avalanche of this new nightmare, this vaguely human-shaped thing with some sort of hat, possibly a Stetson such as a cowboy might wear.

Human-shaped; but not human. This was no man.

It resembled a man in the most basic sense. It had two eyes, a nose, a mouth; even a torso with four limbs. But there any semblance ended. This… thing, had two glistening black orbs mounted too far to the sides of its head for human eyes, and where the nose should have been was a downswept beak – a beak like a mad cartoon bird, that curled so far down across its face that it bisected the thing's slitty black reptilian lips.

I felt warmth on my inner thighs and a pattering and pooling around my feet.

Great.

First Contact, Day One Protocol: Laura Keeble pisses herself.

On the left breast of the creature's dark, smooth tunic shone a disc divided up into twelve segments, each flickering a weak light of a different colour. A smaller, unlit white disk protruded at the centre of this weird array and, as the creature's beak rose slightly to allow its hideous black lips to stretch apart, the small white disk lit up bright in the gloom.

"*Laura,*" A soft, sibilant voice whispered, deep inside my mind.

Too much. Way, way too much. Its insipid voice slithered through me, touching every private recess of my mind and leaving smears like snot and slugs, as welcome as an uncle's tongue between my legs

the light swirled… dizzy, nauseous

My bedroom.

My ticking clock.

Basil the Bear.

Gasping, tangled in wet sheets, my skin chilled by a sweet leaf-rustling breeze, backlit in ghostly blue-white by the moon. Clammy and terrified, I was back in my bed. Safe.

I moved gingerly and felt, with a sinking feeling, a sloppy wetness rapidly cooling on the cloying sheets matted around my legs.

With a mortified groan I peeled the sheets free, my body still trembling from the fear wrought by the dream but my mind wracked by the humiliation of wetting the bed like a fucking kid.

-2-

While others with more sense were just awakening to a gloriously bright summer sun pouring through their windows, with the realisation of its being Monday morning still some minutes away from ending their joy, I already stood, dressed, smart but bleary-eyed before the alter of the office coffee machine.

A coffee machine that didn't seem to like the idea of making me a damn coffee.

Fighting the urge to grind my teeth together, aware of what the dentist had said, I waited as the steel-sided bastard whined, clicked and clonked instead of filling the piteously tiny cup I had placed so appealingly beneath its spout.

"Bastard."

I could smell dust from the worn carpet tiles of the coffee room, the faint greasy tang of machine oil, but no scent of coffee at all, no glimmer of hope that a pixie deep in the belly of the damn thing might be busily brewing away on my behalf. That is how these things work, right?

My right hand came up and touched my lips and I hastily turned the knuckles toward my teeth before nibbling could start to happen on those fingertips and their succulent nails. Another warning from the dentist.

Besides, it'd cost me a lifetime of tending and cultivating to get that measly millimetre of white to peer over the edge of my fingertips, so I was buggered if I'd lose them now just because some anus had forgotten to service the vending machines over the weekend.

I lowered that same hand to my hip and smoothed out my work skirt, humming a tune faintly, drawing my eyes away from the machine with some difficulty, yet determined to feign indifference.

I don't really care if you give me a coffee or not. It's your professional pride at stake.

My bluff that seemed to trick the machine.

I concealed my relief, my gratitude as a splash of coffee emerged, to be followed by a more persistent pattering tumble of brown liquid into my cup. The brief moment of tension over, I pressed my lips together to stifle a yawn that had crept up on me unawares as I reached for the cup.

"Heavy weekend?" asked a voice from behind me.

I turned to see a man. I had the idea that his name might be Michael, but really my overall feeling was that I didn't want to speak to his rough face nor listen to his harsh voice. I wanted coffee, not men. No, not men today. Men belonged in a different compartment of my life, in which I enjoyed the best romance and the steamiest seduction that literature or streaming could offer.

I had pulled the plastic coffee cup free of the machine's clingy clasp and was moving it toward my lips when Michael the Man grinned, revealing off-white teeth that leaned in all directions like the oldest of the gravestones in the boneyard opposite my house.

"That'll be me then," he said, making no sense at all.

The cup stopped close to my lips and a frown crinkled into place above my eyes.

He pointed at the machine. "I'm next at the caffeine fountain, pet."

Did this dick think he knew me?

"Excuse me," I said curtly as I moved to pass him and tried to sip coffee at the same time. Bad idea. The on-the-move sip cost me a sloppy scold of hot liquid against my pursed lips, setting off a buzz of pain and possibly a blister for me to enjoy later. Fucksake.

I glared at Michael as I departed, allocating blame where it genuinely belonged.

"Blimey, that really was a heavy weekend–"

The slam of the coffee room door silenced his twat remark and spared me any more of his prattle.

In the main office, coffee cup pinched between finger and thumb and bag hugged against my breasts, I made straight for my desk, the first grin of the day splitting my face because I was in so, so early; I'd beaten almost all of my I.T. Co-workers into the office today.

Well, apart from Michael, but fuck him, he was on a different project to me.

I reached my team's four-desk bay, or 'pod' as the nerd establishment had re-branded them, where I grabbed another hasty sip of coffee before dumping the cup onto my 'Gold Coasting' coaster so I could fumble in the cubby under my desk for my laptop.

The laptop clacked down onto my desk and my faithful black 'work' bag dropped to the floor.

My job didn't suck, really. Sometimes, I quite enjoyed it.

I logged in from a standing start, squinting and tapping flat little keys as my bottom sank comfortably into the richly padded office chair behind me, my left hand plugging the power cord into the little port on the laptop without checking the battery. Fuck the battery; company-issue machine. Mains was best – no risk of the stupid thing cutting me off mid-sentence if I ignored the low battery warnings.

Nope, this wasn't a bad job; and the pay was better than a kick in the tits.

I opened my email for a quick check of the latest updates to my work, but the laptop wasn't connected to anything yet, so I decided to worry about email updates later and instead focused on the some twenty sheets of crumpled A4 piled across the desk. I'd been a smart Laura and printed a lot of shit out on Friday, just in case there was a Monday morning lag on the server connection while the I.T Support nerds downstairs finished wiping off their weekend wanksite material from the company machinery.

There was no way their glistening little penises were going to prevent me capitalising on being the first of my team to get in. I'd even beaten Ben today. Monday victories were small but satisfying.

Just as well, too, because if Ben had beaten me in he'd have had a bitch-fit over the paper print-outs I'd left on my desk over the weekend. *Clean desk policy, Laura.* Another dick I was forced to deal with.

I cast an eye over the first sheet. Tossed it aside.

Tried a second. Tossed that aside too.

Then a third.

"Fucking hell, Jen!" I hissed, careful to limit my volume now that there was an initial hum of other people's voices beginning to percolate through the office.

It was a project Jen and I were teamed-up to work on, with her designing and me writing the code. Except the design materials she'd completed, the ones I had so diligently printed out, were bollocks.

The whole pile was a waste of the paper it had been printed on, no more like a design spec than the cheap paperback novel jutting out the top of my bag. As usual, my friend had failed to come up with the goods, but more annoyingly I had stayed behind late on Friday to print this shit out. *And* I'd got in early today, all ready to impress the boss with my early delivery on a first-cut prototype.

I could have so easily knocked the shit out of a prototype before Ben even arrived, except for my bitch so-called friend, whose shoddy work had let the side down again.

I puffed my cheeks, leant back in my chair, tugged in the bunchie holding my ponytail until it drew the hair painfully tight, and played it through in my mind. I had been early, ready to go, go, go – so none of this could possibly stick to me. I'd just have to throw Jen under the bus. It was her fault, after all.

A voice behind me completed my misery. "Good morning, Ms Keeble."

I turned to face Ben, our team leader, as he slid a shiny blue suit jacket off the narrow slope of his shoulders and straightened the ocean of white shirt bagging loosely around his pencil-thin trunk.

I sighed. "Morning, Ben," I said, smiling but ensuring he could see that I was putting it on.

He gave me his customary curt, humourless smile. "Good weekend? Caught up with your sleep?"

Somehow, I was more famous for my insomnia than my work, but regardless, there was no way I wanted to reinforce Jen's gossip-mouthed rumour-mongering by discussing my sleep problems with my team leader.

None of his damn business. Sometimes I didn't sleep very well. So what? I'd had a rough start in life, seen my parents die in the twisted wreckage of the family car and had to live with the most miserable bastard-shaped grandfather the world had even known. So, fine. Sometimes I didn't sleep too well. He could fuck all the way off and stay there for an extra week.

I silently shrugged off the wave of resentment. "Ben, we need to talk."

His right eyebrow lifted and his lips pursed very slightly. "Let me guess."

I gave a half-shrug.

"Ms Sullivan."

The crumpled A4 was bunched in my hand already, though I had no memory of grabbing it. Still, I held it up like a brandished sword and waved it at my boss. Well, *line manager;* Ben was hardly senior management material.

I shook the crap in my hand. "Ben, just look at this shit!"

My voice sounded appealing, not assertive. Bad; not the right tone at all.

Ben held up a hand. "Well, well. Easy now. What's the *actual* problem?"

"The *actual* problem? The...?"

Too far the other way, I wasn't angry with Ben, I Needed him on my side.

I took a deep breath. "Sorry. Sorry, Ben, but it'll take me all day to sift through this crap and sort out the design logic, I mean she knew I was going to work late Friday and I got in early today and if she'd done the updates I asked her for...."

His face was blank, his eyes glazed, his mouth set in an impassive line. Badly handled, Keeble; badly, badly handled.

I drew a deep breath. Tried again. "What's the point of breaking my neck to get in early if Jen's going to let me down like this?"

"Right. OK." He sighed. "I'll have a chat with her, Laura, but are you absolutely sure this time?"

"What? Yes. Ben, I just... thank you."

"Good-ho." He span his chair to face his desk and shortly afterwards his laptop landed on his desk, his work now able to start.

I kept my head down to crack on as much as possible for the next thirty minutes, confirming that Jen's design model really was as crap as I'd first thought, so even as I sat poring over the now-crumpled hardcopy, I felt reassured that, even though my friend was in the shit, at least none of this reflected badly on me.

"I think I'm gonna need another coffee," I muttered to myself.

About to rise, I sensed Jen before she arrived. Probably her perfume. It gave me time to prepare myself. She was my best friend, after all, but I could not afford to back down, not even for her. This was business.

Career, romance, friendship. Perspective.

A distinctly acrid tang of perfume wafted into the pod and was followed, a moment later, by the slim-hipped, bouncy-breasted blonde form of Jennifer Sullivan, all long bronze legs and no knickers, a pack of silk cut and a slinky winking mobile phone clasped together in a single crimson-taloned hand as her ultra-high heels clacked against the floor and sent her hurtling toward her desk.

I watched, in peripheral vision, as my friend dumped her lumpy woven shoulder bag onto her desk, flicked her shoulder-length tresses of luxuriant blonde hair away from her face and flashed a vampiric crimson-lipped grin my way.

"Allo, Laur!" she cried, a pearly-white grin detonating at close range and threatening to take me down with it. "I'm all yours as soon as I get myself outside of a fuckin' coffee, babe!"

There was no response time available as She banked sharply back out of the pod with just time to ruffle Ben's hair as she flashed past him. "Mornin', Benny *baby*!"

Ben's flinch and mortified grimace happened behind his feigned absorption in his PC screen, resolutely ignoring the reality of the oestrogen warhead that had just flown off toward the coffee room.

When she returned a few minutes later, a plastic coffee cup snared between her red-painted talons, she drew her chair toward me and flashed another pearl-white grin at me. And a glimpse up her skirt that proved she *was* wearing panties, after all. Nice, crisp, white ones. Satin, from the momentary glimpse.

I smiled. Couldn't stop myself. She had that effect on me, even when, as now, I was trying to cling on to my righteous anger.

My friend was gazing expectantly at me, now.

I had to say something. "Good weekend?"

She nursed the hot coffee cup between both palms and leant forward across bare, bronzed, folded legs. "Fucking shit, babe. You?"

I shrugged and mumbled, knowing that I would *never* get away with failing to share gruesome, preferably sexual details; true or otherwise.

But surprisingly my friend squinted appraisingly at my face and pouted. "Fuck, babe, sorry! You really did have a shit one, didn't you? You OK?"

"Erm, look, Jen," I said, cutting across the small talk with a professional tone as polished as her nails. "This design you left me…"

"Ain't it grand?" she gushed, her breath all mint and her eyes so, so alive.

"No," I answered, fighting hard against her charm. "It's a total mess, I don't know where to start."

Her eyes flicked to the side, as though she could sense the disapproving frown Ben had now aimed at her back, could perhaps hear the echoes of my betrayal.

Her eyes narrowed, lips tightening slightly. "OK. What's the problem?"

"It, it's just—" I began, my confidence decaying like a dead rat on a summertime patio.

"Save it." She lashed a talon in the direction of my laptop. "Bring up the designs and show me the problem."

She rolled her chair closer, all business now that I had challenged her to a cage fight.

I pulled the laptop closer and tapped through to the shared folder on the company network drive. Clicked into a sub-folder called 4.1.1, where the design in question was stored.

She wasn't going to catch me out this time; the evidence was right there for all to see.

"Erm, what you doin' there, babe?" she asked innocently, her voice as sweet as syrup and suddenly as loud as buggery – intended for Ben's ears, although I still couldn't see how she could wiggle out of this one.

I glanced at her and faced her innocent, silken pout. "You said show you the designs. These *are* your designs, aren't they?"

Her finger stabbed at the screen, the nail puckering the thin membrane and the pad leaving a greasy print on its surface. "That's 4.1.1."

"Yes—"

The reply died in my throat.

I could see it now, and there was probably an email in my inbox telling me, too.

"You been working from an old version, Laur? You should be lookin' at 4.1.2, babe, didn't you see my email?"

I knew Ben was listening to this whole exchange with poisonous interest.

Jen tapped the screen again. "Four-One – *Two*."

Oh, bukkake.

Why didn't I wait for my emails to update? Fuck. I had printed out version 4.1.1, logged off and gone home about twenty minutes before an email arrived from Jen telling me she had fixed all the issues in the latest release, version four-point-fucking-one-two.

Oh, my dying ego. The updates in the 4.1.2 files were *all* from Friday.

I *had* to save myself. My *boss* was watching this bitch-queen's size two stiletto slice off the floppier of my two breasts.

"An email, Jen? You sent me an email? I didn't get it 'til it was too late, I was here at the crack of dawn…"

"Save it, Laur, OK, just don't. Have some dignity."

Now there was anger burning my cheeks and stinging my eyes. "No, you, you!"

Time to shut up and row the boat *away* from the crocodiles.

"Sorry, Jen," I said quietly.

The word tasted like a swig of someone else's vomit.

She briefly touched my shoulder. "No harm done, babe. We'll sort it together, right?"

Ohhh, she was going to milk the graciousness cow til its tits bled, now that I was lying dead in a pool of my own stupidity.

I turned face-on, looked her in the eyes, touched *her* arm and leant in close. "Really," I said. "Sorry."

"I know." She nudged my arm and grinned at me. "C'mon, let's just fucking do it, eh?"

She leant in close, the fleshy tops of her breasts wibbling in the periphery of my vision as her already low-cut top gaped and her red talon took control of my laptop, genuinely intending to help me get started.

Oh, such a beautiful thing that had cut me down and left bleeding and pissing on the office carpet tiles. And now, despite my being a total bitch, she was going to work with me to get it done.

I stared into her piercing green eyes and wondered what to say. My shallow friend had shown so much more character, more integrity, than I had. I felt pressure behind in my eyes and looked away quickly before I blubbed and made a show of myself. *More* of a show of myself.

She let me have a moment.

"OK, babe," she murmured conspiratorially, "while we're pretending to work, how about we make plans for the week? A few late-p.ms to help the time go by, no?"

I felt like I was adrift. I glanced up at her. "What?"

"Plans," she repeated. "This week. Tomorrow. You, me, partying. Bock, rock and cock."

I knew which of us would be doing all of the cock. Er, penis; *men.*

"Oh Jen, I don't think..."

"Just as well, babe, it's better when I do the thinking anyway. 'Yes, Jen, I'd love to.' There, that was easy."

There was a pause while I studied her earnest green eyes.

"Oh, Jen!" she cried suddenly, startling me. "you're the bestest pal a girl could ever have!"

I laughed and she joined me, the terrible hatchet job I'd planned for her almost forgotten now as we settled into the accustomed rhythm of our friendship,

Her smile faded a little. "Hey, babe, you would say if you didn't want to go, right? I mean, I know I can be pushy lately."

"It's fine," I replied gently. "I know it's been tough since you and Steve..."

Oops. The dreaded subject: Jen's ex. Ouch.

Luckily, Ben broke into our conversation, inadvertently saving me from my *faux pas*. "Do you ladies have enough to do, or should I assign you some more work?"

"Leo's, tomorrow night." Jen flashed me her ultra-white grin before turning in her chair. "We're in it, on it and over it, Benny Baby!"

I focused on my laptop, ready to ride out the tide of shit Ben was about to wash over me, but he left it at that. For now. There was going to be a reckoning, I was sure.

Jen and I were left to crack on and we did, with the hours flitting away and the coffee going down smoooth. We missed lunch completely, which I saw as a plus given that I had my eye on a dress that currently only existed in sizes *one* to *not-for-you-chubby*, and by the time everyone else began to switch off their machines and call goodnight in scattered enclaves around the office, we had most of the work done and I had a faint but persistent headache.

When Ben left before us, I knew I'd had as good a day as I could ever have hoped to claw back after that dismal opening humiliation.

Laptops in our desks, cubbies locked, we gathered our stuff to go and after a quick ride in a stuffy lift I hit the cloying London streets and its beer-stale warm air.

It was the end of a scorching day and the streets had not yet given up all their stored heat, while people sweated into shirts and blouses and feet reeked from within designer shoes. There was a foamy sweet aroma of booze in the air, too, as people made the most and grabbed a drinky-poo on the way home from work.

Jen only lived one town over from me, but it was enough to put her on a different train, so we said goodbye at Liverpool Street and took our respective tubes of hot sweat home.

As my train pulled into the station, I saw my yellow MGB Roadster, 'Mickey', sitting patiently on the cooling tarmac of the carpark, and knew I had made it through the day.

The corrupted remains of a once-strong man twitched feebly on the bed. He would have been beyond hearing me even if this were not a dream, but it was and, more importantly, I knew this time that it *was* just a dream.

"Darling," the man's wife murmured close to his face, her cumbersome skirts and bulky upper garments rustling as she bent low over him. "Darling, what do you need?"

He moved his head a tiny fraction to the left, and a thin stream of drool oozed from his dusty lips and painted a moist trail across his flaky baked cheek.

I moved forward so the wife wouldn't block my view as she glided attentively about the bed, her rumpled brow catching the weak glow of the gas lamp as she fussed about the dying man's pillow, doubtless wishing there was something she could do actually do for hubby.

On tiptoes I could peer over her bony shoulder to watch the man, and as he came into view I picked up a faint smell of stale exhaled tobacco. A familiar, acrid smell remembered from early childhood, back in those few brief, warm years when my father was alive.

Daddy always remembered come up to kiss me goodnight late on Saturday nights, when he returned home from his club, and always in the dreamy phase between waking and dreaming that same tobacco smell would come to me blended with the tang of alcohol. Daddy smell.

I started and shook myself, pushing away the melancholy memory.

"Easy, James," the wife was saying, her fingertips gently pressing his breastbone as he tried to rise from the smeary yellowed pillow. He sank back down all too easily, even the small effort of rising momentarily drawing a hiss of hard-earned breath from between his splintered lips.

"James?"

I realised before the wife did, that this latest exhaled breath had been too long, too sustained. That it was, in fact, his last. I stepped around her now and saw the wetness of life already fading from his still eyes, his skin losing what little pinkness it had possessed as it set into the waxy bloodless whiteness of death.

Finally.

A terrible thing to think, I know, but he was just a dream person, not real, and I was keen to be on my way.

There was a soft sob from the wife and, somewhere behind her, further back in the room, beyond the weak yellow pool of lamplight, a rustle of skirts as someone else left the room.

I found myself drawn, fascinated, to the dead man's eyes. His wife, his bedroom, the lamp, were reflected faintly now in the rapidly drying moisture held there, although my own reflection was, of course, nowhere to be seen.

The Daddy smell was gone from him now. No more breath.

A rustle of skirts behind me signalled the arrival of some person whose task would be to lay out the body for the relatives to view; all except the wife, of course, whose memories had been forever tainted by bearing witness to his passing.

My attention snapped back to the recesses of those eyes. I had seen movement.

Impossible.

Silly fool! Of course there hadn't been…

I had no time to cry out as I was sucked from the room. My body, such as it was in this dream state, was wrenched from the musty brown room and pulled *through* those cooling dead eyes. I was plunged headlong down a vast flickering red tunnel, glimpses of places and moments hurtling past as I fell deeper and deeper, unable to cry out as I helplessly followed his unbound soul on its final journey downward.

As shockingly as it had started, the journey ended. My feet slammed down hard onto rough cold stone and I felt the chill cut up through my toes and heels. Just like the previous dream. The shock of cold was too real to ignore and I gulped a sharp intake of breath that pulled thick, rank, wet air into my lungs.

Suddenly, this was much less like a dream.

I squinted into the shadows, although I knew what was out there, its cold dead form my companion sharing this tomb of grey stone, the chill of death sunk right through it. I had not followed the path of the man's soul, whatever that means, but the path taken by the flesh he should have left behind. Why was his body here – was this his family crypt?

The staleness of the cloying air was peeled back for a moment as a chill waft of air blew gently across the body that I sensed, more than saw, through the gloom.

Either the light got stronger or I started to dream more vividly, because the shrouded corpse of the man called 'James' was visible now. It was not in a coffin. There was a wooden casket nearby, but it was split open and cast aside against the far wall. The body itself had been lain on a stone slab, still tangled in a grimy shroud soaked in seeped bodily fluids.

As the wind blew again, the shroud was rolled off the corpse, exposing its softening white flesh. This was a breeze with purpose.

A moment later, I sensed a presence. Instantly I felt a warm dry breath at my right ear. A shudder trailed fingers down my spine and the knowledge that this was a dream didn't prevent a gut-gnawing claustrophobia from cramping my body.

I was not alone with this putrefying corpse; there was an unseen spectre lurking here too.

The corpse jerked as though electrified. Then, the entire body began to ripple, its skin undulating in the half-light, a fleshy sack being filled anew with some sickening parody of life. False life.

I backed slowly away with a growing sense of horror, as the body began to swell from within. The muscles beneath its skin creaked and swelled, the head lolled back and rolled to one side. Suddenly I was staring at the dead man's face. one white cataract of an eye lolled slightly open and gazed lazily at me while the other fought to cling to its eternal sleep, the mouth open and lopsided in a final grimacing protest.

I heard a scream and knew it must be mine.

Both of the corpse's dead blank eyes sprang wide open, the dry lips cracked as the mouth opened too, and then my scream was joined by another, the scream of a soul pulled once again into the flesh it had fled, and then I was looking at piercing pale blue eyes, alive once more but filled with sickened dread at the ghastly feel of its own rancid flesh.

It reached out appealing hands to me, but those hands began to deform hideously, to take on a new form, a hybrid form emerging now from this poor man's doomed earthly remains.

-3-

Tuesday at work was a bitch. All our hard work and not a groat of fucking appreciation from that little turd, Ben. By the time I finally had the inside of my front door to my back, I was ready for a serious night out with Jen.

"Grandma!" I called out. "I'm home!"

No answer.

I'd no cause to be worried and shrugged off the niggle of dread. Grandma had been my constant companion in the house that had once been hers, and since she'd raised me from childhood I was determined to look after her until I absolutely couldn't do it any more. Her mind had been going for a long time, taking her further from reality with every passing year, but she was family. The only family I had.

"Going to grab a snack, OK? I'm going out with Jennifer!"

I kept my voice chirpy and light, but I could feel the oppressive weight of dread pressing down as I crossed the hall toward the stairs, fear gnawing deep inside my belly.

I glanced into the doorway to my right. "Grandma?"

The sitting room door was propped open as always, but the room was empty, discarded newspapers and magazines scattered on the creaky old mismatched armchairs that had stood in their anti-slip cups on that worn hessian hearth rug since before I'd been a schoolgirl.

Upstairs or downstairs, first?

I crept down the hallway, past the back room door also on my right (no way would she be in there, that was Grandfather's old room), and entered the kitchen.

"Damn."

The cooker was cold; the breakfast bits were still on the drainer. Grandma had left the dishes all day. Grandma never left the dishes all day.

I bustled more hurriedly back down the hallway and turned and took the stairs two at a time, which wasn't easy in my increasingly tight work skirt, my skin feeling as cold as the cooker had been.

As soon as I reached the top I made for the dark, dry and musty silence of Grandma's bedroom.

The curtains were closed, the bed unmade. Her weary bedside clock tock-chocked its old, slow monotonous beat as it always had, while light dust drifted down onto the mahogany dresser, caught in the glare of a chink of light sneaking through a gap in the closed, heavy curtains.

An electronic screech shattered the silence.

I felt my soul leave my body, though somehow I managed not to blow my digested lunchtime sandwich out at the far wall.

"Fuck," I said, surprised at the high pitch of my own voice.

I grabbed the handset of Grandma's bedside phone, tempted to spit at it first.

"What!" I barked into it.

There was a dry fizzing behind my eyes and a wet scolding in my chest and stomach as adrenaline washed through my system, using every vein and artery to fill my body before it was recalled to silence by recognition of this false alarm – I wasn't about to be murdered by the Daleks after all...

"*Laur?*" said the voice at the far end. "*Laur, it's me, I wanted to check if you're all set for tonight, but... what's wrong?*"

"Hey, Jen, just–" I swallowed hard to force my thudding heart back down my throat, and then spoke. "Give me a sec, will you? I can't find Grandma."

"*Oh, Laur!*"

" I'll be right back, OK?"

The receiver clunked down on the wooden tabletop as I left the room, but just as I stepped out, the toilet in the bathroom flushed at the far end of the shadowy Landing and there was the sound of running water being splashed into the sink.

"Ah," I muttered to myself. "You dopey cow."

The bathroom door groaned open and Grandma shuffled slowly out, draped in her baggy white nightgown, a frown on her brow and her gaze angled to the left and far, far from the place where her body was to be found.

"Grandma?" I queried, which was pretty fucking stupid because I knew it was her.

"Oh. Hello, dear." Her eyes angled vaguely in my direction for a moment.

"Grandma, I've been calling you! why didn't you answer?"

I felt angry. It was irrational ; even caught in the moment, I knew that much, but couldn't help myself.

"I must have... mm. Are you off to work then, dear? Give me a kiss, would you like a packed...? Erm."

A smooth dry cheek was offered for a kiss, while a hand reached back toward the bathroom for the pots and pans.

Now I felt guilty for biting at her. I knew this set of symptoms well enough, these creeping changes to her mind, her personality. And today, she was having a pretty bad day.

She smiled and looked straight at me, her wrinkly white face crinkling even more. "Just leave the letter at the factory gate."

Behind her, in the bathroom, her glasses remained perched on the sink where she had placed them. Having put them down, she had promptly forgotten about their existence, even though they would have been in her line of sight as she washed her hands.

I sighed, unhappy and alone.

I knew to my distress that trying to get through to her when she was like this was painfully unrewarding. She edged toward her bedroom and I let her pass, with her hand extended but not quite touching the wall, teetering in her slippered feet as she went.

I followed her into her room and waited until she ran out of crazy ideas, which took about a minute, and then I quietly took control and guided her onto her bed. She might as well sleep if this was her state of mind tonight. She'd go out like a light and stay out for the night – she wouldn't, I selfishly reasoned, even notice that I was out.

Once under her duvet and her absurdly unseasonable eiderdown, she closed her eyes compliantly and left this world completely for a time.

I sighed. Watched her for a moment. One day soon she would fall into one of these fugues and I'd not get her back.

"Shit!"

I remembered the phone, grabbed the receiver beside Grandma's bed and hissed quietly into it.

"Sorry, Jen! I'll pick up downstairs!"

I hung up and trotted down the stairs, where I headed into the sitting room and flumped into the lumpy wingback chair nearest the phone. I scooped up a far more modern handset and brought it to my face.

"Hey. I'm back."

"Everything alright, babe?" I could hear the frown in her voice.

"Yeah, it's fine," I said, reaching between the two wingbacks to click on the table lamp that snuggled in the recess on a small wooden table. It was light now, but there was no guarantee that Grandma wouldn't go wandering later, and the darkness was a killer at her age.

"Grandma had a bad day?"

"Yeah."

"Sorry, babe. You're gonna have to think about putting her somewhere she can get proper—"

"NOT a fucking chance!" I snapped.

"OK, OK, I got no plans to have that fight with you again! You still OK for tonight?"

I laughed to myself. Jen was such a... single-tasker.

"I'll pick you up at eight," I told her.

"Nah, girlie! I knew you wasn't listening today. I'm driving tonight, remember? You won't get me in that old boneshaker of yours."

I smiled, although the expression worked the corners of my mouth without ever quite reaching my soul. I needed a night out. Grandma would be fine.

"You leave Mickey alone," I said, feigning indignation. "That's a classic MG Roadster, I'll have you know. Steve always said I could easily double my money if I sold…"

Oh whoops; big fat buggerfucking whoops. Twice in two days, what the fuck was wrong with me?

"Shit, sorry, babe. I didn't mean to bring Steve up."

There was a momentary pause on the line. *"We need to start gettin' ready. I know you all too well, Mzzz Keeble, and I do not want to get round to your place and find you still in your knickers."*

"So you say, but I've seen you peeking." Now I smiled for real.

"Eight?"

"Yeah."

"Later."

After that, time passed. I knew time passed because I showered, washed my hair, dried it loose so it hung down onto my shoulders in all its chestnut glory… OK, conceited, but a girl can wash 'n' wish, can't she? And 'dull brown' sounds so much less poetic… yeah, so anyway. I was dressed and back in the wingback and with all that done, I *knew* that time had passed. But perhaps only for me. Somehow, Jen seemed immune to the passage of time and its cheeky suggestion that we all ought to be ready on time, there on time, just bloody *on* time!

My fingers drummed on the arm of the chair.

Those same fingers drummed on that same spot half an hour later, and then again as eight-thirty went sneaking past on the clockface on Grandma's mantelpiece. Time sneaking, creeping.

And still no Jen.

"Fuck's sake."

Clothes that had been fresh an hour ago now clung on at my breasts and beneath my arms, where perspiration was reminding me to never again take a hot shower on a summer's night, while despair led me into imagining a nightmare evening that lasted for all eternity and in which Jen never came – and yet, for some stupid reason, I just sat. And waited. And waited.

The doorbell rang.

I glanced at the clock. How lovely it would be to leave Ms. Sullivan standing at the door. It'd serve her right – but sadly I needed to get the hell out of the house to save myself from being poached alive in my own clothes.

The pink dress clinging to Jen's perfect contours had the thinnest straps human technology can yet make, and the web-thin fabric was so strained by her protruding nipples it seemed certain that they would puncture it at some point during the evening. Her legs were bare, waxed and a gleaming seven-foot length of glorious slender bronze that would redefine the meaning of the word 'Amazon' for any slavering male who caught a glimpse of them. The bitch.

I glanced her up and down, from toe to tit. "Even *you* have to be wearing knickers under *that* dress."

She grinned. "If not, you better hope I had time to shower."

I pulled a face and, without letting that idea form into an image, I gestured toward Jen's car. "Come on, let's get going."

Jen peered at me. "How 'bout Grandma? She be OK, babe?"

I shrugged off her concern, a little irritated that I'd been reminded about my responsibilities. "She's fine. She's down for the night. She's fine."

"OK, then." With a grin, she turned on her heel and clippy-clopped down my path, out the gate and out across the road, rather foolishly assuming that Tiler's Hill would be quiet at this time on a Tuesday night.

Her enthusiasm was infectious and, frankly, I wanted to be carefree, so I pasted a similarly vacant grin across my own face and crossed the road, albeit with my eyes and ears more alert for traffic than my friend had been – and grabbed the door handle of my friend's tiny, gleaming Audi bitchmobile, parked with its snubby nose angling at a lopsided tangent to the curb, the bumper almost scraped up against the low stonework wall of Chadbury graveyard.

No pedestrians tonight, who might tut at Jen's car, bumped up across the pathway.

I fell into the bucketseat and twisted my body so I could wrestle the seatbelt, which saw my discomfort and locked itself inside the reel, preventing me from pulling it out.

Jen turned the key and punched the throttle – trust me, the fierce roar of the engine was unmistakable. She whooped with delight as the engine settled down to a juddering growl.

"You don't get that with a 'seventies classic', babe."

"No," I agreed. "You have definitely got the hairiest little sports car money can buy."

I wrenched the seatbelt again, too hard in my frustration, as I realised when it unlocked and unspooled, my hand flying forward so I very nearly punched the dashboard.

The mad little car lurched and wrenched free of the curb, bumping and then immediately biting road and lurching into violent acceleration as I clung to the still-undocked belt clasp.

All flailing hair, bouncing breasts and churning stomach as we raced into Chadbury, I slammed the belt clasp into the dock just in time as Jen threw us into an eight-hundred degree turn out of the backside of my home town, all the time churning out dialogue I wasn't listening to, knowing that this was her usual pre-night-out feat of cramming two and a half hours of chat into a fifteen minute drive, so she could dump me in the club as soon as she found a suitable penis to surf on.

And then it was over. Jen threw the car onto the parking area and flew too fast toward the garish neon sign that proclaimed 'Leonardo'S'.

My friend stomped the break and spun the wheel; two actions that did not seem to warrant her success in lining the car up in a bay. It would have taken me three tries to get the car that damn straight. Like I say. Bitch.

At the nightclub's entrance we were greeted by a heavy browed, dent-headed bouncer, whose body appeared as though it must have been inflated after he was packed into his tight black suit.

"Evening Ladies," he said.

Jen smiled and stood too close to him. "Hi. Busy tonight?"

His eyes appraised her nearly-naked body. "Never *that* busy," he said with an ugly grin.

She slithered against him in a way I could never imagine myself doing, even if my life depended on it, and then waited until he stepped aside. Jen was in, cigarettes and mobile phone clutched in one hand as she clattered through on the spiky heels of her fuck-me-twice shoes.

The bouncer stared after her, his cock visibly protruding against the front of his trousers now. I passed him without getting noticed, and paid for both of us.

Absorbed into the multi-coloured neon twilight of the nightclub, our faces and bodies were painted in every colour as I followed the spectacle of Jen's elegant form gliding across the vacant dance floor to the bar.

I was so far in her shadow; but at least I knew it.

The place was getting busy already, but not so much that I missed the reactions of all the males as they ran appreciative eyes over my friend's lithe body. I smoothed my skirt, aware of the vacuum that had formed around me in Jen's wake.

She disappeared into the cluster around the bar.

I picked up the pace and immediately slammed straight into a hard, solid object.

Grabbing a startled breath, I stared up. Well, it was a man, but damn it was a *big* one! At least six and a half feet tall, his eyes brilliant in the crazy-neon as he stared into my soul over the empty pint glass I had just helped him to spill onto the floor.

I floundered under his unmoving gaze before mumbling an apology. "Sorry! Sorry, I–"

"No problem."

His voice emerged in a shockingly rich, deep oak of a timbre. Husky yet melodious, I would say.

I suspected I was grinning gormlessly at him.

When he smiled back, an eruption of white teeth seemed backlit in his lightly tanned face, each reflecting the lights of the club perfectly. "So," he said calmly through his smile, "are you going to buy me another?"

"What?"

Oh, man, he was big. Tall but thickset and solid, a bodybuilder perhaps. Not my type, if I'd ever really progressed so far as to *have* a type, but man, he was *big*. Did I say that already?

His smile stayed naturally on his face. "Are you alright?" he asked.

"What?"

Get a grip! A little voice told me. "I, er, yes. Fine. You…?"

"Sam," he then said, extending a huge slab of a hand toward my body, his eyes still alight with some inner joy. "A pleasure to meet you."

He said it the way he might quote romantic poetry. Yikes.

"Yeh, OK. I'm…"

"Laura," he finished for me as he put the emptied pint glass onto a high table fixed to a support pillar. His smile was still steady, still even. "I know who you are."

Oh shit.

I glanced around myself, suddenly vulnerable in this safe public spot. I didn't know this man, he could be anyone and he had me at a hell of a disadvantage. I'd taken self-defence classes for this very reason, but now it was all too real, all too now. I needed a time-out.

The giant, Sam, must have sensed something in my posture, because he grabbed my arm and pulled smoothly, evenly, drawing me inexorably through the milling drinkers littering the neon haven. I wanted to pull away, I wanted to cry out, I wanted to fight back, but somehow all my self-defence training seemed so dreadfully theoretical in the face of a great big real man who had me by the arm.

What was I supposed to do? What had I been taught?

I tugged against his arm and achieved nothing. I tried to get angry but couldn't. Fuck, I'd always assumed I'd feel so good when the moment finally came to use my new powers of invincibility, but all I wanted to do now was cry.

Six-fifty a time those self-defence lessons had cost me. Six- fucking – fifty. Thieving bitches.

He pulled me toward him, eyes far inside mine. His balls were in line with my knee; I'd never get a better chance. But staring into his face, I saw it and realised who he was.

The face, the build were all wrong. Even the face was different, but no. This man, what had he called himself? Sam; yes. Sam – who had the eyes, the *exact* same eyes as the man in last night's dream, the dying man whose wife had called him 'James'.

But his eyes…

Sam moved off toward the crowds forming at the stand-up tables, pulling me in his wake like some can clanking stupidly behind the newlyweds' car.

I glanced around frantically, but of course everyone was fixated on getting their booze, or their designer drugs, or the bodily fluids of someone else all over their genitals. In short, no-one gave a toss about poor me or my plight.

But then, suddenly, a fattish young man with a half empty pint glass in his hand swayed into Sam's path and stopped him.

My delight was so short-lived we should call it 'de-'. The fattish man was a long way into his beer and was swaying, his gaze barely even registering the giant in front of him.

"Step aside," ordered that deep ominous voice from my captor's throat.

Still trapped, with my arm in his grip, I edged around him, thinking about those balls again. One hard…. But then he glanced at me and I froze as the twilight of the nightclub lit his expression in feral angles.

Shit!

Teeth bared and parted ready to bite, heavy brow furrowed down over pinpoint eyes, he looked utterly inhuman.

But his rage was not for me. His feral stare fixed on the fattish man. I felt a hard draft of air as he lunged forward, and then my arm was free and Sam was crashing into the drunk, catching his shoulders in his large hands.

I knew I should run, but I was fascinated by the sights before me. Still holding the man with his left hand, Sam belted him open-handed across the jaw with his right and the drunk's head snapped violently sideways at shocking speed.

Far to my right, a couple of young men were running, closing in, yelling increasingly excited abuse at Sam.

Sam flicked open the fingers of his left hand to pointedly drop the man to whose aid those others were rushing. I had an overwhelming feeling, a conviction from the sight of the way that he fell, that the man on the floor was dead.

Sam turned to face the two new arrivals and his cheeks swelled as he grinned at them. One of them muttered something about his 'bruvver', but whatever he'd threatened in retaliation for his brother being felled, it never happened because at that moment Sam's bulk shot forward.

It was all so frighteningly fast. Straight fingers extended, Sam went through the man, those thrusting fingers punched into the centre of the man's chest so hard it made a *thunk!* that was audible over the pounding music. The man jerked, shuddered and slumped backwards onto a table, a gout of blood spurting from his mouth as he convulsed. Then he tumbled off the table and fell, dead-weight, onto the floor, where he lay gagging, eyes bulging, more blood seeping from between his lips as he lay there twitching weakly.

I stared in stunned disbelief. Even the thought of escaping and saving myself was washed away by the realisation of what I was looking at. The man on the floor was dying, his face visibly bleaching to white even in the psychedelic lighting of Leo's, and his friend, the chubby one who had inadvertently failed to help me, well he just lay there with his head on wrong. Not moving at all; not blinking or breathing. I covered my mouth just too late to stop a desperate sob escaping.

The music cranked up to deafening proportions as the dancefloor lights began to spin up to full speed. Sam kicked the third, and last, man right in his balls. He sprang into the air, landed half on tiptoes and then collapsed like a puppet with cut strings, his eyes screwed shut with an agony I could only imagine, as the crowd finally sensed something going terribly wrong in their midst and began to shuffle back away from it.

The man Sam had finger-punched was immobile now, the dark pool of gurgled-out blood no longer expanding onto the floor beside his gaping, still mouth. The drunk who had started all this lay where he had fallen, arms splayed out to the sides and head still lolling at that sick angle that would have given an owl the shits.

And Mister No-Balls, of course, the poor bastard who now lay on his side, knees drawn up, hands clasped where his sex organs used to be. I suspect he might have preferred to die than have to come to terms with *that*.

Sam grabbed my arm and wrenched so hard I cried out, feeling muscle pull momentarily free of bone.

"Uugh!" I cried. "Please, please don't! I didn't see! I won't tell! Please, please don't hurt me!"

And then the lights were obscured by two six-foot-high solid squares, which was great from the point of view that it shut up my humiliating whining and pleading. Sam pulled me, trying to steer around the two bouncers, but I resisted and made myself just awkward enough that he could not manoeuvre me, or himself, out of their way in time.

I felt so, so smart. I think maybe I even smirked at the giant.

"You!" one of the men snarled.

Sam did not hesitate. He stepped in close to the bouncer; 'toe-to-toe'. The bouncer's shoulders tensed, his arm muscles bunched under his white shirt sleeves. It was only then that I noticed he'd taken off his jacket. These two meant business.

"Weapons, Frank!" his partner yelled, intending a helpful warning, but concealed weapons were never going to be the issue here.

When Sam slammed his forehead down onto the big man's nose I heard the crunch. As the bouncer staggered backwards I saw more blood spurting from that face than I would have believed *could* come from a face. He clutched his face as he staggered backwards, and Sam took advantage, punching the edge of an open hand against the man's exposed throat.

I clamped my eyes shut, sickened. There was a limit to what I could bear to see or hear, and the ghastly noise of cartilage crunching, followed by a horrible animal noise as the man fought to get a whistling, gurgling breath through his crumpled windpipe; yep, that crossed a certain line for me.

This last sound alerted me that the music had stopped. I opened my eyes in time to see the second bouncer's beefy fist thud into Sam's belly, the second fist already arcing over the top for a downward chopping blow to the back of the falling man's head, but this opponent, Sam, was never going to fall.

He grabbed the bouncer's jaw in his hand and wrenched downward. I saw his lips twitch into a brief smile of delight as the bouncer jolted and yelped and a pistol crack of breaking bone reached my ears. This man went down, wide-eyed, to his knees, cupping the split sections of his jaw and making weak mewling sounds as blood streamed between his fingers.

What the actual fuck...

Beyond this wounded man, I saw the first bouncer lying very still on his back, one hand across his throat; where he'd left it just prior to dying; and the other flopped onto the floor.

I wondered if the second bouncer had yet realised how lucky he'd been tonight. The only one of Sam's victims to escape with both his life and his sex organs.

Out of the corner of my eye, I saw another bouncer approaching. "Frank!" he yelled. "John!"

Sam pulled me toward the stairway and I knew better than to resist. The best I could do by resisting was get someone else hurt, and the worst was to get myself hurt or killed, so I went with him up those stairs; he two at a time, me with my legs flapping frantically to keep up on one rung at a time.

I had only one hope, now. Once outside, I might find a way to escape this monster, escape whatever he had planned for me. I didn't really believe that. I wondered what he could need from me so badly he would kill or maim five men. Then it occurred to me I did *not* want to find out.

The new bouncers who'd come to the aid of Frank and John must've called ahead, because the two doormen rushed forward into Sam's path as he dragged me across the entrance lobby.

Sam did not slow. He rammed headlong into one and swatted the other with a massive arm as he passed. Both were flung off their feet so hard that their bodies flew backwards, almost tracking our progress toward the door.

I seem to remember it in slow motion. I don't know why

Sam and I ran through the exit doors. The two doormen burst out through the plate glass windows each side of us. The tinkling of glass was followed by the sharp sounds of human bones splitting and shattering under the heavy impact. Then there were sprays of blood in the air as arteries or veins were opened by the heavy falling shards of glass.

Gouts of crimson were lit purple in the neon lights outside the nightclub, and, now, there were corpses on the ground. A siren and blue flashes. Sam fleeing down the pathway that ran behind the club and my arm, suddenly free as he forgot his mad purpose for me.

I gasped and sobbed, my cheeks wet, my breath short in the aftershock of my mad, terrifying flight.

A moment passed. Maybe a minute.

I rubbed my arms to warm them, clamped my teeth together to stop them chattering. It was summer. Why was I so cold?

I sensed movement and turned toward the glass-spattered doorway of the club, where I saw another (the last?) bouncer standing staring at me. I opened my mouth, imagining I might have something to say, but he was too far behind me and noises were starting up around us now.

He stared at me. His jaw bulged as he ground his clenched teeth. His lips pulled back in a feral snarl.

I wanted to say sorry, tell him it wasn't me, I had no control, but why should he care with his friends dead or bleeding, so before he could act I turned and staggered away, taking the same alleyway around the back of the club that Sam had taken.

I fumbled and grabbed my mobile. Keyed in Jen's number, not thinking to use *contacts* or fast-dial.

The sound of sirens was growing louder as the Police approached the charnel scene. I laughed harshly. Just in the nick of way too late. If Sam had wanted, he could've done several fucking awful things to me by now.

I pulled in a ragged breath as I heard Jen through the speaker of the phone I'd forgotten I was even holding. I gasped out some broken sentences while she struggled to hear over the music back inside the club. I had no idea how she might get enough from this insane non-chat to realise I was outside and needed her help.

I stood frozen in time, now-silent phone in my hand

and suddenly Jen grasped my arm. "... happened?"

I focused, saw my friend, still hooked on the arm of a skinny youth whose balls were not yet due to drop.

My friend could her the sirens, see the carnage. In this regard, she was no fool. "Time to be absento, babe. Tell me on the way."

I was aware that the skinny youth, four parts child and only one part prospective lover, was called Roddy, although I had no specific awareness of any words being said to me.

I was guided a back way toward the taxi ranks further into town, which would not yet be under police embargo.

Tonight, Jen was the best friend a girl could have.

Thought Soldier

-4-

My hands were shaking too much to dial anything into my mobile, so I had to call my home phone from the landline in Jen's flat. It rang out and went to voicemail.

I clicked off and redialled. Same.

I slammed the phone down, hot tears stinging my eyes. *"Fuck!"*

A hand landed softly on my shoulder. I did not need to see the crimson talons to know it was Jen's.

"Hey, babe," she said. "What is it? Grandma?"

I nodded.

"You tried Aunt Potty's?"

A smile pinched the corners of my mouth at the mention of Grandma's oldest and barmiest friend, the self-styled 'Auntie' Dot. Couldn't believe I hadn't thought of that.

I keyed the number, unchanged since I'd been a kid, and got the crazy old girl herself, chirpy and full of beans and sorry but she hoped I didn't mind but since I was out and my 'Grenny' wasn't feeling too good...

Yikes. I shook my head and grinned at the buzzing, yammering handset, happy to let it enjoy a life of its own. Normally, Aunt Potty got on my wick, but tonight, with all the crazy shit happening to me, she seemed like an oasis of sanity in this roughest of seas.

Dot wasn't related to me, but the polite title I'd inferred on all adults as a kid had struck a chord with the old girl, so she'd stuck with it to this day, whilst Jen had delighted in pulling my tits about it for almost as long.

All that actually mattered was that she had decided to take Grandma back to her house, so she was safe; specifically she was not at home where that monster Sam, who had clearly targeted me tonight, might find her.

I used polite pleasantries to shut down the manic chimp dialogue, thanked the old girl and hung up.

"She's safe."

Jen shrugged. "Course. Look, Laur, it's always nasty when it kicks off in town. There's some real fuckwits about. But you can't let a pub fight get you this stressed and paranoid."

I hadn't told her about my involvement in events; it had been enough for her that we'd been there – that was all the trauma Jen needed to trip her into mother-hen mode.

I certainly had no plans to tell her that the events of tonight involved me, that as the real target I had good reason to think that my only family might be at risk. That Sam had *sought me out*, for fuck's sake.

I needed to get my own head around that, first. Me – why me?

"Stay the night," Jen offered, and when I looked at her eyes they were warm and kind in a way that they seldom ever were.

I smiled my thanks and followed the clacking of her heels on the wood flooring she'd insisted on having throughout her flat, heading into the lounge.

Inside, I sat on one side of her fluffy white two-seater sofa, while Jen perched beside me, revealing bronzed thighs that shone smooth and unblemished in the light from her two lamps.

I shook off the impression, alarmed at how I was luxuriating in my perception of her warm flesh. Damn, Laura!

"So-oh," I said, "how'd you, er, leave things with... what was his name?"

"Roddy." Jen's red lips pouted momentarily as she fixed me with eyes that were cat-green and gleaming in the lamplight. "And I'm not sure." She pursed those red protrusions, her eyes narrowing. "I think he was interested, but maybe not enough to wait 'til another night."

"Damn." I knew what her conquests meant to her; proof that she still 'had it', which was getting more important to her as the years slipped by. "Sorry, Jen."

She gave a curt shake of her head. "Hey," she said, her eyes going wide green and her lips going pout-rich red again. "After what happened tonight, we're all shaken up. Anyway, he can either like it or he can fuck off. Harsh but fair, that's my policy."

I smiled back and barely noticed that I was entwining fingers with her. "I really appreciate this, Jen. You're such a good friend."

I held her hand, stared into her eyes while their hot green depths accepted me in...

I snapped my gaze free. Shook it off. "Erm, so what about your car?"

She coughed loudly, drew her fingers out from amongst mine and stood up, smoothing her skirt down over her thighs. "Err, yeah. I'll go get it in the morning, 's fine. You, er, you want a coffee, babe, er...?"

I hesitated, unsure what had just happened. "Um, yeah. Yes. Please."

As she hurtled into the kitchen I got off the sofa, paced a few steps, realised she would hear me clopping on her wooden floor and dumped my hide into the wide white leather chair I was sure she'd bought just to bring out the kid in me – shaped like one of those giant spinning teacups at the fair. It did. Spin, that is. So, hence, I span a little.

Twirling in my chair to offset the weirdness of *that* moment, I settled facing Jen's slitty side window, squinting at the starry sky through the narrow view while my friend clattered about in the kitchen, making coffee. A warm sense of home settled over me and I felt the weight of my eyelids suddenly increasing.

Jen's door chimes erupted into life above my head on the wall. I jerked violently and slid down on the leather, my skirt hitching halfway up around my hips as Jen entered the room, saw me, looked away, looked back, widened her eyes in mock-horror, and then vanished into her hallway to answer her door.

Fucking hell, the wheels had fallen right off tonight.

Only as I heard the latch on her door go, did I think to warn her to check who it was before she opened up. But hey, why should she change the habit of a lifetime?

-5-

I grabbed at the floppy leather arms and levered myself up, determined not to be brutally murdered with my frontie showing. As I righted myself on the chair, puffing from the shock and the unexpected exertion, I heard Jen's voice from the door.

"Hallo Peters, what you doin' here this late?"

Her visitor must have replied but I caught very little of it. Then, I caught the last of the words, spoken in a soft, lilting but nonetheless masculine voice: *"Sorry, love, I was worried about you."*

"What are you, my fucking mum?"

I smiled. My friend's wit was always sharp, but if the man at the door minded, he didn't express it. He must know her pretty well.

Jen flicked the ceiling light on as she returned, swamping the cosy glow of her lamps and cutting ribbons into my retinas.

She was followed into the room by an athletic-looking man whose rough, craggy face might have put him anywhere from an old-looking thirty-something to a young-looking fifty-something. He crinkled his nose and used his middle finger to push dainty wire spectacles up onto its bridge, while the cold white lights reflected off the little square lenses.

"Laur, this is Peters," said Jen. "He lives across the hall."

Still squinting, I clambered to my feet, careful to ensure that my knees didn't part too far – it was a pretty low and deep seat. I held out a hand to meet his and the grip I received was firm yet moderated, just as the muscles in his arms seemed to be; not unfeasible yet clearly toned.

"Oh," said Peters, holding my gaze. "We've met."

"Have we?"

It was late, but he still smelled faintly of some cologne; bittersweet, with the soapy odour of soap beneath it somewhere.

He nodded curtly, just once. "At Rachael's party."

"Did…?"

Shut up, Keeble.

I smiled and returned his grip. "Laura. Laura Keeble."

He smiled too, now. "Tom Peters."

Oh, *Tom* Peters. The full name triggered a vague memory of a chatty, sensitive and interesting man who'd grown less and less interested in me as I'd gotten more and more pissed – and had finally been offered my unintentional contempt when I'd blown cheese, celery, garlic dip and red wine (one careful owner) all over his shirt.

Yikes. Oh fucking deary me…

"Rachael's... er, party...." I was saying, even though my brain didn't want my mouth to speak right now.

He watched my face with a compassionate half-smile. Ahh, shit. When you've let a bit of wee out on the vicar's couch, there's only one thing to say, right?

"Look," I said. "I'm really sorry about that night. My behaviour was... oh, I've got nothing, Tom, it was fucking shocking, wasn't it?"

His smile sprawled, his craggy face erupting into a smile full of surprisingly white teeth. "Naah, don't stress it. Not a highlight for either of us, but as being yacked on goes, that was one of my favourites."

I hadn't noticed his accent before. It was sort of hidden, but still there; a cockney accent peeking out from behind an education that had taught him the proper way to pronounce his words.

He stayed where he was, gazing at me. It was really intense.

"Can I have my hand back, now?" he asked.

"What? Oh. *Shit.* Sorry."

Released, he turned and swept across the room to the two seater.

Jen cast me a glance that wasn't entirely friendly as she passed me. "Coffee?" she offered our extra guest as he slumped onto the two-seater. He nodded with a grin.

"Right, then," she said pointedly. "That'll be *three* coffees. Better refill the kettle, coz I only boiled enough for me an' Laur."

"Oh, I *do* apologise," Tom said ironically, the corner of his mouth still lifted by the remains of his grin.

Jen smirked and made a show of turning away huffily to retreat to the kitchen.

Although I only knew Tom from, well... that party vomit incident, I knew he and Jen were close, had been friends for years, in fact. I was getting my usual nervous belly, now that I was stuck with someone whose opinion of me was actually going to matter at some point down the road.

As my friend left for the kitchen, I considered sitting back in the retro chair, but somehow I didn't fancy it after my dignity issues. Tom had already seen the contents of my stomach, best if he didn't get the full upskirt tour thrown in, too .

I perched awkwardly on the sofa, the presence of the man just to my left causing a tangible and unexpected re-mixing of my body chemistry.

I glanced his way and suddenly, unexpectedly, he flashed me the most honest, massively white-toothed grin I'd ever seen, his whole face splitting open to cope with its joyous abandon, the whiteness of those pegs dazzling against the backdrop of his tanned, weathered face. I fell into his eyes then, those pale grey-blue discs that somehow managed to be boyish and manly all at the same time – their colour might have been washed-out, but somehow the life, the energy behind them gave them a glister they might otherwise have lacked.

He wasn't my type. Not at all. What the fuck?

He leant toward me and I now noticed how hard his chest was, just muscular enough to bulge, while his belly was nowhere to be seen beneath the tightish white tee-shirt, lost in the same place as any excess his narrow hips and legs might have gotten away with if they'd wanted to.

Shit. Don't look at his... too late.

Must be the shock. Or maybe sluttishness *was* contagious.

I swallowed hard and met his eyes. Couldn't think of a damn thing to say. Decided to sweat instead.

He pushed his dainty little glasses up his nose once again. "That, err, that club you were at, they had some trouble, tonight. I was saying to Jenny, but y'know, she always lets me know where she'll be, y'know, in case of incidents an' that. So anyways, it made the News and, er, someone died."

He was gabbling like a crazy person. He seemed as nervous as I felt, which sort of made me feel better, put me, if not into the driving seat then at least, no longer in the luggage compartment.

I asked him how he knew Jen and we stumbled through the early beginnings of what might yet turn into a grown-up conversation.

Jen returned with three mugs, her awkward grip clearly causing the edge of one mug to burn her left hand so that she dumped my mug onto the wooden floor beside my foot, slopping some of my drink.

As she crouched to dab, I was offered a view up her skirt that would have earned a cry of 'cut!' on a porn movie set.

Tom, however, was blessed with her most sickly sweet smile as his mug was held daintily out for his pleasure. The arm he stretched out was muscular, the forearm tapered from a full bicep, yet the hand with which he took the mug was surprisingly dainty, the fingers fine and the nails neatly clipped.

I didn't want to care, but I was drawn into the enigma. He had the hefty upper arms of a builder or a weightlifter, yet possessed the fine fingers of a pianist or a surgeon.

Jen whumped down on the sofa, the *two-seater*, between us, fitting the gap too intimately so that her hip brushed mine and, presumably, his too. Tom swung his mug to keep the liquid from brimming over as he was jolted.

Tom sipped and winced. Too soon, too hot. "So, erm, Jen, I was saying to Laur, pretty grim in town earlier, right?"

"Oh, yeah." She flicked her head in an attempt to get that unruly over-bleached rug out of her eyes as she cast a glance at me. "We saw some nasty old carnage as we were leaving, right, Laur?"

She didn't know, I hadn't told her, yet her green eyes were sharp and I wondered if maybe she'd seen through my attempts to lie to her. After all, she was probably the person who knew me best in all the world, now Grandma was… well, not as wily as she'd once been.

I held her gaze for the longest moment my guilt permitted. "Pretty nasty, yep. I was kinda shook up by it."

An instant change hit the mood and Jen's expression burst open into a smile. "Good thing for us you called me when you did, babe, eh?" She leant into Tom. "Laur called me from outside, got us out of there! The old Bill are probably still grilling everyone stupid enough to stick around, but not us!"

"You said us?" said Tom. "Laura called 'us', so who's 'us'?"

I saw Jen's smile go taut. "Don't fucking start. Nothing happened."

Tom brought the mug to his lips. Sipped. "You keep screwing everything with a pulse, you're gonna end up hurting yourself, babe."

Jen's pretty face had grown dark, ugly. "And you keep thinking you're my Dad, we ain't gonna stay friends, so back the fuck off!"

I was surprised Tom would poke that particular bear. Jen and I were pretty close, but I knew better than to attempt an intervention where her 'love' life was concerned, no matter how well-intentioned.

I realised with horror that I was staring at him. I'd just forgotten to move my gaze but he was staring right back, now, so I'd kicked my own arse straight through into the land of Creepy Weird.

"Somethin' up?" he asked.

I snapped my gaze away. "Shit. Sorry, Tom."

Still, a look had passed between us. Not the creepy-weird thing, but something… nicer. I was always terrible at reading signs, but the look that we exchanged in that moment was too clear, too intimate for even me to miss.

"Oi!" Jen interrupted, clearly not finished with Tom yet. "Don't think I'm letting you off the hook, Peters, you don't get to chew my tits and then dismiss it."

He withdrew his eyes lazily from me and turned his head. "Jen, turn it in; I'm sorry, yeah?"

"Nah," she retorted, and I knew that tone. She was spoiling for a fight. Sexual frustration, would be my guess.

I think Tom knew it, too, because I'm sure I heard him sigh.

"Nah," Jen went on. "You've got a problem with me seein' other men, Peters. You're aching for a bit of what I'm offering."

Ahhh… this was now *banter*. Jen's way of accepting Tom's apology.

"Oh, really?" he replied, airily.

"Yeah, you toad. You know it."

"Well," he replied. "If you ever fancy a change from all those aimless, pretty-boy minge-jockeys, you know where to find me."

She snorted into her coffee

"Bastard!" she laughed.

Tom turned his gaze my way, leaning across Jen conspiratorially, as if our friend wasn't sat wedged between us. "So, Laura, who's this latest conquest she doesn't want me to know about?"

I found myself pinned, fixed to the spot by those pale blue-grey eyes, their twinkling mischief held in check by the glinting lenses of his little spectacles. Intimately close to him, I could see the mirth in his gaze for what it was; a shroud drawn over a deep and haunting sadness forever concealed behind his jovial façade.

"Shut your pie-hole, Keeble," Jen warned, casting me a mock-warning look while still dabbing coffee from the edge of her lip.

"Oh, you know me, Jen," I declared, "the very soul of discretion! I'd never embarrass you by mentioning the boy-child, Roddy, who is, as far as I–"

"Roddy!" Tom exploded, his gaze now pinning Jen. "Bugger me, fucking *Roddy?*"

Jen pouted at me and turned to Tom. "What of it?"

Tom's shoulders bobbed with the work of holding in a belly-laugh. "Fuck kinda name's that, Jenny? Roddy? Are you sure you heard him right, babe?"

I grinned. "It's short for–" I started, but choked off into a laugh before I could say *'Rhododendron'*.

But Tom pounced. "Rhodo-fucking-*dendron!*"

He'd stolen the gag straight out of my head but he'd made it sound much funnier than I would have. He and I were full-on into shits-n-giggles now, with Jen holding her coffee out away from her in case one of we two chucklers should nudge her and cause a spill.

Jen folded her arms trapped on the little sofa between her chortling nemeses. "You two laugh it up. At least I'm getting some."

"Fresh from the cradle!" I blurted, and then immediately regretted it as my friend's mouth opened and then closed, dumbfounded.

Too far, Keeble. Too far.

"Thanks, Laur. Nice one; on that note, I'm gonna turn in. You two feel free to..."

She left the concept floating between us as she pulled her slinky form out from the middle and retreated down her own hallway.

"Hmm." Tom pulled a face. "I think maybe you hit a nerve there, Laura."

"Ya think?" I puffed my cheeks. "Still, what's new? I've done well if I can get through any night of your choosing without at least one social hysterectomy."

He laughed sympathetically. "I think we should go after her."

We got up. Well, he got up in a smooth flexing of sinew and I lurched out of the chair with the dignity of a rat trying to escape a food blender, compounded when having forgotten that I was wearing evening shoes, I slipped and stumbled into him.

I fell against him and plummeted into his deep ambivalent eyes in what must have looked like *such* a blatant attempt to get into a cinch.

Holding my elbow, he eased me to stability. "You OK?" he asked. "You want—"

I shook my head. "I'm fine."

He was holding my elbow, just my elbow, yet it somehow felt very intimate, but as fast as it happened the moment passed and he started to move off, his gaze on the hallway.

Shocking no-one more than myself, I placed a hand onto his chest to stop him. Felt the heavy pads of his pectoral muscles.

I had words to say. *Let me, Tom / I fucked up / You should stay out of it, or she'll blame you by proxy, along with me*

But words just fell away. This was an alien event far from Earth for me.

He leant down to bring his mouth closer to my ear. "Er, Laur, what...?"

I would never know what he was going to say.

I grasped his head in both hands and pressed my mouth to his, before I could chicken out or he could fight back.

The moment seemed to linger.

It was at that moment I knew; I had fucked up.

It was brutally crass, I'd seen it done in films and I'd acted without thinking but now what the fuck was I supposed to do, wait here forever with my lips sandwiched against his in the hope that the universe might end and spare me what must now inevitably come next?

I felt his rough stubbly chin scrape my chin, his cooler drier lips squashed to my wet anticipating ones. I smelled again that faint, spicy, bittersweet tang of cologne, but then a hint of mint beneath the grainy punch of coffee on his tongue and I felt his fingers press to my cheeks, his lips part, his body relax against mine and the instinctive seeking and entwining of our tongues.

It had never happened to me like this before and I was lost in the joyous, mutual intimacy and had no idea how long I was adrift but I did grab his bum because I remember the lovely firmness of it.

We separated and as quickly as it had come, the moment was gone. Tom stroked my cheek.

"Wow. OK then," he said, as lost for words as I'd be if I dared try to say anything.

His face looked as hot as mine felt. He seemed to want to say something but we had fallen into that trap of two adults who'd acted on a very teenage impulse and, now, had nowhere to go with it.

"Night, then," he said, and slipped past me down Jen's hallway.

He glanced back momentarily, held up his hand, the movement hesitant, tentative, betraying how out of character the passion had been, then he passed through the front door and it clicked shut behind him.

Jen's bedroom door opened and she peered out.

Ah-ha. *Jen*. Apology time.

She frowned quizzically at me. "Did you two...?"

So, my appalling faux-pas was in the past, my friend in her pink-and-black lacy bra and pantie set only interested in the gory details of something that was, to her, far more interesting than garnering an apology for something that, deep-down, she knew hadn't been *too* far from the truth.

"Can I *help* you?" she asked me, a laugh in her voice.

I was staring at her breasts.

She glared at me, hands planted knuckles-first onto her narrow yet slightly curvy hips. "Enjoy your trip to my tits, babe?" she asked. "Fuck me, Laur, you're hornier than me tonight!"

"Sorry," I murmured. Shook my head. "Sorry, Jen. Don't know what's wrong with me."

She came close and grasped my arm, leaning into me and whispering conspiratorially. "Don't apologise, just tell me *every-fucking-thing* in minute detail, babe. You an' Peters!"

I glanced up, to the left, down – anywhere that didn't require me to meet Jen's gaze, but she snared me anyway and her eyes widened as she realised.

"You actually did!" she cried, her lips curling at the corners with mirth. "You're shittin' me! How far?"

I grinned. Couldn't help myself. "We just kissed, but.. it was nice. Really... nice."

She slapped my arm. "I've got his number in my phone, babe. Just don't go marrying him on your first date, you fucking great ninny!"

I twisted under the absurdly heavy quilt on Jen's spare bed, lightly poached by the summertime air but unwilling to face going to sleep without some comfort. On my back now, I stare at the ceiling.

Jen's spare room was a ghastly, closed-in chamber with a window that opened about a nothingth of an inch, the air always stale and warm even in winter. In summer, it was practically unbearable, and tonight I was feeling unsettled even without the added discomfort.

Somewhere out on the Woodford Main road, a car whooshed along, the sound seeping faint and distant through the dull white window above my head, while the ghost of its headlamps trailed in an ellipse across the low ceiling of the room.

I always felt faintly claustrophobic in this flat. The house I shared with Grandma was very old, which meant that it conformed to a standard that demanded high ceilings and picture rails. This modern place had low ceilings and was entirely made from spitty fag papers and glue – all in all, I struggled to shake the idea that the whole thing was on the verge of collapsing in on me.

And it was hot.

That car gone, off to wherever its driver needed to be at this time of night, all that lit the ceiling was the faint smeary amber of the streetlamp on the corner of the 'cove', as locals tended to describe the cul-de-sac of cheap houses accompanied by a single block building of flats.

The night's events invaded me as an unwanted replay in the recess behind my eyes. The images came in a pouring cascade, each replaced by the next before I could gauge my emotional response to them.

Tom Peters, that strangely charming, cheeky yet somehow vulnerable man whom Jen had been successfully hiding from me all these years;

Jen herself, first in her sulky guise and then in a sultry frame, dressed in her undies;

And then, shockingly, those terrible blows raining down as Sam turned feral and punched, kicked and crushed

Their bodies, helpless on the ground, all their strength and virility ripped away as blood seeped from their broken bodies.

And now, suddenly, horribly, I was aroused.

"Whaaa...?"

I drew the wandering hands back up over my belly and tucked them under my buttocks, my brows crumpled down at the horrible prospect of getting aroused – not by Tom, nor even by my slutty friend but by Sam's violence and the victory of it over the weak flesh of his victims. Shit. What was *wrong* with me?

But sensations deep in my lower belly overtook my rational mind and those fingers slid down my belly once again, stimulating and setting off warm gushes as they pressed into my tenderest parts and probed deeper. I gasped as my belly clenched against the waves of spasming sensation rippling through me.

I bathed in the warm after-glow of orgasm for quite a while, really really spent and unconcerned if Jen had heard me bucking and gasping. In fact, in the heat of slowly-subsiding arousal, I dared her to walk in and witness me, right here and now, duvet tossed off, legs open, fingers and inner thighs smeared wet. I *wanted* her to intrude, so I could force her face down between my legs and into my wetness.

But slowly the elation faded and I was left, once more, on another wet mattress. I should have leapt up and flapped about in distress; normally would have, at the thought of coming all over someone else's bed, but no. Not this night.

Even as the wetness cooled and got soggy against the cheeks of my bottom, the remembered ferocity of my arousal refused to leave me, the glorious blend of sex and violence that had made me come so fucking hard...

I must have drifted off about then.

A young boy lay on his bed before me, his face obscured by an obfuscating haze. Naked but for pyjama bottoms, he lay still, and I knew him to be focussed on something I could not see. I had a horrible feeling I knew what he was about to do, he was a boy, what do boys always want to do? – but before I could groan in dismay I was grabbed from this room and thrown violently out into space.

A smeary blur of reality was wrenched past my face and then I stood (hovered might be more accurate, perhaps, because I had no sense of the ground beneath me) on a lamp-lit street some fifteen miles away from the boy, yet still in touch with his mind and conscious of the presence of him here. I was in the scene he was impossibly studying, aware of him, this scene, and that this scene was under his orchestration.

The first light of dawn tainted the night sky as I spotted a gaunt yet stately gentleman standing immobile before me.

What the–

I struggled to comprehend what I was seeing.

The old man wasn't standing, he was in mid stride. Utterly still like a startled rabbit, his eyes wide with the same terror such a rabbit must feel when it belatedly spots the car coming, he had one foot raised off the ground, the knee up, whilst the other foot touched only the toes of its sharply-polished brogue to the ground. His entire body was off-balance and angled heavily forward. He was not standing, nor strolling – he was freeze-framed in a moment of running headlong. *Fleeing.*

The scene was frozen. Waiting.

For me.

And at the moment I realised this, time resumed with a jolt and an audible pop.

The old gent's polished brogue clacked down and was followed by the other, the pair creating a frantic clack-clacking tattoo against the concrete that echoed around the empty night-time street as he hurtled headfirst right through my non-corporeal presence, a harshly fought-for breath erupting as a bellows hiss that pumped white steam into my face.

He passed through me and I rotated and drifted along behind him, keeping pace.

The old man flew into an alleyway, his pursuer's scolding breath at his collar, and then a brutal hand suddenly grasped at his flailing coat tails and wrenched him backwards. His expensive leather soles lost traction, whipped away from the hard pavement. He lunged for support with his hands as his legs tap-danced desperately for balance.

He spun and twisted awkwardly and *I* felt the sharp tearing pain in his side. He reached out for balance and the sharp stone edges of the rough wall split the skin of his palm open in a crimson zigzag, and after a moment's weightless drifting his body slammed down hard on the concrete. His teeth clacked together hard and I tasted the heavy copper flavour of blood spray back into my throat as his tongue was pierced.

If I'd been corporeal I'd have shuddered at the disorientating, nauseating sensations I was sharing with this man I was watching. As his audience I was sharing in his pain. It was horrible, elating and intensely dizzying.

The old man I was both witness for and empath to sat amongst his bundled coat and looked up fearfully, blood drooling between the cracked and freshly-sharp edges of his front teeth and out onto his chin.

His lip began to tremble and I felt such pity for him I could have wept, the shock of this terrible ordeal more than could be borne by the youthfully strong, let alone by this tired yet distinguished old gent who ought to be enjoying a peaceful end to his days. Anything but this.

Aware by virtue of this weird share-and-tell that his tongue was cut through, his teeth cracked, I now became aware of his pursuer.

The old man pushed out his chin and glared upward.

His pursuer towered over him, a patient goliath who obscured my view of the old man. The figure folded its arms, lost in silhouette as the halo of the streetlamp lit his bulky outline. "There, there, old man. Get your breath, now."

I could not see the face of this man's violent tormenter, but I didn't need to – I would remember that rich deep voice, oily with sarcastic tenderness, the rest of my life, even if I never again met its owner.

It was Sam, the maniac from the nightclub.

Now I felt confused as well as disorientated. Was I cobbling a dream together to cope with what I'd experienced? Or was I...

A rip of pain was followed by a suffocating sensation as the old man struggled to control the aching wheezes of his breaths, suppressing a pained cough with the speckled back of one hand. His gaze held his attacker.

"Who are you?" he demanded, trying not to let the terror leak out into his voice. "What do you want?"

By way of an answer, his attacker lifted a foot and swung it. A moment later I felt the hard blunt impact in his chest, heard and felt a crack, had a moment of razor-sharp rib-piercing pain. He howled miserably, helplessly, and I felt like joining him as I endured the wet, torn sensations in his lungs as he dragged in precious air and fought to live while liquid seemed to bubble up from inside to drown him.

He kept his eyes squeezed shut now, perhaps afraid that if he opened them his tormenter might see him cry. He tried to pull in a lungful of air, but a dry lumpy hiss sounded and I felt a heaviness, like wet cement, slopping about inside his lungs. I gagged on that horrible sensation and faintly admired the old man because he coped better than I did with what was, after all, exclusively his own pain.

He coughed, choked. Then he cried out with what little vocal power he had left to him. "What... ahh.. d'you want... with me?"

He was greeted by silence.

He opened his eyes, glared up at the terrible adversary he faced.

Sam. I knew what this monster was capable of. He stood over the old man, smug and evil.

"Please," the victim appealed, but then, seeming to hate the sound of his own weakness, he sharpened his tone. "Please leave me alone!"

"Come come, old man,"

The reply was calm, passionless, that voice deceptively deep and rich in timbre and seemingly incapable of belonging to such a mindless thug as Sam.

"You can't really want that," the monster went on. "Would you really choose to go on living this pitiful existence? Would you really want more of this, this... life? Be honest. Go on. Look at yourself."

A hard toecap plunged into his ribs again, as if to punctuate Sam's question.

So bewildering was this experience that I was unsure whether I heard or felt the crack that accompanied his pain. Both, I think. Such minutiae seemed a distant luxury as I endured this poor old man's terrible torment at the hands of my newfound nemesis.

Then the shared pain hit me, sharp and pointed, and I did no more wondering at all. It stabbed deep into his organs and radiated out, making him and me feel sick and weak.

"This is no life!" Sam berated. "What's left for you to look forward to, old man? Really, be honest now. Your 'twilight' years? Incontinence? Senility? The slow slow march to the cremation fire?"

Sam sighed, seeming almost like a teacher reprimanding the class layabout.

The old man went to reply but he had no breath at that moment.

Sam held up a placating hand. "No, no, no, old man. You must not see this as a bad thing. Far better to go out gracefully, don't you think." I saw Sam clearly then, and he was grinning. "Well, as gracefully as my sadism will permit, eh?" It was a sick grin left dead by his cold, sharp eyes.

The old man hugged his ribs but held the monster's gaze, his eyes defiant, and I so admired him in that moment I could've wept for him. "You must be very brave to set about an old man like this."

"Oh, I assure you," the deep smooth voice said serenely, "it's nothing personal. I do not get to choose my... targets."

The white-haired head snapped back sharply as a shoe came up under his chin, jolting jawbone and teeth, but then the foot jerked and glanced up along his face until it flicked up under his nose. I lost focus for a moment, as the old man must've done as his head was hurled back under the force of the blow, but I got my vision back in time to see a glistening streamer of snotty blood slurp from his nostril and onto his trouser leg..

The old man gave his head a sharp shake and brought his left hand up to his burst top lip. "Please, *please!*" he cried, sobbing, his dignity failing him in the face of such violence. "Just stop, please just – tell me what you want. What do you *want?*"

The huge figure crouched slowly, easily, before him, and even the weakling orange light of the streetlamp behind Sam was enough to lance the victim's sore eyelids and pierce his aching brain, dazzling me in my shared perception.

Huge rough hands grasped the papery old face, their grip threatening to splinter his facial bones. "Show me your fear, old man."

Taking as deep a breath as his sodden lungs could muster, the old man threw his weight forward and shoved the big man back, clambering desperately to try and rise to his feet. He was onto his haunches, legs splayed, when Sam casually swung a brutal kick to a terribly delicate place.

The pain was indescribable, the brutal hardness of a toecap slamming into the soft tissue of genitals.

For the first time in my life, I could fully understand why men are so utterly incapacitated when they get kicked there. I stood immobilised, stunned by the deeply internal wrenching, gouging pain that exploded from those little balls to engulf his entire body, clawing up into his belly, through his kidneys, back... Fuck, but it hurt *everywhere!*

He folded instantly to the ground and I would have joined him if I'd had a body to fall down in.

I knew it hurt for a man to get kicked there, but I'd had no idea. I was stupefied.

Staggered by the shocking intensity of this exclusively male agony, I lost focus and did not see what happened next, but when I did look again the old man was huddled in the tangle of his coat, moaning at a nausea I now perfectly understood, his eyes closed, his trembling hands flailing hopelessly at the ruined genitals between his legs.

He was rolled unceremoniously onto his back and must have glimpsed the very last dawn sky he would ever know.

His head was grabbed roughly and wrenched up away from the ground. Sam was strong enough that he was able to lift the paralysed old man up into a kneeling position by pulling his head, but he wasn't planning on helping him up. Oh, no. He threw the head away and down, hard.

I heard and felt a whistling rush of air past the old man's ears that was not painful, but then I watched his helpless body following his head in a graceful arc, the flailing tails of his coat gracefully billowing, and knew what was coming.

"No, no, no!" I cried, though no-one could hear me, screwing my eyes shut and instinctively cupping a skull I did not possess as I braced for the pain that the old man was about to receive.

There was a flash of light in his eyes and a jagged crimson flower of pain that splintered and blossomed at the back of his skull as brittle bone struck unforgiving concrete.

The rusty flavour of blood came into his mouth, the intense pain slicing through his skull and brain, but then he seemed to slightly disconnect from me. The pain fell away, becoming more distant.

His useless hands flailed to stave off the inevitable as his killer's voice drifted calmly through the warming air of the brightening dawn.

"You know, I really do have much more to give. I can hurt you much more than this, and much more artistically. That's what I like best, you know; the pain, the suffering. And to be honest, as long as I get the job done, how I go about it is entirely my own affair."

Sam knelt, grabbed his victim's gory head and gave it a shake. "Violence, see? And… yes, sometime I like to add sex to the mix, although if you don't mind too much I will draw the line somewhat before you on that score, old man. I hope you're not too disappointed."

The white-maned head, now streaked with reddish-brown down the back and one side, gave a sharp shake left and right, surprising Sam. The old man forced himself to return his murderer's gaze.

Seeing this spark of defiance, the mask of serenity slipped and I glimpsed the crimson flush that roiled across Sam's face. The giant screamed abuse in such a fast stream that he became incoherent, but I got the general flavour of it and so must the old man have done.

A heavy fist crunched onto the gent's left eye and his head was sent slamming against the concrete again. The pain was sharp, but that was nothing to do with the cry of horror I let out at that moment.

"Oh, no! *Please* not that!"

I saw the attack plan as the old man lay sprawled on the ground, legs, once again, apart, while the giant lined up, braced and drew back a foot.

"Noooo…" I whined as the old man's dazed eyes began to comprehend just after it was too late to save himself.

The leg swung.

I felt the hideous, alien agony of testes splitting open as they were pulped by this second, more violent slam from the hard, unforgiving boot.

I felt it with a detached nausea, because the old man's ability to feel the pain was diminished by the damage inside his split skull; and because I was a woman experiencing a man's emasculation, so I could acknowledge the horror of it without quite feeling completely engaged.

But oh; then the pain came.

A dying brain should accept its fate and stop craving life. That way, the suffering might be over sooner.

Doesn't work like that, though.

His brain had found a way to go on, something had re-wired itself.

And the pain came.

"*Ffff-f-fuck ME!*" I screamed as a burst of such razor-sharp pain tore through his internal organs that I saw pretty coloured lights go dancing before my eyes.

He must have simply laid there, shuddering on the ground, helpless. I wouldn't know, I was in my own private world of *uuurgh*.

Then his head was clamped in strong hands and wrenched up. He was forced into a kneeling position, the pain of his burst testicles discarded by his failing body as it reached a final survival mode of some sort. His hands flailed in a vain attempt to free his skull, to survive at any cost, but he had no strength and could only wait at the mercy of this monster, knowing the creature had none.

I had drifted whilst in my agony (*his* agony, of course...), but now I saw the benevolent smile on Sam's handsomely sculpted face. "All done, now, old man," he crooned compassionately. "Time to go."

The old man shrieked a pitiful shriek of horror and pain as his head was wrenched violently to the left, his neck joints crackling in protest and his mind recoiling at the knowledge of death gone from imminent to immediate.

It didn't hurt much at all, now. A mild, headachy sensation, no more than that.

His head was snapped back to the right, then fast to the left once more. There were cracks and pops coming from his spine, a vague awareness that the spinal cord was being twisted, distorted as supportive bones failed and broke apart.

A wrench to the left, pain lancing up into his skull this time and a distant echo of his hysterical screams as death rushed headlong at him.

Another wrench, more violent this time.

Suddenly I saw and felt his head jolt, pop and snap sharply off its pivot with a muted crunch that reverberated through his skull, accompanied by a sharp but short pain that drew a final gasp. From me, not him, I think.

Sam dropped him and stepped away.

The air sighed slowly out of his lungs in an almost peaceful surrender to the end of bodily existence. I vaguely felt his body crumple to the ground as I watched it do so. He must have wanted so much to hold on to that last breath, knowing it would be his last, but his lungs knew best and they let it gently escape so that his soul might follow it out and as the last of his air left him so, too, did his pain.

I saw Sam smile, give a little wave and stroll calmly away, before I fell into the broken doll body where the old man's soul still clung briefly to the cooling flesh. We waited together, him and me, companions in his dead body for a little while after his breathing had stopped. But all too soon his vision greyed out as his eyes dried and the optic nerves stopped talking to his suffocated brain.

Unable to gaze at the sky anymore, he let go and fell into the blissful darkness.

While I, released, awoke.

-6-

An anxious midweek bustle had settled over the computer centre when I arrived on Wednesday morning. I guess for some people, the impending conclusion of the week stirred up the fear that their manager was going to ask them to work the weekend, that most dreaded request-that-isn't-a-request which dooms all mortals to a conjoined, twelve-day working week.

Everyone got inspired, at about this stage of the week, both to review deadlines and to be damn sure they were either on target to finish everything on time, or to re-plan the *shit* out of it so it could wait two-and-a-bit days.

Personally, I never saw the problem with having to work the weekend, although for some reason I never understood, I was hardly ever asked.

I yawned and shuffled my way through the throngs of the immaculate and scruffy, all of them rushing to be at meetings or at their next caffeine fix, while I could barely find my desk through the haze over my gritty eyes.

Worry about the weekend? I wasn't sure I was going to get through the *day*.

I stopped dead. I couldn't face Ben yet.

Rubbing fingers against the gnawing ache in my temples, I turned and fled back through the double doors from the main floor and out into the lift lobby. There, across from me, was the door to the coffee room, its round portal window catching glints off the overhead lights.

The lobby was quiet. All the action that ever happened here, went on behind me in the office, except for the odd impromptu 'stand-up' meeting, but it was too early for that, yet.

I crossed to the coffee room door and leant my full bodyweight against the heavy old door, grabbing my weary old shoulder bag to stop it rolling off my shoulder.

I always saw the main coffee room as a place for relaxing; a social hub. This was where people came for lunch when they had time to get away from their desks, to escape the mad bustle for an hour (or more like a half hour), and where they could gather to eat, sip tea or coffee, maybe read a book or play cards, listen to some music.

To be honest, mostly these were wistful memories. The coffee room could comfortably house forty, maybe fifty people, with its clusters of quasi-comfortable low seats gathered around low flat tables, but these days it was mostly used for meetings when all the meeting rooms were booked.

It was never empty.

Today, it was empty.

I stared up at the vast leviathan of a coffee machine, one of a pair that had stood sentinel in this room since probably before I was born.

It hummed quietly, as if it were afraid to break the silence.

With a sigh I stabbed in the code '248' (Black Coffee with Sugar) and the machine whirred, clonked and then spurted its black treasure into a cheap cup. Realising that this machine never seemed to let me down, I thought resentfully of the higher-tech but very much more wanky coffee machine at the coffee station. I had cheated on this, my caffeine lover.

Fuck me, it's true that tiredness kills. It had killed my wits *stone dead*.

"Thanks," I told the hefty beast chirpily, strapping a fat grin onto my face. It was false joy behind that grin, yet somehow it helped give me a lift.

With my steaming prize pinched between finger and thumb I established my bag firmly across my shoulder and then left the gently humming peace and solitude of the coffee room in favour of the clamour and insanity of the main floor.

As I pushed through the heavy door into the main office, I was greeted with absolute silence. The place was deserted.

I was alone in the office. Utterly, impossibly alone.

Then, I heard the rush of voices, taps and clicks and Michael burst past me, narrowly missing my coffee cup with his arm as he shot away to something he clearly thought was important.

I shrugged off the momentary weirdness, the certainty that I had been standing in an abandoned office, as another sign of my intense weariness.

It was ten-thirty when I stepped into my pod, and Jen was already hard at work, her bright nails clacking down onto her keypad, an occasional push of the wrist steering her mouse across the desk surface. Great, just what I needed to see. Jennifer Sullivan in perfect working order whilst every nerve in my body was frayed right through and my eyes were glued to the back of my skull. Bitch!

I sighed as I passed behind her.

The perfect blonde bob flicked as she reacted to me, glancing up with a bright, white, perfect smile of alert joy.

"Hey, Laur!"

Too chirpy. Far too chirpy.

"Jen." I grabbed my desk to stop myself from going under the waves and put down my coffee with observed care. Collapsed onto my chair carelessly.

It hurt my bottom. "Shit."

As I was rigging my laptop, Jen trundled across to me on the coasters of her office chair. I glanced up in time to see a folded piece of paper pinched between two blood-red talons.

"Tom," she said simply.

My whole head filled with blood and it all poured into my cheeks. I snatched the little scrap of paper with Tom's number on it and swung toward my desk. If I couldn't see my friend, then perhaps she couldn't see the nuclear fallout of my blushing cheeks.

The printer behind us whirred into life and an unconscious reflex caused me to glance up.

Ben, our glorious leader, swung his gangling, multi-jointed climbing-frame of a body out of his chair and collected his printout, which was duly dumped on the desk as he stalked off out of the pod.

Jen lazed back in her chair, gaze fixed on me. "You good?" she asked.

"Me? I suppose. You? How's little mister teen tight-balls from last night. Roddy?"

She grinned. "Dunno yet. I'll have to call him."

"Look, I'm sorry we took the piss last night. Tom and me, I mean." I pinched my plastic coffee cup and raised it for a sip.

"Tom and you," she muttered with a smirk. "Sittin' in a tree… It's OK. All good. F'get about it."

Ben returned from the coffee station at that moment, and knowing how he was, especially first thing in the morning, I made what I imagined was a clear both-eyes-to-the-side gesture to warn Jen that his eminence was indeed back among us. Cut the chat. Look busy.

She didn't get the message.

"Just watch yourself there, babe, OK?" she went on, now unintentionally sharing my love life with our petty and judgemental team leader as he angled his bag of bones body down onto his seat. "Peters, he's got a lot of history. I don't want to see you get caught up in all that, get hurt."

Ben flounced across to the printer in the corner to collect his output. "No work to do, ladies?" He queried, his reedy voice piercing the air. "Perhaps you're ahead of your deadlines and in a position to take on extra work?"

I had a performance review coming up; I could *not* afford to piss him off.

Jen had no such concerns. I caught Jen's eye just in time to see her mouth a particularly fruity obscenity and thus got myself dragged into her little game. Ben saw it. He was meant to.

His gnarly twig of a body leant closer to Jen, his lips near her ear.

"I don't *care*," he hissed, "what you choose to say about me behind my back. But don't *ever* disrespect me like—"

He flinched hastily away as she spun her chair, chin jutting and eyes feral. "Get the *fuck* away from me!" she snarled, spit gathering between her teeth. "You think you can bully us, you tin-pot fucking shit-head?"

"I run this fucking team, Sullivan! You will show me some fucking—"

She jerked forward as if to rise and lunge at him and Ben backed off two panic-fuelled steps. He was never going to match up to Jen in full rage and he knew better than to push the bluff too far.

He glared red-faced and wide-eyed, his cock pulled off now he had been forced to so hastily back down.

He tipped his chin, smoothed his shirt front and cocked one eyebrow as he instantly dismissed the humiliation as an event that had never happened and then pasted his dignity back on.

"Keep pushing me, Jennifer," he said as he took himself back to his desk. "Just keep pushing me."

He deliberately failing to see Jen's single-finger salute as her other hand smoothed her skirt. She was almost as red as he was.

I cleared my throat. "I need the ladies."

Excusing myself and unable to meet the gaze of either of the combatants, I left the pod with my head down.

Drying my hands in the Ladies, I was oblivious to events around me until the door flew open and banged back against the wall to my right. Two women hurtled in through the doorway and staggered to a halt.

I stared at them. They barely noticed me.

The first woman was skinny, in her early twenties, with greased-back black hair. The other was older, with eyes that were red from crying and whose straightened brown hair had re-curled into its natural waves as a result of stress-related fiddling. The skinny woman was holding the older woman's arm, gently, as a kind of comfort/support.

The older suddenly pulled free and ran to the nearest sink to splash her face with cold water, then with water pouring off her cheeks and eyebrows, as well as the forward locks of her hair, she leant heavily on the sink and stared into the mirror, her breaths coming in short ragged gasps.

"Hello?" I said. "Are you OK?"

The younger woman flashed me an unfriendly look and snarled something I didn't catch at all.

The older woman spun the tap back off and hoisted herself off the sink, turning to her companion. "Ease up, Sam, she's just being friendly."

She rested her buttocks on the edge of the sink, leant backward and let her elbows angle out to take her weight. She cast her reddened eyes at the thin and, I now saw, slightly Emo-Punky-looking girl.

The girl looked away from that red-eyed stare and turned to shrug noncommittally in my general direction. "Sorry," she muttered without much of a hint of apology in her tone. "Bad day."

The older woman turned and tugged down a paper towel to pat her wet face with. "I'm Susan," she said, glancing at me through her patting hands. "This is Samantha."

The main door flew open again and bounced off the wall.

My heart fell out my mouth. Fuck's sake.

"Fucking door," Jen declared without much genuine irritation as she flounced in.

Samantha watched Jen impassively, whilst Susan fidgeted and pressed her bum into the sink.

"Sue, just heard you heard 'bout your accident," Jen said with a concerned frown. "You OK?"

"Jen." Surly, the older woman lifted her arse off the sink and folded her arms. "I'll be fine."

"So," I said quite loudly, intentionally cutting in. "Someone want to tell me what's going on?"

Susan shuffled on her feet again and so I looked her way. "I… nothing. I just had an accident."

Samantha grinned. "A *water-sports* accident. Bye-bye knickers!"

Susan barked a dry humourless laugh and glared at her friend, pressing her hands to her hips. "Nice! Thanks, Sam! I think I've had enough of your kind of help, thanks."

The punky girl stared at her.

"Fuck *off*, Samantha."

Jen laughed, flashing pearly white teeth between her red-painted lips. "Is that it? Is that all this accident was?"

There was a twitching muscle in the soft pad beneath Susan's right eye. "It happened in front of *everyone*." Tears welled in her eyes. "Absolutely everyone – my whole team."

She backed away, bumped a cubicle door and shot inside. The door slammed to shut us out.

I glanced at Jen, but Samantha caught my eye as she flashed us a grin and then flounced out of the toilet. "Laters, girlies!"

I watched the door slam shut behind her. "Can't say I like her much."

Jen shrugged. "That's Sam for ya."

"Twat?"

My friend grinned. "Wanna-be rebel. Maybe a bit of a twat, too. Never mind her, Laur. Are you OK?"

"I'm fine. Just tired."

"Still not sleeping? I thought crashing at mine might've helped?"

I felt hotness in my eyes.

She rubbed my arm. "Babe."

I shrugged, feeling suddenly very emotional and vulnerable, standing in the office toilet with the smell of disinfectant strong in my nostrils. "It's getting worse, Jen. The last month or so. The dreams…."

Jen grasped my arms and pulled me into an embrace. "We been friends since we were kids, babe. Talk to me, OK?"

She kissed my cheek and stepped back, still holding my arms possessively and holding my gaze to enforce her point.

Jen's aunt had lived two doors down from Grandma and Grandpa;

meeting her that summer had been the *best*. We'd just played and played... Ever since, however bad it got, I could always remind myself that I'd always have that first summer with Jen, the one time in my whole life that was just pure joy, fun... happiness.

"You always keep it in, babe," Jen was saying. "The dreams, ever since your parents... Y'know."

She wanted to talk about this. I didn't. I gently eased her hands off my arms and stepped free, holding her gaze. "I'll be fine, Jen. Have to be, don't I?"

She frowned, ready to say more, but at that moment a toilet flushed and Susan emerged from the cubicle, dropping something into the waste bin with a decisive sigh. "I'm going home. This much embarrassment, I need Vodka. Wine, gin. Hell, at a push, I'll go with bleach."

Jen took the woman's arm and co-opted my help by default as we took her back to her pod to collect her stuff.

Back in the office, I learned, mortified, that Susan's boss was the man named Michael, which was bad enough after I had been so shitty to him on Monday morning, but was made infinitely worse because he was so caring and supportive to Susan as she gathered her belongings. He was a *nice* guy. Bastard!

As I angled my head to ensure I did not inadvertently catch his eye, I instead snagged the gaze of another man, seated opposite Michael, whose ghastly appearance caused me to unconsciously recoil before recovering enough to feel the need to backtrack and make good on such an appalling reaction.

I smiled.

The ghastly man's thin lips parted into a cool, meagre smile.

"Hello," he said, his voice warmer than I expected, with a faint American twang to it. "Alan Mendis."

I tried to conceal my instinctive revulsion toward him, although I had never seen a man I so badly wanted to avoid touching. Everything about him seeped sickness and poor health; from his stumpy, pot-bellied trunk to his reddened scaly face, framed wetly by collar-length brown hair that seemed to have been dipped in a pot of grease before being glued in limp and lifeless strips to his bulbous skull. His eyes seemed to be in shadow even in this brightly-lit office, even though they were not terribly deep-set, as if they preferred the dark and carried a little of it around with them.

He extruded a chalk-stick arm from his frog-bellied body and before I could flinch he had seized my hand – yet oh, so *very* gently, which was more shocking than a tight grip would have been. He raised that hand from my side, trapping me in the cool of the shade with his sharp possessive eyes as the clammy wet-paper hand held onto mine.

"Erm," I coughed. "Laura. Laura Keeble."

His jaw sagged and his eyes flashed wide, the darkness falling away. In that instant, gone before I could really process it, I saw cold, piercing grey eyes glaring up at me and felt a shudder course through my body – of dread yet also familiarity, as though those cold eyes were a terrible reality I had already come to terms with.

And then, the moment was gone.

"Keeble, you say?" he asked airily, as though masking curiosity with offhandedness.

Instantly, no trace of that moment in his eyes now, his composure fully re-glossed and his limited charm seeping up at me.

"You wanna watch him," said a voice beside me. I turned to see Samantha, the punky girl, leaning in close to my shoulder, her cold gaze fixed hatefully on the little troll.

His lazy gaze locked onto her. "That'll do, Sammy," he said soothingly.

"Fuck you."

His lips peeled back off his crooked teeth. "You know better than to go causing any problems, don't you?"

"You," she started, "You can *fuck–!*"

"*-Shut!-* your mouth, Sammie," he said, the sharp cry of the first word soothed by the mellow tone of what followed.

His already-red face was reddening still further. It felt to me as if she were backing down, but Alan clearly saw something different, something he did not like, because I was hit by a thing. A thing aimed at her.

It was so far beyond anything within my experience that I was unsure for an instant if I might be imagining it. But it built rapidly and there could be no doubt.

A wall of force, of energy, shuddered through my head and made the base of my skull grind and ache.

I smelled apple pie for *no* reason *what*soever.

It was in me. *He* was *in* me.

What the fuck was… a power was emanating from him but it was rippling all through me, and it was a power that meant to gobble up poor little Sammy and spit out the bitch's scorched bones…

Fuck.

I started at my own sudden, cold hatred toward the punky girl. I didn't even know her, there was no way I could hate her that much.

The force welled up.

It was not my hatred I was feeling; it was his.

How?

This man, Alan, was going to use this impossible power rippling through me to kill Samantha. But, no; I couldn't let him! What could I do…?

There was a sharp pain at the back of my head. Something within me surged. Pushed back at him.

I cried out.

He cried out.

The power from him vanished and as my gaze met his, he was grinning at me.

"Well, look at you, Laura Keeble! It's a real pleasure, a *real* pleasure!"

That expression of pleasure, from a man I did not even know, would be the last of my day.

Jen ducked work to escort Susan home, which Michael approved and hence which was met with Ben's utter outrage – and on the day, as it turned out, that he had scheduled my career/performance review.

The one meeting of the year that would decide my payrise (if any) and set the tone for my entire year. The one for which I desperately needed to catch Ben in a good mood. And Jen, with whom I was always lumped together, had naffed off early.

My review began badly and went rapidly downhill from there; at one point, Ben even told me he *liked* me.

Ouch. The consolation prize for everyone who ever got stitched up by their boss. *'I like you, but..'*

Oh, dear.

And then: "Yes, there has been some *moderate* improvement in the quality of your work."

I protested at the faint praise, then, but Ben's de-construction of my self-worth was far from over.

"Laura, you don't back up your ambitions with the kind of hard work that would get results. Time and time again you tell me how you're going to put in the hours, go the extra mile, take ownership. But what do I see? A brief improvement, but then you're back in your old rut, arriving late, leaving early, no focus. Far too little."

I reminded him of my duty of care, my need to look after Grandma, but this was interpreted as passing off my responsibilities.

I played my first ace, at that point.

"What about Jen? Way she acts, yet I'm still junior to her!"

He told me in no uncertain terms that my attempt to use his dubious relationship with Jen was mean and bitchy, but ultimately beside the point. He did not like her, never would, but he did put up with her because she always delivered.

Sensing disaster, I played my final ace: a project I had taken on and delivered two full weeks ahead of time – only to learn that this had happened because Ben had enlisted Jen and Susan Blake to work on it without my knowledge. He trusted me so little that he had let me run the show but had made sure all the heavy lifting happened behind the scenes.

I had been set up to fail, and Ben's co-conspirator had been my best friend.

I left work that day knowing that my hopes had been discarded like soiled bum-wipes and, all in all, I was free to assume I would not be getting promoted to the board of directors in the very near future.

-7-

A strange yet familiar sensation.

He glanced up in time to glimpse the back of a female figure passing his pod, and for a moment he was tempted to rise to get a better look.

He lowered his pen. The sensation had been very strong. Could this person be connected with the interloper he had encountered last night, the intruder in his realm? He had to wonder if his decision to come here, place his cover story in this place, had been subconsciously driven by some knowledge of her.

His hand wandered to the shirt stretched across his rounded belly and he began to scratch absent-mindedly.

"Oo-oo-oo," cooed a voice behind him. "Is that your girlfriend, Al?"

The voice startled him from his reverie and he turned to Susan Blake, who flashed a cool grin at him.

"Excuse me?"

She nodded toward the corridor where the woman had just passed by. "You took a long enough look."

"Do you know her?" he asked.

She shrugged. "She's on Jenny Sullivan's team, I think. You want an introduction or somethink?"

He leant back in his chair, causing it to groan faintly. Smiled his most ingratiating smile at Susan. "That would be nice."

Her smile faltered. "Well, tough. I wouldn't do that to my worst enemy."

He felt pressure on his jaw as his teeth clenched together hard. "I see."

Susan leant toward him and he absorbed the briefest glimpse of breast flesh as her top sagged momentarily. Oh, the trappings of biology.

She was asking him something. Banal, mundane concerns that he did not trouble himself to take in.

His fixed his gaze on her. "Now, Susan, I'm afraid I'm gonna have to insist. What do you know about the lady?"

Samantha had risen from her seat, supporting her friend from across the pod. How sweet. "Al, what is your fucking problem today?"

Samantha was irrelevant for now. He would deal with her later.

He needed to know everything Susan knew about this woman who had touched his mind.

"Who is she?" he asked, but no longer because he expected or needed a verbal answer.

He clenched her mind in the fist of his own and forced the question through, his eyes watching her eyes glaze over as he pulled their joint focus down into her inner self / pushed past the barriers into the core of her mind / stripped out chemical bonds that got in the way / sought the right nerve bundle to trip / WHO IS SHE? / There! / Found it.

He pushed, ready to soak up the memories that were about to flow unhindered straight down the wire... but something was wrong, the trigger was too close to something else, something connected to the complex nervous system in there, joined in turn to muscles that fired when they should not fire and he felt his control snap as the physical overwhelmed the mental.

"Uh, uhhh, oh no!" Susan was crying out.

Alan shuddered as her mind was snatched away from him, still feeling a residual link to her as her conscious mind was swamped by mundane bodily functions.

She let out a weak whimper and the pattering sound of her urine pouring onto the carpet tiles beneath her chair made it clear his foray into her mind had come to an end.

"Oh no, no, no, this can't be happening!" Susan gazed around in horror at her team-mates, tears welling up in her eyes.

Samantha was on her feet. She scurried across the pod to her friend's aid, flashing Alan an angry but unfocussed glance as she passed, as if she wanted it to be his fault so she could blame him.

If she only knew. He smiled to himself as he turned back to his desk.

He had learned nothing. Still, there were other, more direct ways to force information from people. Susan Blake, prepare to meet a very dear friend of mine...

I stirred in my bed, Laura again for a moment. I glimpsed my ceiling, my lightly billowing curtains.

I knew I had been dreaming but I could not shake free, yet. The dream I had experienced was a prelude, I could feel myself being pulled back in.

I was drifting and my mind lost focus. Without knowledge of an actual moment of transition, I sank back into my dream and it picked up on a new thread.

I looked around and saw a quaint suburban road lined with identical houses, their owners having now stamped them with individuality through paint, or quirky hanging baskets, or lawn ornaments or hedges.

I felt a contempt that was not my own for such homely considerations.

The faint pattering sounds of a running shower reached my ears from an open upstairs window as I approached the porch of the house I was aiming for. No, not *my* ears. I was someone else.

I glanced at the upstairs window.

Felt the strangeness of the body around me; the bulge of muscles pressing against the sleeves of a shirt, the loll of a penis inside my trousers.

Sam. It was Sam who glanced up at that window, Sam who had arrived at this house. I was with Sam, but fully immersed in him this time, not a witness to his deeds but his co-perpetrator.

He approached the front door. My vision sharpened as his did, attuning in readiness for what was coming.

I pressed the door bell.

The shower pattered to a stop upstairs. I waited... *He, not me, he...* he waited patiently.

No rush. If anyone challenged him, he would act. He was quite unconcerned.

The door was answered by a woman whose body was wrapped in a towelling bathrobe, still using a smaller towel to scrub her wet hair.

"Mrs. Blake?" he asked. "Mrs Susan Blake?"

She frowned. "Who are you?"

He consciously held his gaze off the soft skin around her collar bones, the delicate throat.

"My name is Sam." He offered her a business card. "I represent Andrew's Fabrics. I've brought the samples you requested." He raised an arm full of sample books, weaving his deception.

He was strong; I hadn't even felt the weight of the enormous books of fabric samples.

He scented her hesitation. Really, he did. I felt the sniff of air and had an immediate sense of alert nervousness. She would bolt if he tried to move on her. He was faster but did not want to risk making this too public a scene.

Sam made a calculation. I could tell that this was not the first time he had done this, he knew how to manoeuvre his victims, he was efficient, good at it.

"Well," he said, pulling a face (I felt the facial muscles contract; it was very odd). "Your husband arranged this appointment weeks ago, but if it will not be convenient..."

Her expression altered. I wasn't sure what the new look meant, but Sam felt satisfied that he had cracked it with her.

"Oh. No," she said. "No no. My husband wants to get things moving. Far be it from me, eh?"

It seemed that she was more scared of what her husband might say, perhaps do, than she was of letting this huge stranger into her home.

"Come. Come in."

I felt the brutal satisfaction of a spider netting a fly. He really was loving this.

Inside, he surveyed the room and let his eyes rove over the soft furnishings in the lounge beyond, as she would expect him to do. Then he dropped the heavy books he had been carrying, letting them thud down on the floor before he knelt over them, his right hand loosening his tie. "Let's have a little perusal, shall we?"

As she leant over he glanced up, drawing in a breath to savour her scent. There was a peachy soap aroma coming from her. He preferred the raw animal smells of the feminine body, but the soap was pleasant, too, in its way. A little clinical, perhaps.

"So," he said. "Do you know what you want?"

She did not answer, instead holding his gaze, staring down at him with moist eyes and the smoothly-fleshed mounds of her towelling-swaddled breasts hanging loose as the robe feel away for a second.

He let his gaze linger for a moment and then looked down to peel open one of the large books, rotating it toward her on the floor. "The prices will vary quite considerably, but I do feel that there is a balance to be had between cost and quality, would you not agree?"

He had an amazing voice, deep and rich, and when he pasted on that slightly haughty, assertive way of speaking, he was really quite affecting. He was affecting me, and I was wedged inside his body – I could only guess how Susan was feeling.

She took a pant of air and stared down at him, the fingers of one hand lightly pressing on her lower belly through the robe. His body was finely tuned to detect such things. He was what Grandma used to refer to as a 'sex fiend' back when she used to have the wits to comment on the evening news.

"Can I get you a coffee before we start?" she asked.

"Oh, very kind." I felt him smile. "I'll see if I can't give you a few more ideas." He smiled and flexed his bicep under the close-fitting shirtsleeve, under the pretext of moving a book.

She practically bolted into the kitchen. Still smiling, he listened to the hasty splashes of water, the clumsy clonking around, the chink of mugs. A bitch on heat, young enough to still crave sex, but old enough to struggle to get enough of it. *Such* an easy kill.

I felt a thrill of deep-rooted pleasure, excitement that I would later be ashamed of, as I realised that Sam was here to kill Susan.

Still, it wasn't real. Even while still dreaming, I knew that I *was* dreaming.

Sam rose smoothly onto his feet and crept toward the kitchen, his eyes locked on Susan's back. She had no idea he had moved, lost in her own, deeper thoughts. He watched as she eased her hips gently forward, pressing her groin against the rounded handle of one of the floor-level cupboards.

I was amazed that any woman could be so stupid in this day and age, when we hear every day of some new horror visited on an incautious, unsuspecting, *trusting* person.

Even Sam seemed astonished by her lack of any caution, her apparent absence of any instinct for danger.

But he did not let her foolishness deter him. Studying her bottom, round and firm-looking through the robe, its neat shape pressed out against the cloth, he began to salivate and took a heavy lumbering step toward her.

Too many things happened at once. The kettle hissed and thumped off. She heard that heavy footfall and started. He stepped forward and pushed her hard against the worktop, his body to her back, his groin pressed firmly to her delicious bottom.

"I'd like sugar with mine," he crooned.

He coiled an arm around her midriff, face so close that her warm skin fed him hot soapy peaches. He let his lips brush her earlobe and felt her shiver with tense arousal.

She actually wants this, he thought, seeming genuinely shocked by the realisation. Clearly he was not the kind of man who asked for permission or willing participation as a rule.

He pressed his hand onto her belly and rubbed, drawing a gasp from her, then he eased his other hand into the front of her robe and pressed into the space between her breasts. He pushed his rough cheek onto her soft face, and her head lolled back onto his shoulder.

In a smooth motion he peeled open her robe and pressed his fingers deep into her soft fleshy breasts, then trailed his fingers down onto her belly, gouging the flesh with relish. Pushed his tongue against a vein on the side of her neck, then pushed his hands down, down, down. Then inward.

She wriggled and tried to turn, but his elbows pressed into her sides even as he groped at breast flesh with one hand, the other wedged deep between her legs, fingers intruding.

Now, finally, she recognised that, although she might have fantasised about this happening, it was not actually taking place with any consideration for her consent.

She was not in control, didn't even have a say in it.

And he was very, very strong.

I felt Sam's feral triumph, his... need. Bloodlust or lust, I could not tell. The two seemed tightly bound in him, almost one thing, a beast that hungered as it thirsted.

He knew she was his and, as he began to feel her, the primal stink of a victim, his blunt feral arousal overtook him completely.

"Please," she whispered. He panted with excitement.

She took hold of his forearms, tried to pry them away, whimpered when she found them utterly impossible to move. His thick, jutting penis seeped against his underwear.

He violated her with his rough fingers and kissed her neck. No, he was biting her neck, digging teeth just enough to taste meat but not enough to tear the skin.

She continued to beg with increasing desperation. I wanted him to. I wanted him to hurt her, to use her, to violate her in every way possible and then to take the little life she had left to her because even that was more than we could bare to spare her.

She struggled to pull his hand away from her privates, the indignity as bad as the violation, but she could not break his grip without seriously damaging herself so, now, she started screaming.

Her screams were piercing. Someone must surely hear.

Sam did not get angry or alarmed. He simply wrenched his fingers free of her genitals and shoved against he to push himself back, away from her.

She banged her hip on the worktop, hard, then staggered before she regained her composure and turned to face him.

He grinned and enjoyed the full frontal view as her robe hung open, but Susan Blake, to her credit, did not cower nor cover up, but stood erect, jaw jutting defiantly as Sam bathed in the wonder of her large pendulous breasts, her soft belly and thick untamed bush.

Her face was a mask of false defiance in the face of overwhelming odds, but her bottom lip wobbled as she spoke. "What do you, why are you doing this?"

"Why?"

"What do you want?" she demanded with a little more strength to her voice.

"Well I'd quite like to fuck that rather sweet-looking cunt of yours, Susan."

She gulped visibly and tried to edge around him, sure now that she was dealing with at least a rapist, probably a murderer too.

A little of me emerged from the blend I had formed with Sam. *For fuck's sake, you silly bitch, do something to save yourself!*

Sam moved easily, keeping her on a short leash, using his body to trap her close to the work surfaces.

He had an erection pulsing like a police beacon against the front of his trousers. I could feel it. It was strange, an alien organ, yet it felt oddly akin to my own arousal at that moment.

"Fuck you!" Susan screamed, and kicked Sam in the testicles.

Finally! My mind cried in exasperated relief, even as I braced for the pain, that pain I'd experienced for the first time through Sam's previous victim.

I knew it hurt, sensed that there was pain, perhaps damage, but it didn't matter. Sam was unconcerned by it and, as she bolted for the back door, he lunged and dropped an anvil hand onto her shoulder, feeling a pleasant cracking of bone as his grip shattered something, and then he hurled her back against the kitchen unit. She squealed sharply as the jutting worktop crunched into the small of her back.

She had enough sense to know that if she went to the floor now, that would be where she would end. Grabbed at the edge of the worktop to stay on her feet.

She stared, terrified, gasping, tits swinging uselessly as she stared at him through the tears of pain in her wild rabbit eyes, one hand clasping her broken shoulder. "What the *fuck?*" she cried in disbelief. "All this and you ain't even got any balls?"

Drool escaped her mouth, the lips pulled askew by her grimace of pain.

He raised an ugly serrated knife in one hand. I hadn't felt him pick it up. "Pain is what you make of it, Susan."

She frowned at him, at an utter loss. A rapist with no testicles, now apparently just a psychopath who liked to play with his food.

"Irrelevant. Now, I have a mission to complete, Susan Blake, so why not give me what I need from you and, you never know, perhaps I might show you a little mercy."

She stared up at him, a glimmer of hope in her eyes now. "Need to know? What? What d'you need to know?"

I felt the smile on his heavy face, as though the smile were playing on my own face. She thought 'mercy' meant survival. It did not.

"Tell me about Jennifer's friend."

Her wild terrified eyes stared uncomprehendingly at him, her knees buckling as she sprawled against the worktop and tried to balance. "Jen's... What? Why?"

Me? Sam was still after me?

"I won't take kindly to games, Susan. Now, pay attention. Tell me about Laura Keeble, and this will all be over."

"No," she sobbed. "No, please, you have to promise to let me go if I tell you. Please, please!"

She sobbed, her eyes expressing such misery that I felt a tiny glint of pity – not enough to overcome Sam's bloodlust, though, which coursed through me like an addict's first hit of the night.

"I cannot do that, Susan but I pretty-promise it won't hurt much at all, which is a good deal when you consider my track record in this area."

"Oh, please, *please!*" she suddenly cried, the last reserve of courage draining as the certainty of her own death, the end of her existence, was placed before her and begging was all she had left. "I'll do anything, *anything!* Please, just I don't want to die, please!"

She fell to her knees and her eyes gushed salty rain onto her tiled kitchen floor as she clasped her hands before her in appeal, as though deliberately posing for the front cover of a cheap detective novel.

Sam stared down at her and allowed a momentary pause. "Think very carefully. This woman is very important, you see. I have been seeking her for most of my life, but now my master's need aligns to my own. It is meant to be."

She shook her head, desperately trying to understand, to be a good little victim and give Sam what he wanted. "I don't..."

"I am telling you because I think you can help me, so please try to understand. My master needs the information because she has become an interloper in his realms, but this is personal for me. Laura Keeble was present at my birth."

Susan was all tears and uncomprehending fear, still desperately seeking a glimmer of hope that this monster might at least spare her life. "What, what do you need?

I felt Sam's mouth tighten into what may have looked like a smile but was actually a grimace as he bit down on his rage.

She was not co-operating and there was an animal in him that could smell her sweat and a hint of piss and it wanted to fulfil her role as his prey. And despite his disabled balls, he was still male and her robe was still hanging open; she was a naked female and there was more than a little lust in him, crying out for playtime despite any bruising he might have sustained.

He reached down and gently took Susan's elbow, guiding her up onto her feet. Standing her before him he tried, one more time, to get a rational answer from her.

"Now please listen," he said. "This is the question that decides whether you die with dignity, or screaming and begging and pouring out blood, bowels and urine. Are you ready?"

She nodded.

"Good. Where does Laura live?"

I wondered if Sam had no conception of social media, but then the little that was out there was all friends-only, and of course the house was in Grandma's name, not mine. My social incompetence had finally paid off!

Susan had just told Sam she didn't know where I lived – and I knew this was true, but mind traffic in this dream was one way. He wasn't picking up my thoughts at all.

She sobbed loud and hard and a bubble of snot burst against her left nostril.

"Oh, hush now," Sam murmured comfortingly. "Perhaps I can help you, hmm?"

He slashed the wicked knife across one bare breast, the left, just nicking the nipple and scoring the flesh beside it. The blade snagged her robe and caused it to flick off her shoulder.

Susan let out such a deeply distressed howl of pain and shock as she tried to cower, knees buckling so that she edged back in a half crouch. Sam held on to her elbow, more than strong enough to keep her in place before him.

"Please, please, *please!* No more, don't hurt me, no more no more no more...!"

She sobbed and clutched her wounded breast, her scared-rabbit eyes beginning to glaze at the horrific comprehension that there would be more cuts, and that they would end only when her heart stopped.

Sam sucked in a deep breath. He loved this moment the most. The musky odour of her brief sexual arousal blended with the acrid scent of an animal body in mortal danger. It was a heady blend.

The moment had come.

Suddenly, perhaps sensing that he was tensing for the kill, she threw her hands up defensively.

"Wait! Please! Please, I do know her, I do, I swear!" Her eyes darted down to where the knife waited in my hand – in *his* hand. "Please..."

Sam waited motionless, giving her her moment.

"If I tell you...?"

He watched her.

"Please, it hurts I can't bear being cut?"

Silence.

"Jenny!" Susan suddenly blurted. "Jenny knows her. Jenny Sullivan, OK? Jenny Sullivan."

"And where does *Jenny* live?"

She told him.

Of course she did.

It's hard to imagine how desperate you can get with a sharp knife and a violent man against your naked body.

"Is that enough?" Susan was saying, still fighting for her life the only way she could. "Is that what you needed? Coz there's no need to hurt me. Look, I'm sorry about your balls, but if you're up to it I could maybe make it up to–"

The vicious blade punched sideways across her throat in a hooking arc. Sam danced nimbly away from her as the ragged gash squirted out little pumps of blood.

She mouthed the word 'no' and clasped a frantic hand to the yawning red maw of her throat as if she thought she could stop her soul from pouring out somehow.

Her eyes widened, her mouth worked, she tried to draw breath but could not. Sam knew that the hot purplish-red sauce running down across the backs of her hands was also flooding into her lungs, and a moment later he was rewarded with a delicious wet gurgle that accompanied each hopeless stranded fish attempt to gulp air into her dying body.

She choked, spat a throatful of blood, her bulbous eyes still imploring him, begging, even though it was far, far too late, her last desperate appeal happening in the very moment of her dying.

She flopped to the floor like a hooked fish.

She bucked and jerked on the floor, her crimson-stained gown splayed, her vagina yawning open as her knees fell apart in a mockery of the equally red opening at her throat.

Her hips pulled in reflexively, her body convulsing. Slowly, slowly, her motion stopped. Like a clock winding down her movements slowed, her face relaxed, her back relaxed and her corpse lolled down into her gory robe, her feet slid outward, closing her now-redundant sex organ for the last time as her legs slid closer together, and, as he watched, Sam saw that the fear was gone from her eyes.

It was strangely peaceful. The struggles of life were over, there were no more bills to pay, no more alarms to wake her for work, no more decisions about where to go on holiday. For Susan Blake, all these things were *done*.

Sam wadded some paper towels and hunkered down to wipe her face clean. He dabbed her slit throat but was careful to leave most of the blood behind. Then, he took out his hard jutting penis and rubbed it violently until it welled with semen, and at the critical moment he staggered closer and took astonishing care to ejaculate across her cheek and nose.

I felt his orgasm and it was oddly bleak; the necessary release that failed to give him any meaningful satisfaction. For all his apparent power over her, Susan had achieved this one small victory. He had failed to sate himself through her brutal murder.

His work done, Sam left Susan Blake's house and stepped into a glorious summer's afternoon, content that he had made excellent progress on his mission.

As he slammed Susan Blake's front door, I awoke.

Just a dream. Yet I was troubled that I'd enjoyed Susan's murder. More troubled that no matter how hard I insisted to myself that it had been no more than a dream, I didn't believe myself.

Susan was dead and I had watched her being murdered. I knew that just as well as I knew that the poor cow had given Sam exactly what he needed.

The monster I'd shared kill-time with was still coming for me.

-8-

Morning sunlight fought to cut through the dust floating in the still air while I sat nursing a rapidly-cooling cup of coffee in the front sitting room. I still had the place to myself, with Aunt Potty taking Grandma off to the coast for a 'constitutional'.

Jen had called, already. First thing in the morning, for fuck's sake, and me barely getting three hours' sleep with my close encounter into Sam's foaming brain. I could barely recall the details of my friend's call – the faint kiss-and-suck of her smoking a cigarette, some grumbling about that teen angst boyfriend of hers, then the revelation that he'd dumped her.

He had dumped her, if you please. Jen had chewed through some really wonderful boyfriends in her time, but always with the same outcome. She'd shit on them, cheat on them and then cast them aside, often leaving them to come crying to me as the best friend with a hotline to her heart. Me, who would have loved any one of them for life if they'd ever even seen me just once.

I sipped my coffee, easily disregarding Jen's chapped-arse emotional state whilst considering a second cup before I headed into work. I was particularly smart today, in a rather slimming grey skirt and matching jacket, a creamy-white blouse and a small amulet on a chain at my throat. I was dressed to impress.

Dressed to impress Ben, of all people. My life in a bin liner!

The front doorbell rang.

I went into the hall and, only as I pulled the door open and was confronted by a vast bulky figure that blotted out the sun, did I belatedly remember my derision of Susan's carelessness in last night's dream.

Fortunately for me, the figure at my door was not Sam, was nowhere near as big, fierce or magnificently terrifying, being only human-sized and athletic, with those tiny, almost dainty spectacles perched on the bridge of his nose.

"Tom," I said. "What a surprise!"

I smiled into his uniquely craggy young-old face as he stood awkwardly on my doorstep, no doubt trying to understand the sudden relaxation of relief in my posture.

He smiled with his usual toothy grin, but his eyes carried a trace of apprehension. "I hope this is OK?" he asked.

"Jen gave you my address?"

He shrugged. "Thought you might fancy a trip out today. Not, y'know, a date. Unless you, er..."

"I'd love to, but I have to go to work."

He tried to keep smiling but he fulfilled the definition of crestfallen. "Oh."

"My boss will cut me a new orifice if I call in sick, he's a bit of a bastard to be honest."

"I understand, Laura, it's fine."

Ben that shitty pencil-shaped prick. What the fuck was I doing?

I reached out and touched Tom's arm. "You know what, why not? Yes. Let me change into some jeans and then I'll call work."

His grin right then would probably have kept the Earth alive if the Sun had gone extinct. I returned a lower-wattage smile of my own and invited him in while I changed.

As I changed upstairs in my room, a little bit of me wondered about letting a man I barely knew into my home, but Tom wasn't like Sam, he wasn't a monster. I just knew this to be true.

I stopped and my skirt flopped to the floor. I stared at myself in the mirror. Shit. What if I had to let him see me naked? I had so nearly joined that gym last year. If only, but no, I was lying to myself. I had never really been close and this was the body I had which, for whatever reason, didn't seem to have put Tom off at all.

In my favourite jeans and a white tee shirt over a white bra (no slutty black show-throughs, thank you), I untied my hair and let it fall free. It was clean from the shower, so I could risk letting it loose on the world, not that I exactly had great long locks; my hair was thick, brown and onto my shoulders, but it was hardly what the ads like to call glossy or sleek.

Meet Matt Brown.

Downstairs, I found Tom neatly stored where I'd left him, waiting in the front room. I led him out of the house whilst fastidiously ignoring his compliment on my clothing, which he followed with a cheeky glance at my backside as I passed him.

I felt a little proud. He'd eyed me up. Check out my radiation dial.

Outside in the mild warmth of the early sun, Tom eyed my beautiful MG-B roadster, Mickey.

"You expect me to get in that?"

"Oh, don't you start, Tom. That there is a proper classic car."

"Looks like a boneshaker, you want to go in my car?"

I squinted at him. "Has Jen been prepping you, Peters?"

He laughed. "Erm, maybe."

"You'll love it," I assured him. "Roof down, the sun on your face and the fresh air pouring over you. Besides, we come as a *package*."

"Well, shit." He grinned at my super-serious expression. "You win."

After a few minutes to fold the roof, being a proper convertible that had none of this easy convenience bullshit of touch-folding, we clambered into the low bucket seats and I caught him looking up at the sky and drawing in a lungful of air.

Yeah, told you so, laddie.

"Where to?" I asked, sure he'd have a plan for this impromptu meet-up.

He wound his window down, fascinated by the manual winder. "What? Oh, how about we go into town, grab a coffee and have a mooch, see where the mood takes us?"

With a throaty burble we blew through the gateway of my drive and I threw the wheel to send us down Tiler's Hill, right at the bottom and on into the town centre.

As I throttled Mickey up to get us back to town, I glanced at Tom and decided he had until the coffee was gone to show me a layer; a bit of content.

I'm no Jen, I don't expect it all, but, seriously, he sat in silence beside me, squinting impassively into the oncoming wind, and I couldn't see him turning this around. Impulsive kiss notwithstanding, I was damned if I'd do all the legwork.

The open-plan coffee area in the shopping centre was far from the best coffee-house in town. Frankly, the only decent coffee houses were all far from town.

Still, it was nice. Well-designed plastic seats came with padded cushions to nurse the weary bum, while a mini-picket fence ringed off the area and made it feel a tiny bit apart from the shopping throng.

I drew a deep ragged breath. Stop it. It was nice to sit with this man. He was a nice man, except that fuck it I wanted this to be more than nice; I wanted romance and passion and other things a girl like me might wait a lifetime for and never get.

I did not want *comfortable* – that's what my favourite winter fucking sweater was for.

I sipped my coffee and tasted the pungency of the beans, the hot smell of the steam prickling my nostrils. I thought of Sam, that huge brutal bastard. Damn. My dream had him measured out about right, based on what I'd seen. Mindless, lusting murder consumed him, violence and sex blended into one lust, all sated by brutality. So why did I get all tingly when I thought of him?

Shit, Laura – stop it.

I shut the thought out, tried to focus on Tom. "So, how's the coffee?"

"Hmm?" he glanced up over his white mug. "Oh. Nice, yeah. Good coffee. You?"

I nodded, biting down on the impatient twitchy urge to jump up, dance around, shake my tits in his face – *anything* but this.

I saw his brow crease. "You OK?"

I nodded. "Sorry. Headache."

"Oh. You, er, you want me to go and get something for you?"

I shook my head. "I'll live."

"So." He slurped coffee. "How long you known Jen?"

Wow, hit me hard and fast with a question!

I grabbed another quick sip and launched into a potted history, telling him how we'd been friends since we were little, with a few gap years when I went one way, she went another. How she had got me in at the company where she was an I.T. Trainee. Exciting stuff.

"Lifelong pals, eh?" He leaned forward, picked up his whole piece of carrot cake in one broad veiny hand and lopped off a huge bite that smeared creamy topping onto his lip and the tip of his nose.

I smiled and pointed a finger at his nose. "Would you like a tissue?"

"It's not that exciting, love."

"What?"

He grinned a cake-toothed grin that slowly slipped away as I did not reciprocate. By the time I realised he'd cracked a funny about ejaculation, it was too late to even feel nauseous about eating the creamy topping of my cake.

"Classy, Tom, real classy." I handed him a tissue. "Cake face, nose and lip."

He took the tissue and wiped his nose sheepishly. "Damn, girl," he said. "We narrowly missed out on a tacky romantic-movie moment just then."

I laughed. "No, you just made an entirely inappropriate semen joke."

He widened his eyes. "Don't come over all indignant!"

"Funny man, is this how it's gonna be? Cake face and jizz gags?"

"Sounds like a good name for a double act, perhaps we could corner the market."

"Arf arf! So, I guess you and Jen are pretty close, too. Were you ever?"

"No!" He snorted. "Come on, give me some credit, Laur! We're friends is all, and that's all we'll ever be. Just friends. Close friends, I'll grant you, since my, erm…" He glanced down at the table so I wouldn't see his eyes go dull, but he was too slow and I did see.

I leant forward. Did I ask? Leave it well alone?

He tried to glance up but his eyes wouldn't co-operate. I saw his hesitation in the twitching of his fingers and the way he kept his head down. Then, when he did look up, his expression was set.

"Look. This isn't something I talk about, OK? I mean, not ever. It was years before I ever told Jen, and she's the only one. But with you… I want you to know who I am from the start, how I got to where I am, now."

Well, it was my own fault. I wanted depth. Now, I was going to drown.

He sighed. "I can see that expectant horror in your eyes, but it's nothing like you're thinking. I was married, once."

"But not any more? Coz I don't want to go down that road with anyone."

He shook his head. "It was a long time ago and it ended badly. Very badly. There was violence, there were kids got involved…"

"Violence?" I blurted. Idiot.

"Not from me." He squinted slightly at me, but gave no other reaction. "It was my ex. She had some problems. Drugs. To be blunt, Laur, she was a lifelong junkie and nothing I did ever seemed to help. She'd go off the rails, I'd help get her straight, we'd be good for a while and then it'd start up again."

"Oh, Tom."

"There'd be no food in the cupboards, the savings account would get emptied and I'd know."

"Shit!"

He nodded. "Oh yeah. Off her face on the settee every morning while our kids got their own breakfast, still there when they came in. I had to go out to work to keep us as broke as we were, but it was a real killer. Work all day, get the kids their dinner, get them settled for the night and then deal with Emily."

Damn. I didn't know what to say to him.

His mind far away, back in those dark times. "I used to hide money for the kids' school stuff, food, bills, but she found it one time and really turned. She got rough with me and I soaked it up, told myself 'I can take it', but when she saw it wasn't working she turned on the kids."

"Did you get the police involved? Did they put her away?"

"I had to defend them, it all happened in the moment. Emily was going to hurt them, she couldn't control herself but she didn't leave me a choice."

He drew a shuddering breath.

"Anyhow, that's how I got to know Jen. She was a witness, saw it all."

"Jen? She'd have been a teenager, surely?"

"Babysitter for the neighbours, making a crafty quid on the side for herself. I'd seen her around but apparently she paid more attention to me than I realised."

"Ah, OK." That sounded like the Jen I remembered.

"In the end, Emily got professional help, straightened out, got a divorce, a new man and custody."

"Tom, that's bullshit! You have a right to see your kids."

He smiled a humourless smile. "Funny. I thought that, too, but the new, clean Emily and her shiny wealthy manfriend thought I'd stir up the past, confuse things – talked me into giving them space. Weeks turned to months, months to years, they'd started calling him Daddy. I'd become a reminder of shit they were just starting to be able to forget."

"Hey!" he cried, pulling off his spectacles and wiping the back of a hand across his eyes. "Damn! I brought you out on a date and just *look* at me! I am so sorry, Laura!"

I held up a hand. "It's fine. You needed to say it and I'm glad you trusted me with it."

"You and Jen ever talk about it, now?"

He shook his head, replaced his glasses on his nose. "She was there for me when I really needed it, I'd probably've got prison time without her. But we're… light friends, y'know, keep it fun and lift each other up." He smiled. "Bright smiles and no gloom."

"Sometimes that's what we need, right? Someone who'll make light of the really shit days for us?"

I suddenly stiffened, straightened up sharply in my plastic seat as I felt a bizarre tingling at the base of my skull.

He cocked an eyebrow at me. "Someone walk over your grave?"

"No. I had the weirdest – *Onw!*"

I grabbed the back of my head as the tingle momentarily became a sharp stab of pain, cutting into the base of my skull.

"Laur, you're worrying me. Is it your headache?"

I winced as the pain stabbed again. "My what?"

And then, in my peripheral vision, I glimpsed a large figure slip inside the clothes shop opposite the café area.

Surely not...

Tom was saying something but I no longer cared. I sprang up. "Stay here."

Suddenly full of resolve and certainty, I sprang from my seat, clambered over the low picket fence and strode across the mall concourse. There was an insistent tugging at my senses triggered by that tingle deep in the stump of my neck; it had to be answered.

Tom called my name – twice, I think – but he was now completely outside my field of interest.

I entered the shop.

"My *dear* Laura."

I would have felt his presence behind me even if he had not spoken.

I felt a squirt of ice water flush through the centre of my spine and into my bladder at the sound of that deep, rich voice. I turned sharply but kept my voice calm.

"Hello, Sam."

If the lights in the mall had seemed stark, the glare inside the shop was positively nauseating. It was hard to believe I had been unable to see him until that moment.

"Whoah!" Tom stumbled to a halt beside me. "You're a big fucker, ain't you?"

"I told you to wai–"

The huge form suddenly surged forward like a steam engine strapped to a rocket and as he grabbed my arm I was save from being slammed to the floor because Tom had anticipated and immediately shoulder-slammed Sam aside.

The hand that had me really had me, its grip like pliers plucking the muscle off my arm bones.

I cried out as Sam pulled me to the side with him.

Tom didn't hesitate. He threw a hook punch that slammed the giant's jaw, immediately followed by a straight punch that caught Sam's chin; enough, I would expect, to floor any normal man, but utterly ineffective against this monster.

I could feel the layers of tendon peeling away on my arm and wanted to scream and wail, but something in me refused to give Sam the satisfaction.

His punches having failed, Tom hunched over and slammed himself shoulder-first into Sam, which dislodged the monster's grip on me. I stumbled away, off balance and with a heart that was hammering to be let out of my chest as I saw Sam teeter, regain his balance and clamp a great meaty shovel of a hand down on my defender's shoulder.

It was Tom's turn to cry out as he was snared in that inhuman grasp, while the smiling giant had eyes only for me – cold and malicious. *He is suffering for you now, Laura*

With a yell of outrage a shop security guard came at Sam. Well over six feet tall, he was almost Sam's height and not far off his build, but Sam did not even look at him. He swung his spare arm so fast it was a blur, and so hard that the only thing louder than the thud of the back of his hand hitting home was the sickening crunch of nose bone and eye socket splintering in unison.

Ignoring the horribly injured guard, who had hit the floor quicker than he had charged into the shop, Sam returned to Tom, still gripped by the shoulder and trapped at arm's length, but who was punching the same point on Sam's wrist time and time again, obviously hoping to cause a fracture.

The monster flashed me a smile.

No, I thought. *No!*

I saw the blow arc down and pushed at it. I was too far away to touch him but I grabbed his fist nonetheless and instead of caving in Tom's face, the blow thudded into my new friend's chest.

What did I just do?

Tom flew backwards about three feet and smashed into a rack of clothes, his trailing legs disappearing into the waving flags of cloth as he went through, bound for the floor somewhere beyond.

"Fuck!" I cried, staring at his legs, protruding straight and still from under the chaos of clothing. I needed to get to him, that impact had sounded bad, but Sam was focussed on me now.

I turned to face the monster, terrified that he might be right on top of me.

But Sam stood where he'd stood before, lazily aiming his gaze at me. "You should know better than to encourage your menfolk to fight *me*, Laura Keeble. Surely enough males died for your sake in that gaudy den of iniquity."

"Den of…? You mean Leo's?"

He shrugged, his smile turning down into a more world-weary expression. "It is a place of noise and stupidity, Laura. Of debauchery and evil."

I gawped at him. "Are you fucking shitting me?"

Sam laughed gently. "I claimed no particular values for myself; merely observed that such a place is… no better."

He did not seem to want to attack me, so what was this all about?

I edged a step toward Tom's prone form. "I'm going to check on my friend now, Sam. Are we going to have a problem?"

He said nothing; did not move.

I hurried to the heap of clothes and let out a cry of relief as I saw Tom flapping wildly to free himself from the tangle. He sat up, fumbling awkwardly to straighten the spectacles that had been tilted across his nose as I hunkered down beside him.

"You're tougher than you look," I told him, too relieved to feel much else at that moment.

"You wait 'til I get hold of that fucking"

The great slab of Sam's arm reached over my shoulder and grabbed Tom's tee-shirt, wrenching the cloth taut, as Tom's eyes momentarily welled with fear but then grew sharp, hard.

"Fuck—" he grunted, *"You!"*

He lunged forward, launching himself from his hunkered-down stance and assisted by Sam pulling him, so that I was tossed aside and arse-up by these two slabs of male meat intent on pummelling each other.

I tumbled awkwardly against a clothes rack and my elbow took a painful, fizzing wack, though I was lucky that's the only harm I did suffer.

Here we go, I thought, although a big part of me knew I was being ungenerous. Tom was trying to protect me and I don't know why I wasn't livid at Sam.

I clambered hastily up in time to see Tom swing his arm in an arc, his fist slamming home at an angle to Sam's jaw. Sam's head tilted but he remained impassive, unharmed by the hard blow. He kicked out a leg with unexpected agility given his size. The foot took Tom full in his belly and, with a muted noise like a grunt, he folded gracelessly to the floor, where he knelt, doubled up in pain.

Sam turned to smile at me again.

I decided that he was going to pay this time.

There was heat behind my eyes, a pulsing at the base of my skull and a sudden look of alarm on Sam's previously-smug face as I rocketed across the shop floor and slammed the palm of my hand straight into his face. His head snapped back, but he brought it lazily around again to aim a cold grin at me.

But I could see the cold dread in his eyes that belied his grin. He *knew*.

Both his great spades of hands clamped my waist to break me like a dry twig.

My hand slamming into his chest was accompanied by a sharp pulse at the base of my skull and Sam flew backwards as if he'd been snagged in the jetstream of an aircraft.

He hit the rear wall with an echoing thud and slumped heavily to the ground.

I stared, immobilised by the dream-like defiance of natural law, but a groan from the floor reminded me that Tom needed attention.

I turned and knelt beside him while behind me, Sam arose uninjured from his breakneck voyage. I didn't see him clamber awkwardly to his feet; I was not looking his way. And yet, I knew it was happening and, even as he skulked away like a hurt puppy with his tail between his legs, I was able to watch him whilst also attending to Tom.

I heard a shout outside; perhaps the Police were there. Perhaps Sam would not escape this time.

Tom was sitting up, now. "What the hell happened?" he asked, wincing with pain as he rubbed his back.

The fizz in my head had faded and, now, I could no longer sense things outside of my actual senses. I shook off the memory of my brief, scary hyper-awareness and helped Tom with his painful climb into a standing position.

He had kept a floral dress gripped in his hand as he stood. He now held it up now, his wry grin left a little hollow by his evident pain. "Can you see me in this?"

I glanced behind me. People were gathering around two people whom Sam had swiped and hurt when he flew across the shop, others were tending the wounded and unconscious security guard.

This is bad.

"Come on," I told Tom sharply.

He nodded and I helped him along for a few paces, until we were able to fold into the crowd gathering in the shop and melt away. Security were already herding onlookers out of the shop, and in doing so they unwittingly insisted that their two star witnesses leave the premises too.

-9-

I left Mickey's roof up when we left the mall.

As I signalled and pulled out of the carpark, my silent passenger found his voice. "Who the hell was that big fucker, Laura?"

I swallowed hard. "I met him at Leo's."

"You..." Tom drew in a sharp breath. "That massive fight! That was him, wasn't it?"

I nodded. "Tom, we have to go to Jen's place."

Tom cocked an eyebrow and I noticed a faint bruise above it. "We have to go to the police."

"It'll take too long. Jen's in danger right now."

"What is all this?" I could hear the exasperation in his voice. "One minute we're on a date and the next you've introduced me to Chadbury's answer to the fucking Terminator!"

"I can't explain now, Tom, but that maniac might have Jen in his sights."

I couldn't explain it to him properly. A madman was hunting me, he knew where Jen lived and I knew that from a dream where I saw him murder a woman called Susan. Tell him that and see if he wants to stay in the car with you.

"Jen's place it is," he said.

I pulled the gearstick into fourth as we thundered over the top of the hill, and as we rolled onto the decline down the other side, I flicked the overdrive switch. Cutting left I got us onto the road to Woodfield Heath and the shortest route to Jen's flat.

Maybe we'd be lucky. Perhaps she had gone to work and was entirely oblivious.

Shit! I didn't call in sick; Ben was still expecting me to show up!

The stupid things you think of when your life gets flushed utterly down the toilet.

Tom had to shout over wind noise. "What we gonna do if we get there and find that big fucker waiting for us?"

The wind cut across the car and made the roof flap over our heads.

"I don't know, Tom. I really don't know."

I swung off the main road and took the bend too fast. Mickey's tyres squealed but I showed him no mercy, throwing the car into the communal carpark behind the clusters of two- and three-bedroom flats where my friend lived.

Swinging into one of the parking bays I hit the brakes, killed the ignition and wrenched up the handbrake.

As we left Mickey, he was pinging and ticking frantically as he tried to lose the scolding heat of being mercilessly overworked. but Tom was halfway to the security door, so I hurried to catch up, relieved I'd put my worn but practical boots on with my jeans.

After a minute or so of Tom pounding on the door and calling her name, it became clear that we were not going to get an answer.

He turned to me. "She must've gone in to work."

I studied the door. "No."

"C'mon, Laur, be reasonable."

I stared at the door and just knew. To convince my companion, I reached into my jeans pocket and pulled out my mobile. "If she's at work, she'll answer this."

I was certain that Jen would not be answering this call. I dialled it and put it on speaker, so that Tom heard it ring, then ring, then ring – then click and divert to voicemail.

"Y'alright, this is Jen, I can't take your call or I don't like you, but if you're—"

I cut the call and raised an eyebrow at Tom.

He shrugged. "Could be in a meeting, in the toilet, on the boss's lap."

"Have you *met* our boss?"

He laughed and I smiled, but this was all wrong. Jen was in that flat and she was in trouble – if we didn't get in there it was going to be too late.

A lie was required.

I pretended to start with surprise. "What was that?"

Pathetic effort, really.

He frowned at me.

"Seriously!" I insisted, pointing at the door. "I heard something."

I was full of shit and he knew it, but she was our friend.

"Fuck it," he said. "Let's get in there." He drew a deep breath and then slammed his solid athletic shoulder against the door. And bounced off it.

"Erm, ow," he said, rubbing his shoulder and glaring at the door as if it had resisted him just out of spite. "Right, you want it that way?"

He took a half-step back and kicked his foot out hard. The door juddered and I heard it split, the white veneer finish cracking beneath his hard black boot. He kicked again, nearer the latch, so that this time the doorframe split and the door slammed back hard against the wall of Jen's hallway.

He was inside, swiping the door with his arm as it tried to bounce back into his path and then we were both hurrying into the flat.

Her living room was dark. The curtains were drawn.

It was gloomy but not quite dark, and had that chill that only a closed and darkened room in summertime can ever quite achieve; the deprivation of warmth on a warm day.

A small, sad bar of light was creeping around the almost-closed kitchen door, casting a yellow hue on the area around the sofa.

A lone figure sat on the sofa, hugging itself. The quiet twittering of a daytime radio programme emerged into the silence and almost covered the sound of quiet, desperate sobbing that seeped from the hunched figure. Beside the sofa, a collection of dead lager cans caught the weak light from the kitchen, lying in random assembly around an ashtray filled with ash and crushed cigarette filters.

"Jen?" said Tom, his voice low, almost reverent.

I smelled something rich and gamey that reminded me too much of meat that was on the turn, or old, old cheese. A knot formed in my throat and my stomach wanted to bail out.

The figure slowly looked up and I caught a glimpse of something shockingly wrong. Just a glimpse, not enough to fix properly on what I had seen, but enough to make me want to run screaming from this place, to *not* face whatever this was, whatever dreadful fate had befallen my friend; this thing wearing my friend's robe and yet not entirely Jen any more.

"Babe?" I whispered, my voice thick and ruined to my own ears.

"What's *happened?*"

The figure lowered its head and covered its face. I distinctly heard its whimper this time.

It spoke.

"Plllleeeease."

An aching chill cut through my spine at the sound of that voice, so thick, phlegmy and coarse, still *her* voice, but no longer her. It was sick, ruined and it exhaled that rotten meat and old cheese stench that already clung to the lining of my nose and the back of my throat.

Suddenly I wanted to stop myself being sick because I was sure that if one end of me expelled, the other would too.

Thing started to drag itself up. It was slow, moving painfully. I backed away, as did Tom. We exchanged a panicked, desperate glance *what the fuck do we do?*

Its dressing gown flopped down around its legs as the figure straightened into a crooked stoop, and then it began to shuffle toward the door, its movements hampered by an apparent discrepancy in its legs; one slightly longer than the other.

My mind was full of my own screaming at the knowledge of this thing right here with me, this horror happening right now and I was trapped in it, couldn't run, had to help her but can't *cope...*

I backed into Tom. He clasped my shoulders and I felt the tremor in his hands. I couldn't look at him. If I saw the panic, the horror I felt, reflected in his eyes, I was done for.

The shuffling thing was between us and the way out – the *only* way out of this flat that wasn't a blatant suicide attempt. We were trapped.

But as we stood paralysed and I, for one, grew heady as I fought to avoid breathing the stink of its decay, it seemed to forget about us and shuffled into the gloomy corridor that led to Jenny's bathroom.

I heard the pull-cord just as light flooded from the bathroom and splashed the purple hallway wall opposite.

It had passed inside before the light came on. I still hadn't seen it.

I lashed a hand behind me for Tom's hand. Found it and grabbed on tight.

"I don't," I hiss-whispered. *"I don't think I can do this, Tom!"*

I didn't want to and suddenly I took a faltering step forward. I heard a gasp and realised it had been me. I looked down at my legs as if seeing them might make them part of me again, but now Tom gently yet insistently pushed on my shoulder, gallantly edging me into taking the lead, the fucking tosser, and my shoes shuffled on Jen's carpet once more.

The eternity to her bathroom was not long enough as I reached the doorway.

I heard mournful whimpering, but as I passed into sight of the room the dazzle of the lights blinded me.

I squinted and fought to see. Something stood hunched at the mirrored cabinet.

"Jen?"

My eyes adjusted to the light but my brain couldn't. I wasn't seeing this. It wasn't this that I was seeing.

There was enough left of her to recognise. Just.

"Fu-, fu-, fu," Tom uttered, and I felt him back away and leave me in the doorway with this creature two arms' lengths away.

"No," I said stupidly. "No."

The right half of my friend's face was still there, still recognisable, although pale grey and dusty-looking. The left half, though, was just *gone*. A thick, rough, blistery grey fungus filled the concave area where cheekbone, cheek, lips and chin were supposed to be, a spongy mass that bubbled, cracked and tumbled to the floor as dust as she turned fully to face us.

As her face came fully into view I saw that Jen had only one eye, now; and that eye, the right, was so swollen that the bulbous orb seemed ready to pop free of the tight, dull skin that surrounded it. The left eye was just gone. There was not even the carnivorous fungus in the socket; just a curved hollow of bone.

Her lumpy misshapen body rocked and heaved under her bathrobe. The remains of her lips, the still-human right side of them, were black rather than red, and the absence of the left side of her face gave her a twisted sneer, yet despite this horror, her lone eye welled with tears of gratitude.

"Gl, Gl, Glad, chLauraa," she managed through that ruined mouth. "Nll, nllot, not alone."

"Oh *Jen*," I gasped, my own eyes wet from the horror of my friend's condition.

She raised her right hand to her face.

I knew there had been a hand protruding from her robe when she began to raise it. I *saw* it, I knew it had been there. But when her arm came up, the hand was gone, replaced by a wrist stump, neatly sealed with a greyish crust as though cauterised by this sickening disease that was eating my friend alive before my eyes.

How could that be? *Nothing* could do that!

Jenny moaned, the utterance distorted by clumsy unworkable lips and a thickly phlegmy throat.

The fungus beneath her empty left eye socket crumbled suddenly inward and a deeper crater opened up, revealing something reddish-blue inside. Her nose folded down toward that crater as though it too were being sucked in.

"Fu-uuck-fuck!" I cried out. "Uuuuh, fuck, fuck!"

A sound escaped Jenny. It might have been a sob, but it was hard to be sure. How could she still be alive? How? This was sick, it was wrong, it was *impossible!*

Her lips twisted again, but they were hampered by the loss of much of her chin to another grey-crusted hole that was now working to crumble away most of her lower jaw.

The hole ran along the side of her jaw, and just visible behind the grey crust, her one remaining bottom tooth on that side leaned precariously in its bit of socket, dried now by the lack of spit.

Suddenly in a moment of horror beyond any I had ever known I heard a deep sucking sound and Jenny's remaining eye pulled back, as though a vacuum cleaner had sucked it back through her head.

She emitted a dry squeal, cried my name, her stump-ended arms flailing to find me as she screamed and sobbed, blind and dying horribly.

All she wanted was for me to stay while she died. To not die alone, blind and in utter terror.

All I had to do was stay, be a comfort for a few seconds more. I should have been that brave.

I wasn't.

I turned and fled, Tom right with me as we flew from the flat.

I think I heard Jen's last word as I smashed against the front door on the way out, her anguished how sounding so very like my name, desperation and desolation.

We finally stopped running when we reached Mickey, who sat waiting in the glorious summer sunshine as if the world had not just changed forever.

I grabbed Tom's arms and stared up into his moist eyes. "Come home with me?"

-10-

Mickey's engine gurgled as we bumped along the road, the sun beat down on the black canvass roof just an inch above Tom's scalp. Somehow, unbelievably, the world was carrying on as if the laws of existence still applied, as if this was still the same universe it had been twenty-five minutes ago.

"Fuck," Tom said, elbow on the window and knuckles resting against his gritted teeth.

I drew air in but the heat in the car was stifling and just made me want to hurl. The heat in here should have eased the chills coursing through my body, but it didn't, which was probably due to the fact that they were being caused by infectious little worms crawling beneath my skin and ingesting me, severing my veins, chewing off nerve endings…

"Stop it!" I told myself.

"Huh?"

The voice beside me was dull, numbed. I turned my head and focussed on him, noticing only now that he was crying silently.

"Tom?"

No response, just the elbow on the glass and the little ledge beneath it, and the knuckles at the teeth as the tears fled his eyes.

"What did we just do?" I asked, turning back to watch the road as I drove; as if that mattered any more.

"Something we have to try and live with, Laur, that's what."

"We could go back...?"

"No. No we couldn't."

A hot swill of bile emptied into my throat and I was sure for a moment that I would have to blow sick onto Mickey's steering wheel. "No, we can't."

Finally, we reached Tiler's Hill and then we swerved between the open, rickety gates of the house where Grandma had once tended me as a child, and where I now tended her at her sunset.

The tyres bounced on the uneven drive and, when I'd gone far enough in to be able to swing the gates shut behind us, I stomped the footbrake and then cranked the ratchet up on the handbrake.

After I killed it, Mickey's engine tocked and pinged gently under the glowering shadow of the ancient Semi where I lived.

The house, in shadow, was all hard red bricks and cold straight lines. It seemed oppressive as it cast a broad afternoon shadow over us, despite it being only about lunchtime.

"Am I the only one shivering?" Tom asked.

The very bricks of this place I called home were soaking up all of the day's sunshine and draining the warmth from the air until we wept heat from our very bodies.

I shuddered but then got a grip of myself. We'd had an awful, life-changing experience and now the home I'd known nearly all my life had turned into Frankenhades.

I opened the driver's door and found the usual comforting audio wallpaper of my part of town (distant traffic, birds in the trees over at the peaceful graveyard opposite) – completely absent. It was unpleasantly like awakening from a nightmare in the deathly hours of pre-dawn; an experience I knew all too well, the rest of the world at peace while I lay trapped in the shivering horror of it.

"Bleedin' spooky, eh, Laur?" said Tom, slamming Mickey's passenger door way too hard.

I looked up. The shadow around the house was not shadow at all. The sun had gone away. Turning, I saw the other houses along the length of the hill also cast in gloom, whilst the trees standing sentinel in the graveyard across the road from us were backdropped by a grey-and-black streaky bacon sky that looked full of all the rain in the world.

Tom was already at the porch step so I hurried to be nearer him.

"It was summer when we left," I said softly.

He shrugged. "Let's get inside and warm up, eh?"

There was a dreamlike haze over my mind as I jammed the key into the lock and let us in, as if I only knew what I was doing it at each moment, the rest of everything seeming to fall away.

With a twist of the key, we were in.

After the almost complete absence of sensory information outside, I was damn near floored by the sudden musty, cloying stink of damp wallpaper bubbling with mould; carpets made wet by boots and left to stay wet until they rotted; and wall dust too thick to attract even the prickliest of corner-dwelling spiders.

I heard Tom cry out in protest and knew he'd been granted a sample, too.

My eyes adapted to the gloom and the shock of what confronted me hit home.

Never actually modern, the house had slowly evolved under my influence, since that cold wretched old bastard of a grandfather had died, until it was close enough to modernity that visitors didn't have to worry whether they'd fallen through a rip in time. Still quaint, Grandma's house had become at least passingly contemporary.

Not any more.

Now, all that had been undone. The hall was a sodden, decrepit mess. Wallpaper hung off in mildewed tatters, brown and glutinous with damp; the threadbare carpet was full of ragged rips, its pattern bleached away, its edges curling near the walls in ragged hessian strips as though trying to rise up in protest. The white banister rail I had lovingly painted less than a year ago was gone, replaced by a bare, stained wooden ribcage that jutted splintery edges as though to catch unwary limbs and leave them bloodied. The rail and the bars were yellowed with age, the thin paint cracked and blistering. The same yellowed, peeling paint adorned the room doors and doorframes, too, but the hallway was not the extent of the ruin that had been re-inflicted on my home.

My gaze had been drawn to the kitchen.

That semi-modern workspace I had bullied Grandma into investing in, was gone. In place of that drab but happy place, where we had baked cakes on most Sunday afternoons before her decline, was a dark and intimidating scullery with a filthy chequered tile floor scattered with rickety yellow-and-green cupboards, brown walls and a few cracked pieces of hardwood worktop on little hand-cut iron legs.

"You've been burgled," said Tom.

"This is," I said, awestruck. "This, this is…"

I felt a strength-sapping nostalgia of dread well up and leave me useless. That thin-lipped old tyrant had never spent a penny to make Grandma's life, or mine, a little more bearable. This was the house as it had been under *his* regime, when every penny was counted and every sin paid for in full. The house Grandma had struggled to keep clean while the walls threatened to fall in on us, overlorded by grandfather.

Just after my parents had died, when I first came here.

I thought I heard a voice.

I glanced at Tom as he crouched to pick at the edge of the carpet. "Did you hear that?"

He didn't respond at all, picking at the carpet as if he were assessing it for replacement. The voice came again, from upstairs. This time I heard it more clearly and knew it had called my name.

A woman's voice, but not old like Grandma's – yet one I had not heard for many long, sad years.

Mumma.

It called my name again and a cold like nothing I had ever felt before sliced through me.

A single, yellowed, old style lightbulb taunted me from the upstairs landing, refusing to overcome the winter gloom up there.

I turned back to Tom, feeling suddenly very alone in the gloom, the filth, the musty damp.

He was gone.

Panic closing my throat and dimming my vision, I whispered his name; then I screamed it.

My voice fell flat, refused to echo in the dead and the damp.

How had he heard the voice, too? Gone upstairs? It didn't make sense but that no longer mattered, because I needed him, I needed anyone so I would not be alone facing… *this*.

I forced my foot forward in a dragged half-step, determined to edge toward the stairs but fighting base instincts that could overrule and put me into panicked flight at any second.

Is this what had happened to Jen? Was I infected, hallucinating because that horrific fungus was invading my body? Perhaps I should run outside, leave this house and fly free in Mickey, my sweet wheeled companion… but this was the only home I had, besides which, as lame as our date had been, I couldn't bring myself to abandon Tom. Not after Jen. The sting of her cries – not just the terror in her voice, but the hopeless misery as we left her, let her die alone.

My foot kicked against the first stair and now I had to choose to either find him or live with my cowardice, twice-played.

Moisture gathering under my arms drooled down my sides and caused me to shiver even more violently than before.

I took a deep breath. Held it, released it. No help at all.

"Fuck this," I muttered. Too many monsters, too much I could not control. This, though, terrible as it was, could be controlled, managed. I had a say, here, today.

Placing a foot on the first stair, I pushed upwards, overruling my flight urges and driving up until I finally stepped onto the landing and felt an overwhelming pull from the main bedroom.

As I approached the door to Grandma's (and Grandpa's) room I heard a man's voice, which seemed to be half groan and half cry of distress.

"Tom!"

I threw myself into the bedroom and was immediately brought to a cold hard stop. Sensing me, the couple separated and exposed the full vista to my horrified gaze.

Tom gaped as though he had just awoken from a nightmare. His jeans hung open and from them his long fleshy penis dangled out, wrinkly and lined with faint bluish veins that were still distended from his now-wilting erection. There was a roll of skin that had been drawn back off the bulbous head of it, and from that head hung a stringy loop of whitish semen. As he stared at me, his trousers slipped off his hips and dropped to bunch around his ankles.

He held out a hand to me, but his penis twitched and a little extra gout of sperm was discharged onto Grandma's carpet.

But this was insignificant, his penis meant nothing, compared with the horrible truth of *who* he had just shared this vile intimate thing with.

Standing behind him, behind this man who I had dared to begin having feelings for, her lightly tanned and perfect skin naked and glistening from her pert pointy breasts to her brazenly bald-shaved vulva, was Jennifer Sullivan.

Her gaze was fixed on me, but there was no apology in it.

Her naked body was perfect but I saw now that she had no eyes; just two black pools of nothingness welling up from within the sockets, the surfaces flat and dull. Impenetrable, gross, cold.

I had a tiny hint of brainpower left in that moment and it wondered how the eyes had not been the first thing I noticed in this charnel sex scene.

She grinned at me, like Death might.

Tom was hastily gathering up his jeans and packing away his treacherous penis, staring at me, but I could see nothing but Jenny. Fuck Tom, though, he was just like the rest of them, but Jen, my friend Jen, this bitch who had always, *always* got every man she ever wanted and had now robbed me of even the briefest illusion of romance.

Tom's glasses had fallen onto the floor as he'd discharged onto or into my best friend, and his jeans were rumpled with the belt buckle twisted, which all served to hamper his attempts to put his treacherous prick away. Cunt. *What* had I ever seen in him?

But he had been mine – mine to at least fail with, at least.

And Jen was dead. I had seen her die, rotted and ruined. How could she be here, so hot and glorious?

She moved, began to pass me before I had even registered the change, her bare shoulder brushing me as she went by, tainting me with cold from flesh that looked vital but was in truth anything but. She had left the bedroom on her way to the stairs before I could react, hips swinging and breasts swaying.

Impossible. She had walked right up to me and past me and I'd barely sensed her at all until she *touched* me.

No!

I spun on my boot heel and lunged after the departing nude, but Jenny slipped to the edge of the stairs and blurred into a downward smear of colour, her ghostly presence fading fast until I stood alone at the head of the stairs.

I stared down that empty staircase for a few seconds. Tom approached me from behind, calling to me in a whiney voice that helped me to understand why Sam might enjoy killing and evisceration, so since I had no way to catch the ghostly Jen I rounded on him, to find he, too, was losing substance, growing transparent as his warmth fell away from me.

I went to cry out in frustration but I had no voice. I felt the pressure of the threadbare carpet under my shoes weaken, fade, saw that the sodden brown-papered walls were growing pale, fading into translucent nothingness.

The walls of the house bowed, rippled and melted away, heading into oblivion.

It had to be me. Somewhere, in my real house, Tom was cradling me, probably watching my body succumb to that evil fungus that had claimed Jen. Unless he lay beside me in the same state.

Plague. The end of the world, just as I was about to land one of those fish that the sea is supposed to be full of.

Fuck, such bullshit; so unfair.

Unless this was real, especially because the pain of being pulled, wrenched apart in at least three directions at once, was all too real and becoming hard to ignore. The rest of the world had just finished melting away with the last droplet of floral wallpaper and the pain of my body intensified.

I kicked my legs into vacuum, nothingness, with nothing to grab onto, stand on or touch as panic brought an acid surge of bile into my throat, but it wasn't dark or cold now, it just *wasn't*; there was nothing to sense, no concept of up, down, solid or gas.

The sense of everything was gone and now it began to lose any sense of self as it, too, ceased and
folded into nothingness
merged with nothingness
became *nothing*.

-11-

Something.

Existence, but only as thought; as mind without flesh; as will without influence – but it flew, was drawn with purpose to another place, to another life, someone else's, not its life, not *my* life: an observer again.

The woman's name was Samantha Parker, and as she sat blow-drying her hair in a bedroom, I came to be near her but not part of her. An observer, only.

She smiled into her mirror at the reflection of a man and I somehow felt knowledge of his name, *Greg*, as he approached her. She pushed back her long reddish-black hair with one hand and fired the dryer into its mass.

He took some hair and sifted it between his fingers. "I like your hair like that!" he called over the dryer.

She turned the dryer off. "Well, I don't."

She shook her hair free of his hands and spun the lid off a pot of hair gel, stabbing four fingers into the goo and scooping out a quantity to rub in her hands.

A moment later she had smeared the goo into her hair and created her characteristic greased-back style. Her glossy red-black mane now glued flat against her skull, I recognised the monosyllabic emopunk friend of Susan Blake, who had intervened to warn me away from the man called Alan.

I heard the doorbell. Greg grinned, sat and then flopped back in a sprawl on the bed, folding his arms behind his head.

Samantha glanced at him, still smearing her hands over her sloppy hair. "You gonna get the door?"

"No."

She stood. "Lazy bastard."

She pulled the bath sheet tightly around her body and left the room. I studied Greg for a moment. Tall, with wiry arms and a narrow chest. Perhaps he was handsome? I was only nominally female now, and had none of the hormones needed to judge sexuality well. He looked masculine; that was as much as I could say.

I lost interest in him and was instantly in the hall, behind Samantha. I felt a momentary and detached apprehension at the sight of the mountainous man who stood on her doorstep, his heavy frame blotting out the reddened evening sky.

"I've come about the car," her visitor said, his voice a deep and rich colour that I knew only too well. "I realise it's rather late."

Sam flashed Samantha a disarming grin and I knew her body had responded to him in an unintentional and animal way.

"I better, ah, I'll get my, er fiancé," she bumbled, her attitude so deferential I almost expected her to curtsy.

Watching the transaction progress I was, as I would have expected to be, entirely drawn toward Sam while the couple organised themselves to try and secure the sale of their unwanted car. While they faffed with documentation, the giant wandered aimlessly around the room, peering at their pictures and ornaments. He seemed to have no objective, but I knew him better than that.

Suddenly, after a discrete glance at the cute couple, he reached down into a tiny ornamental saucer on the telephone stand and took out an object. I could see that it was just an old, inscribed silver watch, which made no obvious sense.

Sam turned to the couple, slipping the watch into his pocket so deftly that even I wondered if it had ever been in his hand.

He smiled, resolved the paperwork and handed over an amount of cash; all notes. He left with the keys to their old car, and as soon as he was gone, Greg gave a loud sigh through a huge grin of relief.

"I swear, I *don't* believe we finally got rid of that poxy car!."

Samantha smiled. "Now we've got a few quid, we can pay Luke back."

They made the most of celebrating; down to the pub, where they'd been getting ready to go before Sam had called, and then back home for some more alcohol followed by a lot of sex, both of which, apparently, were equally delicious to them, although as a disembodied passenger I got very little from any of it.

Later that night, as the pair were cuddled up watching some crap on a streaming channel, the doorbell intruded on them once again.

"Damn it!" Samantha cried. "Greg?"

Greg lolled on the sofa, arm still draped around her. "You get it."

She slapped his arm away and clambered up. "You're a pig, you know that?"

"Uh-huh."

Samantha pulled open the front door with ill grace and muttered under her breath as she was confronted by two Police officers.

Samantha held the door and tilted her hip. "What, now? Fucksake, I've told you lot before, he doesn't deal any more!"

The officers tried to tell Samantha why they had called but she was determined to tell them in detail exactly why they should fuck off, and how soon.

Just as Samantha was in danger of shutting up long enough to hear what the police were actually saying, Greg appeared behind his woman and pitched in. Aggressive from the start, he didn't hear anything the two visitors were saying.

I caught a bit of what they were saying – their car had been at the scene of a murder, and Greg's engraved watch had been found right beside the body.

The victim was Michael Williamson, whose name seemed faintly familiar: a memory of the unreasonably cheerful sod who'd tried to flirt with me at the coffee machines.

"Sir, if you'll just calm–"

"Why? Why? Always the fucking same with you bastards…"

"Sir, please just–"

"Go fuck your–"

And all too soon, Greg was dragged clench-toothed from his home, with Samantha in tow. Having decided to twat one of the officers in a last-ditch attempt to rescue her errant man, the girl earned herself a place in the back of the car too, so that both were dumped unceremoniously into the back of the vehicle, where they fell into a resigned silence.

As the police car pulled away I found myself unable to follow it. My disembodied self was being pulled away and suddenly the scenery around me blurred and I was some distance away in the presence of the large man to whom I had been drawn.

The watch made sense if this was a clean-up. Sam had used the couple's car to dispose of Michael and frame the cutesies to pull Samantha out of circulation. If so, though, why had I been drawn to his bloodlust? Surely he was done.

Sam drew a huge lungful of cool night air, rich with the scents of peaty soil and tangy fertiliser. Headlight beams briefly dazzled him as a bobbing vehicle negotiated a bend ahead on the twisting road.

As the vehicle approached, Sam lunged from his position by some hedgerow, waving a torch, flagging the car but far too close for it to actually stop. The car, a police car, I could now see, swerved to avoid hitting him, but Sam had chosen his position carefully and the car, swerving just enough to avoid hitting him, dropped a wheel into the concealed ditch and was wrenched off the road violently, flipping on its snagged wheel.

It was a muted crunch that reached my ears as the car landed on its roof and safety glass popped and split. The giant approached the wreckage while steam sizzled and hissed from somewhere at the front of it.

It lay upside down on the hard dry mud of the field, headlights still illuminating the gloom, the twisted metal of its frame and shell still pinging in reaction to having been so roughly punted.

Crouching, Sam peered through the front passenger window. A policeman's glazed eyes stared back, their view of the world forever obscured by death, and I faintly felt the large man's pleasure, his satisfaction.

We were not linked yet; at least, not as we had been for Susan's murder.

Another man, the one I knew as Greg, was embedded within the flat pack created between the roof and the back seat. He, too, had gone to a better place in a single sticky splash, his body pulped.

The big man stood and circled the car, peering through the driver's window. I drifted behind him, feeling the tingling of his excitement as though it were mine and, as he moved away again, I saw a hand hung limp over the steering wheel, a head with tied-back hair laid beside the hand, lit by the weak green glow of the instrument lights.

The cap the policewoman had been wearing was gored beyond recognition by her own blood, copious quantities of her unravelled brains coiling out of a jagged hole in the top of her head and weeping onto the roof of the upturned car. This lady's arresting days were over. The big man smiled and, faceless though I was, so did I.

Sam's sickness was contagious.

He peered through the last window of interest and I no longer needed to will myself along beside him; I was anchored to him in our shared joy at this carnage.

The girl, Samantha Parker, also appeared dead for a moment, but then she moaned and moved her head. Sam grinned broadly with delight. Lovely.

She twitched a hand as she saw him standing over her, her eyes appealing to him so that he was bathed in warm pleasure and I felt it with him; so filling, so satisfying.

He assessed her.

The collapsed roof had pinned poor Samantha down, trapped her amidst the tangle of jagged razor edges without any of those metal juts and shards having actually punctured her body. She had been neither crushed nor pierced. She was, conveniently, completely trapped in a compacted space between the partially collapsed roof and the seat she had been strapped into.

"Help," She whined asthmatically, unable to fully inflate her lungs. "Can't... breathe."

Sam smiled benignly and I felt the deep primal rage and lust that drove him, hidden just behind that façade of his.

"I regret, my child, that help is the very last thing I might offer."

"The fuck?" she cried, forcing a painful wheezing cough from her. "Don't be a dick, mate, I need – hey!"

He climbed easily onto the upturned underside of the car, carefully avoiding the hot exhaust pipe. *Didn't want to ruin his skin.* I understood.

Beneath him, Samantha took the extra weight of him onto her already-squeezed ribcage.

"No, for fuck's – uughh...! What!-you-fuck-no!-cunt-you-yuuh!"

His weight squeezed her between her seat and the car's roof, forcing her already twisted body toward the razor-sharp edges of torn metal that she had narrowly avoided in the crash.

Sam braced himself, stood, drew a breath and then took a huge leap into the air. He rose up and up, graceful and free, and then plummeted, accelerated down until his feet slammed hard onto the car's underbelly, causing metal to pop and split and the structure to collapse in on itself.

There was a thud below him and a wheezing shriek as the wicked edges of metal were driven down into Samantha's body, forcing the air out of her lungs, squashing her flat and hopefully piercing her. He knew she must be in agony now; sharp, awful pain in her belly as her organs got wrenched from their proper place or squeezed and popped like blood-rich spots on an acne-ridden face.

He had suffered such agony once, at his birth, and he so, soooo loved to share.

He jumped up and slammed down hard again. The last intact window popped and shattered below him.

Was she still suffering down there, or was it all over already?

Sam jumped gracefully down off the car and leant toward the window to see, curiosity mingling with bloodlust and a burgeoning arousal that was stirring his sex organ.

The seat had slammed her twisted hips very violently downward and her right leg had been twisted from its socket like a chicken leg in the hands of a hungry man. It looked like his own special *art*.

Her chest bulged forward as though packed out with extra organs (which it probably was, he thought delightedly), and her head was raised halfway out of the side window by the brutal pressure on her body.

Only when she uttered a phlegmy sob, too fucked up now to really scream, did he realise with delight that she was still alive, still suffering, and I felt his delight like a tangible tingle in flesh I did not have.

She whimpered softly, fully intimate for the first time with the spectre of her impending death.

Sam leaned close and pushed a fallen strand of hair back into her slicked style; so gently now that she was cooperating in feeding his need.

"Tell me how it hurts," he murmured, stroking her forehead tenderly and sounding for all the world like a lover whispering intimacies.

"Please, *urch,* help, mmm, m-meee!" she appealed, her voice backed by a hissing from a hole somewhere in a tube within her, the effort of speaking almost too much as her lungs were stretched to bursting point by the pressure on her chest.

She blinked and for a moment her eyes focused right on him.

"It... hurts... so much," she murmured; an appeal rather than a description. Of course it hurts, you stupid fucking bitch.

Sam had a full, throbbing erection, now. I could *feel* it, the heat of its pounding.

But suddenly Sam jolted violently and straightened up. His eyes zipped from side to side as if expecting an ambush.

He edged away from the victim he had trapped in that wreckage, his animal instincts now turned to combat. He had *felt* something. Something new. A presence in his mind.

I knew, because I had felt the contact at the same time he had.

And unlike Sam, I had recognised that presence. He was sensing *me*, my link to him and this meant that the link was not a one-way stream of consciousness. I had a purchase on his half-animal mind and maybe, just maybe, I could interfere, perhaps even cause Sam some of the pain he seemed to delight in inflicting on everyone else.

If I could have grinned maliciously, I would have done so right then.

I stared straight into his face as he looked around, panicked and afraid, unable to see me. Now I would make *him* suffer – for hurting me, for hurting Tom, perhaps even for killing Jen because it seemed he must surely have had a hand in that somehow.

It seemed so obvious, now. I would force him to feel his own victim's pain, to endure this poor girl's misery *with* her. I knew how to do it, too. The knowledge was inside me.

I opened myself to him, but also to *her*.

A transient thought process, nameless but equating to an idea *We are one*

A moment later we both saw and felt through Sam, but we both also saw and felt through Samantha's dying body, too.

He jolted violently, his eyes widened but then a huge grin sprawled across his face. "Ohhh, thank you!" he cried to the air.

I felt his gross physical response to the sensations being endured by his victim's dying flesh. His tingling skin, his watering mouth and his hot, insistent erection.

UR HERE

Alight with pleasure, he grappled for a hold on the upturned car and felt the thrill of horror that seared his victim as she realised that he actually meant to, wanted to, kill her. She struggled to draw a ragged breath and he and I felt the raw, ragged pain she felt. It hurt so much, as she fought to use lungs that were fit, now, only for the dogmeat factory.

I had not slowed him by making him suffer her pain. He was glad of it. He was excited by it, and now he was indulging in his hideous pleasure as he had never done before.

He was moments from killing Samantha, feeling her need to let out a final protesting scream, but above her miserable fear rose a potent rage against this murdering bastard who was about to take away her life, a need to hurt him, inflict this misery on him, instead.

I kindled the spark, encouraged her anger by opening myself to her and letting the rage mix and mingle with my own against this monster.

And then, Sam and I both received a flood of violent, brutal images as

Samantha's rage blended with my hatred of this huge filthy killer and translated it into images of vengeful violence.

I felt Sam smile. She really was a very wicked little girl! The images slipped in and out of our mind like some slideshow.

She held his eyelid back and flicked the lighter on, held the flame to his eyeball until the cornea shrank and popped like a bubble;

She slid a razor lengthways down his penis, opening it along the line of his urethra; he screamed on and on as his flesh opened like a split banana;

She thumped a large hook into his belly and sliced upwards to his ribcage; he gurgled and spewed blood as his wet red guts poured onto the ground;

She poured petrol over him and lit, then watched as his useless arms flapped against his scorching skin, the tissue blistering and weeping his fluids, his agony continuous until the loss of fluids depleted him and his heart failed…

Wow.

I would never know how much of that was Samantha's last burst of rage, how much came from within me. All I was sure of was that Sam liked her monstrous choices so much he hesitated, actually considering for a moment if it might not be too late to spare her.

But of course it was way too late for her.

Atop the car once more, he jumped again and

she felt a lance of pain through her chest and a flood of heat expanding into the cavity within her ribcage. Suddenly she could no longer draw any breath; there was nothing, no ability to pull air into her desperate body.

Pressure built in her chest, *need air*, pain as if her brain were pressed to the inside of her skull, about to burst free, her eyes felt like they were being squeezed and there was a sponge filling her mouth; going dark now but it still hurt as the last working bits of her fought for oxygen, *dying*, her head ready to burst like an overripe tomato.

Sam jumped one last time.

A piercing agony split her body in two. She felt her face flush, her head pound and she felt sick but even that couldn't get out because of the pressure, trapping and closing everything, and then darkness pushed in on her and took the world away from her, just vague glimmers as she collapsed into a singularity and she knew where she was going, that this was the end of everything that Samantha Parker ever was or could be and there was a horror to it but she had no adrenaline, no heartbeat so the biology of terror was lost to her as her contorted body relaxed… and she was gone.

For a moment, Sam stood gasping atop the wrecked car, then he leapt down, scanned the area to ensure he had no cause to flee, and finally he crouched beside the crushed vehicle, leant in through the shattered window and kissed Samantha's gory red-splashed mouth, tasting her swollen, distended tongue with his own and gazing into her bulging, rapidly dulling eyes.

"Goodbye, my beautiful, wicked girl," he said softly as he stood.

Her eyes, more like glass than life now, stared out at the sky without seeing it. All too soon, those glass orbs would be milky and sunken. No more Samantha.

I tried to pull away from him, sick with the horror of it, the horror of the joy of the horror of it, and Sam and I… divided.

Now, I was alone. Formless, I stood in the fields some way from where Samantha Parker had died so terribly.

It was quiet, peaceful here. I could dimly sense the wind blowing through the place where I apparently existed without contributing to the weight of the world. There was a crescent moon awakening in the sky off to my right and there was a vague after-tingle of Sam's deeply intense arousal.

I sensed a weight in the air behind me. In whatever way I was able to do so, I turned.

I achieved a new level of disbelief at the sight of a vast wave of intense blackness that roiled across the gloomy night-time fields, erasing everything like a child scribbling over a drawing with a huge black marker pen.

Oh. OK, then.

I wanted to flee but was now paralysed. With no anchor to the world I had no power to make myself go here or there, so I could do nothing as this monstrous thing swished across me and I plunged into utter nothingness once again – a plunge into an ice-cold winter pool, the scolding chill creating the sensation of all my nerve endings being boiled away.

It lost all sensation once more and was gone.

-12-

From the emptiest void something formed. Something… a mind. A mind re-formed from nothing.

Memories pooled and became *me* as they coalesced in the cool ether and the disintegration was undone in a maelstrom that drew together both me and the world that needed to be around me.

Fragments of time, being and matter ravelled and entwined, healing the rift, closing the cuts and restoring the semblance of causality. A flicker, a moment of light, the laying on of mass, and the collapse of redundant memories as she re-joined reality.

I became again.

In that moment of formation I felt myself become complete and yet, not quite; something vague, something missing and not just from me, the memory of it no longer in the world, non-existent because it was in nobody's memory.

I was returning but reality had been changed somehow, although I knew I would no more no this when I was Laura again, than anyone else would know to miss it.

In those last moments before I was truly restored, I saw how fragile reality, matter and even time itself really were. How they could be bent to make lies of the truth.

-13-

A car horn blasted behind me, a prolonged and angry burst. I snapped my eyes open. *Shit!* The back of the traffic queue was now some three hundred yards further up the road and I had no idea when it might have moved.

I cast a hasty glance at Tom, who gestured after the traffic with his hand.

I rolled my eyes at him. "Thanks, that helps."

I hastily wrestled the stumpy gear stick into first and booted the throttle, so that we lurched forward and I was then forced to stomp the brake to stop us hitting the tail of the car in front.

"I know it's a lovely day," said Tom, "but you ain't gotta sunbathe in the car."

I wanted to fire a witty retort back at him, but to tell the truth I was really confused, with no idea why I might have blacked out back there. I had no recollection of closing my eyes.

Taking in my surroundings, my confusion abated somewhat. The roof was down and Mickey's engine was burbling, it was a beautiful day with sunshine blazing and Tom and I were having such a great time. Pity to spoil it.

We had really hit it off. Coffee in town had turned into an impromptu drive into the countryside and been followed by a stroll through the woods, what Tom rather drily referred to as a 'constitutional', before deciding to go back to mine for a late lunch.

I shrugged off my confusion and flashed Tom a smile. He smiled back.

The house was shaded from the sun as Mickey bumped up onto the front driveway. The gloom swallowed us whole, as though the very bricks of my home were soaking up all of the day's heat.

"Is it me," said Tom, "or has it turned a bit nippy?"

I wriggled my shoulders to help suppress the urge to shudder and had a sudden dizzying snap of recollection, unformed, evasive, but familiar; as though this moment had already happened and we were re-living rather than doing this all for the first time. Déjà vu, that most ridiculous of brain-farts.

I killed Mickey's engine, so that the summertime chorus of birdsong filled the void left by the absence of his throaty burble – a pleasant backdrop of summer for the more than half a day I still had left to spend with Tom.

Like a couple of silly kids without a care in the world, we practically skipped to the front door and I gave Tom a playful shove so I could reach to jam my key into the Yale lock, but as I turned it my smile froze for a moment.

Something. Something troubling. A moment of trepidation when there's a little chill in the spine because you know something bad is coming.

"Come on!" he said, and the sensation flitted away.

I was greeted by the familiar scents of home (plug-in air fresheners and Grandma's floral air sprays) as I cut through the hall and into the kitchen.

"Cup of tea?"

He didn't answer and I turned to him. Tom was gazing around the hallway, a finger pressed to his lips. "Hmm?" he asked absently.

I took a step toward him. "You OK?"

"What?" His gaze moved lazily to meet mine and for a second he had a worried, far-away look in his eyes; but then they sharpened and the moment of reverie was gone. "Sorry. Sorry, Laura. What?"

"Tea," I told him. "Cup of. You silly-bollocks."

He laughed. "Yeah, yeah, that's great. Thanks." He still seemed distracted. I left him wandering the hallway while I headed for the kitchen.

The kitchen being at the back of the house, there was a lot of direct sunlight on the window and not much ventilation. As a result, I was hit in the face by a curtain of face-melting heat as I crossed the threshold and had to brace myself so I could reach the radiantly-hot back window and unlock it with a tiny silver key kept nearby.

Sadly, all the window let in was birdsong. The air outside was as hot and clingy as the air trapped in the kitchen.

"Bloody hell."

Trying not to gasp, I turned to the work surface on my immediate left, where a cheap, tired white plastic kettle sat wearily awaiting my bidding. Making yet another mental note (the twentieth?) to get a new one, I grabbed it and crossed to the steel sink, a sink that I'd only recently persuaded Grandma to needed, to replace her ancient enamel Butler.

"Laur."

I started at the voice, right behind me, a sudden unexpected intrusion into my inane thoughts. I turned to see Tom at the kitchen doorway, a frown creasing his already crinkly face.

"Didn't you have to call Jen?" he asked.

"No," I said. "Any particular reason why I should?"

He pushed his little glasses up his nose a tiny way. "No, I s'pose not. Forget it, I reckon I've got a touch of sunstroke."

I patted his arm. "Nice cuppa should fix that."

Leaning to fill the kettle, I barked my shin on one of two cream doors that stood ajar in the green wooden unit beneath the sink and I cursed sharply.

When I turned, Tom was still there, leaning against the doorframe.

Grinning, now, after my little swearing session.

"You swear like that down the docks?" he asked.

"Yeah, alright. It hurt."

He pouted at me. "There, there. Sadface."

I glared at him. "Don't emoji me."

He gave me another pouty face. "OK, then. So, where's Granny today?"

Had we discussed Grandma? I didn't remember.

I dumped the kettle onto its base. "She's out with her friend." I clicked the kettle on. "Hungry?"

He rubbed his hands together, which I took as a yes. "Go sit down, I'll be mother."

He resisted an incest joke and left me to it.

When I had sandwiches and tea, I loaded a tray and took it into the back parlour, where Tom waited.

As I entered that old, old room I was suddenly, horribly struck by how my home must look to others – and especially to Tom.

Damn.

The parlour was as drab as the rest of the house, made up entirely of brown florals in the form of wallpaper, carpets and furniture. The furniture, though, was especially ghastly, comprising a hotchpotch of four mismatched armchairs, all in various shades of brown or beige floral print, their arms and feet a suitably sombre dark dark wood.

It was an old lady's house.

This room, like so many others, reflected more of Grandma than of me. I'd always supposed the day would come when this house would be mine to alter as I pleased, but in truth I had that freedom, because Grandma was rapidly slipping away, but somehow I think that this horrible truth made me cling to what little I had left of her – her furnishings being the most obvious thing I couldn't bear to part with.

Anyway, the parlour was saved by a pair of casement doors at one end that looked out onto our beloved garden, where the sun was busy pouring its warm golden glow onto our shrubs, while bees visited our flowers and hovered to savour the sweetness.

Tom sat in the rightmost of a pair of armchairs that faced the casement doors. It was – no, in happier times, it *had* been – Grandma's chair. Wood-framed, the varnish scuffed off the arms, with a brown-and-beige contoured pattern still visible in the hard, fading cushion, it was about as comfortable as it looked, but Tom seemed fine with it. He sat with a large hardback book resting open on his lap, its hard scaly back upward, its pages down. He lifted it to show me.

"Yours?" he asked.

I shrugged and nodded, hoping that dismissiveness would conceal my embarrassment.

"What they call this, then? Classical Romance?"

I heard a ghastly nervous laugh escape my throat and deflected, held out the tray. "Shut up and eat your lunch."

Taking a plate and a mug from the tray, he placed the mug on the floor and took a huge bite of sandwich. Then, I watched his face collapse into a convulsion of horror as he chewed, until he was prompted to lift the edge of the sandwich and peer inside, as though expecting an alien.

When he looked up, his expression suggested he'd found one. "What's *thish?*" he appealed through a mouthful of half-chewed bread.

I crossed to the casement doors and opened them, letting in a feeble breeze, then crossed and perched on a chair with my own plate. "Chocolate spread."

He grimaced and shook his head, swallowing hard. "If you want me to go just say so, there's no need to give me a dogshit sandwich."

A guilty pleasure. I'd never been allowed it as a child, so it had become first an obsession, and then over time, an addiction.

I laughed as he took another hesitant bite. "There's gratitude for you!"

He ate, but he looked like a thirsty man trying to chew rock salt. Still, he tried, bless him. Only when he glanced up at me from his 'feast' did I realise that I was staring at him instead of eating my own food. I hastily got to my sandwiches, revelling in the rich gooey texture and unreasonably sweet fatty flavour.

After we'd eaten, we took our mugs outside and then went out and sat on the low brick wall that separated the short patio from Grandma's great expanse of back lawn. We chugged the last of our tea and listened to the birds, while a rogue squirrel decided we looked like trouble and made a bolt for the old birch tree down by the end fence.

Tom took out a green packet from which he extracted a scrawny cigarette paper into which he twisted some hairy-looking tobacco.

I watched as he rolled a smoke. A long association with tobacco had begun, for me, with my grandfather. That cold, narrow-eyed old man had smoked a pipe, and the only time he had ever been tolerant of me was when he sat in his chair in the front room and filled the thing for his evening smoke.

No, actually, my father had smoked, I realised. A faint memory pecked at me and then flitted away; Daddy smell, whisky and tobacco, kissing me goodnight.

Tom finished rolling the cigarette and lit it. I watched for a moment as he inhaled, savouring that first headrush – I knew how that felt. I'd experimented with smoking myself, but somehow it never really took.

He was staring at me. "What?" he asked.

"What, what?" I tried to ask innocently.

He pinched the cigarette between thumb and forefinger and smiled at me. "You were gawping."

"Sorry. Lost in the past, I guess. My Grandpa and my Dad smoked."

A slight crease appeared in his brow. "Past tense for both of them?"

I nodded. "Past tense."

I knew I would tell him the woeful tale of my life, eventually, but at that moment in the sun, warm and relaxed and full of life and hope, I didn't want to draw that cloud back over myself and, bless him, Tom didn't press me on it.

He squinted at the sky, leaning back whilst grasping the low brick wall in his hands. "You wanna lie on the grass?" he suddenly asked quite casually.

I shrugged, but he wasn't looking at me, so I said yes out loud and then he did look at me. He held out a hand, left his baccy packet on the wall and led me to the grass.

It sounds like nothing, but lying there in the sun, resting in the crook of Tom's arm on the dry yellowed grass, I felt as contented as I'd ever felt in my life. He didn't try anything and I knew he never would – not in a bad way, rather I sensed he was going to let me decide the pace we went at.

Jen would've laughed and called me an old lady; told me to 'get in there'. It didn't matter. This was my time, my *moment*, it was fuck all to do with my slutty friend.

When the afternoon sun finally lost its punch and a coolness brushed over us, we reluctantly clambered up and went inside.

Back in the parlour, Tom dropped onto Grandma's chair again while I slumped onto a shabby beige armchair near the doors, facing him – feeling hot, weary and contented.

He looked as shattered as me. I rubbed my moist face, delighted to have avoided sunburn – not an issue for Tom, of course, who had the weathered, salty face of a hardy old sailor.

"Got anything to drink?" Tom suddenly asked.

"In the kitchen," I answered lazily, pointing. "Help yourself."

He sighed and eased himself up from the chair, then went into the kitchen. While he was gone, I closed my eyes and listened to the distant humming of a neighbour's lawnmower, and the nearer noise of water splashing into a glass in the kitchen. I realised my tongue was dry, stiff and immobile in my mouth, and when a moment later Tom entered the room with two long glasses of squash I reached eagerly for mine.

"Ooh, thanks."

The first chilly gulp splashed down my throat and felt so glorious that I greedily gulped down more, taking half the glass at the first go.

Tom had downed his in one. "I could've murdered a beer," he said, smacking his lips. "Still, that hit the spot." He lowered the glass to the floor beside his chair.

"Well–" I hesitated.

"What?"

I leant forward and draped my hand, half glass and all, over the arm of the chair. "You want to go out for a drink? Seems a shame to quit when the day's been so full so far."

He shrugged. "Works for me."

"OK."

He wanted a shower before we went out and I suspected I might benefit from one, too, so I led him upstairs to get him a towel, the odd choice of showering here, at mine, not entirely lost on me, since he had no clean pants anyway.

Tragically, Tom realised and halted on the stairs. He turned back to me. "Hang on. I need clothes," he said.

"I know," I took another step up and pushed his back. "But shower here anyway."

He gave me that massive, wide grin of his. "Oh."

Upstairs, I realised with a fluttering belly and a heartrate of about six hundred beats a minute that this was actually going to happen.

In the relative coolness of the bathroom, he stripped me hastily as I wrenched at his belt buckle and dragged down his zipper.

I had his big swollen balls and shockingly engorged penis in my hands in an instant, while he wiped the caressing chill of air off my naked skin with desperate, exploring hands, the sensation of someone else's touch almost unbearably new and glorious.

Naked and feeling slightly self-conscious, I closed my eyes allowed the moment to engulf me; the feel of rough male hands pressing into my skin, clawing at my belly, rolling onto my breasts and puckering the nipples with a tingling that reached to my spine, while I rolled his balls in my hand, the other grasping his penis and feeling the pulsing of it, our sweaty scents becoming musky now and suddenly his mouth pressed to mine, his tongue parted my lips and delved, hot and merciless inside my mouth.

He thrust his hips and I could feel his foreskin rolling freely in my hand, while he pawed my flesh, the roughness of it more arousing than I would have imagined.

I gasped as I felt fingers, fingers that were not my own, press gently and then more insistently between my legs, their presence igniting my lower belly with sensations that radiated outward and provoking thoughts that would make Jen blush.

Don't think about Jen, for fuck's sake

His mouth left mine, his head bowed and he kissed and licked my neck. Every inch of my skin was lighting up, as if my body had been asleep and now, finally, it was awakening.

I kneaded his balls and pulled at his penis with wild abandon. His fingers plucked insistently and he suddenly hit the spot full on, I think I gasped, I don't know my whole body was on fire and my voice, my cries were far from me.

I heard another voice.

"Easy, easy," Tom was saying, his hand coming to mine as I must have come close to pulling his penis out at the root.

"Sorry, I gasped, but I wasn't, I wanted to be rough, I wanted to love him, hurt him, play the whore and have every experience my pathetic life had denied to me until this moment.

I eased up on the penectomy and he rewarded me with an arm around my back that sent his hand to my bottom, where its hard kneading of my cheeks gifted me a new surprise, new sensations of arousal. Who knew?

There was a salty taste in my mouth and I realised I was licking his firmly solid chest, but his insistent fingers ruled my body and I reflexively pulled back from him as my back arched slightly, hips thrusting forward, hand pulling his penis toward the source of all the glorious sensations lighting up my flesh.

Our mouths came together again, hot tongues meeting and wrapping each other as my knees buckled. Tom, more prepared than I was, held me and eased me to the cool tiled floor, where he laid his heavy body on me.

Lain on my back, I waited for him to push into me, but instead, he slid down me and his face vanished from my view.

His kissing, sucking lips and flicking, teasing tongue left me blind, all my senses shut as all of my reason began and ended with the increasingly rapid manipulation, and when he suddenly sucked hard, pulling my engorged bud between his teeth I was nothing but rhythmic muscular spasms coiling and uncoiling and, somewhere in amongst them, an inexperienced little girl unable and unwilling to swim against the tsunami of orgasm; hot, wet, bright and deafening.

I was still lost in the universe his cruel mouth had sentenced me to, when I felt the weight of his body atop me once more and then, below my waist, came the hot, wet push, my throbbing lips gulping his penis up into me. Joined at the waist now, I felt my hips rising and falling in the rhythm of his pushes, massaging me open, pulling back to close me behind him, just enough that the next push repeated the sensation inside me; again, and again, and again.

Ecstasy had become indistinguishable from agony now, the need for release as tortuous as the desire for more, for ever greater heights of tension, but something inside me broke in that instant and it was as if I had fallen into fathomless hot water, the crashing splash of overwhelming, juddering joy throwing me carelessly across the universe through light and sweat and a joyous animal stench and the chill of air on my exposed tongue, until my back flopped down with a wet plop onto the bathroom floor and I saw once again the insides of my eyelids.

I opened my eyes and saw the pretty white of the bathroom ceiling, heard the rough gasps of my own breath, felt a chill tingling my nipples and an afterglow from the last dying embers of my fading climax.

I snuggled close to Tom on the cool floor, ignoring the wetness and the rapidly chilling sweat for as long possible because I could hardly bare to live outside that moment and needed to cling onto it as long as I could.

Tom wriggled so he could look at me, eye to eye. He seemed smaller now, slumped on the floor beside me, his soft wrinkly penis flopped across his thigh like a dead soldier.

"I don't ever want to feel any different than this," he said.

I smiled through tears but find I couldn't say anything in reply.

Mickey crunched to a halt in the gravel carpark of a small country pub as I stomped the brake pedal. Then, I jiggled the stubby gearknob into reverse and spun the car back into a parking space.

Inside, under the low ceiling of the oak-beamed bar, a thick silence draped the empty, high-backed wooden chairs huddled around low, dark tables, while the creamy-perfume scent of furniture polish tried but did not quite succeed in smothering the ghostly musk of yesterday's beer.

In that silence, seemingly wedged in as a further fixture, a barman in a white shirt stood behind the polished hardwood bar and wiped a pint mug with a tatty cloth as his droopy eyes studied us. He seemed determined to be a cliché, so who was I to argue?

His dour expression was unaltered as Tom grabbed my hand and pulled me across the aged, stained yet wonderfully thick carpet, nor did he react when Tom released me and rubbed his hands briskly together, declaring, "Pint of best, please."

This was clearly a term Ye Olde Barsteward understood. He did not ask, 'best what?', nor did he glare disapprovingly as I had half-expected him to do. A thick glass mug vanished under a large varnished pump handle and with two grunts, two long pulls and a short, and a quick glance at the outcome, the dour, ageless man dumped a dimpled pint glass full of heady-smelling beer onto the bar in front of Tom.

I grabbed Ye Olde's attention and managed to earn his disapproval by asking for wine. He listed off such a sorrowful catalogue of white wines that I decided being the designated driver tonight was no big loss at all.

I held his gaze with what I hoped was a withering look. "Half a lager shandy, thanks."

The barman humphed his *utter* disapproval. It seemed hard to believe that this ray of sunshine had no other customers.

Once we had our drinks we crossed to a little table next to a small, smeary window.

Tom landed his glass heavily onto the table and grabbed a chairback, pulling it out to allow me to sit. Sorta old-fashioned, but I sorta liked it.

I lowered myself and nestled my bottom onto the polished hardwood chair as Tom eased it carefully in behind me, before dropping onto an identical chair of his own.

I glanced around. This place had been my suggestion. A friend of Jen's allegedly drank here all the time, although this now felt like a bit of s stitch-up on my friend's part, perhaps meant as a joke but maybe deliberate, to hammer home what a social dogturd I really was.

"Nice place," Tom said, and I found I had no idea if he was taking the piss or not.

"Sorry," I said. "Blame Jen."

"Oh, like that, eh?" he smiled. "Well, I'd rather be able to hear myself speak, although honestly, if I listened hard for it I could probably hear my *pulse* in this place."

I sighed and pressed the curve of my back into the surprisingly comfortable slatted back of my wooden chair, before resting my drink down on the table.

Tom cleared his throat. "Y'know, I've been thinking." He paused, as though he'd expected a gem from me that would save him *having* to continue. "OK. We've been together all day, now, right?"

"Yes, clearly."

"And we've..." he waved a hand ambiguously. "Y'know."

"Yeah I know, I was there, remember?"

He cupped his hands around his pint mug and met my gaze. "Well, I just, I think that, we... well, we barely know each other, properly I mean."

"I suppose." I shrugged. "What d'you want to know?"

Unexpectedly, he grinned at me, slumped back in his own chair and blew out his cheeks. "Ahh, this getting to know you lark's bloody tricky, ain't it?"

I grinned back and felt myself relax. Not just me, then. Good to know.

He grabbed up his pint glass and took a big chug of beer. I smiled and reciprocated, sipping my shandy, which smelled like sick and tasted like slightly sour lemonade.

"OK, Peters," I said, challenging him. "So, tell me what you do for a living."

He lowered his pint only just enough to speak over it. "You first."

"OK. I'm an escort."

Tom snorted and fought to swallow the mouthful of beer he had just taken.

"Hey, how the fuck d'you know I'm joking?" I demanded, feigning indignant anger.

He grinned back at me, all straight white teeth, and used his index finger to slide his spectacles up his nose. "Yeah," he said. "Yeah, I see what you're sayin'. Sorry, Pretty Woman, no offence intended, I'm sure."

I cocked an eyebrow at him. "No-one likes a smart-arse, Peters."

"Except the ass's wife." He went to sip his beer but hesitated and put it down, instead. "No, seriously though. I know you're not an escort coz you work with Jen."

"Oh, and what would *that* prove? Well, yes, OK, I *am* in IT; an architect, which is just a fancy name for a designer. System solutions, very dull."

"You like it?"

I thought about it for a second and shook my head. "Truth is, I'm a *junior* designer, Tom, and not a great one if my boss is to be believed. I mentioned my boss earlier, I think. Well, he's a dick. His name is Ben and as far as I can tell he was put on this Earth to screw my career up."

He nodded slightly and waited for me to continue.

"Well." I shrugged. "One of us has to be wrong."

He frowned. "This boss of yours. Ben. Bit of a macho man, right? Big ego, likes to have control over women?"

I laughed, startled by how far off he was, and gave him a quick summary of my scrawny nemesis.

He laughed with me after that.

He leant forward, his expression relaxing into something like sadness. "Y'know a minute ago, you called me 'Peters'. Reminded me of Jen."

"Jen?"

He nodded. "That's what she always called me."

I couldn't understand why I felt so sad, but I knew something he had said was wrong. It took me a second to realise what it was, but as soon as I realised it made me cold inside; more than it should have.

I hesitated before speaking. "You said 'called'."

"Eh?"

"You said 'called'. Past tense. That's what she always *called* you. Why'd you say that?"

He shrugged it off, but I watched his brow crease. "It's nothing. Slip of the tongue. What's the big deal?"

"The big deal is that my first reaction wasn't to challenge you on it. It felt like you were right."

He stared at his beer, the glass held between his hands.

I wondered what the fuck had just happened, but whatever it was, a spook in the air, it was *not* going to ruin the best day I'd ever had.

I hastily changed the subject. "So, come on, then. Your turn. You've heard my weary tale of woe, so what do you do for a living?"

"Me? I'm a historian."

"You're... Oh, OK."

It threw me completely. He seemed so physical, so I'd assumed he would be a fitness instructor, a builder; something that explained his hard athletic body. But no, he was an historian, a gym-dodging library ghost. Well, not gym-dodging, clearly.

When I looked up, I found his eyes alight with mischief. "Surprised?" he enquired casually.

"No," I lied. Then laughed, because I was kinda busted. "OK, teach me to harbour stereotypes, won't it, but seriously, I'm interested. So, what's your area, your field?"

He hoisted his glass and took a swig of beer.

"Right now," he was saying in answer to my hastily fumbled-out question, "I'm leading a team working on a local history project, going right back to the first settlements in the area. Did you know that on the site where Chadbury now stands, there's been a village of one sort or another for at least seven hundred years?"

"To be honest, I've lived here nearly all my life and I know sod all about the place. So come on, any dark secrets? Witch covens and devil worshippers?"

"Bloody hell! Take it easy, H.P. Lovecraft!"

Still, I'd had a feeling he wouldn't be able to resist and I was right. "Well, you know," he said conspiratorially, placing his pint to one side and leaning on the table, "there might be one or two sinister tales that the good folk of Chadbury don't talk about." He tapped a finger on the table. "Dark *secrets.*"

"Really?" I realised that I actually wanted to hear about the murky past of my home town.

He leant back in his chair, scooped up his pint and downed the last of it. Then, he tilted the empty glass toward me and angled it to point at an open door near the back of the place. "Fancy going out to the garden?"

"Are you stringing me along, building anticipation? Alright, but this story had better be *seriously* juicy."

He insisted on getting the next round, since I was driving, so I went through the doors into the rear garden to choose a table.

It was still warm outside, but the light was weakening and the first hint of an evening chill was just discernible in the leaf-scented air whispering between the trees. Most people just didn't fancy it, I supposed, because all but one of the ten round wood-slat tables scattered at jaunty angles across the uneven lawn were empty, the exception being nearest to a pond running up to the trees of a dense woodland behind the pub. Backdropped by the woodland and the reds and ambers of sunset, sat a couple holding hands. At the feet of the woman was a carry-seat from their car, presumably holding a baby.

How sweet.

As I waited form Tom, I was glad I'd put a sweater on over my tee-shirt – perhaps a fringe benefit of being a convertible driver was knowing to bring an extra layer even in summer, in case of a chill in the air being blasted past. I didn't mind giving Tom a second chance to see the shape of my nipples, but sticking out half-chafed through a tee-shirt wasn't a great look, as far as I knew.

I grinned at Tom as he placed drinks on the wood table. "Story time!" I gleefully insisted.

"What are you, three?" he huffed, but I saw the twinkle in his eye as he perched and took a sip of beer. "This goes back to the war, right? There was this bloke and, well, he had a rough war, came back from the front lines, but when he came back, he came back… different."

"This sounds a bit familiar, Peters. Isn't everyone changed by that sort of experience?"

"Don't call me that, Laur. Now pay attention."

I picked up the fruit drink he'd bought me and peered at the murk. Sipped and tasted sweet sticky pineapple. "What the fruity fuck is this?"

"It's good for you." He resumed his story.

A man, a myth from war-time, who had supposedly had an *experience* while he was out there in the trenches. Something terrible; life-changing, yet when he came home no-one could get him to talk about what had happened. Nothing unusual in that, though. There were probably more who came home unwilling or unable to talk, than otherwise.

Tom plucked off his glasses and peered at the lenses. Then, satisfied that they were fine, he lifted them on and pushed them up onto the bridge of his nose once again. "Yeah, damaged, affected by the trauma, that was pretty common, but it was the stories that others told that made this man so interesting. Stories about what he'd done – about what he *could do*. The ones who'd fought with him kinda revered him, but they also feared him. He'd saved lives, but it was how he had done it that meant they all steered clear of him."

"That's pretty sad." I sipped my drink and got a tangy hint of citrus fruit and a *lot* of artificial nastiness; chemicals and sugar forming a strangely acrid-sweet flavour. I grimaced. Good for me, my left tit. "But not the juicy story I was promised, Pete– Tom."

"Well, It's all kinda vague, Laur, it gets an odd footnote mention here and there but nobody took it seriously. Still, from what I could piece together, his comrades said he could blast an entire battalion across a battlefield, with just a look."

I had a momentary thought that seemed like a memory, a sense of a feeling at the base of my skull, but I couldn't grasp it and it flitted away.

Tom seemed to need prompting. "What happened to him?"

A breeze blew between the trees across from us, causing a faint chill that puckered the skin on my arms despite the woollen sleeves that covered them. There was a hint, a distant smell of wood smoke mixed in with that breeze, and it hung rich and heavy in my throat.

"For a while there was interest in the story, desperate for something that could take them away from the mundane daily horror of ordinary people dying for no sane reason. Here was a nice bite-size fantasy that everyone could chew on."

I decided against finishing the vile fruit drink and pushed the glass away from myself across the wooden tabletop. A bird (a bat?) fluttered from a tree across the pond, departing for pastures new.

"Anyway," he said, continuing. "To wrap up this little tale, he wasn't lynched or hanged by a mob or anything terrible like that; but what started out as a harmless story to tell at the winter fireplace did turn pretty ugly, in the end. Folk began to question the *real* reason he was shunned by his fellow soldiers – he didn't really have mega-man superpowers, so why were battle-hardened soldiers scared of a man that they all said had saved their lives countless times? It didn't make sense. What had he really done out there?"

I could see where this was going. To live as a pariah in your own village; it must have been terrible. "So his own friends and neighbours were judge and jury?" I asked.

Tom shrugged. "Pretty much. Tight-knit community, a once-familiar face now a stranger to everyone."

I shook my head. "That's terrible. So, what was–?"

The sentence hung unfinished as I was hit by something, a memory wrapped left chilled and unwanted for years. Mum's obituary, buried in Grandma's paperwork box, found by my inquisitive little hands.

"Tom, what did you say his name was?"

"Esagen. Jack Esagen. Took me a while to recall it, which is odd coz it's an unusual name, isn't it?"

"Yes." I stared at the table, my thoughts far away. "Very unusual."

He could tell something was up, but bless him, he tried to paste over it.

"Well, anyway, he gets married to some girl who was as much an outcast as he was, according to the horribly unflattering report of their wedding in the local press. Didn't say if she was… *special* like him, and frankly that was that. The pair disappeared from history. Sorry, it maybe wasn't as juicy as I made it sound in the sales pitch."

I lifted my chin and smiled at him. "It's fine. Nice storytelling skills. This three-year-old is very happy. What d'you say we talk about something cheerful, now?"

"Good shout. Tell me all about you, Laura Keeble."

I snorted a laugh. "I said 'something cheerful', my story's anything but. Parents and brother killed in a car wreck when I was young; raised by my grandparents; lost Grandpa when I was ten, but stayed with Grandma." I felt a wistful sigh surface. "Grandma was my family, really; I even took her name, but now I'm getting to see our roles reversed as she shrinks away and I have to take my turn to look after her."

"It's bad?" he asked.

I shrugged dismissively but that dull ache in my soul had started up. "Most days she doesn't really know who I am. Or worse, she thinks I'm still a little kid."

"Wow, sorry," said Tom, sincerely.

I shrugged. "Price of getting old."

"Tough on you, though. You thought about, you know, a care home?"

"No way."

It wasn't that I was such a great or caring person, but Grandma had given up a big chunk of her life to raise me. I just *couldn't*.

"Fair enough," he said. "Although you'll probably have to at some point, so you need to be prepared for that. How long's she been like that?"

I hadn't ever really thought about that. "I don't know, I started this job about four years ago and I think it must've started around then. No, wait!"

It hit me, right then. "No, it started *exactly* then! Grandma first went into decline when I started this job I'm doing now. What the hell, that can't be a coincidence!"

He tipped his head. "Course it can, Laur. All coincidences seem like they're more, don't fret about it."

"You're right. Of course." I frowned, irritated. "It's a coincidence. Course it is."

I took a shaky sip of my drink and remembered why I'd pushed it aside as my tongue convulsed under the sweet, sticky fruitlessness of it.

"Hey," he said, his hand landing atop mine.

I looked up, realising that I was staring into the drink cradled in my hands. His gaze was so tender, I had to look away. There were emotions trying to escape from me. It felt like I had lived a long time with nothing to show for it and it really fucking sucked balls.

You silly cow, I chided myself. *Get a grip.*

"Sorry, Tom," I said to this poor sod, who was no doubt wondering what the fuck he'd got himself involved with. "I'm a walking bummer with shoes made of sad fuckeriness."

He held my gaze for a moment. Then burst out laughing.

"Fuck off!" I pulled my hand out from under his.

"Sorry," he said, still laughing. "I'm not laughing at you it's just, you've got such an, erm, unusual turn of phrase about you."

He took a breath, reached for my hand again.

I let him take it and he cradled my fingers.

"I wasn't laughing at you, Laura, I swear. We've got sad fuckeriness in common, haven't we, you with your childhood and me with my marriage? I guess you must've been close to Granny and Gramps, if they raised you from a kid?"

I felt a half-smile, but I'm not sure how much of it actually made it to my face. "Grandma, yes."

"Aah." He squeezed my hand almost imperceptibly. "Not Gramps?"

I looked at him then, and I knew my eyes were cold. "No," I answered flatly. "Not Gramps."

I dropped my gaze to a knot in the wood of the tabletop and didn't see it anyway, my eyes disused and my mind's eye aimed backwards half a lifetime, emotions flaring in me like a crossbow bolt bursting a rotten apple, as the face of that cold dark man flared up into view once again, coldly alive as if we had never buried him.

"I try not to think about him," I said, letting myself feel Grandpa for a moment, his memory for so long buried. "If I close my eyes, I can still see him, standing over me in that mouldy old cardigan, pipe in his mouth, hands on his hips. Eyes as cold as the abyss."

Fuck. I was in danger of resurrecting that old bastard. I closed off the memory, pushed the image of him back down where it belonged.

Back to the grave, you evil old bastard.

"I didn't cry at his funeral."

Tom went to speak.

"Can we drop this, please?" I asked.

He was still holding my hand. I'd barely noticed. Now, he lifted it, drew it toward his lips and kissed it. "I really am sorry, Laur," he said softly.

"It's OK," I told him, and it very nearly was.

-14-

I awoke with a violent start in a darkness that could only mean midnight.

I had no memory of dreaming, which was a blessing, but was seriously disorientated, chilled by a cold breeze tickling my back. I crawled off the edge of the bed carefully, to avoid waking Tom, wedged into my bed with me and making low beer-snores with his throat, pulled down my tee-shirt to cover as much of my behind as possible, then started toward the bathroom.

A soft voice teased my ears with the barely perceptible sound of my own name across a seemingly vast expanse of the cool night-time air.

"Laura…"

I stopped at my bedroom door. Wary, I crossed to the window, curiosity and sleep-daze reducing my ability to have a sane reaction to that light, ephemeral voice.

Beneath my window, the bluish light of an autumnal moon cast a ghostly light on Tilers Hill and lit the silhouettes of trees in the graveyard opposite. The air was not cold, yet it was certainly too cool for summer. The season had changed – something I'd encountered before, but only in a dream.

This could not be a dream. I was cognisant of the possibility of this being a dream, which surely meant I was thinking with a waking brain. Something else was going on here. Something *really* odd.

Then I saw who had called me.

A lone woman stood by the graveyard wall across the road from my house. Her face was slightly obscured from my view by moon-cast tree shadows, but that was not what had caught my eye. She was misshapen, lumpy, her form smudged as though she had been drawn using children's crayons.

I glanced over my shoulder, suddenly nervous and spooked, but there was nothing but a few patchy moon-shadow tree shapes on my back wall, and Tom snoring contentedly into my pillow.

The woman called to me, appealed to me, begged me to come down to her.

I felt compelled, then, to go to that figure. This was not a dream, I was more sure than ever, yet whatever danger that strangely-shaped woman posed, my feet decided for me and moved me to the pile of clothes I'd left on the floor.

I resisted the overwhelming urge to go downstairs until I had scrabbled into a pair of jeans and a teeshirt, but then the bizarre autopilot took over and I passed down the stairs, through the pale moon-lit hall and outside, into a cold night lit by a bleak winter moon.

It was autumn, maybe winter, there was a dreamlike vagueness dulling my mind, yet I remained certain I was awake.

The chill of the pavement shocked and curled the soles of my feet. Familiar. This had happened to me before. This time, though, I had for a moment had the choice of putting shoes on. It just hadn't occurred to my stupefied brain.

The wind sliced through my tee-shirt and crinkled my nipples pinching-tight. My breath formed a cloud. No smells, I realised. There were no smells in the air at all, as if they had been removed from reality.

Perhaps I was dreaming, after all.

My eyes flicked and found that gloomy patch across the silent night-time road, in the shadow of the vast ancient tree that held an open-hand of thick branches up over the dead, where the figure stood.

The figure moved forward a step and the misshapen quality of it vanished with the shadows to reveal someone familiar.

"Susan?" I said, my voice a croak. "Susan Blake?"

I crossed the deserted road to where she waited, arms folded, her thick, swaddling, towelling bathrobe gathered tight around her. She, too, was barefoot.

Shit. The bathrobe. The bathrobe she had *died* in. OK, what the actual fuck? The memory was there, but I hadn't seen her die. Why did I remember it, why could I picture it so vividly? Regardless, it must have been a dream because here she was, alive and well, on a clod winter's night… in the middle of summer.

I had the same headache a computer gets when you ask it the meaning of life.

"I know you," she said. "You're Jen's friend, the posh one."

I felt my eyebrows rise. "The what one, now?"

She flashed me a sad smile. "So he got you, too."

She wasn't making sense, and I was getting seriously cold. "Let's talk inside, it's freezing out here."

She nodded, but continued to frown at me as we crossed the road.

Tom must have awoken, because he was waiting at the open front door. He had slipped on my best dressing gown and he looked absolutely ridiculous. On me, that robe was a fitted and flattering green satin wrap that managed to look tight yet not show bulges I'd sooner get away with concealing. On him, it stretched across his chest and hugged his upper thighs and made him look like a mad bohemian thespian on a bad-hair day.

Still, I found my gaze drifting toward the bulge of his big balls against the taut satin at the front, and when I glanced at Susan I found her gaze visiting the same spot for *her* vacation, too.

"Hey!" I swiped her arm.

She cocked an approving eyebrow at me. "He yours, girl?"

I disdained her and led into the front sitting room. Somehow, the back room where I'd shared sandwiches with Tom felt too much like it was *ours*. I wasn't prepared to share that with anyone, especially another woman.

The cold, silent TV glared at me like a blinded, disapproving eye as Tom went and slumped into one of the wingback armchairs, as if he owned the place. Susan went and leant against the fireplace, elbow and forearm across the mantle and her foot just kicking the silent ornamental fire.

I stood awkwardly, still in a state of confusion but a little reassured to be in a room I knew, with people I knew.

"Well, you're here," she said, her gaze flitting from one to the other of us. "So I guess Sam must've got to you both."

I frowned at her. "What d'you know about Sam?"

Her eyes widened. "Know about him? What do I know about him? All I need to fucking *know* about him, is that he fucking *murdered* me – sliced me up and left me to bleed to death on my kitchen fucking floor, the evil cold-hearted cunt!"

I felt a cold thrill at her description, which perfectly detailed Susan's death as I had witnessed it in my dream. The only difference was the bit where Sam left her to die. He hadn't, of course, but it made sense from her point of view. She was, mercifully, too dead to be aware that he had wanked himself off over her corpse.

"Killed…?" Tom cried incredulously, leaning forward in his chair. "Are you a bit fucking merry, love?"

Susan glared at him sharply. "Don't!" she snapped, although there was more fear than anger in the glints of her eyes. "You can't pretend we're not here. You know this is real, same as I do."

I thought for a moment. "No," I said flatly. "This is a dream. The only one of us who is going to exist in three hours from now is me."

Tom scratched his cheek and peered up at me. "A dream? Laur, we're not asleep, love."

"Really?" I smiled coldly at him. "So how do you explain the fact that it's winter outside, instead of summer?"

He shaped a 'W' with his mouth, as if to echo the word back at me, but he frowned and stayed silent.

"You're right," Susan said, pulling my attention back to her. "You're right, it is winter here, but that's because we're not in Chadbury. At least, not the real one. Trust me though, girl, this is no dream, either. Waking nightmare, maybe, but we're as awake as dead people get."

"Yes," I whispered, somehow *knowing* it to be true.

"Oh come on, Laur!" Tom cried, exasperated. "This is batshit fucking crazy, love!"

"Tom!" I rounded on him, aware that my anger was a displaced. "Open your eyes! Look. Think! *Feel* it. This isn't a dream, we woke up into this world, but this isn't the world we were in before. It's winter!"

He pressed his lips together.

"Seriously, babe!" I cried, exasperated.

He sprang from the chair. "This is fucking stupid, I'm going back to bed. You two do what you like."

He left in a swirl of satin robe and I was left with Susan, who stood anxiously at the fireplace, eyeing the room warily as if expecting it to fall out from under her.

I moved a step closer to her. "I saw Sam kill you. I was… kinda there."

"You were *there?*" Tears welled up in her eyes. "Why didn't you help me?"

"I couldn't. I… I was there, but, but I wasn't *there*. It was like, like a dream or something, except I sort of knew it wasn't a dream and, and I saw what Sam did to you."

She pressed a finger against the inner edge of each eye, then swiped the back of one hand under her moist nostrils. "You… saw."

"I'm sorry."

She stifled a sob with the back of her left hand. "I died gagging on my own blood and pissing myself. He hurt me *so* much, Laur!"

Hurt me.

Hurt... *me.*

And then it happened.

I was suddenly, shockingly, hit by a stark image of Tom with his trousers open, his eyes pained with guilt and distress, and another woman there with him, just outside my field of vision.

"What the fuck?" I cried, no doubt startling poor Susan, who had vanished from my perception completely.

The memory crashed into me, as though the world had fallen away and I was right there, watching that horrible event all over again, yet for the first time, an event that both had and had not ever happened.

The day it happened. An entire day I somehow remembered differently.

"Laura?"

I heard Susan's voice and felt her hand touch my shoulder. Faintly. Distantly.

"Laura! Laura, can you hear me?"

"Not right, not right at all," my voice was saying.

"Laura? Laura?" Susan's voice was growing desperate in that far off place.

"It all started again," I murmured in wonder, seeing the joins for the first time.

My grip on reality was collapsing faster, now, as the fixed thing that was the time I had lived through became flexible. My mind was invaded by a cascade of incoming memory over which I had no control

– of arriving home to a radically changed house, no longer a home at all, just as it had been when I was little, that sick dark place, all musty rooms, gloom and the oppressive presence of Grandfather.

of Mummy's voice, calling

of Tom, exposed, spent, sated by the other woman there present; Jenny

but not Jenny. Jenny was   already dead by then

- Jenny was *dead*

and then Jenny; Jenny dying, my oldest friend crying out to me, please, her best friend, please don't leave me... Yet I did. We did. Tom and me.

In a moment of utter clarity, I could see both versions of that day layered clumsily over each other, the complexity of existence momentarily revealed to me. It was in flux, yet it should not be. Something had re-written it for my benefit, but the original reality still existed in my head.

I was the sole beneficiary of the change. I was at the eye of the storm. I was the only one who saw it. It was not at all random, nor driven by some outside force. I had been the catalyst, I had done this somehow.

In a world with no logic, there was logic to this revelation. The choice of my mother's voice to draw me in, the choice of Jen for Tom's betrayal, all to provoke me, to drive me to – what? Re-write reality?

Laura Keeble, moderate failure in life and general nobody. How could I have had anything to do with it?

I saw myself in the shop, throwing the giant form of Sam across the room. Not with my hands. A dull pulse at the base of my skull.

It was me. Somehow it was me.

There ought to have been a 'why me' moment, but despair fell away to unbelieving amazement. How could this be, but more importantly, what did it mean for me?

Too many thoughts, too much to deal with.

"You OK, girl? What you doing downstairs?"

I looked up. "What?"

Tom stood frowning down at me. I glanced down and saw myself slumped in the wingback armchair, the two of us alone in the room. "Where'd Susan go?" I asked groggily, still feeling the aftershock, sickening swirl of universal truths slopping around me.

"Who's Susan?" he asked blankly.

"Are you OK? Who the hell's Susan?"

Tom's eyes showed concern for me, but no recognition of the name. For him, the visit to the Winter Chadbury had not happened. The walls of reality had closed again. Wherever Susan was, it was not here.

I stared at Tom. He still looked worried about me, but he had no memory of Susan and, somehow, it made perfect sense to him that he had slipped on my satin robe, even though he had presumably not stepped outside the house nor felt the chill of autumn in the bedroom. For him there was a perfect, unbroken and singular reality, moving smoothly from cause to effect just as reality had healed for me after our visit to the nightmare house the previous day.

I felt a little sorry for him. Tom would never remember, nor understand nor faintly glimpse the scale of reality, the layers I had seen.

I sighed. "I'm fine, Tom. I'll be fine."

I wasn't. I remembered both realities now. Jenny's terrible death, the disjointed causality. I suspected that, after tonight, I would never be able to go back to the way things had been.

I let Tom lead me upstairs, fighting with each step to cling to the clarity of my knowledge, fearing that I could feel it starting to slip away, driven back by a deep-rooted craving for normality.

I fought my own weird gift, desperate to hold on to the truth. It was vital. I might be alone in the world, the only one who understood. I could not let myself forget.

-15-

Dazzling sunlight hit my eyelids and flash-lit them red as I turned in my bed. Awake, I flopped and flailed for a moment, then winced at a stab of pain in my head as I sat up, gazing around groggily.

The bright morning sun poured its light uncompromisingly through my thin curtains, warming air awash with the cloying tangs of sweat and beer-breath. I blinked hard and winced again at the pain that twanged behind my temples.

I stood up waveringly and, as I did, Tom's crumpled bulk twitched, stirred and rolled within the cramped confines of my bed.

His swollen eyes peered out at me. "Ohhh, damn that evil thing that we call 'beer'."

I slapped his arm. "Hey! I was driving, why have I got a headache?"

He groaned, turned awkwardly in the tangled quilt and aimed his bleary gaze my way. "You haven't. Mine's so big, it's spread to fill your head as well." He licked his top lip. "What time is it?"

"Seven. I'm going to be late for work."

He grimaced. "Sorry."

"Don't worry."

I felt sure that, had my life not been poured out into a swill bucket of insanity last night, I would be worried about getting myself put on a disciplinary at work, after skiving off yesterday and now looking at being late today, but no. Things had changed.

Some of the previous night was a little blurry, but I had held on to enough to still perceive the impermanence of the formerly fixed path of my life.

As for work, well, I had a real dilemma about how I was going to face it, take it seriously, knowing what I now knew.

Tom rolled off the bed, all big shiny biceps and big swinging balls. He grabbed my dainty robe again and wrapped himself in it before heading downstairs.

In the kitchen, I clicked the kettle on while Tom went and slumped in the front sitting room. Lucky bastard, he didn't remember a thing; as far as he was concerned, this was the world and it was progressing as it always had. He could blame the beer for his headache and ignore the fact that he hadn't actually drunk enough to be quite that hung-over.

I took mugs of tea into the front room and pressed one into Tom's lazily extended hand, before perching on the arm of the wingback he'd slumped into.

I sat and cautiously sipped hot tea from the smooth rim of the mug.

"You could have a go at making the tea next time, if you like."

He muttered something unintelligible and I felt more annoyed with him than I should have. Perhaps an echo of my resentment at what he had done in a timeline that he could no longer even remember so, yes, unfair, but to me, he had still done it.

"Tom, do you remember the last time we saw Jen?"

He stared at the TV and sipped like a nouvelle zombie immersed in 24-hour news. "Yeah, it was the night we met. That a trick question?"

"No, I just…" I struggled to phrase the question so I wouldn't sound like a crazy person. "Do you think she's.. alright?"

There was a silent pause and dust danced lazily in the loping arms of those sunbeams.

"Mug's heavy," he said, his gaze still on the TV.

"What? Well put it down, then. Do you need any other life advice? Nappy change? Bottle of milk?"

"Where?" He continued to stare at the TV.

Perhaps he hadn't escaped last night unscathed, after all. I hesitated, baffled by his sudden stupidity. "On the coffee table, Tom."

Just as he daintily pushed his glasses up along the bridge of his nose, I noticed that he had them on once again. When had he picked those up?

"I can't," he said bluntly.

"Can't what?"

"Put it on the coffee table."

"Tom, what the fuck are you talking about, you're really starting to annoy me, now."

He stared straight at me. "I can't put it on the coffee table, coz it's tea. See?"

Twat.

I frowned down at him. "How could you be bothered? Seriously?"

He shrugged.

I hated the knowledge I had been cursed with. It wasn't fair. Was Jen alive or dead in whatever reality existed now? If I called her number would she be back, real and alive again, to answer my call? I fumed silently at Tom, who could sit and relax and believe the lie that was the 'world' news. And to make matters worse, he was acting like a total dick this morning as if to reinforce my reduced opinion of him.

I had to get a grip, somehow, but it was so much to take in.

Maybe the certainty from the day before would fade, leaving me in peace again. Yeah, right.

I drew a deep breath and picked up my mug, nursing it. The tea was hot and the steam that tickled my nostrils as I held the mug up was faintly herbal.

I glanced at Tom as he muttered at something that was happening on the news item on-screen. I could still all-too vividly picture him, penis out, with Jen. It didn't matter that the situation had been manufactured, that it hadn't really been Jen; it still felt like a real betrayal to me.

I slugged my tea and stood up. "I can't deal with this, I'm going to get ready for work."

As I stepped toward the door, Grandma shuffled through it on her flat slippers. "Hello, dear," she murmured in her frail whisper.

"Grandma." I leant and touched my lips to the dry cheek she offered up. "I didn't know you were home. You want a cup of tea?"

When had she come home? Had she been here last night? I didn't remember seeing her curtains drawn, her room in use, at all. I think I just hadn't been looking. My grip on reality was coming apart badly and, now, someone I cared about had fallen through the cracks.

"No thank you, dear," Grandma replied. "I'll get my own tea, I'm more than capable."

Though she was shuffling her feet, her eyes were sharp behind her dense glasses, her mind very much back in the driving seat.

Her head suddenly swivelled, aiming those thick lenses at Tom. "And who might you be?"

Tom rose from his chair and extended a hand. "I'm Tom, Mrs Keeble."

She didn't correct him over her name, merely humphed a laugh - a thing she often did — and ignored his proffered hand. The head swivelled, the glasses were aimed at me. "Breakfast, dear?"

Shit. Hell, no. I was no way going to be forced to eat one of Grandma's breakfasts. Some sacrifices are just too much to ask.

"Sorry, Grandma." I touched Tom's arm. "Come on, time for work."

Grandma stared, her face still blank but, I was sure, a faintly amused glint in her eyes.

As Tom stepped toward me, Grandma suddenly snatched at the sleeve of his robe, pulling it part of the way open so I saw his dick swinging.

"Mrs..." he started.

"She can't hide from him any more!" she said sharply. "Keeping them apart was the wrong thing to do!"

She stared fiercely up into his eyes for a moment, then turned and shuffled out of the room.

Tom turned to me, aghast. "What the buggery was *that* about?"

I shrugged. "Sorry, Tom. Told you she's not right. Come on, before she starts blowtorching bacon."

We hastily got ourselves ready and left before the ominous clanking of pans could snare us in their deadly breakfast. I grabbed a dubiously greyish-black skirt that was only alluring to men who wanted sex with old ladies, and a white blouse that I suspected (but was unable, in my haste, to prove) had a stain somewhere on it; and then, with black shoes to clippy-clop in and a black patent-and-suede bag that could easily carry a housebrick, I led the now-dressed Tom away from the protesting cries of perfectly good food.

By the time shook off Tom and got to Chadbury West Station, any hope of making it to work at a forgivable time was long lost. I bolted for the 8:58 as the door bleepers went, and took comfort in the fact that at least I would have a seat on this late train, as consolation for the bullshit Ben was going to ladle onto me.

Reality felt rather real again.

I didn't know I'd fallen asleep until I woke up with a jolt. It had been a peaceful and gloriously dreamless sleep, rocked by our journey over rails in a steel tube bathed in sunlight, so I felt more refreshed and alive than I had in a long while as the train eased in alongside a platform at Liverpool Street station.

I clambered up, grabbed my bag and flounced off the train with a spring in my step, landed on the platform and followed the handful of people who had shared the train with me. I felt inexplicably good.

Emerging through the ticket barrier I was slammed back into my nightmare.

I staggered to a halt.

This place was still recognisably Liverpool Street, but only just. In the 48 hours or so since I'd last stood here, the great vault of the station roof had been distorted beyond all sanity.

It was still a great expanse of ornate ironwork stretched outward in a radial frame, but far too ornate, all green-painted flourishes of ironwork, resembling the way someone might romantically paint the place rather than how it was supposed to look.

I drew my gaze down and glanced back. "Shit," I murmured.

The ticket barriers I had unconsciously passed through were nothing to do with the Liverpool Street I knew, either. The modern ticket gates that I always worried would one day slam shut on my breasts and kill me stone dead with pain, were gone. They had been replaced by waist-high, curved green iron turnstiles unlike anything outside of a nineteen-twenties poster in a how-we-used-to-live museum. They were wonderful and impossibly incongruous, but not to the scant few passengers wandering through, who accepted them as correct and proper, and nor to the ticket inspector who nodded at passengers and seemed unconcerned that they were free to walk through without swiping their tickets or cards on a reader.

The sleep on the train had cured my headache but now I felt its returning shot across the bow. My chest began to ache – I realised I had been holding my breath and let it bellow free.

Deciding to get out of there and worry about what it meant later I stepped hastily forward and was poleaxed once again.

The great open expanse of the concourse swept grandly away in all directions as ever, but the second-level row of shops was gone, there being no second level at all, now; just the pale brick of the outer walls sweeping up toward the green-painted framing arch of the ceiling.

Before me, rickety wooden free-standing stalls stood arrayed against the furthest wall, tended by ordinary looking modern people who appeared to have no awareness that they seemed to be shopkeeping from some gothic re-imagining of a Charles Dickens novel.

I moved hesitantly forward, past a seven-foot-high ornate red pillarbox standing sentinel in the middle of the concourse, its overhanging top resembling some ostentatious mayor's hat, and made for the escalators to street level.

"Oh, fuck right off!" I cried, provoking some old-fashioned looks from others in the station.

The escalators, too, had been replaced with something insane. No longer did steel rungs slide up and down between metal and glass supports as they had done for all the years that I'd been commuting. Now, a set of chunky wooden rungs chugged up to street level, accompanied by two heavy black rubber handrails travelling on polished brown hardwood supports. A faint yet nauseatingly-familiar tangy-stale smell of slightly singed rubber reached my nostrils from the mad old contraption.

There was nowhere to run to. I was in a world gone mad and I could do nothing but suck it up and carry on. No-one else could see anything wrong; it all made perfect sense to them.

On street level I found to my relief that the rest of London had kept its sanity, so averting my gaze I headed to the office. All normal. There was no guard in the security lobby, which was unusual but not unheard of. Ted and Barry were getting on a bit, neither had the best bladder for holding tea for too long.

I still felt shivery from the dazzling cascade of wild change I'd been subjected to in the last twelve hours, but I swiped my card, passed through the turnstile then took the lift to my floor, where I was greeted by cathedral silence under the eerily sterile blue-white lighting.

There were no smells. No machine coffee, no morning bacon rolls, not even sweat from the likes of Matt P or Greg, who generally left a wake of it like sharks trailing blood.

"Damn," I uttered softly, and then, clutching my ample black bag to my chest I stabbed the lift call button several times before noticing that the lift doors were still open.

This was all wrong.

I leapt into the lift and stabbed the 'G' button.

I controlled my breathing as I watched the descent as a countdown of floor numbers until, by the time the 'G' lit up on the panel, I'd got a slow rhythm of breaths going and my heart had stopped hammering at my ribs. I planned to leave the office, escape London and go home. I needed familiarity. I was horribly aware of how quickly Grandma had lost her mind. Maybe my brain wasn't waiting for old age to set in to play that cunt's trick on me.

The 'G' winked off.

"What?" I stabbed the button again, but too late

The bag I'd been clutching fell through my hands and hit the floor with a muted flump. "No," I uttered. "Oh no, no, no-no-no…"

All the air had poured out of my lungs. I swallowed hard and sucked in a breath.

The lift continued smoothly down until finally the 'B' lit up, and only then did the doors ease open onto a world of midnight-deep gloom. I didn't feel myself edge backwards until my back pressed against the rear wall of my metal cell, where I caught myself breathing hard in the heat of fear, too scared to imagine what twisted horror had now been formed from the embryonic chaos overtaking my world.

Nothing happened. I told myself to move, to get at that fat black button with an orange-lit 'G' at its centre, but that gaping black maw in front of me held my attention and kept me frozen.

Silence, darkness outside the fragile safety of this cage.

I had faced far worse than a dark corridor, both sleeping and awake, yet it seemed to be more than I could manage too just take that step and a half across the small square metal floor to press the damn button. I'd be on my way back up to the Ground Floor and this would all be behind me, yet I couldn't move, couldn't face taking my warm body any closer to that cold dark opening, even if I had to do it in order to escape.

Until that moment, I'm not sure I'd ever believed that it was possible to actually be frozen with fear.

I knew my fear was irrational but somehow it was a physical constraint that held me immobile. I refused to cower. *Refused.* Grasping control of my ragged breathing, *in-one-two-three, out-one-two-three*, I willed my left foot to edge out from beneath me.

My wayward body reached the list control panel and my finger extended, trembling a little, OK a lot, and then stabbed that 'G' button so fucking hard it was amazing that it didn't pop straight out of its housing.

Nothing happened.

"Oh, shit in my mouth."

The doors stood there like immoveable sentinels, mockingly welcoming me to the palace to where I had no choice but to be.

"Fuck it." I smoothed my skirt and stepped out of the lift and into the gloomy corridor.

As I hastily clippy-clopped across the concrete floor my eyes adjusted to the gloom, until I could see that it wasn't all that dark at all, just gloomy relative to the brightly lit elevator, which even now cast a bright white expanding triangle of light across the floor as I headed toward the green 'fire exit' sign over the escape door.

I reached the door, my path to freedom, and grabbed the pull handle. It moved toward me an inch and then clunked and ceased.

Locked! A fucking fire door!

OK, keep that grip you've just about got, Keeble.

To my left was the 'Clean Room', the sterile operating room where the company's more potent machinery was able to hum and buzz safely, secure from dust, flies and human moisture with an uninterruptable power connection and a backup generator. The Clean Room usually had a small skeleton staff on shift rotation, but I guessed they too would have vanished into the ether in what was, today, The Crazy World of Laura Keeble.

At least there were lights on in there. Their white glare peered around the sides of the doors.

I opened the door and eased myself cautiously inside, painfully aware that I had been herded here like cattle. And we all know what happens to cattle, right, kids?

Lauraburger, anyone?

There were long banks of tall white machine cabinets, some with racks of equipment visible, others just blank and white, all standing in rows like a sixties sci-fi imagining of a paperless library.

And there, halfway down one of the walkways, between the white stacks, stood the tall, bulky, unmistakable form of Sam.

I guess I should have known.

My nostrils tingling with the acrid tang of ozone from the always-on machinery, I had to suppress the urge to cough, which was starting to make my eyes water.

He smiled. "My dear Ms Keeble, you are becoming emotional. Are you glad to see me?"

I smiled back, coldly. "Look at you. Fresh from my dreams. And my eyes are watering because you leave a stink in every room you go in, Sa–"

He pounced so fast that he was on me before I could finish. A vice-hard hand gripped my shoulder, another much more tenderly cupped my left breast. The pressure of his touch against my nipple, even through my clothes, felt as gross as a wriggling maggot would feel on my tongue.

I shrieked with rage and there was a sharp pain at the base of my skull.

Sam jerked violently, let me go, staggered back a step and then stared at me for a moment. "What...?"

The expression of wide-eyed bewilderment remained on his face as he tipped over backwards and thudded down onto his backside, legs splayed.

I turned on my heel and thought I told my legs to run, but I went nowhere before a sledgehammer slammed down hard onto my shoulder. I cried out as he gripped and a lightning-sharp pain lanced from my shoulder down through my chest.

He spun me and I stared up at the grinning malevolent face above me. "That's the second time you've done that to me, bitch," he snarled through his pearly-white clenched teeth. "It's going to be the last!"

His grip tightened and the pain became horribly sharp, brittle, and I was sure I heard bones groaning in preparation for being snapped.

"Rest assured, it will be the last, you worthless little hag!"

Behind me, distant yet sharp, the Clean Room doors flew open. Sam shoved me away and his sharp blue eyes re-focussed.

I staggered back, hunched in pain and grasping my shoulder as shards of pain split the muscles and bones apart.

When I could focus on anything else, I saw a bizarre figure confronting Sam, dwarfed yet defiant before the giant.

The newcomer was an unremarkable-looking little man dressed in a tired-looking grey suit, the dull white shirt beneath left open at the throat, with no tie, whilst the overall effect was gift-wrapped by a shabby, creased grey coat. A dark brown hat, similar to a cowboy hat but much less well-made, sat perched on top of his head, which gave his whole appearance a shambolic insanity in keeping with the day I was having.

He seemed unaware of how dangerous the giant before him was.

I staggered toward him, still holding my shoulder. *"Run!"* I screamed at him, legs already at DefCon One for my escape move.

Poor dumb idiot was five-feet three at best, with his slight frame justifying no more weight than about ten stones – Sam was going to purée him.

"Come on!" I shouted at the little man. "He's gonna kill–"

But something spooky/impossible happened, instead.

The newcomer stared up at Sam and something must have changed in his eyes, or something – I don't know. All I know is that Sam took two hasty steps backward, away from the much smaller man who was facing him off.

"No!" the big man yelled in rage, but his eyes were not angry but terrified. "You *cannot* do that! You are *forbidden* to interfere!"

The newcomer simply stared.

"No!" Sam screamed almost indignantly, but he seemed to decide on discretion and turned on his heel. Bolting away between the machines at a speed only he seemed able to achieve, Sam was gone.

A moment later, I heard the bang of the Clean Room doors.

I turned to the smallish man. "Wow," I said. "I've never seen him scared like that before, how'd you do that?"

He stared at me for a moment. He had a rather nice face, slightly lined by time and yet still kind. Almost a miniature Tom.

I smiled and offered my hand. "I'm Laura."

He smiled back… well, he tried to.

A scream rose up through my body. I managed to prevent it bolting free only because I was so scared that my throat had closed. The hand I had held out to him wilted on its limb.

He had attempted an approximation of what he must have imagined a smile to be, but he seemed to have limited connectivity to his facial muscles, or perhaps was unfamiliar with how to use them, because his face collapsed, convulsed into a hideous rictus and twisted out of shape, the mouth twisted down on one side, one eye half-shut by the strain of it.

I let out a guttural cry of horror and charged at the exit doors, finding that Sam was suddenly the least terrifying of the two not-quite-men in this prison. The little man made no attempt to stop me as I fled into the gloomy vestibule and went headlong at the lift.

Whatever had kept the lift here before, its influence was gone. The moment I punched 'G', the doors slid shut and I felt the capsule slide upward toward safety.

I started at the *ting!* of the lift, light-headed with the toll of the stress I'd just endured. The doors slipped open to reveal the ground floor. I bolted across the lobby, my heels and toes clacking and slipping at the polished flooring, my eyes fixed forward so I couldn't see if either of my personal monsters were coming after me.

I reached the secure turnstile out of the building. Secure. I needed my pass card.

"Shitfuck…."

My bag! I'd had it when I took the lift that stranded me in the basement, but I could not remember having it after that.

"Shit, shit, shit…"

And then, I saw it – sat on the floor of the lift where I must have dropped it all that time ago in the basement.

Another expanse of floor to cross, which was beginning to feel like a habit that was haunting me, yet at least this expanse was familiar and well-lit. I charged at the lift doors, my cloppy heels trying to slip on the polished floor, then slowed, edged into the steel capsule, knelt, reached and grabbed the mock-patent handle and whipped the black patent-and-suede bundle toward me.

Still safe. Still no new nightmares to face.

Staggering out into the sticky heat of a summer's day was a shock after the chill of the deserted office. I packed my security pass next to my Free-Latte-One-Day card in London and called Tom as my heels clacked across one pavement after another, tasting the fat greasy fumes of the traffic as I hurried back to the station.

"Tom, I'm coming home but I need to see you."

"You OK, you sound out of breath?"

"Fine, where are you right now?"

"Eh?" I could picture him pushing his little glasses up onto the bridge of his nose and frowning in that crinkly way of his. *"Erm, at the library. Chadbury Library, I've got some research to do. Is something up?"*

"I'll meet you at the library, see you in about forty minutes."

I hastily ended the call and got back to Liverpool Street Station, which had reverted to normality when I reached it, suggesting the really scary prospect that in fact I really was just going batshit – but that was a worry for another time. I needed Tom. Maybe because I just needed reassurance.

-16-

The volume setting on my shoes was way too high for the hard, polished floor of the silent library as I clacked along between two columns of dustily populated book cases, heading toward the back of the library where the microfiche readers sat, grey and stoic, a relic of an earlier technology that still clung to usefulness in such ponderous institutions.

I passed all the way through the stacks and reached the open ground-level area where the reading tables sat populated by a few dusty cardigan types, but there was still no sign of Tom so I trotted up the little flight of twelve stairs to the 'upper level' - a wood-floored study area with several desks and an air of studious silence.

Tom was leaning back on a hard-wood swivel chair at a table piled with dusty old books, arms folded behind his head, biceps swelling his tee-shirt sleeves in a nicely under-stated sexy way. As he saw me, he hastily swung the chair upright and swivelled toward me.

"Hey. You OK?" He smiled at me uncertainly

I hurried forward and leant to give him a quick peck on the cheek (his momentary lip pucker suggested a mis-reading), before grabbing a hardwood chair of my own and dropping my suede bag on the floor. "Tom, there's something I need to explain to you, something you need to understand."

I saw him draw a deep breath and couldn't help wondering what he imagined I was going to say. Whatever it was, he was certain to be wrong. "No problem, tell away."

"Some stuff has happened, Tom. Some of it you know about–"

"Mm-hmm. Sam."

"Yes. But there's a lot that you don't know, or don't think you know, because you've forgotten it."

He frowned but half-smiled, too. "Wow." He rubbed his right eyebrow, pushing his glasses crooked as he peered at me. "I was expecting a 'Dear John', not sure what's worse."

"Why would I come all this way to dump you? You not heard of texting?"

He laughed. "Fuck off."

"Right." I took a deep breath. "I know how this is going to sound, I really do, but you have to believe me. Things are happening and it's all getting more and more insane and if I don't tell someone I'm gonna go mad."

He reached out and took my hand, holding my gaze. "Whatever it is, I'm listening."

Oh, where to begin!

"It started in the nightclub. That's where I first met Sam. But, but I suppose everything started going *really* crazy the day we went out for our date."

"You make it sound like months ago, Laur. That was yesterday."

Yesterday? No. No way, it couldn't be. I realised I had about two days' worth of memories in my poor, sore head because of the reset, but he was right, I'd only been to bed once in all that time.

"Look," I went on, my head aching from the confusion of it all. "I know stuff you don't know. It's hard to explain, though, coz I can remember stuff that your mind has decided to forget. No, alright, maybe not *decided*, exactly, but.."

He held up a hand. "Stop, back up a bit! Give me the wiki version, OK?"

I pushed hair back off my forehead, realising that the hair was lank with old sweat and more than a little way short of catwalk-ready. To be fair, though, fashion models didn't have to fight their way out of haunted fucking basements.

I gathered my thoughts. "You remember Sam, right?"

"The nutter at the shops? Oh, yeah."

"Good. Well, after that fight, we went back to my place, you see."

"This the bit you think I've forgotten?" he asked. "You've got self-image issues, girl."

I laughed at that, but the moment of mirth died as the heavy weight of what was happening to the world around me re-settled on top of my soul and farted.

So, Tom remembered the fight with Sam, and he remembered going back to my place. I had a slightly tenuous grip on what had happened *both* times, and what had happened only once.

"Tom, answer me this one. As far as you remember, what happened after we left the shopping mall?"

He shrugged. "We were pretty shaken up, so we jumped in that freaky old car of yours, what's it called? Mikey? And then we drove up through town, and then... and *then*..."

His eyes widened and he stared into space for a few seconds.

"Fuck me," he uttered.

I felt relief that was tinged with a little hint of guilt, because I knew I was making Tom open up his mind to the insanity of the world where I now lived.

"There it is," I said to him. "The hole in your memory."

"But..." He rubbed his stubbly chin as his bug-wide eyes stared at me. "We just, we just *forgot*, Laur. I mean, I *am* remembering it right, aren't I? One minute we were leaving the mall, seriously shitted-up after that fight, and then the next second we were half-way back to yours with memories of a whole loved-up morning, sunbathing in our car seats and then back to yours for lemonade and dogshit sandwiches."

"You see it, don't you? How the memories don't fit together?"

"That's... Laur, that's fucking mental!"

"You should try being me right now," I said. "Now, do you remember what happened to Jen?"

"What about her?" I saw curiosity in his eyes, so... not yet.

I felt the hotness of tears in my eyes and the cold hollowness of sorrow in my belly. Having to say it out loud was going to hurt almost as much as having to live with the knowledge.

"She's dead, Tom. We saw her die, we were there."

"Nah, come on," he said immediately, but I saw his eyes. *"No,"* he murmured, his voice hollow but the conviction to deny too weak in him now.

"It was awful, some fucked-up wasting disease that ate her away in front of us."

"I don't–"

"I know you don't, Tom, but trust me, we were both there. It was horrible and scary and we didn't come out of it with much heroism."

Fuck! It hurt badly enough to tell him she was dead, let alone to explain out loud what we'd done, how we, how I had failed Jenny.

"I wanna tell you shut up, or call bullshit." He pressed his lips together. "But I don't have that luxury any more. I can feel it's true even if I can't remember."

There was a terrible, empty look in his eyes. He rolled his head back and I heard a little pop in his neck.

"Fuck," he told the domed ceiling above the upper reading tier.

"I'm so sorry, Tom. I didn't want to involve you, I don't even know why this is happening to me, why I seem to be the only one who can see the changes, I mean, I'm nothing special or any—"

"Oh!" he cried, suddenly reanimating and startling me. "Come with me."

Before I could protest he bounded down the stairs with me clopping along in tow, along the main floor and through the wooden tunnels to a bookcase at the gloomy rear of the library. He turned to me, straightened his dainty glasses and said, "Fish files."

I thought that was what he'd said, as he peered at the bookcase. I could see a set of binders wedged between the thick spines of proper books on the upper shelf.

"I do not have a single clue what you're talking about, Tom."

"Here we go," he said, apparently ignoring me as he selected two binders, a blue and a light grey, which he pulled free and tucked under his right arm.

"This way," he ordered, before marching away further into the abyss between the stacks, like a librarian pied piper, assuming I would follow him.

At the very back of the library, cuddled by the chill of the cold concrete wall and bathed in the sterile light of six underpowered strips, three dull blue hooded screens sat impassively on a rough-edged wooden bench.

The penny dropped. Tom had called these things 'fiche files, because they contained microfiche cells, miniaturised photographic images on gel sheets that cold each store every page of several years' worth of newspapers, or whole books, all on a sheet no bigger than a pop tart sachet. I'd seen these things before; years before. Apparently, though, the library still used them.

Tom perched on a wood-framed swivel chair in front of the blank pale blue screen of the middle reader, thumping down the two hefty binders he'd taken from the bookcase. He extracted two of the little greenish-black plastic sheets, which he loaded into the reader before him. Actually, they were smaller than I remembered – not quite as big as a pop tart sachet.

He edged his backside left to right on the wooden seat, seeking comfort as his attention remained locked onto the large blue viewing screen.

"Tom?"

"You need to see this," he told me.

His fingers worked the Reader wheel with surprising dexterity. "You probably think I can't handle what you've just told me, or you think I'll say you're nuts, but I'm no fool, Laur, I knew something was wrong from the minute we met your loony pal Sam, so I did some digging and... *here.*"

He slid his chair aside a few inches so I could see, and I leant over to peer at the display. The reader had a 20cm screen and there, magnified however many times from the cell below, was an old newspaper page, faded to light grey print on an ivory backdrop.

Central to the page was a picture, something quite rare from the era when this paper was printed, but clearly it had been important to someone to record an old photo of a gang of local friends. Who they were, I could not say. They were certainly all long-dead, but on the day of this picture they were all young, fresh and about to head off into war together.

I felt a cloying frustration at the impending chaos clawing at the walls around me while Tom wasted my time with ancient news. Historian or not, he had to know better. I laid a hand on his shoulder. "Tom, I'll give you one chance to show me something helpful, and then I'm gonna reach into your trousers and pull your cock off."

"Oh, I *say*," he answered in a ridiculous voice as I felt my face flush.

"OK, that came out wrong. But the day I'm having, please don't waste my time!"

"Look." He pointed to a particular place on the image on the 'fiche screen.

I frowned, leant and squinted at the picture. It was blown up as big as the screen allowed, but it was smeary with time and lack of original quality.

The front row of men were crouched low to the ground on their haunches, hands dangling between their knees; the second row were hunched across the backs of those in the front row, hands pressed onto their shoulders as though about to hopscotch their way to freedom. The back row stood upright.

"What am I supposed– fuck!"

In that last group, to the far right, one man stood slightly apart from the rest, his burly white-sleeved arms folded across his chest, a long, heavy, straight wooden tobacco pipe protruding from his mouth. His eyes glinted out coldly at me across the decades, their icy malevolence untouched by the years of fading this picture had endured before it had been preserved on 'fiche.

"*Grandpa,*" I hissed, shocked at the amount of bile I still felt compelled to pour into the saying of that one word, as I met that cold-eyed, dead-hearted old stare....

I straightened up, glared at Tom. "What the fuck are you playing at?"

He didn't look at me and he didn't react to my mis-directed rage. Instead, he pointed at the display. "Look. Properly *look!*"

"Fuck look, Tom, just fucking *tell* me."

He sighed. "Read the names, Laura."

I blew out air, feeling spitefully angry with Tom, but I leant over and squinted at the screen anyway. I saw a name, *his* name, springing out from the meekly backlit transparent image that was now preserved for all eternity.

Jack Esagen.

That cold, cruel old man who had so cursed his defenceless orphaned grandchild with a loveless life, that nightmare from my childhood, had been given the name of the soldier from Tom's story at the pub, the man who had been made a pariah after the war for supposedly having 'powers' or some such.

"No, Tom, it's a mis-print, that wasn't his name."

He peered up at me through his lenses, lips pursed. "I don't know why," he said gently, "but you're remembering wrong, Laura. That was his name."

I nodded, numb.

He pressed a hand to my arm. "You may not have taken his name, but you're descended from Jack Esagen."

I brushed his hand off me. "Did you know when you told me that story?"

"No, that story just… sort of came to me," he said, frowning. "With everything else lately, I'd struggle to believe it was a coincidence."

I felt an angry reflex to challenge him, but he spun away from me and began to hastily re-load the reader with another thin gel sheet.

The screen filled again. A local news report. Old, but nowhere near as old as the previous one; maybe twenty years or so. A Wednesday. A car crash. A family car that had careered off a narrow country road between Chadbury and Woodfield Heath.

My parents' car. Ohh, not good, where was he going with this?

"Tom, just don't, OK? This is too much."

"You have to see, have to get it."

I didn't need to look. I knew what I'd see – it was an event I had been a witness to, although the memory of it was faded, distorted by time and blurred even at the time by shock. It had been horrible, terrifying, and it had brought to an end both my family and my childhood.

The details, the smells, the emotions were all as lost in time as the smudged words on that sheet were faded by it, but I'd never needed to see it before.

"Look," Tom urged.

I did. Ronald had died at the scene. Dorothy had died later, on the way to hospital. A little girl was found alive, bruised but unharmed, in a ditch nearby – a little girl who would awaken in hospital to learn that the world she had believed was unchangeable and filled with joy and magic had been destroyed in an instant while she slept, to be replaced with a nightmare of misery and loneliness that she would have to drag along behind her for the rest of her life.

I sighed as a heavy wistful sadness weighed me down.

But Tom's deft fingers worked the scrolling wheel again and now I was looking at another article, printed two weeks after the first. An appeal. The couple's son was missing. No-one had raised the alarm at first, but for all that Grandpa was a cunt, even he wasn't prepared to let Peter lie dead somewhere, unfound.

"D'you see?" Tom asked.

A photograph, issued by the Police in an effort to try and jog someone's memory, I suppose, for all the good it had done. They never did find him.

"Do you *see?*" Tom urged.

I huffed an irritated sigh at him. *"What?"*

"Fuck's sake, Laur, I know it's hard but you've gotta try!"

Returning my attention to the picture, to shut Tom up more than anything else, I saw the grainy image of an oldish photograph printed on low quality paper, and now shrunk down onto a little plastic cell. Yet I knew the child in that picture at once.

I smiled and felt the pressure of tears in my eyes. I remembered him so fondly, my sweet brother, that quiet, scruffy-haired little man who had been half of me and had shared with me just a very few of my summers.

And suddenly, as Tom had known I would, I saw it.

I'd forgotten the details of my brother's face over the years, retaining only a warm fuzzy memory of loving loveliness – the only way the bereaved ever do remember those they have lost. But now I could see what Tom wanted me to see, the discovery that he had been so excited about.

"No," I muttered to myself, mortified by the truth. "Not Peter." The image before me grew blurry as the wistful tears in my eyes turned coldly bitter.

"I am really sorry, Laura." He slid off his dainty little spectacles to rub his eyes. "I tell you what, it was a fucking shock for me, too, when I first saw it."

It didn't make sense that I could forget such a striking feature of someone I'd once been so close to, but there was no denying who Peter took after in our family. He had the same sharp, cold stare as Jack Esagen. Our grandfather. I felt sick as the last sweet memories I owned turned sour. How could he have that old bastard's eyes?

Tom turned in his chair, probably meaning to rise and embrace me, but his eyes went wide and he sprang away from me, throwing me off-balance before he grabbed my arm. I went to ask what the hell he was doing, but the words were left unformed as I felt a pulse at the base of my skull – a sensation I had felt before, and whose meaning I was beginning to understand.

"Shi-it!"

Tom's glasses clattered to the floor with a silvery tinkle and a second later he dragged me up the book aisle that ran parallel to the one through which Sam was coming at us. We emerged breathing hard at the wooden staircase up to the reading platform.

"No," I gasped. "We'll be trapped!"

Sam was coming, we could never hope to slip across his path toward the exit. The best we could do was make our stand somewhere where we could keep out of reach of his frightening grasp.

As we drove up the stairs, me with hot, aching legs already, I glanced over my shoulder and wished I had not. A large mass reached the foot of those scant few steps and bounded up without hesitation.

I cried out as another pulse juddered through the base of my skull. I swayed, felt my legs crumple and realised I was going to fall back down the staircase, into Sam's final embrace. I was grabbed but happily not by the monster, as Tom saw me teeter and got me to safety. We stumbled a few steps onto the platform and turned to see the vast bulk of Sam swell into view on the top step, blocking the stairway completely.

"Well, this *is* a happy reunion," the monster said, his rich melodious voice flowing from that handsome blue-eyed face.

"Are you following me?" I asked sarcastically, unaccountably engaging in banter with this hateful creature.

He lumbered up onto the platform, his toned face swelling into a broad grin. "If you only knew," he said.

I stood my ground, pushed out my chin and hoped the boneless wibbling of my legs didn't show. "Why don't you leave us alone, Sam? We haven't done *anything* to you!"

The giant's grin faded. "Oh, I beg to differ." He advanced a step, cocking his head to one side. "And you know, I am going to enjoy this so very, very much."

Tom threw himself past me with a bellow of rage, but Sam flashed forward in a blur and, before Tom could reconsider, a great broad fist slammed against his chin. His head snapped back. He back-pedalled three paces and crashed into a wooden chair, managing to roll his body enough to go down hard on his backside and avoid falling headlong to the floor.

I stared up at Sam, who glared down at me with brilliant sapphire eyes, the prone form of Tom no longer of interest to him.

Well, that was my assumption.

The giant charged but, even as I braced myself, he rushed past me and dragged a blast of air across me as he went, his shoulder barely clipping mine but the force of it enough to send a jolt of pain through my bones.

Tom had managed to lever himself up and was on his feet, more angry than scared now, pumped full of testosterone and thinking himself much tougher than he really was.

Sam thundered across the platform and I saw, just before the monster smashed into him, that Tom wasn't actually standing where he had fallen. He had moved position and then made a show of getting up from beside a different chair than the one he had toppled against.

Why, was answered a moment later.

As the giant reached him, he stopped standing his ground and, with the giant fully committed, he threw himself sharply aside.

The safety rail of the upper reading platform came into view and Sam slammed straight into it. He emitted a bull's cry of rage, folded at the belly, flipped headlong over the rail and plummeted. His cry grew shrill for an instant and then got cut off by a hard *clack!* followed by a wet crunch.

I stared at Tom, whose expression was grim but whose eyes revealed the smirk he was hiding.

Crossing to the balcony edge, I peered over with him.

The hard floor below had a dark patch on its wood – but no broken, defeated body slumped immobile where it ought to be.

I turned fearfully to Tom. "He *can't* have just got up after that!"

He pursed his lips. "This is *not* good."

There was a footfall behind us.

I turned sharply and froze, staring.

As Sam grinned at me, it still carried all its former malevolence, but the lie of its beauty had fallen to ruin. His lower jaw was offset, clearly dislocated, but that was the least of his injuries. The impact on the hard wood floor had taken a toll. His one remaining eye glinted at us with hideous rage, but on the other side of his nose there was a gaping hole, the cold black socket oozing a sloppy curdled mix of eye juice and blood down his cheek, the void sucking the saggy redundant eyelid inward, as if his face wanted to forget that it had ever had an eye there.

"Shit," I heard my terrified voice murmur.

He shifted his weight from foot to foot, his body twisted as if his shoulders, spine and ribcage were no longer properly aligned, his posture twisted slightly off to the left.

His grin widened malevolently, revealing several gory sockets where he had lost teeth, but his damaged face could not cope with the grin and, with a sickening *snick!*, a sharp splinter of shattered cheekbone twisted free and punched through the smooth skin of his cheek, a sharp, bold white icicle jutting through a straight crimson line that drooled blood.

"Hhlleee," said Sam, loops of bloody spit drooling from his twisted lips.

He seemed broken. He wasn't.

The hunched figure launched forward in a blur of movement, a fist grabbed Tom and flung him headlong across the width of the reading area.

There was a thud and a splintering crack behind me as Tom landed but my gaze was fixed on Sam, all my focus on how *I* might survive this encounter.

A young, cardiganed man, the librarian I think, appeared on the stairs from below, looking frightened but determined to sort out whatever was going on. Somehow.

Sam turned his body and lined up his single eye on the librarian, who was armed with some handheld device (probably no more sinister than a phone). The young man stared at the monster, his mouth agape.

The giant drew a small black object from his pocket.

I watched the polished black orb as Sam held it up in his palm. The size of an orange, it seemed to be black yet it seemed also to contain some sort of inner light that did not glow. A black glow in a black orb.

Deep inside my head, I felt Sam's vile and joyful anticipation and I knew that violence was coming, although at that moment I could never have imagined the form that violence would take.

I edged away from Sam, abandoning the librarian to his fate in the hope of buying time to help Tom.

The young man was wavering, his mobile held out defensively, his expression uncomprehending.

There was a harsh bark of noise and a dense clump of utter blackness spat from the orb and flew at sickening speed across the space between them. It thudded into the librarian's chest with a dull *whump*.

A thick, rough, undulating mass of blackness spread out from the centre of the young man's chest, an octopus of road tar that sprawled and engulfed his belly, legs, throat and then crept up onto his face. It was caustic, because as his high-pitched screams echoed throughout his library I smelt the sweet, sickly-rich stench of honey-roasting pork coil into my nostrils and saw his meat shrivel inside its tomb of all-encompassing black venom.

The man's screams achieved, for a moment, a pitch higher than the vocal limits any man should ever reach, until the glistening, living filth swelled up onto his face, his throat crumpling below, steam pouring from his mouth. Then, as the stuff poured itself into his mouth and gouged into his eye sockets, he was silenced forever.

His legs folded, the flesh gone and only tar-engulfed skeletal bone left to hold his weight up. The whole black mass, body fully inside like a fluid binbag full of corpse, crumpled onto the floor, its size reducing as it finished its meal.

It had all taken moments. I had stared transfixed and surrendered my momentary advantage to shock.

Sam pocketed the orb and crossed the reading platform before I came to my senses, still staring in awe at the librarian's remains, not even a skeletal corpse but a collection of bodyparts, bits, burned and entombed in their black sheath.

By the time I pulled myself back into the game, I was too late to help Tom as my enemy grabbed and hurled him like a rag doll. I cried out his name and ran to where he was rolling across the floor, but Sam was on him again, but again Tom's frantic scrambling was less random than it seemed and as the giant grabbed at him he threw himself back, forcing Sam to overstretch and I saw the now-dry black pile of the librarian just as Sam tripped on it.

In a blur I saw the tumbling Sam grab Tom and the two of them went over the edge of the top stair and tumbled away.

"Tom!" I cried, as helpless as I had been useless to this point.

Dodging the charred corpse I took the stairs as fast as I could, really not thinking about what I was actually going to do against a man who seemed to have no idea how to lie down and die.

At the bottom of the stairs, I stepped on the librarian's phone and hastily kicked it aside. Sam and Tom stood about three feet apart, facing each other.

Sam took out the orb and held it up.

I opened my mouth but failed to say anything.

No...

That harsh whump of sound echoed around the library once again and Tom staggered back under the impact, his chest smeared with the engorging tarry amoeba of the terrible, alien weapon.

A moment later, the library shook with his shrieks of agony, echoing peals that hammered off the cold library walls as his body was gouged, scolded, melted by the hungry, relentless fluid.

I closed my eyes, unable to watch him die, wishing I could not hear his desperate cries and uncaring that Sam would now turn his weapon on me.

Enough. I give up.

I felt him. I felt Tom; his terrible suffering as skin and flesh were peeled away; more intense than I would have thought possible, but quickly exceeded by a horrible rending ache as internal organs boiled in the cooking force of the orb *stuff*.

I felt him; I was with him as he weakened and failed.

Tom Peters died. And locked onto his mind, I was pulled down into death with him.

-17-

Jennifer Sullivan, my dead friend, wrapped her dressing gown tightly around her body and tugged the belt tight with an angry flourish.

"So," she said curtly, her fists pressed against her hips as she glared at me. "Do *you* know what the fuck is going on?"

I shivered in sympathy at the sight of her, standing in her gown and slippers on the cold pavement, her skin seared by the same chill wind that was cutting through my summer work blouse and puckering my nipples, shrivelling them inside my bra. At least she wasn't crumbling and mouldy any more, a memory that still brought bile to my throat and shame to my cheeks as I recalled it.

"Well?" my friend demanded.

We were standing at the bottom of Tiler's Hill, the road where I lived; although I knew full well, as I stood there with my two dead friends, that this wasn't really *my* Tiler's Hill and even if it was, I very probably did not live there any longer.

And this really was *not* Tiler's Hill. Not the one in the real world. Whatever real was. No, it was clear as we stood in the middle of the tarmac-coated road and didn't get mown down by a rabid driver that there was no sign of any life here at all. Just us.

"Well?" Jen demanded. "Spit it out, what the fuck is this place?"

"Easy, Jen!" Tom said in his gentlest, most reconciliatory tone. "We all got dumped here, none of us knows what's going on."

"That right?" she directed her gaze at me "No-one knows? You?" She folded her arms now, pressing her breasts back down into their warm cot. "It all started with you, Laur."

I wanted to challenge her on what she meant but she rounded on Tom.

"And you! I expected better of you, Peters!"

His expression hardened. "Fuck yourself, Jen. You got no *idea* what I just went through!"

She glared. "Oh, poor thing, and what about–"

He turned his back and skulked away to the curb, where he stopped to swing one black-denim leg and scuff its booted foot against the jutting stone.

"Oi!" Jen yelled unhelpfully.

"Tom?" I called, feeling caught in the middle of shit I didn't understand.

I flashed Jen a frown and crossed to Tom. The wind cut deeply into me through my pathetic summer blouse, and I wondered how Tom stood there in those jeans and just a white tee-shirt without shivering his bollocks off.

I reached up and laid a hand on his shoulder. "I know it's shit, babe, but try and keep it together? For me?"

He looked straight at me, seeming to search my eyes for an answer. "Am I dead, Laur?"

Shit. I had no time to put up defences. "I think so," I answered him flatly. "Yes. I think we all are. Sorry."

"Hmm." His lips drew taut and then he glanced up along Tiler's Hill, squinting slightly. "OK, then." He grinned at me. "Into town, or up the hill to your place?"

I laughed and stuck a thumb up over my shoulder. "Town," I said decisively.

"That's my girl." He turned. "Goin' exploring, Jen, you coming?"

She was still huffy, though I could hardly blame her after what we did just before she died, but still she tagged along, seemingly deciding to let us off for our sin, for now.

"So what was it?" she demanded as she bounced along beside me.

"What?"

"You and matey, there. Died together, did ya? Happy couple?"

I went to answer but I glanced and saw her eyes, realised that her happiness was a pasted-on veneer, a lie – her question was deliberately pointed.

"So," she went on, still smiling at the mouth but cold at the eyes. "No fucker of a so-called friend left *you* to die all alone, then?"

I stopped walking and turned face-on to her. "Jen, please."

"No!" she screamed at me, all semblance of a smile gone. "Do you know what that was like? Lying there waiting for the pain to end, alone and scared fucking shitless!"

Tears blossomed and poured from her eyes, but before I could react she grabbed my arm and her face came in close to mine, her eyes wet and her breath warm and stale.

"You don't know, Laur! You can't *imagine*. It took *forever*. Pain, terrible pain and no hope, just death and I wanted it, I wanted to die because I was blind, paralysed and I hurt everywhere. You left me. You fucking *left* me!"

I was useless and I wanted to cry myself. Her eyes poured and her mouth worked. My friend had never looked so helpless, so desperate, so utterly *small*.

"My *friends*," she said softly, bitterly. "My so-called fucking friends."

Tom had come back to where we stood. "Come on, that's not helping anything," he said.

Jen went to speak but he laid a hand on her shoulder. "Look, I'm sorry, Jen, but I don't remember it. You dying. There was a lot of weird shit, but that bloke that walked out on you when you needed him, that's a Tom I don't even recognise. It's not me, babe, I swear."

"And that makes it alright?" she asked, pouting.

"No, of course not, but right now we're all in the same sea of shit and if we don't swim together. Well, I don't plan to swallow."

She laughed for the first time and many of her tears were shaken off her cheeks by it. "You make a joke about me always swallowing and you're dead, Peters!"

"Too slow," he said. "Already there. Come on. Together? What d'you say."

She pouted, but there was a twinkle in her eye now. "Yes. Fine."

I glanced at Tom. "Me, too. Sorry."

I caught the look Jen flashed me as we set off again and suspected Tom was a bit more forgiven than I was for some reason, but that would have to be a battle for another day as we followed the tarmac that would take us to the bottom of the hill, after which we would be able to veer off left for the town centre.

But at the bottom of Tiler's hill, we stepped off the world.

"Well," I said. "This is a new level of buggeration."

"What the fucking hell is going on?" Tom cried, exasperated.

Our last step on Tiler's Hill road, right at the junction where it merged into Chadbury Way, had caused us to fall suddenly and shockingly out of Chadbury, out of the chill of winter, and into a different world altogether.

I squinted against a blazing, blinding morning sun that beat down fiercely upon the wild grassland where we stood, surrounded by the sound of chirruping birds and the rush and sigh of the long grass that surrounded us, swelling and ebbing under the relentless pressure of a warm, dry wind. As I gazed into the rough wild grass, tall enough to hide a large dog, I glimpsed the shimmering glint of water a little way off into the distance.

A faint noise reached me. *Tock, tock, tock, tock.*

In the false Chadbury it had been cold, wintry. Here, we stood at the bright beginning of a hot summer's day.

I turned to look behind me and was confronted by the true depth of the insanity into which we had been plunged.

We had stepped off Tiler's Hill, alright, but it was still there. It had been brutally cut, or dropped into place, but whichever was the case, I faced a jagged, open edge of concrete that jutted onto the grassland where we now stood, buttressed tightly up against the start of the grass as though a concrete ship had crashed here.

But that rudely blunt joint of land was not the worst of it. I was able to look back up Tiler's Hill, as far as the bend where the graveyard started, and to follow the line of the dull, grey, wintry sky back to here, where it, too, ended.

"That just *can't* be," I murmured.

Two incompatible skies;, the grey winter cloud of Chadbury winter and the shimmering blue of the summer grassland, were pressed together in a straight line, like a bad artist's cut-and-paste – none of the winter storm clouds ventured across the line to the grassland, while not a glimmer of the brighter summer sky seeped into the iron-grey of the winter sky.

"Fuck," said Jen. "I guess we really *are* dead, then."

"What do we do now?" Tom asked, his tone suggesting he didn't expect an answer.

I dragged my gaze away from the inexplicable join before us. "Assuming we're stuck here, now," I suggested, "We should probably take a look around, see where this place goes."

"Hang on!" said Tom, starting to sound more scared and pathetic than he should let himself be. "Why do we have to go anywhere? We may not have much of Chadbury, but it's gotta be safer than wandering off. We could fall off the edge next time and find there's no ground to catch us!"

He had a point. "No, Tom. "We can't go back up there. That isn't our town, it isn't *any* town at all! If we go hide in one of the houses, then what? No shops, no food. We have to find out where we are, what this all means."

He cast a glance out into the grassland, squinting, fearful. "I know," he conceded. "I just... No, I get it. Lead on, then."

Jen remained silent when I looked her way, merely cocking her head non-committally, so we pushed on into the grasses and made our way cautiously forward, my friends probably checking the ground with every step, as I was.

The water I had glimpsed was not as far as it had seemed. I stepped out of the grass and found myself on a slope of ground that curved down and grew muddy, boggy, with tall reeds flanking the edge of a narrow river, flowing silently past at a sedate, gleaming pace.

Tom stepped carefully into place alongside me, Jen a pace behind him. "This place gets weirder and weirder the more ordinary it gets."

I smiled. "That makes sense in banana, penguin."

I glanced at him so I could enjoy his bewildered frown.

I squinted against the glint-glint of sunlight flicking off the water and saw, across the water, a crumbling, grey-wood building, a boathouse of sorts, half-sunk into the reeds and mud of the bank and leaning backward at a lazy angle into the grassland behind it.

The boathouse sat in a fenced yard which also contained a second building, this one looking well-maintained. Painted a vibrant white and blue, it gave every indication that a sailor might step out for a turn on his boat at any moment. From the low roof of this building, a single white mast pole reached up into the sky, a line tied securely to it, doomed to wait forever for someone to run a flag up it.

There was a whoosh of wind across my face and the grass around me, and as that wind hit the mast, the line flexed out and tapped back against the mast pole.

Tock, tock, tock, tock, tock.

"Hear that?" Tom suddenly asked.

I glanced at him. I must have pulled a mean face, because he scrunched his eyebrows.

"The birds," he said simply.

"Tom, have you bumped your head?"

"No, love; listen. The birds. What's wrong with this picture?"

I frowned at him but, to his credit, he was right. I could hear birds. Gulls, ahk-ahking somewhere; somewhere... else.

"I didn't notice them before," I said. "Why?"

He smiled. Smirked, actually. "See? That sound wasn't there until I thought to myself, 'where are the birds?', and then there they were."

"That's just fucked, Tom."

"You know what else? We can *hear* them. Can you actually see even one bird, anywhere?"

I knew I hadn't. Not even a glimpse of movement in the sky, not since we had stepped onto this weird plateau. "Damn."

Jen cursed and teetered on one leg while she pulled a limp, soggy slipper off her foot, baring a tanned leg up to the thigh beneath her dressing gown. "This is takin' the piss – what you two conspiring about?"

"It's like… background," I said in wonder, looking up at Tom and seeing my own bewilderment reflected back. "It's… *fake.*"

Flinging both slippers back into the grass, Jen turned to me and pressed her hands to her hips. "What you sayin' Laur? We died and we're in a computer game?"

I wanted to laugh at the suggestion, but as stupid as it was, I didn't have a better explanation.

"Nope." Tom pursed his lips, deciding to be the authority on what was going on. "Doesn't make sense. We *know* we died, right? And that the way we died was, well, messed up but not… tech-related."

"True," I said. "We probably have to assume that this is real until we have proof otherwise, or else what; we can't just sit on the ground and shout 'Exit' until the programme ends."

He chuckled. "Like your thinking, Laur. And hey, this mad reality's got a few perks."

He pointed down the bank at a little wooden rowing boat that bobbed gently in the rippling water a few yards along the river on our side.

I glanced and caught him grinning. "Ain't that a touch?"

"Nobody likes a smart-arse, Tom."

Getting to the boat involved edging along the bank across slightly damp ground and then going down into properly wet mud closer to the water, which left the already pissy Jen with a seriously chapped arse about life in general and her luck in particular, but once in the little wooden hull we sat either end while Tom sat at the oars and rowed.

We were on the opposite bank in a few minutes. Jen piled out and kicked her bare feet into the mud, then staggered up to solid ground, muttering about the "Fucking wooden cocksucker" while wrenching her robe tightly around her breasts.

Tom and I discreetly exchanged a smile as we pushed on up to the shorter grass of this side, but any faint mirth was wiped away as we reached the top of the incline and saw what awaited us.

Tom rested a hand on my shoulder. "I, er… I think I've run out of swear words, Laur."

I placed my hand on his. "I'll lend you a fucksake, my dear."

We stood before absolute and final proof that this was not our universe, or anything like it. The grassland on which we stood sprawled away from us for just a few yards before being brutally cut off by a blunt unyielding wall of blackness. Not a patch, not an *area,* this was a deletion of everything, from east to west, from up to down – a black barrier extending from the earth and cutting up through the clouds and the slicing off the sky.

"This is…" Tom started. "It, it's *insane.* How did we not see this from the river?"

I had an idea; no idea how I came by it. "Walk towards it."

"What? No!"

I gently pressed his chest. "Trust me, you go closer, I'll go back."

I went three steps back down the bank of the river and turned, watching my friends step hesitantly a few steps away – toward an open grassland with a blue sky stretching on into the distance.

"You won't believe this!" I called to them.

They turned to me.

"What is it?" Tom yelled back.

I could see them both perfectly, but they were silhouetted against a blue summer sky out to the horizon. There was no black wall.

"Stay there!" I told them.

I started to walk back, pausing after each step to re-focus on my friends.

Step one, the sky was still behind them. Step two, the same. I kept going and on step five, the black wall re-appeared behind my friends. I stepped back; blue sky. Forward; the black wall.

I returned to them and told them what I had seen.

Tom crossed his arms and glared at the wall, as if accusing it of something. "I suppose I shouldn't be surprised. Nothing else here makes any sense, so why should that thing?"

Crossing the flat region of heathery ground that led to that infinite wall of solid, impenetrable blackness, ignoring Tom's protests, yielded no answers about this vast thing; its surface was absolute, displaying neither the texture of a matt surface nor the reflectiveness of a glossy one, so it might be a barrier, it might be a gateway – possibly benign, but possibly not.

We had to know, or this grassland and the little snatch of Tiler's Hill behind us might be the tomb to which we were confined.

It took so much willpower, such a force of muscle power, just to raise my arm. As it lifted, I opened the fingers and reached out the hand, but then hesitated. Drew back my fingertips from the chilling abyss.

Glancing back over my shoulder I found my friends close behind. Jen stared at me, wide-eyed and fearful, and shook her head once – whether to advise me against this or simply as a denial of everything, I couldn't say.

"You might as well," Tom conceded. "What have we got left to lose?"

I stared at that perfectly flat black sheet of featureless nothing. "Easy for you to say."

"Eh?"

Glancing to my right, I noticed a thick, tall blade of grass that curved upward from the earth and swung into the blackness of the wall. Its tip was missing, presumably sunk into the wall. I edged toward it and reached out, flicked it with a finger and watched as it slipped easily free of the abyss into which it appeared sunk, before bending back and dipping its tip into that unblemished midnight.

Not even a ripple.

"OK," I muttered to myself.

"Careful, Laur," I heard Jen say. *Aww, she does still care.*

I faced the wall. It did not reflect me. Slowly, slowly, I edged my fingertips nearer to that dead unyielding surface, a churning in my belly reminding me I was hungry but also letting me know that my body knew that this was a life-or-death moment even if my mind was too stupid to.

My fingertips touched it.

I snatched my hand back. "Shit!"

"Fuck!" Jen yelled behind me, startled by my reaction. "Shit, girl, fuck, I damn near laid a fresh one ! What the fuck was that?" She panted hard and pressed a fist to her chest.

I shrugged and returned my attention to the wall. "Nothing," I told them. "I felt nothing at all, it's as if that wall isn't really there."

The shock of it had been feeling no change in sensation even as my eyes watched my hand vanish.

I stared at the point on the wall where my hand had touched. Like the grass, I had left no imprint, no impression at all.

I cleared my throat, steeling myself for a literal leap into the dark. "We can't let this be the end of our journey. We have to."

I heard a grassy rustle as they moved closer to go with me, but before my nerve went I snatched a quick breath and sprang forward, squeezing my eyes shut as I plunged into infinity.

Which proved to be a warm quiet country lane at evening time.

-18-

It was early evening and the last of the warm daytime breeze whispered through thick banks of trees that crowded in on either side of the black tarmac road where I stood, those great leafed wooden sentinels held back by dense, low, shrubby undergrowth that fell onto the edges of the road like a giant's discarded curly wig.

I dared to hope that we might have stumbled onto a place where others might have been before us, because the curly wig of undergrowth was neatly trimmed into a line alongside the road, and someone appeared to have hacked a path through the bushwork and into the woods.

I took a step and breathed in, to be immediately assailed by the tang of cut grass mixing with the distant yet rich smell of meat cooking in someone's home – tongue-moistening aromas of meat and potato cooked in some unseen kitchen, the first smell I had noticed in a while, providing final proof that there were people here.

I felt sharp chill in my spine and felt a tug that made me glance over my shoulder, in time to see a crash of jumbled matter burst into existence on the open roadway and resolve almost instantly into the forms of my two friends, standing bodily on the road just behind me. There was a dull whump as air was pushed out to make room for them.

"Now where are we?" Tom asked. He pushed his spectacles up his nose and took a breath. "Whoa, is that a real smell or another one of this place's tricks?"

I frowned. "Tom, you've got your glasses back. You dropped them in the library, when Sam chased us through the bookcases."

He pulled the dainty wire frames off his nose and peered at them. "Bugger me," he said softly.

Jen sniffed. "Dunno about glasses, but I'll tell you what, I'm *hungry*. We should follow that smell, kids."

"Agreed," I said. "It's our best shot at finding other people in this place. But there's something I need to do first."

I crossed behind Jen and cautiously held out a hand, feeling for the point at which my friends had just appeared. Suddenly and with no sensation at all my fingertips vanished, followed by my knuckles. I snatched my hand back.

There was no wall of blackness here, but the gateway, or portal, was as real here as it had been on the grassland.

Tom's peering face appearing at my left shoulder. "We'd better make sure we leave breadcrumbs, eh?"

I frowned at him. "Bread–? Oh, I see. Make sure we can find our way back to the exit. Good idea, but did you remember the loaf?"

His smile was faint and, with nothing else to do, we set off along the lane, covering some distance while the sun eased down into the bedding of the horizon and a mild chill set over us.

After a mile or so, my legs began to ache, but my friends were untroubled; which was remarkable for the lazy and naturally disgruntled Jen – but even as I was mulling that over and wincing at the sharpening pains in my calves, the road split cleanly into two halves in front of us, the right-hand road seeming to move deeper into the forest while the left widened before turning a corner up ahead.

Tom held out a hand and cocked an eyebrow at me. "Your choice."

"Fucksake!" Jen snapped. "What's the problem, Peters? Just pick a direction and let's go!"

I grabbed Tom's arm and leant on him, puffing and sharing my weight. Up ahead, thick bushes grew steadily thicker between the two routes until, a few hundred yards further on, there were trees, suggesting that the roads were separated forevermore.

And something else, something... cold.

"Do you feel that?" I asked.

"Feel what?" said Jen impatiently, anxious to move on.

There was something terribly wrong with the path along the leftward fork. I could *feel* it, but I couldn't exactly *see* it. The road, the shrubbery, the air itself seemed darker, oppressive, a trapped malevolence clawing to break free from that thin veneer of normality.

Or maybe I just had the willies.

Neither Jen nor Tom sensed anything, but I was not willing to go that way and told them so.

"Just please, trust me on this, we have to go right."

"Why?" Jen jutted her chin out at me, her eyes glinty and sharp. "Why do you get to have your own way?"

"Jen." Tom gently touched her arm. "She's been right before, we should trust her."

"Oh, before, eh?" Jen inhaled and pumped her tits up past a double-G cup. "Like when the pair of you bailed and left me to die? *That* before?"

"*Jen!*" He snapped, his higher pitch and sharpness of tone startling me as much as it startled her. "Fucksake, girl you can't keep throwing that back at us!"

I could see in her eyes that he was backing her down, but I also knew Jen and she was going to resent this terribly.

He puffed his cheeks, gathering himself together. "Right. We go *right*."

I hid my smirk or triumph very well (I thought), especially when the right fork proved to be the right choice – since after only a short walk we emerged from the lane and spilt out onto a quaint-looking circular village green.

We stopped and took in the scene, the oncoming gloom of twilight beginning to bleed all the colour away. To our right, its white-fenced beer garden obstruding onto the green, squatted a small black-and-white wood-fronted pub, a few tables with furled umbrellas scattered in its little garden, all of them clean and empty. Following the curve of the green around was a row of six dirty red-bricked houses, all joined together to form a terrace, all of them wearily staring back at us across the green through yellow-framed, heavy-sashed windows.

On that far side of the green was another road like the one on which we stood, apparently leading out of the village in the other direction. There looked to be a house or two along that road, too.

Civilisation?

I glanced at my friends in time to see Jen bite her lip and turn frightened-rabbit eyes toward Tom. "I don't like this," she murmured nervously.

I felt a bitter thrill of anger rendered heavy by despair as Tom placed an arm over her scrawny shoulders. Bitch. Nice manipulation; maybe I felt scared, too, but oh, no, Laura can deal with it. Not pretty bunny-wabbit Jennifer. Oh, no.

I stomped off toward the brick-built houses, too pissed-off and butt-hurt to speak to either of them.

I felt but bit down bitter tears at the thought of my man with that bitch. I wanted to be the bigger person, but I hated that she could do that thing of hers to men so, so easily.

Shoving open a stumpy one-foot-high garden gate, I clop-clopped up to the front door and knocked hard, twice.

It was a shock to hear the sound of a security chain chinking on the other side of that door, the presence of others as unnerving now as the absence of anyone had been a short time earlier. I glanced back; my friends were crossing the green and would be with me in a few seconds.

The front door. I turned my head. The shock of who, of *what* stood in that doorway paralysed me. I instinctively went to hold up my bag defensively and remembered dropping it during the fight in the library.

Naked without my accessories, I tried to scream but found that I also had no voice. I might've fouled myself, but I hadn't eaten for a whole day and quite possibly no longer had the means in this nightmare afterlife.

"Hello," I murmured, the need for politeness making the moment ridiculous.

-19-

A huge old clock tonk-tunked in the hallway outside the parlour, while I raised a violently wobbling teacup to my trembling lips. I managed to get the tea into my mouth with that first slurp, which was a bit of an achievement considering the creature who had served me, who now waited with quiet indulgence as I slurped. A trembling hand returned the teacup to its saucer, the resulting chinkety-clink as unpleasant as it was embarrassing.

I was wedged into a smallish, narrow and very upright armchair, the back of which curved inward to wrap partway around me at head height, while Jen was perched forward on the edge of a matching item to my right, knees off to one side, head forward and her eyes sharp.

The room we sat in was a gloomy parlour containing our two armchairs, a dining table with three straight wood seats, and a darkwood dresser that held plates, cups and a crystal decanter of some brownish alcohol, on a silver tray that it shared with two stumpy crystal glasses. Behind Jen and I was the source of the poor light in here – a small dirty window draped with a crusty, yellowed net curtain that seemed to be trying to stop as much light as it could from falling onto the peeling paint of the windowsill.

The whole room had the dry reek of dust and ancient, flaky paper about it – a dry oldness that tickled my throat and sat very well with the owner of this house.

Tom shuffled on a hardwood seat at the dining table, nearest the dresser, and cleared his throat, the sound intrusively loud. The clock tocked again. Time was not right, or maybe that was the perception of my racing brain.

His name was Edward.

He occupied the seat at the dining table to the left of Tom

His deathly, dusty body creaking as he reached for his own teacup, flakes cracking off the back off the hand he used to delicately seize his refreshment.

The sight of him still made me want to gag, even after twenty minutes. It seemed unlikely I'd ever get over the horror of him, even if I stayed here for a lifetime.

Superficially, at a glance, he might've passed for an elderly gentleman in a dry, dark and dusty three-piece suit – if you really, really screwed your eyes up and forced yourself to ignore his bone-white complexion and, well, bones. Visible bones.

That gag reflex kicked in again and I nearly re-enjoyed my tea. Damn.

Edward smiled at me and skin lifted loose from his cheeks. He coughed, and fine dust drifted down from his forehead into his teacup. He was trying, poor old thing, to comfort and reassure me, but all I saw was the horror of his condition.

He'd been nothing but kind ever since he had opened the door and seen my reaction to him, which only made me feel more of a bitch for being so repelled by him, but he was a monster for one very good reason. He had been dead for a very long time.

His skin was mummified, literally falling off his bones in dry, paper-thin slivers that belonged on some ancient, long-forgotten scroll. Scored with lines and prone to crumbling dustily away whenever he moved, his skin was drawn taut and fragile across jutting facial bones, but it was his eyes that I simply couldn't move past.

Outside in the hallway there was a creak from that dark heavy casement clock I had glimpsed absently on my trembling journey into this dusty parlour. The great timepiece was priming to strike the hour, although time seemed so abstract right now.

His *eyes*. The whites were yellowed like newspaper that had been left out in the sun, but the corneas had collapsed, the liquid pressure of life having seeped away so that the middles of those eyes were as sunken as a ping-pong ball that someone had hit with a screwdriver. The remains of his corneas that gluey and dull, reflecting no light at all.

His skeletal hand, mostly bare, dusty bone nestling amongst strips of creamy-white gristle, raised the teacup to the dry brown lines that passed for lips.

I tried not to notice the thin mauve veins running between the gristle lining his bones like worms left to dry out in the sun.

Tom fumbled in his jeans pocket and pulled out a rolled-up green bundle that I recognised as his rolling tobacco. He held it up for Edward to see. "D'you mind?"

The old man turned his head, a slight movement of his eyes causing them to crackle in their sockets. I think I would move my head if there were a danger that I might split my brittle orbs.

"Not in here, Peters," Jen rebuked.

"What? Ah, come on, Jen, if the old boy don't mind."

When the old man spoke, his voice was gentle, reedy, only slightly roughened by his condition. "Less of the 'old', please, young man."

Tom laughed quietly as if this were some perfectly sane teatime with a jaunty old uncle rather than a nightmare with a hospitable zombie sat corrupting in its parlour. In a dining chair.

As Tom rolled a smoke, it was my turn to clear my throat. The creaky head swivelled clumsily to point those stiff dry eyes at me.

I swallowed hard. Th ice needed breaking and I had questions. "Erm, Edward. Can you tell us where we are, exactly?"

A sigh escaped him – or maybe that was just his breathing. "Are you telling me that you have come all this way and you still haven't worked it out for yourselves?"

There was a school-teacher's reproach in his tone that made me frown defensively. "Well, no. I mean, yes, I suppose, or I wouldn't be asking."

"Hmm. Indeed. Well, you see, the question is less about *where* you are, than it is about *why* you are here in the first place."

"I don't–"

He held up his hand and I saw way too many exposed veins. I wondered if the blood in them had solidified. "Please, allow me to explain."

I shrugged, stifling my gag reflex once again.

"We died," he stated flatly. "All of us. Everyone here is dead back in what you probably still think of as the 'real' world. Why we're here, and not wherever we should be after our earthly lives have ended, is all about the how of our deaths – you see, everyone here, all of us, died at the hands of a power which bridges the realities of what we perceive as *matter* and *thought*. Somehow, as a result, we are preserved here, in a nether region between the universes of each."

"Wait a minute," I said, frowning. "Universes…?"

"Yes, miss Keeble. There are separate universes, one in which the laws of matter hold sway, another where the laws of thought and imagination have power."

"Bullshit."

"Laur!" Jen cried, somehow forgetting the foul-mouthed slut she had always been.

"Is it 'bullshit', miss Keeble? Mind and body, is that not what they say? Each of us comprises both in life, with each belonging to one of the realms of existence."

"So," I said, "That means that Sam–"

"*Sam!*"

The old man spoke it like a curse. There was very little scope for expression on that bone-and-parchment face but his icy tone was very clear.

"Erm, sorry?" I was unsure what I was apologising for.

That dusty old head teetered slightly side to side once, then the old man waved a fragile hand. "No, no, no. It is I who should be sorry, miss Keeble. I have lived – and been dead – long enough to have some grasp of my emotions, but merely to think of that brute… you must understand. You see, Sam murdered me in the cruellest, most brutal manner imaginable."

I frowned, some sense of awareness awakening in me. *I know you, don't I?*

"He… he erm."

Edward was unable to say it but he no longer needed to. I remembered, had seen this poor old man chased down an alleyway and beaten, violated. Murdered. I chose not to say, because knowing his humiliation had been witnessed could only make it worse.

"It's OK," I said instead. "We know what he's capable of, from first-hand experience."

I leant forward in my chair as a connection formed in my mind. "So everyone Sam kills is here? He's got some supernatural power?"

Edward's mouth opened, but before he could speak I saw Jen look up from her teacup. "Laur?"

She trailed a finger around the saucer of her teacup and then put it down on the small table beside her. "When you say Sam," she said, peering at me through her lashes, "you mean that bloke from the nightclub, don't you? From Leo's?"

"Yes, but–"

She smiled humourlessly. "That boy gets around."

I frowned now as I checked back through my memory. "Hold on, Jen. How do you know Sam, he didn't kill you?"

The slight pout of her fleshy lips, the minor twinkle in here eye. "Well, you know how it is, Laur."

"Oh, Jen, you *didn't!*"

Damn it, everyone knew Jen was a box of assorted creams, but *Sam?* She wouldn't. With *that* maniac? Not even her, Surely.

She shrugged. "What can I say? Roddy had just chucked me like a cold turd in a chocolate fountain, felt like utter shit and then this rockie hottie with sweet blue eyes and balls like a boxer's fists bowls up at my door. What am I supposed to do?"

"Oh, I don't know," I said. "Hold your knees together long enough to find out who he is?"

Bit bitchy, I can see that. I'd just been round this tiresome loop so many times with Jen; it was bad enough that she fell open like an old book to almost anything with testicles, but it seemed that she just loved to pick on the men in *my* life!

Still, Jen ignored my comment and went on. "I knew he was OK coz I saw you talking to him at the club that night, so I wasn't worried, and damn, he was really pretty! Plus, he *really* knew how to use his tongue!"

"Alright!" I cried, exasperated but laughing in spite of myself. "Enough detail! We yield!"

She grinned. "So did I."

"So you let him put his sausage in your pastry. Classic you, I'll grant; but it never occurred to you that it might've been *him* that killed those people at Leo's?"

"What?" she asked quietly, finally meeting my gaze full on, her expression locked into a rather comic look of stunned shock.

I nodded, smiling grimly at her. To be fair to Jen, I had deliberately not told her about Sam's – and my – involvement that night at Leo's, so technically, how was she supposed to know?

Her red talons were hooked onto the arm of her chair as she asked me that very thing. "How was I supposed to know that, Laur? You never said a fuckin' word to me, never gave me no kinda heads-up at all!"

"Maybe you've got a point, Jen, but you still let Sam push his way into both your front doors, so there's that."

She puffed at me. "Because I thought he was *safe!*"

And there it was; the measure of what made a random guy fuckable – I might have wanted him. "You mean you thought he was mine, don't you?"

I looked inter her eyes as her mouth slammed shut. "Ain't like that," she muttered, pulling her gaze free and looking anywhere else. I could see her chewing her lip. "It *ain't*," she muttered.

"Tch." I turned away in disgust. I couldn't look at her.

I saw her head turn my way again, in the periphery of my vision.

I was ignoring her when I felt her taloned hand press down on my wrist, which forced me to acknowledge her.

She was close, crouched beside me. "I was lonely, babe, low. I just needed… I didn't do it to hurt you, Laur, I swear. Please."

Her hand moved to just under my chin and she lifted it to align us, revealing genuine pain in her eyes I that moment.

"Sam was attentive, babe. At a time when everyone else had something better to do."

The fuck? "Are you blaming *me?*"

"No, Laur, course not! But suddenly you had Tom and I, I…"

I smiled and softened as the warm memory of an old baby-talk expression we'd once shared returned to me, a sudden stab of nostalgia when I least expected it. "You'd lost your safety blankie, right?"

She laughed silently and nodded, and there was a momentary glint of tears in her eyes.

Now, I laid my hand on hers. "I'm sorry we left you that day, Jen."

She gave a dismissive head-shake, but what I had done to her wasn't right and she deserved to hear me say it.

"Really, Jen. I'm so, so sorry, I was a shit friend and an utter coward."

Her other taloned hand stroked the back of mine, as an eagle might stroke a mouse. "Let's put all this behind us, shall we?"

We hugged, then, while the remainder of this little world re-intruded as I heard a dusty scraping from where the old gent, Edward, was seated.

"It is not always necessary for Sam to kill us to bring on this dreadful fate. He does not choose to send us here; I don't think he even knows we are here at all. There is a connection between his very existence and this realm."

"Wait," I said. I eased Jen way and she slid back to her chair. "I remember... something. A man dying, he was being nursed by his wife but then, then he died and..." I trailed off.

Edward waited for me to gather my thoughts. My frown was seriously creasing my brow as I struggled with the fleeting memory. I was going to need an iron. "He died, I saw him die and I was pulled down and then, then I saw his body. Something..."

Edward leant carefully, dustily forward in his chair. "Do you think Sam was created? Engineered?"

I shrugged, the fragment too elusive, and rubbed my temples. "I think I'm just too tired to think straight anymore."

The old man eased his skeletal dusty frame up by pressing one hand down hard against his hardwood table. "It is getting late, perhaps a night's rest might be favourite for all of us?" He pursed the thin dry forms of his lips. "I would be delighted to offer you a bed for the night. You can decide what your course of action ought to be, once refreshed."

I caught Tom's eye and read the whole story of his thought process – the same one as mine. I didn't know if we could really trust this creature, felt bad for thinking that way when he seemed such a sweetie, but had glimpsed the absolute blackness of night through Edward's yellow-netted parlour window, and the prospect of staying in this house with a kindly monster was far more appealing than being outside in that crazy universe beyond his walls, where we might stumble in the dark and fall into some unknowable force of creation could dissolve us into soup. Or something like that, anyway.

Besides, none of us could seriously imagine that this polite gent was a threat just because he'd gone a bit mouldy. He'd been nothing but kind.

-20-

The little attic room he assigned to me was cramped but cosy, and that first night I slept like a baby in a cot. The next day, although we had questions, we ended up spending what felt like a serene Sunday with our zombie gentlefellow host, who, for his part, so quickly established our trust and made us feel at home, that we slipped into feeling as if this house were where we belonged.

I would never forget how he eased the pain in those first few days; so much so that we almost forgot how lost we were to the world we had known.

And during those first days, Edward became so familiar to me that I stopped seeing the corpse on the outside and instead began to see the kindly gent beneath the dusty crumbling surface, while, in as much as our host became imprinted upon us, so too did the village, especially when the old gent introduced us to the villagers who shared this place with him, meeting most nights in that quaint little pub on the green.

The villagers were all, to one degree or another, in states of decay like Edward. Some lived in this village, but we learnt that there were other houses, some along the many lanes behind the village, some edging into the woodland. None, though, down that left-hand fork that had so spooked me on my arrival here.

Time passed for us in the nether-world into which our strange deaths had condemned us, those deaths that had not been as final as they should have been, although of course being dead we had no idea whether time in here, for us, was anything like time in what we still thought of as the 'real' world.

Jen, Tom and I began to form acquaintances with a few of the villagers, but our greatest bond remained that with Edward, our kindly host, whose house had become our bed and board; he was so kind and, without us, was so alone, that staying seemed the only thing for us to do.

It had been, I think, about four or five weeks by the measure of the village's day to night cycle, when I sat down in that front parlour with Edward for our usual evening cocoa.

I sipped the hot chocolatey drink from my favourite mug. "Have I ever thanked you, Edward?" I asked.

He waved a hand.

"No, I mean it, you've helped us get through a pretty massive adjustment. This after-life would have been pretty scary without your support and guidance."

He nursed his mug in both hands. "You do understand, miss Keeble, that this is not actually the after-life?"

"Kind of, yes. But to all intents and purposes it is."

He peered into his mug, which, being Edward, involved creaky movements of head and shoulders to avoid disturbing his sunken eyes. "No, miss Keeble, it isn't."

I admit I had wondered about the village, the grassland we'd seen when we first arrived and even the false Tiler's Hill, how this place seemed to comprise mainly places I knew, except for this village, the most realistic of the three we had seen.

"OK, I have wondered. Tell me." I sipped my cocoa again and lost myself for a moment as creamy warm velvet engulfed my tongue and billowed into my throat, spilling the creamy-sharp flavour of chocolate as it smoothly flowed. "Mm, Edward, that is delicious!"

"Why, thank you, I certainly try." He chuckled, the mirth genuine even if his bony face could not reflect it. "But you must understand, miss Keeble, that as much as there are a Matter universe, your 'real' world, and a Mind universe that you do not know, there is an interstitial reality between the two. A bridge *and* a barrier, joining them yet holding them apart. The External Mind Reality. I tend to shorten that to 'emr'."

"OK, nice name by the way, but why are there real places here? Why would it look like *our* universe?"

"It doesn't." He opened out his dry arms expansively with a creak. "This pocket of the emr was created and is maintained by the will of all of us who live here. Together, we have the mind power to hold it in place, although some features we learned are an unnecessary burden."

"Such as?"

"You may have noticed that there is moonlight tonight but no sign of a moon in the sky? That is because we don't need one. The illusion of the sun we did create, of course."

"So, no moon. Fuck me."

The kindly old gent overlooked my 'coarse' language. "The point is, miss Keeble, that some part of our minds has persisted beyond bodily death here."

I took a big creamy slurp of Edward's amazing cocoa and licked my lips. "You say that like it's a bad thing. We're happy here with you, we might want to go explore beyond the village some day but, well, I don't think any of us left a life behind that's really worth pining over."

His skeletal fingers tapped his mug, the absence of skin over the bone negating the lack of fingernails. "You don't understand. As long as we hold on to the memory of our physical form, our mindforms here continue to depict us as we were in life; but over time, as the recollection of our old selves fades in the mind, the illusion of flesh becomes harder to cling to. In the end you will be..." He angled his hand back to gesture at his own decrepit form.

"What?" I cried, a thrill of shock squirting adrenaline through my belly. "No! I thought you all looked like that because you were already decayed before you travelled!"

"No, miss Keeble, this is the fate of all in the emr."

I knew I was going to have a few sleepless nights over that one, but I suspected that it would hit Jen the hardest. She'd always defined herself by her looks and had dreaded the day when age started to show on her.

How could I tell her?

My friend was going to take it hard. I was more upset for her than for myself.

Had I known how she would seek to console herself, I might have saved my pity for myself.

-21-

I had only been with Tom, intimately with him, on that one occasion, that day when the world had been pulled out from under me and upended forever. The memory of seeing him with that fake Jenny had never left me, though, so however much I knew it was unreal, a false thing, I had never actually moved past it.

Truthfully, if I had really wanted to try to rekindle something with him, I would have initiated something long before the crunch-point came, because let's face it, there was nothing but time and opportunity in our unending tenure in the village. The feelings just were not there, at least not as they had once promised to be, so we had fallen into white noise, a void of inaction.

And then he'd started drinking. At first it was a social thing, all of us at the village pub – we'd all made the effort. Later though, drinking became the default Tom response to everything: *long day?* - have a drink / *can't sleep?* - have a drink / *still here?* - have a drink.

He had taken the news of our fate far worse than I would have expected and had, as a result, plummeted headlong into an oblivion that would never need to end – without a real body, liver or brain, there was no meaningful risk of permanent harm, which was good but also really, really bad because with no fear of harm there was no necessity for restraint.

Whatever harm the alcohol might or might not have done him, his heavy drinking was out of character and a cry for help – a cry that I didn't care to answer.

Besides, Tom had a new best friend and drinking buddy. It became a regular thing to see him with Jen plugged in at his side, head on his shoulder, laughing along with his inane bullshit. Or just sitting there, smiling into his eyes.

I weep inside at my own naivety in not seeing it for what it was.

And then one night, my eyes were forced open quite brutally.

The weather had been changing slowly in the village reality. The villagers liked to maintain basic seasons, to keep alive the fiction that this place was anything other than a precipice at the edge of a formless abyss. It was colder than any night we'd seen any since our arrival, because the emr village had now moved from its summer season into its cool season, so since my friends were no longer interested in joining me for my evening walk and with outdoors looking chilly from Edward's warm parlour, I decided to skip my exercise and grab an early night.

I crept up the stairs with my chipped but solid white mug in my hand. Old Edward's cocoa continued to be a real winner, being so good and creamy that I barely hesitated any more over the horrible possibility that he may have shared a little of himself into the drink, through that uncontrollable flaking he did so much of.

There was a rich, warm silence to the gloom of the upstairs landing, accustomed and familiar. Edward was always up, sat in his front parlour, while my friends tended to either come in late on pub nights (giggling like ninnies) or turn in well before me, so bedtime always began with this silent, peaceful pad across the carpet and up the five extra stairs to my little attic room.

Perched on my bed, ready for sleep, I took a last yummy sip and then plonked the mug beside the bed so I could shrug off my clothes before donning my baggy bedtime tee-shirt, a gift from some previous occupant of this room. Well, I'd found a few tee-shirts in the built-in corner closet, so with possession being nine-tenths of the law... yeah, that.

I slipped between the chilly sheets and huddled in. As my own body heat radiated to warm the space around my body, the only thing missing was Basil, my silly old teddy-bear. He was back in 'reality'. Possibly buried with me. Shit, that was a gloomy thought.

I sighed. Shuffled. Closed my eyes.

Waited.

The expected soothing lull of sleep just wasn't there. This was a common feature of my new life, the pull of the dreams I used to have now departed forever, which had been the original reason for starting up my evening walks.

I rolled onto my side and faced the wall. Twisted the other way, the covers tangling around my legs. Kicked a leg to free myself, threw myself right over onto my belly and held position, cheek sunk deep into pillow, in case the sleep pixies were ready to pick me up now.

Nope.

I punched the pillow as I pulled myself up, gaining the satisfaction of seeing it collapse in shock at my brutality, then swung my legs over the edge of the bed, clambered up and before the cooler air of the room could dissuade me, pulled the tee-shirt down as far as it would go over my undies and grabbed a pair of jeans.

Kitted out in a warm jumper (another inheritance), my jeans and a shabby pair of pumps I'd been using as slippers around Edward's house, I set myself to taking the walk I should have gone out for in the first damn place.

The landing was silent as I descended my five little steps onto it, the tock-tock of Edward's clock a distant backbeat until a sudden sound startled me.

I froze for an instant with a prickle of fear, trapped in the open, away from the safety of my warm bed, but this place was familiar, it was home. I had heard something but I was unable to say precisely what, so I shook off the feeling and focused on creeping.

It was dark on the landing, but not pitch-black. A glint of light was coming from Tom's bedroom door, slightly ajar yet apparently occupied, which was unusual – even drunk, he was fastidious about keeping his door closed.

Another noise behind me but it was muffled and less interesting than that open door, hanging like a backlit invitation that I edged creakily open in anticipation.

His room was empty.

Wait – what? I frowned.

Another noise behind me. I turned and this time realised what I was hearing, my legs carrying me toward Jen's door even as my brain screamed out a belated protest.

I knew what I was hearing straight away but I would have given a fair bit to be allowed to un-hear it, even to un-know it; the wet flesh-on-flesh slap-slap-slap, the puffs of expelled air, the escalating grunts.

I closed my eyes. Even in the afterlife, apparently, I still came a poor second to my friend where men were concerned.

My eyes filled with tears and I bit my lip, furious with myself as my legs backed me away from that door instead of plunging me through to gouge eyes and rip out hair, pubic and otherwise, in righteous outrage.

I desperately needed to be elsewhere and my legs finally concurred, so we fled as a single body down the stairs and out through the front door, flying headlong through Edward's fussy little front garden and into the cool night air of the village.

Panting for breath, the exertion relieving some of the bottled-up pressure of my misery, I stopped on the green as the springy natural carpet of grass pressed into the bottoms of my limp, elderly pumps and wept moisture into the soles of my feet, the air chilling my throat and creeping under my jumper.

I glared up at the bled-blue moonlit glow of the moonless sky and bellowed a hoarse, hollow laugh at my own expense. "You silly, *silly* bitch!"

As I lowered my gaze I was startled by a lone figure standing motionless a little way ahead of me on the green.

Squinting and tilting my head were, oddly enough, not very effective at bringing the figure into focus, but before I could fixate on why it could be so close and yet remain obscured, it sprang at me in a blur of motion.

"Fuhh..."

A spiky bolt of adrenaline scolded my belly but it was too late to fly and now the figure was a man and he stood right in front of me.

But a familiar figure, at least.

"You!" I gasped, the comedown from the adrenaline rush hitting me like a titpunch. "You scared the fucking shit out of me! What are you doing here, did he get you, too?"

He studied me, that strange little man who had fought off Sam in the basement of my office before changing my world with his shockingly alien attempt at a smile.

He was still dressed as he had been that day, his open-throated pale grey shirt baggy beneath a plain grey jacket, a woollen greatcoat hanging all the way down to his black-booted feet.

"Sool," he said flatly. His voice was smooth and somehow echoey despite the open village green all around us. No doubt seeing my puzzlement, he clarified. "Sni Sool Techkatha."

The echo was actually a faint underlying sibilance to his soft voice, low and almost not heard but definitely there, as if some small part of his voice belonged to a snake. He certainly appeared to be some kind of weirdo, but as far as I could recall he'd never actually tried to kill me or any of my friends, and since he also hadn't slept with my boyfriend, he was up there as practically the best friend I had in all the world, in that moment.

"It is time," he said. "You must come with me now, LauraKeeble."

He had a weird accent that I could not place. He was odd generally, actually, with no body language to speak of; just a little grey man no more than five-seven high, in a grey suit, who as I watched him barely even seemed to blink – and yet here, on a cool winter's evening with no breeze and the bluish glow of false moonlight, he was more at home in this lost place than I could ever hope to be.

But I certainly didn't plan on letting him lead me off anywhere.

"Look," I said, "I don't know who or what you are–"

"Sool is of the realm sentinels."

I laughed in spite of the unnerving weirdness of this encounter. "Did you just third-person yourself? Look, I don't know what you want but I'm not afraid of you, OK? Let's be clear, you try anything and it's going to end badly for you."

Yep, I said that to him, hoping that he couldn't hear my heart thudding as I did so, while I felt the first surge of nausea yet forced myself to stare into his dull grey eyes.

He parted his thin colourless lips and his semi-sibilant voice seemed to intrude upon both my ears and mind simultaneously. "We mean you no harm. We are what came to be to protect the realms. Their sanctity, our duty. But your help is needed. We must leave this place, LauraKeeble. Now."

Then it hit me. The realisation was so shocking that it snatched away any hope that this little man might be just another lost soul who had found his way here. The faint sibilance in his voice was not a sound at all, but a slight delay between my brain translating the actual sound of his voice – and those same words as a parallel stream of thought playing directly into my mind at the exact same moment.

It was insane he could do such a thing and even more so that I could comprehend it.

"Look," I told him, my resolve diluting into an ocean of fearful doubt. "I just want to be left alone, please; this is my home. You can't make me leave!"

I had to wonder how true that was. It was entirely possible that this man with the power to feed ideas straight into my mind in fact *could* make me do anything he wanted.

The dead-fish eyes did not blink. "This is not a place, LauraKeeble. It is... Ee-em-ar."

emr. Shit. The same name Edward had given to this place.

The small man's facial expression remained impassive as he stared up into my eyes and continued. "This is emr. It is extract... no... *extrusion;* of the Mind universe. That place you know?"

I backed away from him, the taste of dear old Edward's cocoa back in my throat. "I'm going now," I told him. "Just leave me alone, please, I can't hurt you anymore..."

"You see this as home," he said. "It is in peril."

I stopped backing away. Somehow when he spoke I felt the truth of what he said, although I was aware that this might be because he was controlling my mind.

Yet, as frightened as I was, the rational part of my brain realised that if he had that level of control over me he didn't really need to ask at all, he could just force me to comply.

I drew in a rather tremulous breath and pushed the vomit-cocoa down with a hard swallow. "Alright, fine, explain it to me. The Mind universe, that'd be a universe where our thought selves live, right?"

"Simplified to say so, and yes. Two universes exist, one is Matter and one is Mind. Separated, with thought flowing into Mind from Matter. We sentinels protect such." He gave a sideways jerk of his head that looked very 80s-dance but was probably an attempt at seeming more human. "I am not Sam. Nor the Other. I am, you say, 'on your side'? But you, LauraKeeble, you are necessary now."

"I'm just too dead to help anyone, now." I felt tears well up in my eyes and was shocked by the despairing chill of saying it out loud. I'm *dead*.

"Wrong," he said flatly. "Being here is not death. The two realities? Kept held apart by this place you are in... it is a, what word? Barrier. Yet also is a bridge."

I was wiping my eyes with the back of my left hand when that word suddenly registered. Bridge. "Wait, we're not dead? We could leave here? Me, Edward, the others?"

"The others exist here only, but you are here by choice."

"No," I told him. "No, I died, I remember. Sam killed Tom and..."

"Yes, he died and is a thought relic. No meat, no... body. He was up close in a second and a seriously hard hand clenched around my arm. "You have the ability of flesh. You chose to come here, but maybe did not understand so. "You have an... ability you have begun to know. In the Matter realm, is your mind in the flesh; here, is the flesh held inside the mind."

I tried to prise his hand off but it was as fixed as it was painful.

"Let go, please!" I appealed.

The vice released my arm and he stepped back, seeming to realise what he had done. "No harm was meant."

I rubbed my arm. "Apology accepted. I think."

"We must go, now, LauraKeeble. The *Other*, too, has your ability. But his power is for harm. You can hide here, help no-one. Or perhaps come, save all."

He turned on his heel and began to walk away across the green in what was quite a childish attempt to get his own way.

"Hey! Wait a minute!" I trotted after him and was panting for breath by the time I caught up, his short legs pretty effective at getting him off the green and out into the lane where I managed to get close enough to grab the grey tweedy arm of his jacket. "Hey!"

He halted and peered up at me, eyes still dead, dark straight hair still lank, with no discernible body odour or breath to confirm he was anything other than another of my mad dreams.

I drew a ragged breath and cursed every cake and choccie bar I'd ever eaten. "Look," I said. "I'm far from convinced about any of this, but I'm not stupid. You might be offering me a way out, so.. just tell me. This 'other'. Who is it?"

"The other *Keeble*," Sool told me casually, as if I should have known this already. *Silly, silly girl.*

"There is no other Keeble; my only family is Grandma."

He seemed to ignore what I'd said, gesturing behind himself with a wave of his hand. "See," he said.

I followed his pointing finger. "What the actual fuck?"

Without moving, we had somehow traversed the whole distance from the village green to the spot where my friends and I had arrived all that time ago, way out beyond the junction in the lanes, where the portal had been.

"OK, how the fuck did you do that? We travelled half a mile without moving?"

"This is a realm. I can amip, no, *manipulate* realm strata."

A smile curled the edges of my mouth. You're down the rabbit-hole now, Keeble. "Glad we cleared that up," I told him.

"This," he resumed, casually disregarding my charms, "is a rip in the emr. Holes, now, cut between all the false places he has built onto the interstice realm."

"Built? So this person you call a 'Keeble'–"

"*Is* a Keeble."

"Come back to that. But, this someone is, what? Creating false realities for fun?"

Sool's face was unchanged yet I sensed a darker shift in his mood. "He sees it as creation, but it is unsound. The emr will... fail. Rips grow, emr collapses, the primary realms fall together."

"The primary realms, you mean my universe don't you?"

He pointed at the portal. "You *must* return to the Matter realm. Stop the other Keeble."

"Wait, what?" The possibility hadn't occurred to me that Edward might be wrong, that we could simply walk through a portal and back into the real world. "You mean we could've just gone home all along?"

"Yes correct." He gave that 80s-style jerk of his head. "You only. Not the others, your friends. They are relics.. Dead." He pointed at the portal again. "Go back. Stop the Other."

Great, except I had no idea who the fuck this 'other' Keeble was or how the fuck to find, let alone stop them. I told Sool exactly that and included the swear words.

"LauraKeeble, you do know. Try. *Look* at what you know."

I felt something push at my mind – not exactly intrusive, just a touch but enough to jolt my brain into a cascade.

Sam was a puppet. I'd seen through his eyes using the same link, the same conduit his maker had used to control him, drive him. Why could I do that?

But Sam had been looking for me of his own volition: why? Because he was connected to me. I had seen his 'birth' in one of my not-dreams, his real body dying and his mind resurrected in that awful crypt. He was driven to seek me out.

There had always been, however, someone else moving ever closer to me. As my dreams had intensified, as reality had become more fragmented, the pieces had begun to pull together.

I remembered the odd sensation I'd felt in Susan's pod that day when she'd wet herself. And then my dream that night, seeing Susan die. And the ugly skinny troll-like man with the pot-belly; I'd seen him at the office, he'd done something to Susan. He had *made* her wet herself, when his probing mind had hit a trigger in her brain.

My eyes widened as my mind saw. *He* was Sam's master, his maker. It was no coincidence that he worked in my office. He had been moving closer to me, consciously or not, for a very long time.

Sool seemed to be following my thoughts. "You see the truth of it? *His* is the power that threatens the realms."

"I do see," I replied softly.

Jen's ghastly death, all because she'd been intimate with the puppet, Sam; Tom's death at Sam's hands, Susan's too – these led back to Sam.

The changed Liverpool street, however, and the do-over day at my house when Tom and I had gone back there, these were something else. Me or this 'Other'? – hard to say. I suspected that I had been inadvertently responsible for the do-over, but Liverpool Street?

"He changes the emr," said Sool. "Treats as if play toy. He bends your 'reality' the Matter realm, too, but not always by intent."

The cocoa was back in my throat as the reality of my life, my very self, seemed to unravel before me. Was I still me, was this still my life? It had mostly been a shit life, but it had at least been mine.

Unravelling, crumbling… rotten.

Hot tears were just behind my eyes.

Sool stepped away from me, taking a pace along the lane. "I will configure this portal. Send you back."

"No, wait, you still haven't explained – why me? Who is this other Keeble you keep on about? I don't understand, Sool!"

He raised a hand. "If the Other continues, all that is matter and all that is mind will be lost. You must stop him now, LauraKeeble. No more delays."

I drew in a breath. "How can I stop anyone, I don't–"

His strangely dull eyes focused on mine. "You have an advantage. He wants you alive, thinks you still could be his sister."

I started. "Wait, his *what?* Sool, wait!"

He gave me a shove and I felt a wrench as if the surface layer of my entire body was being torn off. The lane vanished and I fell headlong into a dazzling funnel with distorted echoes and swirling muddled lights tumbling past all around me.

Unexpectedly, the ground leapt up and slapped the souls of my feet.

Hot air poured in all around against me. I shook my head, dizzy, my vision blurred. Clearly, my questions would have to wait.

-22-

The tall stone face of my office building in Southwark loomed before me. It was bright, warm, humidly summertime warm and the air smelled of tangy, sticky skin and greasy vehicle fumes. It was quiet for daytime, but the faint rumble of traffic in the great city reduced any eeriness.

My jumper and jeans, so sensible in the village, were way too snug in this heat, but there was no point worrying about a little sweat. This was not my world any more, apparently, and I was here for one simple reason. A mission, of sorts.

A car suddenly cut around the corner and bumped along the street, its simple ordinariness shockingly alien to my new perception.

"OK, Keeble" I muttered to myself. "Get a grip."

I drew a deep breath and strode into my office building, where the ugly man in Susan's team would be working away, unaware I was coming for him. Hopefully, anyway.

I stepped into the cylinder of the leftmost of the three steel-and-glass revolving doors, my heartrate rising in anticipation of finding this place empty or altered, somehow alien and terrifying, but with relief I stepped into the lobby to be greeted by a short wave from the security guard as I entered the foyer.

I smiled. "Hey, Doug."

I explained to him that I'd left my pass upstairs when I popped out to get a 'proper' coffee and Doug let me into the office after forcing a temporary security pass upon me.

All I could think about as I caught the lift up to my floor, crossed the fourth floor vestibule and entered the main office, was what the hell I was going to do. I couldn't fight, certainly couldn't *kill* anyone – did Sool really mean for me to do that?

In the office area I stopped halfway along the corridor between office partitions. At least here, in this air-conditioned environment, I was reasonably comfortable.

Damn. It had all seemed so obvious when I'd stood beside Sool in that lane but now, here, reality surrounded me once again. My reality. I was home. What was I thinking?

"Laura!"

I started at the sound of my name and turned to see my manager, Ben Thomson, flouncing down the corridor between the work pods toward me.

"Laura," he said more gently as he reached me. "I've been trying to call you all day. Why aren't you dressed for work?"

"What? Oh."

Shit, I don't belong here any more. I'm at work in my scruffs. I realised, too, that I had no idea what day it was, how long I had been away. Ben wasn't acting as if I had been AWOL for weeks.

Ben was frowning at me. Ahh. Washing hadn't really been a thing in the emr – we weren't alive, it just didn't apply. Now I'd been plopped back into flesh form, what the fuck must I smell like? Yikes.

"Sorry, Ben, I lost my bag, someone, someone stole it and my phone, purse, the lot. Had to stay at a friend's place."

He waved a dismissive hand. "Never mind. We need to talk, Laura. Come with me."

One, Ben had held such power over me, the navigator of my career fate. Now he was nothing to me. Nothing at all. Still, I let him lead me into a meeting room, the heavy veneer door slamming shut behind us as he sat carefully down and began to fastidiously arrange his pen and pad on the table before him. Slowly. Methodically. Fucksake.

"Ben, can we hurry this up, please?"

He peered up at me through his eyebrows. "Please sit down."

He said it nicely and I was programmed by a career-time of weaselling to obey. I plopped myself down on a chair opposite him, pushing the loose sleeves of my jumper back off my wrists.

There was a pause.

I waited, but Ben was silent.

"Ben, seriously. What?"

He sighed. Rubbed his face briskly with both hands. Up. Down. Up. The hands peeled away and he aimed his red-rimmed and bleary eyes at me. "It's Jennifer," he finally said, with a theatrical sigh tagged onto the end.

Oh, shit, *that*. I had to suppress a groan as I realised that this imbecile was going to break news to me that I already knew, and which whilst a big deal in Ben's little world, was old, old, old in my world and really not a priority.

"You know that Jennifer and I never really hit it off," Ben was saying, sounding awkward and vaguely insincere. "but there was no spite in it, really, and I..."

Blah blah blah. Poor, weepy Ben. He actually had tears in his eyes!

I kicked my chair back and stood. "Sorry, Ben, I don't have time for this."

"Laura?" His voice was shrill with disbelief. "Jennifer is dead! I wanted to break it to you gently!"

He seemed so small. "I know she is, Ben. I have more important things to worry about."

"What?" He rose from his seat. "Laura, that's the shock talking. Sit down, please."

He looked lost and off-balance perching on the table's edge with his white-shirted stick arms.

And then he must have remembered who it was who was treating him with such disdain. The podgy girl he'd always got away with using as his punch bag, knowing he could dangle the carrot of 'career advancement' if she dared try to kick back.

"Sit down at *once*, Laura Keeble!" He roared at me.

The door slammed behind me as I strode down the corridor toward what I feared would be a terrible showdown. Still, on the bright side… my life might be a confused, insane muddle with danger and dread at its core, but at least it had put my so-called *career* into shockingly clear perspective at long last.

Outside the pod that housed the man I'd met as Alan Mendis, I hesitated. Just for a moment, though. I was someone new and I had purpose. Sool had given me that.

I stepped into the pod and went straight to his chair. My brother.

How I could have missed it before, I would never understand, yet now I could feel the presence of my brother, because regardless of his mad insistence on calling him a 'Keeble', Sool was right about who he really was. I could peel away the years, the stubble, the grim pale skin of that face and see that long-dead little boy I had once loved so much.

"Peter," I murmured.

His head snapped around. He stared at me for a beat and then I felt a faint pressure at the back of my head as his gaze inspected me, as though his mind were searching mine; which I was certain it was.

His lip trembled at the sound of the unfamiliar name, presumably all but forgotten in his re-invention into this life behind the mask of 'Alan'. Then suddenly, shockingly, he actually pushed into my mind.

It was a tangible presence, a shockingly intrusive sensation of being eased open and entered, followed by an insistent digging and peeling back of layers.

My shock turned to indignant rage. And then, without any warning, some hidden and quite alien muscle buried deep within my brain snapped awake and I felt myself push back at the invading presence, forcing it out.

His head snapped back, he rocked backwards in his chair for a moment and then levelled off, staring at me with a shocked yet faintly amused look on his face.

fuck, sis, that's the first time anyone's done that to me

The words simply appeared in my head with no physical voice issuing them. This man called Alan – my brother Peter – lolled back in his chair and draped an arm over the back of it.

The rest of his team, close by in the pod, were murmuring. I realised why.

"Perhaps we should speak out loud," I said to him.

To the others around us, my words were the first spoken since I had entered the pod.

He leant forward in his chair and stared up at me. "It really is you, isn't it?" he said with his voice.

The base of my skull was throbbing, just as it had when I'd become angry at Sam in the clothes shop.

We stared at each other. I had fantasised, many times, about finding my brother alive after all, but in *my* version, he always turned out to be a pioneering surgeon or some great hero; never once had my fantasy brother been this oily, weasel-looking character.

Still, he was what I had and that was better than nothing.

He grinned. "You know I can hear what you're thinking, sis, right?"

Oh, fuck, what a faux pas! I went to apologise...

no need, sis

He turned in his chair and called out to his manager. "I'm taking an early lunch!"

"Come off it, Al," said the man called Michael. "We need to get this go-Live plan finished!"

He stood, ignoring Michael, ignoring everyone but me, his gaze fixed on me alone as he gestured out of the pod. "Shall we?"

We left, he and I ignoring the insignificant people milling around and trying to get our attention.

-23-

The *Bantam* was a former spit-and-sawdust pub about two hundred yards from our office. Back in the Eighties and Nineties, the place had seen renovation that took it from its working-class roots and set it among the warehouse–chic fashion set for a time. The owners must've been rubbing their hands together with glee in the glory days of boom and yuppies, but they never saw the end coming and as the over-inflated economy sharply bottomed out they had used those same hands, or so the story goes, to blow out their own brains up the far wall behind the bar.

We walked into what was now a fashionably-dressed 'Retro' pub, which is to say, a pub dressed in a mock-up of the way it would have looked in the Seventies if the previous owners hadn't fucked about with it, the place a painful contrast to the charming little pub Tom had taken me to before he'd died.

Before Sam had killed him.

I was here for a *reason*, not a reunion.

We got drinks and sat across from each other at a deliberately chipped wooden table as the One O'clock sun burned through the glass of the pub's windows, its heat cooking the air and sucking shards of sweat up through my skin. Distantly, I heard a man up at the bar thud his sloshing pint down, his clumsiness suggesting that it was far from his first today.

My brother Peter, whose name was now, for whatever reason, *Alan*, picked up his heavy scotch tumbler and swilled it gently. "You hot in that jumper, little Laura?"

I felt an odd little thrill and caught his eye as he momentarily glanced at me. "What did you call me?"

He took a pull of whisky. "Sorry. Old habits."

"Your 'little Laura' died a long time, Peter. About the time you let me believe *you* were dead."

He glanced at my chest and then met my gaze again with a wink that left a cheeky yet pleasant glint in his eye as he raised his stumpy whisky glass in salute.

I felt the corners of my mouth twitch but didn't let him have a smile. Instead, I lifted my orange juice and sipped, the icy liquid leaving a cold trail in my throat that contrasted with the hot stale air of the pub. "Shut up, Peter."

"Aw, C'mon, sis. How long's it been?" He thrust his glass up into the air and a gout of whisky slopped out at his abrupt salute. "Re-united!" he cried, his voice loud in the hallowed gloom of the pub.

Several people glanced our way from other tables or from the bar. A few of their faces were familiar to me; old soaks from my office, the ones you didn't bother going to for help after 2pm. Still, no cause to give them juicy gossip for the office.

I ducked my head reflexively, as if that somehow made me invisible. "Keep it *down*, Peter, what the hell's wrong with you?"

He shrugged. "What?"

There was suddenly a constriction in my throat, accompanied by unexpected pressure behind my eyes as old feelings resurfaced. I swallowed hard. "Why didn't you come and find me, Peter?"

He stared into his glass, unwilling to meet my gaze.

"You knew I was alive, you must have. I lost my entire family in one day."

He flicked his gaze up toward the ceiling. "Oh, spare me! It's all about *you*, is it? Your feelings, your pain?"

The soaks were pricking their ears again, so I lowered my voice. "We could've grown up together, been a family."

"How lovely." He swigged his whisky again, but a little too hard so that some of it drooled down his chin. He swallowed hard and swiped his chin with the back of his hand. "And I suppose we could've lived together under Granny and Gramp's roof? Hmm?"

"Peter–"

He smiled at his glass. "It was all their fault, Laur. They fucking made me... It was *them*. Fucking old cu… they were, oh, whatever."

"Grandpa's dead, Peter."

He still didn't look at me. "I know."

"Grandma's–"

He glanced at me. "Yeah. I know about Grandma." He winced and returned his gaze to his drink, as if the knowledge of Grandma's decline could still pierce his shields.

I realised I was still nursing my glass, so I lowered it to the table. "She's getting worse, now, Peter. She probably doesn't have many more years if you did, y'know, want to see her."

He huffed out a laugh. "Nah, I don't think so."

He slugged more whisky, chinking ice in the glass. "It was all their fault, Laur. If they'd left me alone, kept their damn beaky noses out…" he trailed off.

"What are you trying to tell me?" I asked him. "What happened back then?"

"I got abandoned, is what happened."

"But you still had *me*," I insisted and felt an embarrassment of tears welling up again.

He met my gaze, his grey eyes glistening too. "After the accident, I was gone. I mean literally gone. Lost. By the time I found my way back, well." He pushed lank dark hair back off his forehead and gave a weak shrug. "The world had moved on, didn't care, hadn't missed me at all."

"No, I missed you! Always! I was alone, too, Peter."

"Not the same at all, sis. I knew, right, I knew no-one was ever going to understand. I was… unglued from the world."

I knew that feeling, had experienced it, now, for myself. That sudden realisation that this was no longer the world I'd taken for granted, no longer *my* world.

He shook his head slowly, sadly. "Anyway, you had the ol' folks to take care of you." He leant across the table, eyes glinting and chin jutting as real anger bit into him. "And who came for me, eh? Who took care of *me*? I was just a lost little boy, Laura, all alone! It wasn't *right!*"

He thudded his glass down hard and I just knew the soaks would be taking notes. Well, fuck them.

He was still glaring at me. "Go on," he challenged. "Ask me the question you want to ask me, little Laura."

"I don't know what you mean," I lied.

I needed to know if the accident that had put me in hospital for weeks and killed our parents was really an accident at all. Had the horrible feeling I already knew. Couldn't ask and find out for sure.

He sat back and reached for his glass. "Still, it's funny how life throws you a bone, coz I found my mentor and I never looked back. Funny thing with kids, how you can adapt, use what you've got. Find strengths you never knew you had, with just a little of the right guidance."

I felt lost in memories, doubts, regrets.

I looked across the table at him. "I'm sorry you had to go through so much," I told him.

He shrugged. "It's done, sis. What's passed is past. I'm sorry we missed out on our time as kids but shit is shit, and most of all I'm sorry that you have to take the crash course, now. It's a headfuck and no mistake."

That word piqued my curiosity. "Crash…? What crash-course?"

He stared into my eyes and for a moment the grey irises seemed to melt into blackness, but I was sure it was an illusion, a trick of the light.

What was certain was that he lunged forward lightning-fast and grabbed my wrists.

"Peter!" I cried out, pulling to free myself but failing.

His scrawny limbs were stronger than they seemed.

"Reality isn't what you see, Laura, it isn't what you think it is!" He squeezed my wrists. "This is your chance, you're just emerging now and the possibilities are so much bigger than you know! I can help you."

His grip slackened a little.

I wrenched free.

I glared at him, rubbing my wrists. "I'm not here for your help."

"I know." He smiled coldly at me. "But can you really go back to living as a mundane, everyday Matter puppet, even with just the glimpse you have had now?"

I picked up my drink, sipped the grainy acidity of the cool orange juice.

There was still so much I did not understand. And yet I had a purpose here, a calling; a mission.

"Peter, I'm here to stop you, not join you. You're causing terrible harm and if you don't stop, you're going to destroy both realms and everything in between."

"Realms?" His brow furrowed in mock-bewilderment. "Now where would words like those come from, I wonder?"

"Don't patronize me," I said coldly, "I'm not some silly little office girl."

"No, you're Techkatha's puppet." He shrugged and hoisted his whisky glass for a sip. "For now, anyway."

An old man shuffled past our table, and I waited until he was out of earshot before retorting.

"I'm no-one's fucking puppet!"

"Well, I certainly hope that's true."

He necked the last of his whisky and stood abruptly. "You are so much more than that retarded fucking *sentinel* would ever allow you to be."

My brother aimed himself at the bar and set off, tumbler in hand.

I sighed and watched him go. I'd imagined this being so much easier. He had always listened to me when we were little, so why couldn't I get through to him now?

My long-dead brother, alive to me once again. Sort of, anyway. There was so little of the boy I'd loved left inside this arrogant man with monster-powers, striding boldly across the bar-room, small yet daring *anyone* to challenge him, his gaze intense and his whole presence screaming of barely-suppressed fury.

That big question still lurked, though, still whispered to be heard in the space between us.

He was my brother. I owed him a chance, but if I got the wrong answer to *that* question I wouldn't be able to let him have it.

I just couldn't ask it. Not yet.

Lunchtime was in full flow now, with people barging noisily into the Bantam for a 'light lunch' or a 'swift one'. The noise and bulk of bodies filling the bar-room softened the former, echoey tomb-like feel of the place, so that by the time Alan returned and slumped onto his stool, a fresh whisky sloshing in his glass, the atmosphere had changed.

"Something on your mind?" He asked, his voice raised now to edge over the background chatter and clatter of a busy pub.

I looked up. "What?"

He cocked his eyebrow and glared pointedly at the remains of two mangled cardboard beer mats lying on the table, ripped into little pieces. I looked down at them, unaware that I had set my fingers about them in my mind's absence.

He chuckled. "Same old Laura, you always fiddled with shit when you got lost in thought. Now then, lets re-cap shall we? We just established that a certain sentinel twat has been filling up your head with bullshit."

I picked up one of the pieces of beer mat. "So you know Sool, then?"

"Oh yeah – self-serving, self-righteous fun-vampire."

I laughed at the truth of it. "Very poetic."

He smiled curtly but then he leant forward. "I'm not playing, Laura. Sool's a bad egg from the arse of a rotten chicken."

"He made a pretty convincing case, Peter. And after my run-in with your nasty creation, Sam, I need some convincing that you aren't exactly what Sool said you are."

He coughed. "Sam?"

"Come off it, Peter," I said. "that's beneath you. I've seen first-hand what that maniac of yours is capable of, so don't fuck about with me."

I felt a smile picking at the corners of my mouth and bit down on it as I realised that it derived from a malicious lusting pleasure that still resonated through me at the memory of the kills I'd shared with Sam.

My brother laughed. It sounded forced. "Yes, of course Sam inevitably belongs to me, making me the bad guy in all of this. Sool says so – it must be true!"

"I'd love to believe that you're the innocent party in all this, Peter! Sam killed my friends."

Alan snorted. "What makes you so sure?"

"I was there when he killed Tom. The others told a similar story, so yes, I do believe they all died at his hands."

My brother was suddenly very still, like a child caught with the whole packet of biscuits.

"What?" I said.

"They... *told* you?" he said, his voice hollow now. "H-how? How could they...?"

I smiled and shook my head sadly. "I've met them all, Peter. Their minds survived death, somehow, I don't understand it but it's got something to do with the emr, as far as I..."

I couldn't see his eyes any more. Not that they were not there, just that I couldn't see them, there was an absence...

There was a crunch of pain at the back of my head as my brother forced his mind inside mine, this time much more violently than he had done before.

My vision was erased by white light and white-hot pain in my head.

I cried out.

A voice burst out inside my mind.

which sector of the emr do the survivors occupy?

Pain, confusion, I knew my mouth was working but I had no idea if any sound was coming out because my head was flooded with light and screaming noise.

which sector?

which sector of the emr do the survivors occupy?

A force within me pulled forcibly at the image, the memory, of the village in my mind and I fought to suppress it, to prevent his seeing it.

show me

show me

I tried to cry out again and had no idea, once again, if I'd succeeded.

And then, subconsciously, reacting by reflex alone because my conscious mind was almost gone, crushed to the size of a grape pip, something near the base of my skull, some impossible extra mind-organ, pushed back hard in self-defence.

My mind organ flared, spiking pain through my skull bones and into my spine but pushing the violating force out of me.

Knowledge of his presence in my head vanished. The white flash across my vision diminished and I saw, through tears of pain, that he was staggering away from me, his movements jerky, hands patting frantically at his head as though his hair were on fire.

"Fucking bitch!" his voice screamed at me.

And then Peter was gone.

I blinked hard and shook my head to clear it.

By the time I could focus properly there was no sign of him. I stumbled to my feet and staggered, aware that the soaks were getting the show of their pathetic lives. Well fuck them. They would live or die by decisions made, actions taken by Peter and me from now on. They had no power to judge *me* any more.

-24-

I needed to get back to the emr.

It didn't matter that Jen and Tom were treacherous low-life bastards, I had put them and all the villagers in harm's way by letting my brother know that they were still alive; and however much I wanted to believe Sool was wrong about him, I couldn't get away from what he had done.

Thinking of that violation of my mind made me shudder as I stood outside the *Bantam*, leaning against a brick wall, fresh sweat cutting trails through stale sweat under my already-rank bedtime tee-shirt, now double-insulated by the shapeless jumper that had seemed like a good idea for a night-time walk a thousand years ago back in the emr.

The emr. How the fuck was I supposed to get back there? I barely understood how I had got there the first time.

My brother knew what he was doing, so he could feasibly be there right now, doing whatever messed-up shit he had the power to do.

I closed my eyes. Drew a deep breath. I had to help my friends.

Picture the village. I held the image in my mind and tried to will myself there.

When I opened my eyes again, the street was still under my feet, the lunch-time clatter of the *Bantam* behind me.

"Fuck," I said softly.

This was no Oz and I was no Dorothy.

I tried to open my mind but I had no damn idea what that even really meant. What does that even *mean*? For fuck's sake.

That strange organ buried in my mind had saved my neck more than once but never through my conscious choice. It just reacted, like a little alien in my skull guarding its territory for its own selfish reasons.

I pressed my hands to the rough brick of the pub's wall and closed my eyes again. Tried to picture the village, in the hope that there was some sort of magic thingie that would happen when I least expected it. The solid brick beneath my palms remained stubbornly solid.

Obviously. Silly cow.

"You alright, pet?"

I opened my eyes and saw a lanky city Herbert squinting right into my face. He had a pinstripe jacket over his shoulder and an open-collared plum-coloured shirt crammed scruffily into shabby black jeans. Balding, with a rough yet patchy stubble, he was everything you could want in a complete tosser.

"One too many in the bar, was it?" he asked with a patronising smile.

I grinned at him. "Would you mind fuck off, please?"

I probably looked quite mad, a woman in a heavy jumper on the summer city street, glaring with a feral grin. He scurried away without hesitation.

I decided to take a deep breath, relax and try *calmly* to port myself to the emr.

I drew in a deep breath, closed my eyes and leant against the wall again. Tried to picture the village. Focussed on that spot in the lane where the portal was, in case it was somehow a more potent link.

Clearly it wasn't. Not a fucking thing.

"Great," I muttered without opening my eyes. "Just fucking great!"

A stark image of Tom, gripped in Sam's brutal hands, flashed before me. Worse, an image of Edward, his helpless flaky flesh crackling off, irreparable and ruined, as the monster I had unleashed on the emr ran rampage.

I was getting hotter and hotter under the blazing early afternoon sun and my discomfort was amplified by the horror of knowing I had brought down such pain, misery and death on people I'd shared my life with back in that village.

I felt hot tears sting my lower lids, a prickle along my spine, a little squirt of scolding adrenaline in my belly and, with all these things, a sharp stab of pain at the back of my head.

"Fuck!" I cried, clasping my head. "Oww, fuck! Damn it!"

I staggered away from the wall feeling dizzy and sick and then cried out in fear as I was wrenched with shocking violence off the ground, off the world, with the pain at the back of my head now a brutal pulsing that felt ready to bust my skull open.

Sensations burst against my skin, my eyes, my ears as I tumbled end over end, hurtling weightless through an insane, shapeless tunnel of light and colour that I could not focus on, crying out in terror but my voice snatched away as I fell and fell, my muscles tensing instinctively as my body prepared to be dashed against something hard and unforgiving at the bottom.

But I was dumped onto my feet.

Painfully hard, but onto my feet.

Bent double now, hot liquid billowed up into my throat and burst out, mostly fruit juice but also traces of a malty-looking sludge that was probably undigested cocoa. I belched the acidic mess onto the ground. It splashed onto dry compacted mud in front of me.

Mud. Not concrete. I frowned and straightened up, wiping a drool of bile off my lower lip as I tasted the rancid flavour of vomit on my tongue, but it was all worth it because the mud beneath my feet lay twelve feet from the fork in the country lane.

"Fuck. How about that?" I had done it.

Unbelievable.

The weather had changed pretty dramatically in the short time I'd been away, but it was the emr, alright; no doubt about it. An icy wind razored through my jumper and managed to chill the sweat that the summer sun of the real world had drawn from my pores. There was no smell of any kind on that wind, as if the villagers could no longer be bothered to maintain the illusion of smell. Or they were... Shit.

It was early evening, but the weak remaining light was murky and sad, as if it were waiting for chilly rain to serve as its tears. Out of nowhere I was hit by a stark image of Jen, atop the nude torso of Tom, her wobbling rolling and flopping as she chased orgasms with *my* man.

"Fuck's wrong with me?" I asked absolutely no-one as I wiped a tear with the back of my hand, grimaced and marched toward the village green.

The pub was in darkness when I reached it, the surrounding houses equally lacking the lemon sorbet light of lamps seeping through any of their windows.

I started as I spotted a bulky male figure just ahead of me on the gloomy green. His face reflected too little light to be seen, but I had a bad feeling that was confirmed when he spotted me, because he hunched forward and bounded at me like a pouncing wolf.

"Sam!"

Ready to flee, I braced for the impact of his huge frame, but he pulled up short and stood less than two feet away, hunched and panting.

"I dloo apologise for m-lly appearance," he slurred with a voice that was gravelly and yet wet. A loop of drool poured from the slack left corner of his twisted mouth, where the lips no longer met.

I stared at him in horrified fascination. Sam had not escaped the fight with Tom and me unscathed. The fall from the library balcony had cost him dear, leaving him with a single leering eye, whilst on the other side of his bent nose, with a jagged angle of gristle protruding at the bridge, a hollow socket was loosely draped by a wrinkled, sagging and useless eyelid. His face, his whole head, had the appearance of being bent, which left me wondering how much damage his brain must have suffered.

He swayed, perhaps unaccustomed to his newly crooked stance. He had not hunched to attack me like a predator, as I had originally thought. No. His body was permanently hunched now, with one shoulder higher than the other as though in a permanent shrug, one leg permanently bent slightly outward at the knee, his spine and perhaps a number of his bones shattered or at least severely dislocated.

He should not have been able to stand up, let alone threaten me, in such a broken state – but perhaps the rules were different here. Tom and I had come through to the emr exactly as we'd been when last alive at the library; perhaps Sam had been unfortunate enough to bring his wounds into the emr with him.

Perhaps, of course, Sam as not dead at all, but had been sent in here by someone, a certain someone I may have tipped off like a gullible fucking fool.

He made a harsh noise that may have been a laugh, its clarity lost beneath twisted lips and over what I suspected was a bitten-through tongue. I almost felt sorry for him until I reminded myself what I had witnessed this monster do to my fellow human beings.

He suddenly lurched a step closer and twisted his buckled back to bring his face down from his still-lofty height to meet me at eye level, the act setting off a shrill creaking sound that I could barely believe came from a human body.

"Ylou are gloing to play now," he told me calmly, with almost no malice.

It took me a moment to make sense of what he had said through his bent mouth. *Pay*, not *play*.

"Sam, stop," I ordered, surprising myself by the fact that I was not shaking badly enough to bounce free of my jumper. "Just tell me what you want."

"Blitch!" he screamed. A stringy coil of saliva looped out of his mouth and some of it splashed onto my breasts. The thick jumper suddenly felt like one of my better ideas.

His hands came up, curled like claws. I remembered only too well how strong this monster was and knew I had no physical defence against him, even broken as he now was. If I let him get those hands on me, I was going to die in a burst of pain and flesh-twisting horror.

My fear wanted to run but my rage would not allow such an afront by so worthless a piece of shit as he.

The rage solidified and suddenly Sam was in my grasp.

My hands didn't touch him. At the back of my head, that increasingly familiar throbbing ebbed and swelled as my mind grasped Sam's physical form, gripped it tight and held it in my will, trapped.

His one eye went wide, his already-slack mouth dropped an extra inch – this was beyond his comprehension. His pathetic twisted body jerked and staggered backward, seeking escape.

No, I don't think so.

I pulled him up, straight and immobile, his bent back pulled almost into line by the force exerted on him. In his clawed right hand I saw the black orb he had used to kill Tom in the library.

He had been about to use that on *me!*

Cunt!

My rage was intense, fuelling the organ of my mind and yet focussed. I felt my mind grip every nerve ending throughout Sam's body and I did not hesitate.

Perhaps I should have found it harder than I did, perhaps I should've felt compassion for this monster, but I didn't so I wrenched out his nerve endings like bunches of wires and poured power to light them up.

The power was greater than I could properly control; I don't know how badly I meant to savage him but as his helpless shrieks grew more shrill I felt, distantly, a filtered version of the white-hot pain that gouged at Sam as his hot skin blistered and bubbled off his muscles under the blazing intensity of my mind. It was a gloriously shocking and satisfying sensation and I revelled, not for the first time, in our empathic link.

Tiny hairs on my arms wilted and died in the reflected heat as the muscles beneath Sam's skin split and peeled back off the bone like bacon coiling on a hot grill. The intensity of the scorching was matched only by the deafening sound of my victim's shrieks.

Oh, his agony was glorious.

Our unique bond allowed me to share it with him and I bathed in it pleasurably whilst he was utterly undone by it; suffering beyond endurance, continuing unabated and growing ever more intense until he must surely collapse through physical loss if nothing else, yet he remained conscious and skewered by the agony I bestowed, his inhuman strength now his greatest enemy, his inability to die a terrible curse on him.

Gasping and panting with pleasure, I tore at his glands, his organs, delving beneath the meat and into the slimy entrails, searing these open too. I felt his tiny mind try momentarily to focus through that black orb, to fight back, but agony robbed him of even the illusion of hope and he could do nothing but shriek and writhe in the scolding might of my will. I peeled strips off kidneys and lungs and testicles, all my assorted potatoes being prepared for the pot, and all the while smiling and moaning to myself and aware of yet unconcerned by the orgasm stampeding toward my lower belly.

And then, all too soon, my victim's agony was ending as the last human functions were torn away from him.

I let him go and, emitting shrill squeals that might have been cries or equally may have been the last desperate breaths of his perforated lungs, Sam collapsed.

He was ruined but alive, squirming in the dirt, but I was utterly spent. I could have happily lain beside his poached and stripped body, except that his squeals now alternated with snarls of mindless hatred.

No sense getting killed by my own hubris.

Now, with shame, I felt the cooling dampness that my vagina had wept into my jeans. I hoped there wasn't a visible patch, because I wasn't sure Sam was too disabled to act on his rage if he recognised the extent of my arousal.

His head was burnt, his face peeling away now, and so was his chest, while his belly seemed to be an open cavern and there was something oddly mismatched, too, about his limbs. His ballbag was gone, the goolies inside split and burst, and his penis was just a shrivelled black twig.

But his single eye glared at me with a rage that defied description.

I staggered away from him, my wetness turning clammy and cool and my guilt rising up to replace the thrill of power as I accelerated into a full pelt toward Edward's house, my heart thudding and adrenaline scolding my belly by the time I broke the funereal silence by hammering on that wooden front door.

My knock went unanswered.

I glanced over my shoulder again. The green was deserted, which was even worse than if I'd still been able to see Sam crouching there, broken and tormented. I already regretted not finishing the job I'd started with such zeal.

I started at a loud clunk and had to fight the urge to take a step back as light lit the small windows in the upper part of the door. Someone was answering after all.

The door yawned open to reveal Tom's lithe half-naked torso, his jeans partially unfastened to reveal a little puff of hair which, lower down, I knew, swathed his thick penis and heavy dangling balls.

"Oh," he said.

Briefly, a heavy sadness weighted me down, a sorrow to have lost that intimacy, the loving touch of his hands on my skin, the heft of his balls in my hand; but his indifferent greeting quenched my melancholy with fresh anger.

"You gonna stand there or let me in?" I demanded, feeling my lower jaw jut aggressively.

I didn't wait for an answer but simply walked at him and made him swing his useless self the fuck out of my way.

"Oh yeah, come in, why don't you?"

Passing Edward's sedately tock-tocking clock, I entered the cool darkwood front room.

Tom followed me in, fastening his half-open jeans as he offered me a drink and crossed to the cabinet against the far wall without waiting for an answer.

He pulled out the ledge of the bureau and opened the drinks cabinet beneath as I perched on one of the hardwood dining chairs. There was a chink of glass items.

"Fuck you been, Laur?" he asked without turning.

"Why? Do you suddenly give a shit? How long was I gone?"

He turned to me with two stumpy crystal glasses, a dash of yellowish-brown liquid swilling at the bottom each. "Don't you know?"

I shrugged, not ready to explain where I'd been or why my time and his might be out of synch. He still had no idea I could go back home and he'd given me no incentive to share. "I do, but time's funny here."

He handed me a glass and gave a shrug. "Couple days." He necked his entire glassful and then shook his head violently. "Whoa, that's better."

I wondered how many times he'd been wedged inside that bitch's cockpit during those two days.

I nursed the stumpy glass as he returned to the cabinet for more booze, rolling it between my palms without taking a sip, watching the amber liquid swill and considering where to start. "Sam's here," I finally said, glancing toward his back.

He twisted toward me , his exposed abdomen contorting in a ripple of toned muscles. "Are you serious?"

"He's, I hurt him," I said. "Slowed him down a bit, but he won't give up now he knows about–"

Oh hairy fuckballs. Hadn't planned to give that away! I ducked my head and tugged a sip of the drink and confirmed that it was indeed whisky as it seared its way through my throat and into my belly.

Peripherally, I glimpsed Tom lean against the dresser next to the drinks cabinet. "Now he knows... about *us?*"

"It's nothing I can't handle, Tom."

He flipped himself up from his leaning position. "Save it, Laur. We got a visit from that weedy fucker you slipped off with the other day. What's his name? Sid Snail?"

I started, met his gaze. "You know about Sool?"

He turned back to the cabinet and attended to fixing himself a drink. I heard the slosh of whisky being poured before he turned to me with a quite substantially filled-up tumbler. He wore a cool smile. "Him and Edward go way back, apparently. He filled in some blanks for us. Like who's been pulling Sam's strings. Tiny detail you didn't bother sharing, eh? That the real enemy is your fucking *brother!*"

He slammed his drink down, whisky sloshing onto the table, reminiscent of what my brother had done in the *Bantam*.

"I didn't have time... Sool took me away. I, I'm sorry, Tom."

"Oh," he cried airily, "and apparently you're not really dead, unlike us, which is fucking epic."

"Tom, I'm not the enemy." I hated that I was defending myself. None of this would have happened if he had stayed faithful to me.

"So what the fuck happened with your not-really-dead bro, Laur? You two have a nice cosy chat, did you? Maybe casually mentioned us and our little village in passing?"

I felt my fists press to my hips, angry with him now. "Of course not!"

He cocked an eyebrow at me, then adjusted his ridiculous little glasses. Shit. "Look," I said. "I didn't mean to. I just, it was... it's complicated."

He sighed, slumped down on a dining chair on the opposite side of the table from me and took a gulp from his tumbler. "Fuck we supposed to do? Sam, for fuck's sake. What? He gets to kill us all again, now? There's nowhere for us to go."

I dropped the tumbler onto the table and drew a deep breath. "I made a mistake, Tom. I'm sorry, OK? I wanted to believe in my brother."

He humphed a humourless laugh. "Fuck have you done, babe?"

"Don't call me that." I grabbed the glass again and took a swig. Fucking awful sour burning piss. Fake Mind World Whisky was *not* a good blend. I got kicked by a shudder. "You can't stay here, Tom, it's not safe any more."

"Thanks to you."

"Yeah, well, paint me guilty blue. You think self-pity's likely to save you when Sam gets his game back on?"

He glared at me, his eyes bleary behind his glinty specs. Probably been up all night fucking Jen. "You can go, Laur, we don't need you."

His sulkiness was starting to chap my arse now. I leant across the table. "Yes, Tom, you do! You need me now, more than ever. I nearly killed him just now."

He frowned. "What? How?"

I dropped onto a hard dining chair. "Dunno. I've got some sort of... gift."

"What does that even mean?"

Edward shuffled into the room, followed closely by Jen.

The bitch never disappointed; she'd obviously dressed for my benefit because I knew damn well she and Tom had been fucking when I knocked at the door. Her tight white summer top clung to the ripe swells of her perfect breasts, the nipples, even when soft, protruding through; and then there was the skin-tight black skirt that made headlines of her buttocks and thighs as she moved. It was classic Sullivan.

As the old man began the slow and painful process of settling himself down onto a wooden dining chair at the table, creaks and cracks emanating from his dry old recesses, my former friend cast me a glinty-eyed look and swept across to Tom, leaning down to kiss him full on the mouth, the swollen ends of her breasts dangling against the hands he had just lain upon the table.

He kissed her back, of course, which Jen expected to be a killer blow, a horrible shock to me as their tongues entwined visibly between their slurping lips. Fucking bitch. She thought I didn't know the two of them were bumpin' uglies.

Her eyes slid sideways even as her mouth slobbered against Tom's and she met my gaze deliberately, that old triumphant glint in them. *Back into the corner, plain girl*

She rose slowly from my ex and turned full-body to face me. "So," she said with a very cool stare and her tits thrust out, "I hear you fucked us over."

I laughed, harshly at the brazen cheek of it. "I think you've got the market cornered when it comes to fucking your friends over, Jen."

"Fuck you!" Tom snarled at me. "You led that fuckin' animal here you fucking stupid–!"

"Tom!" Edward snapped, his reedy voice crackling. "There's no need for that!"

"Oh come on, Ed! After what she's done?"

"Tom, it helps no-one to take our anger out on Laura. She is undergoing a difficult transition."

Jen cocked her head at the old man. "You wanna talk me through that one, Ed?"

"Enough," I said wearily, bored with their mundane bullshit. "Edward, how easily can you get everyone in the village together for a meeting?"

"Why?" he asked, still sounding friendly, choosing not to join the Laura-haters society.

"We don't have much time," I said.

"I can visit a few trustworthy people first thing in the morning."

"It's a bit more urgent than that. Sam's here and I may have slowed him down, but realistically I don't think I did enough. You all have to leave."

Edward raised a skeletal hand and touched his bony chin. "Leave our home? Where would we go?"

"I don't know, but until I know I can call on my gift I can't protect you. I need time to figure out how to control it so I can fight him."

"Well," the old man said, absorbing the news and taking it rather well, all things considered. He had lowered his stiff, creaky head but now he raised it to meet my gaze with his dried-out eyes. "Is there really no other way?"

"I'm sorry. It's just for now."

Jen leant against the back of Tom's chair, her hand on his shoulder and the curve of her hip resting against his arm. "This is all your fault, Laur."

I shrugged. "And yet that doesn't help, Jen. Edward, are you sure you can't gather everyone right now?"

He considered. "I think we have to wait. I would struggle to rouse many of the more frail villagers, and besides, if Sam is out there it will be much easier to pick us off in the dark."

I was far from convinced that daylight was any protection from that monster, but I was playing against a deck with very little good will in it for me. I had no choice but to take what I could get.

"Fine," I said. "How long until it's light?"

Jen looked at Edward. "About two hours now, ain't it?"

The old man nodded.

"We're giving Sam too much recovery time," I said.

"You all get some rest," Tom suggested. "I'll keep watch here. I can see right up the path from that window and truth be told, I don't think I'm ever gonna sleep again until that freak out there gets put down once and for all."

I smiled at him. "I'll stay up with you."

He shook his head. "No, you're all we've got. You definitely need some sleep, you're more likely to work out how to do your thing if you're rested."

"Thanks."

He glanced at me but did not return my smile. "I'm not doing this for you."

I glanced at Jen. "No. I don't suppose you are."

If looks could kill, Jen would in that moment have reduced me to a pair of pickled ovaries in a jam jar.

Edward glanced from her to me in the silence that had fallen. "Your room is still made up for you, miss Keeble. I was sure you would be coming back here, eventually."

I smiled at him. "Thanks, Edward."

It rained for the rest of the night. The whoosh-tap-tap of the fake wind and rain against the little window of my room was cosy, somehow reminiscent of home. I slept fitfully, though, because I kept seeing heavy rain sheeting across a village green, and from beyond that curtain of haze the creeping presence of something broken and malevolent edging ever closer.

I had started something and if I didn't finish it, then Sam sure as fuck would do.

The next morning, as I sat sipping tea in the front parlour, I heard the latch on the front door make its discrete yet somehow resentful scree-click as our host returned.

Tom helped the old relic onto a chair. He looked like shit today. It might have been only a few hours, but I felt recharged from my sleep and Jen, resentfully silent ever since the boys went out, looked like she had made the most of the chance to rest.

Poor Tom. From lover to traitor to sap.

I lowered my dainty china cup onto its saucer and looked up at two extra visitors to what I had, until recently, begun to think of as my home. A man and a woman, both equally old-fashioned in their clothing, which was not unusual here; and both badly decayed, which wasn't all that unusual either.

They were hard to look at. These two were *bad*, worse than our elderly host, their skin rotted and crumbled away so that gaping dried-up sores exposed yellowing bone in both their cheeks and foreheads. The man's nose ended in a now-dried open sore that resembled a sick nightmare parody of the tin man from the *Wizard of Oz*.

But there was something starkly unusual about this couple, and Edward's decision to bring them here had been in no way a random choice. Even through the ruination of their dried-out flesh I recognised them.

Old, faded monochrome memories seeped forward to the foreground of my memory as I stared.

The woman absently pulled up the fingers of her black gloves and shrugged off her coat, the hands that she unveiled composed mostly of bare bone, draped here and there in a delicate sheath of flesh that seemed to be the final insult by its very scarcity.

Tom arose from his seat, gesturing at it with his hand to indicate that the woman should sit.

I did not move at all. I was staring. I knew my mouth was gaping open. I struggled to use once more a word, so long disused yet once so precious, that seemed far more alien than anything that I had seen in all the insanity of my recent life. A word no child should ever have to surrender.

"M-Mumma?" The word caught in my throat and I wasn't even sure I'd spoken it out loud.

Edward creaked on his chair. "This young lady has something important to say to the whole community, but I thought it important that she meet the two of you first."

The woman stared at me.

Tears blurred the achingly tragic sight of my undead parents, but the couple looked at each other blankly, clearly bewildered.

How long had it been for them, since the accident? It had been more than twenty years for me, but time passed differently in the emr. Maybe they'd forgotten that they had ever had a daughter.

"It- it's me," I said wetly, sobs catching every breath I managed to tug into my throat. I turned to Edward. "Why, Edward? Why did you keep this from me?"

The old gent had a hand to his mouth. "It has been very, very hard for them, miss Keeble. They lost so much more than the rest of us."

"You mean…?"

"Yes, miss Keeble. You."

I turned to the two creatures standing before me. "Mumma, Dadda. I, I'm Laura."

"Laura?" the woman echoed. Her voice was dry, unfamiliar. She turned her head in that odd, stiff way that Edward also favoured, facing her husband. "*Our* Laura?"

I smiled. "You know me, don't you?"

The man, my father, looked straight at me. "Our little girl," he said softly, staring.

A deep boom deafened me and sent a deep aching pulse rumbling through my ribcage. I cried out and tried to stand as the world went insane around me, but I toppled across the tips of my own shoes.

"Tom!" I screamed, lunging at the one person strong enough to support me as I fell. Already on his feet, Tom was able to brace himself against the table and his strong hand grasped my arm as plaster dust rained down upon us from the shuddering ceiling.

Edward's front window burst in on us, the musky net curtain shredded instantly by shards of high velocity glass.

I fell.

Tom fell on top of me and every ounce of air was thumped out of my lungs as his weight crushed my chest.

And beyond the window an insane voice shrieked my name.

Sam had made his move, and thanks to Mumma and Dadda, he'd caught me with my emotional knickers round my ankles.

-25-

Another blast burst against something solid and sent in a juddering boom from somewhere near to us.

On the floor, unable to fill my lungs with Tom's weight pressing down on me, I could do nothing but blink my eyes to prevent cement dust from the ceiling falling in and clogging them up. There was another blast, then another, and then more and closer together, while I lay trapped and helpless beneath my former lover.

Sam was toying with us, avoiding the kill shot so he could enjoy the terror he could spread, to create that hot sexy thrill I remembered only too well from being linked to him. Anticipation, the building glory of the lust; the scold of the final release.

I had returned too late to save these people.

I bit painfully into the inside of my lip as a really close explosion slapped my eardrums and shook the room violently, the sharp taste of my own blood accompanied by a prolonged groan from the old bones of the house around me.

"Tom!" My voice was wheezy from his weight. "We have to get out!"

He opened his eyes, kept shut until now, looked at me without much focus and clambered off me to sit back on the floor nearby, dazed.

There was silence puckered by an occasional creak or ping from the settling, wounded house, dust floating in clouds that tasted of crunchy talcum, perhaps concrete dust or wood. A sudden ping sounded and then a thudding crunch made my shoulders tense, as a shard of glass fell out of its window frame and hit the floor somewhere to my left.

I forced myself to my feet in an ungainly flail of limbs. "Everyone up! We have to get out of here!"

The shredded curtains billowed tattily away as Jen struggled up from the floor beneath them.

The sound of heard human voices reached us from outside, some baffled, some tautened by panic, or a distress that their peaceful home had been so brutally violated.

There was a creak above us and when I looked up I saw that the rough-edged, grey-brown wooden joists of the ceiling were protruding precariously from jagged holes in the split white plaster.

I glimpsed movement as Jen bolted for the door.

"No, I insist," I called out sarcastically. "After you."

Tom was up. He grabbed Edward, a little too roughly in my opinion, while I was startled by the still-firm grip of my father's skeletal hand on my elbow. I allowed myself to be guided toward the parlour door, well, the hole where the remains of a door now hung in long splinters where we followed Tom and my former elderly host out.

I looked up at Dadda. He was still taller than me and his face had something of that hawkish resolution I always remembered seeing when something had to be done or someone (often me) needed a talking-to. The damaged nose, the paper-thin skin over desiccated muscle tissue, should all have contributed to making him seem less like the man I remembered, yet they didn't – if anything, I think the decomposition had mummified him, kept his face as a dry and slightly shrivelled version of what I remembered – he'd died instead of ageing.

It was foggy outside and it had been raining for a while. The fog, of course, was smoke that billowed and mingled with the rain that drenched everything indiscriminately.

On the green, we joined a scene that looked like it belonged in some graphic, gritty war film. A chaotic churning mass of villagers milled around in the smoke, those with enough face for expression looking drawn, panicky, ready to throw their tits if anything else happened. The rest were bone-faced relics who belonged in a pulp zombie movie, not this war scene. Through patches of grey smoke, flickering swells of orange light revealed where some of the villagers' homes were burning.

I slipped in sodden mud and kicked splashy brownish-grey muck with my shoe but Dadda's still-strong arm steadied me. He stared straight ahead, not speaking. Mumma held his other arm, this firm beacon of calm reason in the madness.

Something dark flashed through the scurrying, panicking flock and several bodies were flung off their feet to plunge headlong into the wet churned mud.

"The fuck?" I murmured – but I knew.

The flock milled more frantically, fish startled into blind action by a shark, muted cries of panic swelling toward hysteria.

There was a harsh bark of noise. More bodies tumbled and I felt a ping of pain at the base of my skull.

"What's happening?" Tom yelled, struggling to be heard over the frantic crowd.

"It's him," I said simply, not sure if Tom could even hear me.

There was another burst of flying bodies before us and before I could react, my father stepped in front of me. I frowned in confusion at the gesture, but although maybe it was sweet of him, he wasn't going to be able to protect me at all – it had to be the other way around. I pushed him roughly aside and surged forward, trying to let my awakening mind lead me to the enemy but not sure I had any real say in what that separate organ within me would choose to do.

Panicking villagers surged past me. I pushed through waving my arms at them. "Stop! You're making it worse! He'll pick you off, you have to get down, please listen, get down!"

A body rammed me and my breath flew out of me. I staggered back and my useless pumps skidded wildly in slick mud, but the man who'd rammed me was so off-balance that he plummeted headlong and landed with a splash off to my right.

I drew a breath. "Hey! Stop! You have to stop! Listen! He'll pick you off one by one like this! Please–"

Another figure burst from the chaos, arms flailing as it stomped the fallen man's head down into the mud and then hurtled straight at me. I was grabbed and pulled out of the way and saw my father and Tom. Tom kicked the wild figure in the belly and it reeled away as the two men moved to flank me protectively.

"They're saving Sam the bother," I cried, staring horrified at the bodies already fallen, the milling forms trampling friend and neighbour indiscriminately in their wild panic.

I heard a terribly familiar voice call out to me from beyond the smoke, its tone cracked but still carrying power. "Oh, Laura, what a dreadful hash *someone* has made of protecting this village!"

I felt a thrill of fear scold my belly. He was close but I couldn't see him.

"Show yourself, you bastard!" I screamed into the smoke, layering bravado over my very real terror.

I was probably going to be dead very soon.

A tall, heavy but twisted figure lumbered through the haze before us, its shambling footfalls squirting mud in all directions as it powered forward on bent legs.

Sam's already ruined face twisted still further as it sprawled into a hateful grin of rage. He held up a black orb in one twisted, black, skeletal hand.

"Hello again," the monster said as sweetly as his charred vocal chords would permit.

The little orb perched in his withered claw seemed to emit a glow, immensely strange because it was bright yet it was utterly black. Black light. Impossible. Black light that cast a purple tint onto the face of the monster wielding it.

This is it

I tried to conjure up rage, knowing that this was how my ability had risen up before, but the blatant terror of seeing my own imminent death seemed to cancel it out. I was too slow; far, far too slow.

Sam fired.

There was a harsh noise like a huge dog's angry bark. A thick glutinous black mass erupted from the orb, but it did not come for me. Instead it snapped through the air across the green and slammed into a young couple standing lost among the milling crowd – but in plain sight from my vantage point.

Sam grinned at me and cocked his head that way, urging me to look. Foolishly I did.

The thick black mass sent by the orb had burst open against the bodies of the young couple to form a membrane that engulfed both of them in its scolding stickiness. I covered my mouth in an instinctive and helpless gesture of horror, any sense of personal danger momentarily lost to horrified fascination at just how horribly, powerfully corrosive this venom was.

Their shrieks were so high-pitched as to be barely human at all as the toxic filth gouged into the skin and meat of their bodies and peeled them like overripe satsumas. It closed around them, scolding flesh and boiling internal organs, their screams silenced by steam that gouted from their mouths until the glistening shroud flowed across their faces and poured into their mouths, their throats. Where gaps briefly opened in that clinging, undulating surface, hot dark blood and scolding steam spurted outward in fierce jets, one such jet hitting a panicked crowd member nearby, setting his shirt on fire.

I glanced and saw Sam still grinning fiercely, his exposed blackened stump of a penis jutting out hard from his burnt lower belly.

The young couple were no longer suffering inside their scorching jellid prison. The boiling substance had stripped them inside and out. A spindly hand briefly pushed free from the collapsing mass, but it wasn't voluntary, however much it resembled a last, desperate bid to escape the agonising death within. The whole mulch lost cohesion, the black stuff losing its glistening lustre as its digestion cycle ended. The pile collapsed onto the muddy green and the deadly venom itself oozed away off the sparse bones, thinning and spent, drooling away into the wet grass.

A couple of veins that had survived somehow, trapped between nude bones, now burst open under the pressure of the boiling blood within and that hot crimson liquid spurted onto the green around them in a final announcement of the banns of their deaths.

There was a moment's silence in which all eyes including mine fixed upon Sam – or, more accurately, upon that orb in his claw.

An instant later the air was blasted by screams of terror and the smoke whipped to and fro as the panicked villagers tried to flee their terrible hunter.

Sam's grin was, however, for me alone and I knew for sure that he had spared me that one time only so I would understand the violation he intended to unleash against *me*, against my body.

"Back to the house!" I screamed.

I bolted, hoping my group would follow. My feet slipped in the quagmire of the churned green but I threw myself headlong because I knew that if I slipped it was over. Falling meant never getting back up.

I glanced back at that horrible harsh bark and saw Sam's orb spit glistening black death again, and then, almost at once, again. Others were dying now - he was patient in his insane bloodlust and could come for me when the fun of killing others wore thin. I was, I knew only too well, the dessert he could look forward to.

The orb spat into the crowd, the scolding black gluts slapping into bodies and sending the acrid stench of burnt animal fats out in a cloying stench cloud that overtook me and made me gag as I ran, overwhelming the woodsmoke scent of the still-burning houses as I ran and hoped that my friends and my parents had run, too.

For beings of thought rather than matter, I thought impassively, the villagers certainly burnt like real people.

Three screaming panicking people to my left were hit by the black stuff and went down in a tangle of seared flesh and tar-like gel, and I understood that this stuff was as hungry as it was stretchy. I did not stop to see what happened to those three nor did I hesitate for them; I knew I could not help.

The house had only been a few yards behind me when I had left it but it took forever to find again. I must have run the wrong way, which meant that I either kept going the wrong way or risked turning back and running straight into Sam's murdering arms.

I stopped for a second, my under-serviced lungs wrenching in air, my poorly-maintained body aching and trembling, while I looked around frantically for the place I wanted to flee to. Safety. An illusion, of course, but all that I had to cling to. Home.

All I could see was smoke and fleeting bodies. More and more of which shrieked and fell around me.

"Fuck," I gasped. "Fuck!"

The panicking crowd seemed to have been herded toward me, because in a matter of seconds I was surrounded. It grew impenetrable. Wild faces, wide-eyed with hysteria, a dense cluster of people following the mindless pattern of frightened cattle. Most were in good condition. The worse relics had almost certainly fallen first, unable to flee and with no-one to help them as their desperate friends and neighbours fought to save only themselves.

Oh, to have been a good person, to be able to say I tried to help anyone. I didn't. In that moment all I knew was the desire to avoid the agony of being boiled alive and then suffocated in that horrible thought-mass from his orb – to avoid it for now, for another minute, for as long as possible. I didn't *want* to help anyone else.

I saw the house and lunged forward. Pushed a face, elbowed a side, kicked a leg, pulled a tit and kicked someone's balls until finally I burst free of the morass of people and saw –

A screaming hysterical woman from elsewhere on the green ran past me away from the houses and then started sprinting *backwards*.

No, she didn't. She got *blasted* backwards.

Her hair was on fire as she sailed by the other way and as she hit the ground on her backside the burning filth oozed down over her head like a funeral veil being lowered, searing skin from her forehead and creeping relentlessly down toward her eyes.

The woman's clawed hands reached toward me. "Oh-o-oh! H*elp meee........!*"

No more of what she said made sense. There were babbled words screamed in high-pitched notes of hysteria, pain and horror as her eyes popped like squeezed grapes and I refused to imagine how much that must have hurt, but then bubbles appeared at her nostrils as she blew and sucked at that sick venom instead of air and her screaming mouth filled up, bringing her cries, and her agony I hoped, to an abrupt end.

Her throat burst in a spray of clumps. I gagged. Then, at once, I fled.

I pounded the ground with flaccid jelly legs, haunted by the gym membership I had never bought, until the familiar of mortally wounded shape of Edward's house moved closer in my field of vision.

I saw Tom, then Edward. Tom was pulling Edward along, the decrepit old man staggering and flailing his arms, his eyes wide. The old relic was in no shape for this; it was amazing Tom had managed to keep him out of the way of the hurtling thought knots.

A staggering man completely covered in the lethal tar staggered into their path and Edward reached out to push him away.

"No," I uttered helplessly, suddenly sure how this would end, instinctively sensing the ravenous hunger of that substance.

The glistering blackness slurped hungrily up onto his hand, his arm, his shoulder and I swallowed hard and forced myself to move as the elderly gent I had called my friend was engulfed and destroyed.

Starting toward him I saw Jen come racing across the green from my left, heading right into my path as she flew toward the old man, her wide wild eyes fixed on his dying form.

Knowing I was heavier than her had been a source of chagrin for many years, but today it finally served me and not her as we collided with a slap. My left breast took a lot of the impact and that fucking hurt, but Jen bounced off me like an overexcited kid on a trampoline. She went down hard and splatted arsewards into the mud, green eyes alight.

A bolt of venom snapped past over her head. Her lank blonde hair flitted briefly in the breeze. She gasped and stared at me in shock.

If she had kept her feet beneath her, she'd be dying now.

This wasn't about our petty fight any more, and we both knew it.

I offered her my hand. She took it, I pulled her up and I glimpsed the collapsing black mess of Edward.

I grabbed Jen and pulled her in against me. "Don't look," I said softly.

"Oh, Laur," she whimpered, her eyes wet. "He was a sweet old man. He didn't deserve that."

"I know. Come one."

We went to move off but I saw my parents through the chaotic milling throng of panicking bodies, the two faces, ravaged by decay but still Mumma and Dadda, flicking into view through the melee, just long enough for me to register them.

I held up an arm to guide them toward me but another bolt of black venom lashed through the crowd and it closed, obscuring them once more.

I screamed their names and hurled myself into the morass of panicking bodies, my feet slipping in the slimy mud as I fought desperately to reach them.

Knowing I was never going to make it.

Someone called my name from behind me. My name as a warning. But I didn't care.

I saw them, saw another thought knot flying at them, my mind seeming to play the moment in slow motion and there was definitely a pulse at the base of my skull and somehow that bolt skitted away from my parents. The relief was so far beyond description and I was so far beyond laughing or crying. I just stood there and let them cross to me, opening their arms lovingly as I remembered them doing so long ago.

I sensed another of the black energy masses; felt its approach. I turned my head lightning-fast and saw it flying toward my face, so close already that I could feel its nauseating heat blossom on my cheek. I felt its need, its almost sentient desire to take me, to *consume* me, and knew that Sam had exploited my desire to save my parents to get at me.

Bastard.

In that self-contained universe of a tenth of a hundredth of a second, the organ I had been trying to summon into action finally succumbed to my will and I pushed at the deadly venom closing on me.

Too late I saw the long game that Sam had played.

My mind pushed the malevolent mass away from me but in doing so it forced it to veer in an arc, passing so close I felt the skin on my cheek singe, but it didn't touch me and so did not get me.

I heard my mother's cry start and cut off.

I closed my eyes, understanding the scope of the revenge Sam had achieved.

I didn't want to open my eyes but I had to or I was dead, too.

The dooming black shroud had engulfed my mother. My father glanced at me for a single second, a brief sad smile on his wilted face. Then, he stepped in close and wrapped his arms around her, letting the source of her death take him too. The venom greedily wrapped him into its embrace and he shared his final step with his wife.

The horror, the rage, were blood-red armour and I donned them greedily as the vile glistening mass that had dissolved my parents collapsed and congealed on the wet ground.

Sam would pay. I sought the hateful wretch, now. Cried out his name like a single rifle-shot into the murk.

"Where are you, you worthless fucking shit pile!"

Ready to hurl myself into the melee to find the bastard, I was grabbed, pulled backwards and herded, before I could properly grasp what was happening, through the front door of Edward's house and into the hallway.

Tom kicked the front door shut behind me and bent over, leaning on his knees and panting for breath.

My plan for revenge against Sam had been a vanity; I knew I couldn't risk taking him on that way. I felt the relief at avoiding such a fight accompanied by guilt that I didn't want to avenge my parents enough.

Still, they'd been dead a long time. To me, and in actuality too.

The hall stank of wood dust and powdered plaster. The air was hazy with dust. The tall, wooden-cased grandfather clock had a big split in its thick wood frame that ran from just below the round face all the way down to the carved wooden structure of its base. The glass that had once covered the clock face, as well as the glass from the casement door that showcased the long pendulum, lay in shards and twinkling pepper-dots strewn across the hall carpet.

That great stalwart of my time here had been silenced forever now, like its elderly owner. I thought, distantly in that moment, that there was an old rhyme from my childhood about a clock that never ticked again after its old-aged owner died.

"I can't," I started, but my will was as weak as my body as the shock and horror laid heavy weight over my shoulders. I slumped back against the wall facing the clock. "I can't believe my brother would do, would do all... *this*."

My pumps were sodden and the baggy tee-shirt under my jumper, salvaged from Edward's spare wardrobe a hundred lifetimes ago, felt as if damp had crept into that, too.

"Really?" Tom enquired, his tone cool.

I sighed and glanced at his face, seeing the same numbness there that I could feel pressed to my own cheeks. "No, not really. I think he can justify anything to himself."

He barked a short flat laugh. "Glad you finally woke up and smelled the blood-loss."

The only valid reaction was to ignore his understandable sarcasm. "I'm pretty sure my brother must have caused the accident all those years ago. It all makes sense now. Just before, I remember him seeming... different.

He'd already decided to leave us. He killed our parents, his own mum and dad. If he could do that..."

Tom pursed his lips. "Yeah."

Jen pushed off the wall she'd been leaning on. "We all got hurt today, we all lost something, but there ain't time for this. We've gotta get the fuck away from here or this is gonna be our grave."

There was a polite knock at the door.

One-two.

It was repeated. *One-two.*

I glanced at my slut friend. "When you're right, eh."

"Back way!" Tom hissed as he pulled me off the wall by my arm, shoving me along the hallway.

"There'd fucking better be!" I muttered as I was chivvied into the darker part of the hall past Edward's parlour door. We had never needed a back door until now, so I had never needed to look for one.

And then something connected in my head and I halted, causing Tom to bump against me.

"Fuck, Laura!" Tom snapped. "Move!"

I grasped his arms and stared, crazy-eyed I suspect, into his eyes. "Go back, we have to go back."

He frowned impatiently, frantic and on the verge of anger. "Are you mad?"

But I knew.

Edward's hall would end abruptly in a neatly-wallpapered box-end just out of sight in the gloom. There was no back door, no kitchen. This house only had to be real enough to provide the illusion of reality. In all the time we had been here, Edward had been the only one to prepare any food or drink – he had absolutely insisted upon being host to us – but not just because he was the perfect host. Every cup of Edward's cocoa was as good as the first, because he wasn't making it – he was creating it at will in the same way that the villagers had created the village. Think it; have it.

And if Sam stopped playing an burst through that front door, there would be no way out for us. Jen was right - a ready-made coffin.

"Open up, little piggies! Fee, Fi, Fum!"

"There's no back way! Move!"

Tom's eyes widened as he reached the same realisation as me. He let me herd him back along the hall toward the front of the house, to the only available path open to us; the staircase.

Lucky for us, the stupid lust-driven monster chasing us hadn't yet tired of his sick sport, the tantalising, the fear he could create through the anticipation of his victims. He was still outside, confident of his upcoming kill.

Jen joined us in the hall. "What now? Fuck do we do?"

"Up the stairs!" I hissed, as if letting Sam hear through the front door made any difference. Unless we could climb out of a window we were still trapped.

We were up on the Landing when the front door below burst apart in a spray of splintered wood and glass shards, a shimmering blackness momentarily taking its place before fading to reveal the immense, twisted, lumbering silhouette of Sam.

Framed there in the scorched doorway, he jerked and staggered as a sudden spasm convulsed his body. He let out a wretched shriek of pain and rage as something dreadful went awry in his ruined body. My blood was chilled wine in my veins at that awful sound.

I had seriously fucked him up, yet I hadn't done him anywhere *enough* harm. With a shriek of rage more bloodcurdling than his previous cry the monster threw himself headlong and bounded up the stairs, hunched, almost galloping up the stairs on all fours.

"My room!" I cried. "There's a window out onto the roof."

Our already slim hope of escape was snatched away as Sam bounded up the stairs much faster than I would have expected with his twisted body, trapping us, crowding us back into the corner by the bathroom door. There was no window in the bathroom, no way out.

He glared at me, one-eyed, his rancid breath hissing between chipped teeth. The damage I had inflicted had scorched off almost all of his skin and much of his flesh, but this had served to reveal what he was made from, the ghastly truth of his once-beautiful form.

Sam was not a man at all. His outer layers had been more than mere skin and muscle, they had been a binding, giving human shape to a sickening jumble of random animal parts from a lunatic butcher's waste bin. I wondered at the sick mind that would be willing to breathe life into so heinous a thing. His right arm was human, but the left was a clumsy insect's limb, the meat-welded nerve endings that operated the human fingers of his now-stripped-off hand still dangling from the crusty, spindly greeny-black shell that bristled with wiry hairs and ended in a wicked-looking pincer. His left leg was meaty red with odd clumps of fur clinging to it, like the leg of a dog that had been in one too many fights, while the right was a grey-green, awkwardly-jointed reptilian thing with a three-toed foot, the flesh welds that kept his human toes in place peeling away now to leave the scaly finish of the limb unblemished by mammalian meat.

Despite my fear, a sense of awe washed over me. "How did Peter manage to make you?" I asked.

The monster swayed a little, as if recoiling from my reaction to him, causing a thin line of transparent mucus to drool from his burst abdominal cavity.

My mouth was watering in a pre-vomit spasm. I'd eaten little since leaving the village to go meet my brother, but I'd had a drink in the Bantam, and that little amount of liquid wanted out.

I fought not to gag – the next few seconds would decide if there was even a possibility of living past this event.

My mindforce attack had burst his belly open, leaving a mostly hollow, red-lined cavity from which a wobbling tangle of glistening red and yellow organs hung out on mucus-slimy threads of internal tissue. A fragile-looking tangle, the pieces slopped and oozed over each other as he swayed, one large glistening purple mass, possibly a liver, slopping in a pool of that transparent mucus, lolling out before being sucked back up under his partly-exposed ribcage.

Jen took a hesitant half-step toward hi. "Sam?"

"*Jen!*" I hissed. Maybe she felt like she had a connection with this monster, but I knew better.

"It's OK, Sam," Jen said soothingly as she took a full step closer to the steaming autopsy that was my brother's henchman. She was close enough now to put a hand inside his burst-open cavity.

Despite the horrors below his neck, Sam's head remained that of a man; badly burnt, blackened by my savage assault, but nevertheless human, and now as Jenny spoke I glimpsed something in his remaining eye, some glint. Jen had touched something deep within the recesses of this monster's brain.

But then the spark was gone and Sam raised the glistening black orb in his remaining humanish hand.

"Sam!" she rebuked.

The monster hesitated, lowered the orb and his blackened brow furrowed.

"You remember me, don't you? You remember *us*, right, Sam?"

That single eye rolled wetly in the blackened crusty remnants of his face, his dry and split lips twitching as he stared at her. "Jenn-fer," he croaked.

His voice was different now, even the phlegmy grating of his damaged throat failing to conceal the change; a softening, a more varied tone. A human note.

"Yes, Sam. It's me."

The hand holding that deadly orb fell to his side, although it did not let go. "Jenn-fer."

He twitched again, perhaps through bodily pain but more likely now through some inner turmoil.

I knew what Jen had done with Sam, what they'd shared that she was now trying to get him to remember and, seeing him now, I wondered just what revulsion she must be feeling at the thought that she'd let this thing put its penis inside her body.

Tom kept his silence up. I wondered if he was having the same thoughts and I couldn't help hoping he was. I'd been dumped so mercilessly by him, but ha-ha, look whose porridge you've been stirring, dick-head.

"L-l-remember." Sam teetered on his feet a little, his one-eyed gaze distant. "I came to you... for infllormation. I was given free reign, so long... so llong as, as I got it. And then.. and then I was to *kill* you."

"But you didn't, did you?" She stared up at him and I heard the tender smile in her tone.

Realisation hit me. *I came to you for information...*

"Jen!" I cried, more in dismay than anger. My friend glanced back at me. Frowned. *Not now!*

Is that how he had been able to track me so effectively? Had she...?

Jen held my gaze for a moment, but then returned her attention to Sam. She was right. Now was not the time. I could be angry later, if we survived; if Jen could somehow pull a fucking massive rabbit out of a shit-coloured hat in this cramped corridor.

Her gaze returned to Sam's ravaged mutant body. If she glanced at his dry-roasted genitalia, I did not see her do it. First time for everything... ain't I a bitch?

"Did you know, Sam?" she asked. "Did you know that your touch would doom me, cost me my life?"

The scarred and blackened tissue of his brow definitely creased this time. "Kill?... No. No, I lllleft you alllive."

"I died, Sam. You *infected* me and, and, I died."

There was real pain in her voice and I hoped she hadn't just blown it with him.

"No," Sam croaked. "I... I am... sorry."

"Would you be so cruel that you'd kill me a second time, Sam?" she asked him.

Smart bitch. I had to approve.

Sam made an odd, low noise and lowered his ruined head. There were reddish patches exposed amongst the crusty black mess on his scalp. Jen's words seemed to be getting through to him.

I could do nothing but wait. If he raised that orb again, it would be the last thing any of us saw before we got boiled alive in that disgusting scolding tar.

But Sam raised his head, not the orb, and I saw that his single-eyed gaze was fixed on Jen.

She waited for him. We all did.

His reptilian arm lifted, gestured at the stairs.

"Go," he croaked, and stepped away from us.

"Sam..." she started, perhaps realising he was the only man who had ever seen her as anything more than a cock-warmer.

"Go... *now!*" He angled his huge twisted body away from us until he was showing us his scorched, red and black back. He let out a soft groan. "I

204

have little control."

Seeing our chance I shoved Jen hard toward the head of the stairs and she snapped out of her reverie. We bolted down those stairs faster than I would have believed was possible and danced across the splintery remains of the front door in the hallway, erupting onto Edward's neat front garden and out onto the green.

The green.

"Oh, no," I murmured as a scolding sting of adrenaline surged through my belly, my head pounded, the flight for our lives placed on pause at the sight of the horrific carnage before us.

The smoke was clearing now. Surrounding the green, there were only the burnt skeletal remains of houses, with no buildings left intact, the last broken teeth in an old man's mouth, the gaps between them filled with rubble and settling piles of dust.

The sky had cleared and the rain had cleared, although streaks of black hinted at more rain to come, but the wet, glistening swamp of churned mud, once a green, had mixed into it the twisted fragments of countless bodies, all scorched black, all skeletal pieces, jagged and jutting, some draped in the remains of the lethal tar that had digested them.

It was the aftermath of an explosion in a doll factory. Re-imagined by a serial killer.

I heard Jen retch just as my own gaze was caught by a discarded arm with a complete hand still attached, a wedding ring glinting against the muddy earth; it seemed to be pointing, which led me to notice a head which the stampeding crowd had stomped into the sloppy mud, one glazed eye still visible, peering balefully up at us from its waterlogged tomb, while rainwater filled up the thing's open mouth. I was spared a view of its neck, though my imagination happily filled in the blanks with an idea of a dry-blooded neck stump, blackened at the point where the tar had finished its work.

All the villagers. Our former neighbours, even our friends.

And somewhere amongst that tangle of tissue lay the last remains of my parents.

"Shit," I cried as tears welled up in my eyes and a sick feeling weighed down my belly. My mum and dad were mixed in with those bodies. Where had they died?

I looked around desperately, needing to see.

Tom grasped my elbow. "We can't do this now," he said softly. "We have to get out of here."

My tears were hot but my bones felt cold. "I have to know where their grave is, Tom!"

The sobs had a life of their own, they pushed themselves out from me. My parents were here, I couldn't just leave them mixed in with this hideous mess.

He pulled on my arm. "Laur! Now, come on!"

I shrugged free, furious at his presumption, this stupid man, this dick of no self-control, but then a brutal animal scream erupted from the house behind us and in that gurgling, inhuman cry of hating, hurting rage came the truth of Tom's words. I nodded to him.

We wanted to bolt across the green, but instead we had to zig-zag awkwardly around clumps of horror scattered in the churned mud. My heart raced with a mixture of panic at our slow pace and revulsion at what we were walking amongst. Walking in.

Sam was coming for us now. We had wasted some of the time Jen had bought for us, yet I couldn't rush, couldn't risk stepping on someone's... anything.

Then I stepped on something solid. Kept my eyes levelled, aimed at the horizon. Refused to allow myself to *know*. Nothing to see down there; just an old, discarded bottle, or some other thing; but not a part of a *someone*, not an object that had, a short time ago, shared blood and life with the rest of a person's body, a living thinking being.

I wanted to tell myself that these were only mind beings, but that didn't alter the fact that their dead bodies were flesh in every way that I could see or perceive and it was *too much*.

Finally, when I feared I could stand no more, we stepped off the green and were at the opening into the lane that led away from that awful charnel scene.

I glanced back and saw a twisted form lumbering carelessly across the broken corpses on the green, not dodging around them as we had done but crashing through and trampling or kicking up limbs and pieces that had recently been people.

His pace was uneven yet relentless. He was catching us up.

I think maybe I cried out. I definitely bolted for my life.

We ran headlong and I hoped against hope that I wouldn't trip, because if I went down it would be all over.

I had changed since all this began, because even as I fled in terror, part of my brain was processing cold logic. Sam's tactical mind would know that our first instinct would be to flee through the portal out of this emr region. On the relatively even ground of the lanes, he would catch us, his lumbering gait slowing him yet his supernatural energy reserves preventing any hope of fatigue.

That reasoning part of me saw our only good option.

"This way!" I yelled as loudly as I dared with Sam on our trail.

I hurtled along the lane, my calves cramped tight and threatening to lock up at any moment, but I waved a frantic arm to get the attention of the other two, and then diverted off to hurl myself headlong into the shrubbery beside the road, crashing face first into the lashing stinging branches but driving hard into the painful tangle anyway, feet slipping in the mulch of wetted leaves lain dead on the ground.

We had to go into the woods. Sam had no reason to expect us to do that, but we had to do it before he came around the corner onto the lane and saw where we had gone.

If the other two followed, they'd survive a bit longer. If not, Sam was going to lunch on them and that would buy me some more time.

Harsh, but there you are. More of my increasingly cold reasoning.

Water and mud slopped inside my pumps as I thrashed at rough sharp branches drove myself onward, the wetness freezing my feet, the sharp foliage springing back to whip at my face and arms.

I heard a startled yelp behind me and without breaking my pace, I snapped my head quickly around to see Jen, the one I'd have been happiest to see get fed to Sam, following me but getting tangled in the briar. She stumbled and dropped onto her arse on the sodden forest floor. Her sexy tight black skirt was half-submerged and her clingy white top was splashed with brown goo.

I stopped my plunge into the woodland and glared at her. "For fuck's sake get up and *shut* up!" I hissed.

Tom grabbed her arm and pulled her up, roughly, dragging himself and her toward me.

I left them to it and drove my aching, cold body through the dense foliage once again, lashing wildly to keep the vicious barbed branches away from my eyes, and suddenly, shockingly I erupted out into a wide circular clearing. I plunged forward and nearly went down face-first onto the open ground as the resistance I had been leaning into was snatched away.

Tom pulled Jen into the clearing a moment later and they, like me, took a second to steady themselves and get their bearings.

"Well," Tom said, puffing for breath. "I'm complaining about this holiday when I get home."

This was a gloomy and shadowy place, the light made a weak green by the leaf canopy overhead. Swollen drops of water still tumbled down into the clearing as the leaves overhead finally let go of the rain they had collected earlier, making a dull plip-plip as they plunged into puddles pocking the mulchy ground. The air was heavy with the cloying herb-like zests of wet grass and moss.

It seemed so shockingly normal, apart from the silence, the lack of chittering birds celebrating the end of the rainstorm.

I rubbed my cheeks, which were sore from the razor-edged branches that had slapped and pinged me.

"We can't… stop," I gasped, still haemorrhaging air from my raw hot lungs. Exercise and panic. Still, if my poor fat-engorged heart gave out, it would rob Sam of his fun; a poor consolation, but my expectations had been brought down a few pegs.

Tom glanced back. "No sign he's following," he said as quietly as he could. "That was a pretty sharp idea back there, Laur. Good call."

"Yeah." I whispered back, peering into the foliage wall we'd just passed through. "But we can't count on Sam falling for it for too long. Even if he goes through the portal it won't take him long to work out that we pulled a wrap-around on him."

Jenny was hunkered down, hands dangling between her splayed knees. Her inner thighs and the gusset of her panties were exposed, and either side of that now-soiled sliver of white cloth the bald, shaved outer lips of her genitals peeked out. I hastily looked away. "This fuckin' sucks."

"So," said Tom. "What now?"

My attention shifted to where we were. "We have to anticipate Sam, be ready to loop back around and get to the portal after he decides we're still here in this emr."

Jenny stood with an ungainly thrust of her legs and tried to wipe mud off of her face, but she succeeded in smearing it across her cheeks and making a bad mess muckier. "Fuck does that mean, genius? Anticipate him how?"

I shrugged. "I don't know. Wait him out, find somewhere we can see when he's coming back for us, so we know when to make break for it. Stay ahead of him."

"Nice plan," my friend replied caustically, pressing her hands to her hips. "We just gonna run forever?"

"No, I said. "But until we have a chance to do anything smarter, staying ahead and staying alive is what we've got. That way."

I pointed at a gap in the trees on the other side of the clearing, which had what looked like a narrow dirt path trailing away into the belly of the woods.

Jen pouted. "Right, coz Sam'll never think of going that way!"

I frowned at her stupidity. "I already told you, Jen, we need a vantage point. Somewhere

uphill from here."

Tom crossed to the opening in the foliage, scratching his head. "Why would anyone clear a path through here?"

"How d'you mean?" I asked him.

He pushed his spectacles up onto the bridge of his nose, startling me because I had been sure he wasn't still wearing them. "Well, it leads from this clearing, but how d'you get into this clearing to use it?"

"One problem at a time," I suggested. "For now, we need higher ground and that's our only option."

I led and Tom followed. As usual, Jen skulked at the rear, but that suited me fine. She'd shield me from the first hit if Sam outsmarted us and started shooting.

The path was just compacted dirt that had been shielded by a tight overhang of young trees and, further up, the leaning boughs of older forest sentinels. It was indeed taking us slightly uphill, but it was still a relatively easy walk compared to the thicket. After a few minutes, it turned left between two large trees and opened out onto a gravelled drive about thirty feet wide.

"Well," I said. "That's unexpected."

At the end of the gravel drive stood a large flat-faced brick and stone house, at least twenty bedrooms, that backed directly onto a dense wall of vast old oaks, whose expansive boughs seemed to grip the building in an impenetrable embrace that trailed around its side walls and over its dull red roof.

Beside me, Tom pushed his spectacles up in that odd way of his, frowning at what lay before us. "What's Grantleigh Manor doing here?"

I went to ask him what the hell he was talking about, and then couldn't be bothered.

The little path was the only means of approach to this house. Tom had been right back in the clearing, the path led to this place, but only if you could find the clearing in the first place. It didn't make much sense.

"I don't care what that place is, I said. "We'll have a view back to the clearing, maybe the road, from one of the top rooms."

"Tue, but d'you think your brother knows about this place?"

"No idea. But he didn't know the village existed until…"

Oh, whoops. Way to poke the bear, Keeble.

To his credit, Tom kept any resentment of me in check. "Fair point," he said, "And it looks like whoever put this place here meant for it to be hard to find."

"So?" asked Jenny, catching us up and retaining a pouty teenage petulance that she was too old to wear convincingly.

"So," I replied, quelling my irritation with her, "it's a good bet for a hidey-hole and gives us our advantage."

"Maybe."

She still sounded pouty. She was getting right on my fucking tits, and more than a little bit.

We approached with caution but the place was silent and still. At the top of three white stone steps was a broad oaken double front door with brass fittings. The other two hung back so I tried pushing the doors and found them unlocked but stiff. They groaned as I leant my weight on them, the rust of disuse making them stiffly resist me until Tom found his balls and joined me, his extra weight and strength helping to drive the creaking, groaning doors apart so we could slip through into a wide, cool hallway with a polished stone floor and whitewashed walls.

The hall was broadly square and the air smelled faintly of dry old dust and musty old leather, the dust creating an irritating little tickle in my throat every time I breathed in, whilst the scarce light piercing the filthy windows picked out dancing flurries around shadowy white-sheeted furniture in rooms through archways to either side of us. stood yawning open in the dusty gloom.

I started violently and felt a squirt of adrenaline scolded my belly as a harsh groan thundered in the echoey hallway.

I spun, my breath suspended by my fear, my breath exploding out with relief as I saw Tom fighting the fouled hinges of the great old front doors in a vain attempt to push them closed.

I glared at him. "Fucksake, Tom! Are you trying to make me fill my pants?"

He leant his back against the almost-shut doors and flashed me a *hey presto!* hand gesture as they slid shut with a satisfying clonk when the latches engaged.

"Yeah, Tom," Jen contributed. "I don't need runny shit pouring down my fucking leg."

Tom laughed and rubbed his jaw.

I gestured at the broad staircase in front of us, its three-person wide carpeting opening out in two directions at the next level up like some grandiose set from Phantom of The Opera.

"Let's head up and set up in the room with the best view so we can–"

"Fuck!" Jen cried from somewhere to my right.

She gone to the window beside the door and, now, she stood panting hard, eyes wide and nipples jutting like cigar butts through her sodden summer top.

"Nice plan, Laur!" she yelled at me, although there was more panic than anger in her eyes. "Nice fucking plan! Fuck me! Right up the arse!"

"What?" I asked, my own apprehension a sheet of ice beneath my ribs.

Tom hurried across and rubbed at the window before peering out. He turned to me. "Plan's blown, Laur."

I had crossed the hall to him and now I saw through the window and experienced the will-sapping horror of seeing that bulky, twisted, awkward shape lurching along the gravel driveway, his staggering steps bringing him relentlessly closer to the house.

"How the fuck?"

It was all I could think to say.

Tom flashed me a hollow, frightened smile. "I think this is it for us, Laur. End of the line, so to speak."

I sighed. Nodded. "We gave it our best shot, though, eh?"

"What!" Jen glared at me, hands on her hips. "Fuck you, Laura Keeble, I am not gonna stand here with my tits on a stick and wait for that cunt to kill me! We can hide upstairs!"

I wasn't even crying. I felt... done. "What's the point?" I asked my former friend.

"Dunno, babe, but we can at least *try!*"

I shrugged. Maybe, maybe not. It bought us a few minutes more of this increasingly pointless life, if nothing else.

*

The upstairs corridors were a uniform dull green and reeked of the overpowering sweetness of lavender hygiene products that didn't quite hide the sickly cloying reek of meat that has gone soggily rotten in a warm kitchen. Hot, wet decay and death.

We didn't have time to worry about that, though, because down below us the heavy thud of the huge wooden front door echoed up to us, forcing us to pick a door and dive inside.

There was no point, really. Our inexhaustible hunter would simply take his time and check every room until he found us. Even if we got out of the house... I wondered about simply transferring back to the Matter Realm, but in my despair I could only envisage being hunted for days, weeks, months until Sam or maybe even my brother himself found me.

I sighed and played along for Jen, although fuck knows why her opinion of me carried any weight.

With the door eased carefully shut, I turned to face the terrifying sight of nothing, absolute blackness, a darkness that was so deep it pressed against my eyes, and worse yet, the oppressive, cloying sick-sweet rotten-meat stink of a butcher's bin. Something was in here with us..

I fought against my mind as it tried to sketch the horrors that might lurk in that darkness.

"Laur," Jen murmured, her voice quavering. "I'm not sure about this any more."

"You wanted to try," I whispered back. "What the fuck is that smell?"

My eyes were starting to adjust. The room did have a weak, very weak, light source somewhere out of sight and I could discern two rows of white-sheeted beds, all of them still and silent, as though empty.

"Come on," I muttered.

We pushed into the room and crouched down between two beds, and for my part as we cowered there with an aching dread of that door opening, I began to feel a bit ridiculous. Who was I kidding? Out of my depth was a kind way to describe this predicament.

Heavy, uneven footsteps echoed deliberately from the corridor outside, growing slowly closer. I felt a hand rest on my shoulder as one of my companions reached out for human contact, whilst a click-scrape from outside told me that Sam was methodically testing every door as he moved ever closer; he would open our door all too soon and this foolishness would end.

I was terrified of the pain, yet I couldn't seem to make myself care about the fact of dying itself.

As I crouched, leg tension fought gut-cramping fear. Between the two effects, I managed to do no more than bob slightly on my haunches, trying to relieve the only discomfort I could affect as I stared at that door, waiting.

As I peered over the edge of the bed I caught a strong smell; different from the general smell of the room – rotten yet somehow mild, almost dusty. There was something in the bed, a shape under the sheet and a thrill of dread cut into my belly as I realised that it was the source of at least some of the sickly, familiar stench filling the room.

Whatever was lying under that sheet, it was utterly still and less than six inches from my face.

The heavy, uneven footfalls outside stopped and the door was ease patiently open.

Jen grabbed my arm in alarm and I just about managed to stop myself crying out like a teenager on a rollercoaster called *'you're gonna fucking die!'* as light from the corridor poured into the room and seemed blindingly bright compared to the gloom. Sam's twisted shoulders were silhouetted against the green-walled corridor.

He chuckled; a sick, torn sound.

My hope withering into a dulling resignation, I thought of my parents, less of my lost chance to reunite with them and more the dimly-remembered warmth of my tiny years with them.

The monster at the door was moving into the room. The same monster that had stolen my parents from me to sate a little of his perverted bloodlust.

I hadn't meant my desperate grasping at memories of my lost parents, certainly had not intended to forge any advantage from it, yet as loss fuelled anger, the rage welled up within me and without even thinking about it I arose into a crouch and aimed my gaze at Sam, who frowned at me in bewilderment as my mind organ made the back of my head pulse with dull pain.

Unconsciously I had primed myself for this fight, even as my conscious mind had contemplated simply surrendering to my fate.

I felt myself reach out to Sam and unleash an intangible knot of rage. Something flashed from me straight at him and before he could raise the orb he was blasted out the doorway to slam back against the far corridor wall.

He emitted a deep, raw scream as he writhed against the wall, his clawed hands desperately trying to gather up some glistening matter that was coiling out of his open belly and ribs.

I could feel his pain, distantly, and I delighted in it.

"He's hurt!" I said sharply. "Move, now!"

I clambered out from behind the bed and expected the others to follow.

"Who's there?" a voice asked.

I started at the unfamiliar, willow-thin voice, just as Sam spun in a circle just outside the door and a piece of something slick, wet and internal splashed onto the floor between his feet. He emitted a low, miserable groan.

The monster stared aghast at that piece of himself, his body tremors momentarily quelled at the shock of losing some of himself. A moment passed. Then, with a hysterical shriek, he launched himself headlong back the way he'd come along the corridor, his fight with us abandoned in his wild animal panic.

"Who's there?" asked that voice, again.

Tom was next to me as I headed toward the door, watchful for Sam's return but unconcerned by that voice.

"Don't you hear that?" I asked him.

He glanced at me. "Hear what?"

I held his arm and halted him. "That voice – there was a voice."

"Yeah, yours, it said 'let's get the fuck out of here' and it was right."

"No, it was... never mind."

"Help. Please, help!" the voice cried again. "Don't leave. Please don't leave."

A sudden piercing shriek from down the corridor came loud enough to lance my ears and send a trail of ice water down my spine. It ended abruptly.

To cocked an eyebrow at me. "You need *more* reasons to take your own advice and get moving?"

"No no, don't leave me, please, please help me..."

I turned, seeking the source of the voice. I may never have been the most moral person I the world but that plaintive cry for help demanded I at least try to help.

"There's someone else here," I told the others as I moved back into the room. "Hello? Where are you?"

"Here! Please, I'm here! It's dark, I can't see you!"

"Laur, what you doing?"

I looked under a bed. "She needs our help."

"Who? Fucksake, who?"

"I'm here, over here."

I straightened up, suddenly apprehensive. The others couldn't hear the voice because it was in my head. It was someone else's thought in my mind. And there was something in the bed.

"Fuck."

Tom was beside me. "We have to go, Laur."

Light from the corridor caught his lenses and obscured his eyes but he was frowning.

"I can hear a voice in my head, Tom. I have this terrible feeling I know why."

He saw me glance aside toward the bed and pulled a face. "We don't have time for this!"

Before I could stop him, he wrenched the sheet back to reveal a nude white skull that glared up at us from between two pillows, its eye sockets dark and hollow, two wafer-thin scrapes of dry reddish-brown muscle fibre still clinging to the bare bone in the angle of its jaw. It rocked slightly between the two pillows propped either side of it, as though glancing around at us with its eyeless cavities.

And then the voice came.

"Help me, it' so dark in here!"

The coarse feel of that dead voice clawing at my brain made me gag with instinctive horror, like a spider crawling across my nipple.

"Is that..?" Jen murmured.

I nodded. "This must be what they do when the decay goes too far. These must have been villagers once, but they've lost the image of their physical bodies, become a mind trapped in a body that no longer works."

Tom grabbed my arm. "Great, Laur, but we need to be fucking off before the mental pot-pourri man gets his act together and comes for us."

He was right. The terrible, tragic fate of the villagers was not something we could fix and we might have only minutes to get away before Sam's rage overcame the horror of his condition.

"Help us, please!"

It was in my head with me. I staggered back, panting, feeling sick. It licked the lobes of my mind with its sibilant, intrusive, plea. Its words hit home. Us.

"Who's there?" "What's happening?"

"Has someone come?" "Can you help us?"

"Please..." "Who is that? What's happening?"

They were in my head, *inside* me, there was no way to block them out. My mind was being violating by sickening, decayed presences.

I reeled away and stumbled toward the door, frantic to be away from the vile intrusion, but the backs of my knees struck the frame of a bed and I skidded, staggered and thudded painfully down onto my knees.

They can't have heard the noise, but maybe my distressed mind transmitted something. Whatever the reason, in that moment all of the entombed minds in the beds around us, trapped in the dark silence of dead, eyeless skulls came to life as they realised that something was happening, that their long, long era of isolation might finally be about to end.

"Help me..." "Can you hear me?" "It's so dark, help me up."

"Hello?" "I'm in here, my name is, my name was, I am..."

"Please save me!" "Have you come to save us?" "Hello?"

"Please!" "Hello?" "Please" "Help us" "Hello?"

"Hello?" "Please, Please!" "Answer us!" "Help us" "Please"

I cried out. It hurt, but worse than that, the overwhelming intensity was dimming my real senses as I was pulled under. As the voices burrowed deeper into my mind, the sights and sounds my eyes and ears were seeing fell ever further from my brain. They were shutting me down, pulling me into their dark silent paralysis.

I had to get away or I would be a drooling helpless zombie when Sam came back for us, but I couldn't find my arms or legs any more. They were out there somewhere, beyond the blinding fog of disembodied thoughts and pleas.

I was shutting down.

And then with sudden violence, utter silence hit me.

The absence almost as shocking as the overwhelming assault on my mind had been.

Light flared before me as I found my eyes. I felt the solidity of my flesh once more and sagged against Tom, supported by his strong grasp, as I pulled in long, deep breaths and waited for my head to stop spinning.

We were in the corridor. Tom had just pulled the door to the relics' ward shut. I slumped against the wall, hands splayed against it to support me, while I slowly reconnected with my meat.

I stared at him. "Did you…?"

He nodded. "What the hell happened to you in there?"

"That was smart," I said. "Thank you, Tom, you have no idea!"

Tom's face was a puzzled frown of concern.

"They were all crying out, their voices were just too much," I said. "Luckily they don't have much of a range."

Jen had her fists pressed to her scrawny hips. "What the hell are you talking about? What voices?"

I sighed. "Yet another fringe benefit of my little gift." I smiled a taut smile. "The fun just keeps on coming."

"Laur…" Jen started.

I laughed a short sharp laugh. "Fuck it," I said. "I just have to get used to it. Come on, before Sam pulls himself together. Literally."

We set off along the corridor, back toward the staircase. I knew Sam was going to be there somewhere, but it was the only exit – the other end of the corridor was a blank wall, much like Edward's 'kitchen'

"Let's go steady here," I said quietly to Tom as he walked beside me. "We still don't know if Happy Harry is up on his feet or not."

Tom laid a hand on my shoulder. "Way he was screaming, I think you maybe did it this time."

I put an arm in front of him to stop him as we reached the final curve in the corridor, just before it opened onto the stairway landing. "I wish I had your confidence. Let's take it steady, OK?"

We edged in tight against the wall, the reassuring chill of the hard stone wall at our backs.

I took a fast peek and took in as much detail as possible in the millisecond my brow and eyes were visible to anything waiting there for us.

A brownish-red smear down the far wall. A splash of oily-looking yellow fluid on the floor, as if someone had been mending a motorbike. A boot scuff on a skirting board and redder, more arterial-looking blood drooling down toward it from a splat about mouth height on the wall. Something crimson, or purple, lying on the floor, surrounded by more brownish-red gore.

I turned to Tom. "He's not up here. Maybe he left."

Tom shrugged. "Or fell down the stairs, I hope."

"Come on, then." I sucked in air, the swell of my lungs a boost to steel me as we pushed round the curve onto the first-floor landing.

Sometimes, silence can be really fucking spooky.

At the echoey, cold stone stairs we saw a trail of gore going down and, at the bottom, a hefty tangled pile of reddish chunks and loops that might be some of Sam, or possibly the busted remnant of *all* of him.

As we stepped off the bottom stair we had to edge around that mass of guts. It sprawled about four or five feet out across the floor and was waist-high, a throat-clogging stench like a bad zoo pouring off it that made my mouth well up with spit as my stomach churned violently.

Glancing at the spilt pile I noticed, within the meat tangle, two stalks jutting out that were just large enough to be limbs, protruding at awkward angles. There was an array of bulbous organ shapes swimming in the glistening pool of spilt blood that lay all around this smelly, repulsive mess, hints of steam curling off them. This was too big to be a spill. This was all that remained of Sam.

As we passed the pile it twitched, a vile blocked-toilet stench of shit billowing out as Sam's bowels ruptured.

"Move!" I said, well, gagged.

We hurriedly scraped overspill of our footwear in preparation for the sprint across the hallway.

"Glurgh…. " gurgled whichever part of that ghastly mess could still be considered to be Sam. "Pleease…"

I stopped. Stared.

Amongst the crimson mulch before us, an eye opened. Jenny backed into me and I pulled away from her as she doubled over and wretched, though her stomach being as empty as mine she had nothing to eject.

The eye extruded from the glistening redness of meat and I watched in a kind of horrified fascination as a wet, blood-enrobed head coiled free seeping goo on a wobbling twisted stump of neck. A split appeared in the head, somewhat beneath the eye, showing me a hole containing a few, now broken teeth.

"Fuck, oh, fuck," Jen murmured through her hands.

The pulverised body tried to lift off the floor, a red-stained hand visible beneath it, pressing to the floor, a webbing of brownish-red clinging between the fingers. As my brain assembled meaning in that shape, based on knowing where the head and one arm was, I realised with a thrill of horror that Sam's body was still in one piece; OK, a twisted, tangled piece, curled up like a ghastly malevolent foetus, but essentially *intact*.

I took a step back. "Run!"

There was a laugh bordering on hysteria that might have been any of us. "Fucking *run!*"

We bolted for the door. Luckily, Sam had not troubled himself to close it on his way in, so we fled outside, into the cold, hard rain.

It was freezing, the rain cold and cutting and a shock after the relative warmth of the house. Jenny took two steps from us, doubled up and wretched at the gravel driveway.

I knew Tom would waste time comforting the silly bitch and we did not have time for it. "Let's go! You wanna chuck or you wanna survive?"

She glared at me from a white, white face. "You're all heart, Laur."

I crossed to her and slapped her arm; affectionately, not hard. "I'm keeping you alive, babe."

There was only one way to go, so we fled back the way we had come, the fierce driven rain turning my jumper into clay and my shoes into skates, until we got under the thicker tree cover and were afforded a little shade.

My one consolation for the misery of this walk was seeing the state of Jen, her shoulders hunched and head down, the clothes that had so flattered her slutty body this morning now mere wreckage, ruined by rain and mud and the struggle to cut our way through the jaggy bushes. Her blouse was now smeared unattractively across her breasts, her nipples protruding enough to make a porn star proud, while her wet skirt flapped in torn strips against her crow-thin thighs, threatening to trip her up at any moment.

It made me want to smile. Is that bad?

Finally we were released from the grip of the foliage and expelled onto the verge of the country lane like a vomited kebab.

Through exhaustion or clumsiness, Jen pitched facedown onto the muddy verge with a gloriously undignified splash. Tom would have helped her, except that in an uncharacteristic moment of possessiveness I slumped against him, forcing him to hold onto me, instead.

He peered down at me, confused, the rain dappering his dainty little glasses.

I kept my weight on him until Jen had clambered to her feet unaided, glaring partly at me but mostly at Tom, her hair glued to her cheeks and her bare knees bleeding.

"You both good, are you?" Her voice reeked of sarcasm.

I smiled at her. Apparently, though, her eyes were developing laser technology as I watched, because it hurt now to look at them, they were so fierce. She still seemed more pissy with Tom than me.

I let my friend simmer for a moment longer out of pure malice and then decided that survival might need to take precedence. "Right, we need to find the portal so we can create distance between us and Sam."

Jen glared, hands pressed to her bony hips. "Who the fuck put you in charge?"

"Jen, come on," said Tom, softly. "Everything that's happened is tellin' us that she's the only one who has any control over what's going on."

The country lane around us burst away from us like a gigantic reality bubble, day vanished, the rain stopped and the world snap-changed.

It was the dead of night and we stood, dazed and a little nauseous, in the Chadbury graveyard, just opposite the house I shared with Grandma.

It was more embarrassing than anything, after what Tom had just said.

-26-

A new reality had slammed into place around us and it was night, probably midnight, with a dim moon filtering morbid light through the spindly silhouettes of cold branches above and all around me. A real moon, not the fake moonlight of the emr village. The skeletal fingers of the ghostly moon-shadows trailed across the tombstones of the dead and buried.

Somewhere nearby, the long-dead remains of my parents lay interred. Their real remains. A momentary pang hit me and I drew a deep breath in through my nose. The earth here smelled mossy and rich, an unexpected layer of realness after the limited sensual stimulation of the emr.

I frowned at that, wondering what it meant. Where were we? That seemed an even more pressing question than the other biggie; how the fuck had we *got* here? Was this a more detailed reality than the village emr, where someone had gone to the trouble of creating smells, and a moon? Perhaps a trap set by my brother?

I turned on my heel in time to see a colourless ripple break the air in front of me. A splash of white appeared at its centre and in a fractured moment that splash condensed itself and became Tom's tee-shirt as Tom arrived.

"Ha!" I said, realising that we had not all arrived at the same instant.

The mossy scent of the graveyard intensified for a moment as the displaced air from Tom's arrival pushed into my face.

"Shit, Laur," he said, gazing around in awe. "You've done it. We're home – wait. How did you manage that?"

"This"

I started violently at the voice

"is not your reality."

A smallish suited man leant on the nearest gravestone. He straightened and crossed to us. To me. "We must insist on your help, LauraKeeble. We cannot act against the other Keeble directly."

I sighed. "What is this, Sool? I've already said I'll do it, what's with the fucking melodrama?"

Sool stopped and stared impassively at me. "The chance to fight the other was missed, LauraKeeble."

I frowned at his still and blank face, so bizarrely featureless and un-memorable. "Look, that was the first time I'd spoken to my brother in over twenty years. You need to cut me some slack here."

His gaze drifted away from me. "As was predicted."

I felt angry and dismayed all at once, having given it my all, so a neatly-packaged 'fuck-you' was fast-tracked toward my lips, held back only because Sool spoke again.

"A lesson in priority is needed. This will be it. You should have known now that this is the reality of Matter."

"Oh, home," Tom murmured pathetically, looking around in awe. "I knew it!"

For the first time since he had appeared, Sool acknowledged my companions. "No," he said, glancing briefly at Tom. "This is not *your* Matter realm. There… has been a shift. A shift in the time axis."

"He always like this?" Jen asked no-one in particular.

"So," I said. "you can travel in time, Sool?"

Jen humphed. "I'm callin' bullshit."

"Yes, correct. Bullshit. Not true travel in time, but in bringing you here did I shift your perception somewhen. You can see, for a moment, what is the world as it will be in future, if you fail to stop your brother."

"OK," Tom cut in, looming over Sool. "Just a sec here, fun-size. Whether we're in the future or whatever, Jen and I shouldn't be able to exist in the Matter realm, I remember Edward tellin' us that much."

I heard such desperate hope in his voice. He was pitifully desperate to be wrong.

"Yes correct," Sool responded. "Cannot."

Tom's shoulders slumped. "Oh. Well, how come we can be here?"

I could answer that one. "Because this is a perception, not the actual universe of the future, right, Sool?"

Sool allowed a moment to pass before answering. "True, but the event we predict is coming, has already occurred here. Even if this were real, the mindforms would function here. The realms have collapsed; a mind being can dwell here as can a matter being."

Tom went to speak, his eyes alight.

"Neither can survive long, though."

I knew we were actually where he said we were. It was instinctive. The air here was wrong, not just the cleanness but the way it smelled, tasted; as if all the dust had settled and there was nothing left moving to disturb it any more.

Sool planned to show me what was going to happen if I didn't stop Peter.

The little man crossed to a tall crusty oak tree by the low stone graveyard wall, stared at the old trunk and then picked distractedly at its crumbly bark for a moment.

He turned back to me. "By this time in your... history, all intelligent life is no more."

"But... the trees?" Jen asked stupidly. *Such* a star pupil.

"They exist but they are not alive. Soon will even existence stop."

He hoisted himself over the graveyard wall so, with a glance at Tom, I clambered awkwardly over that wall that had seemed such a big adventure in my childhood and stepped onto Tiler's Hill, my home, apparently unchanged.

The road wound up past the graveyard and on toward the Woodfield bypass, same as ever. The streetlights were dark but that was not so unusual this late. The sky above us was the same old sky, and the moon sat perched, as so often, at a jaunty angle to the Earth, casting its sinister bluish light across the scene.

It was only when I looked more closely at the houses that I saw any real change, but once I'd noticed it there was no going back.

"Shit."

The house I'd shared with Grandma was still there but the front bay windows and the front porch, once so suburban-average, had been twisted into great gothic arches with dense black leadwork spidering across ironwork and dense greenish glass. Along the road was the house that had belonged to old Gordon Robertson, a once pleasant, paint-fresh old gentleman's home but now vast, looming over everything else in the road, everything else in the *area*, its whitewashed facade now exploded out and up into a huge castle-like structure of light grey stone slabs, a huge wooden fortress door its entrypoint, narrow slits in the stone forming its windows.

All of the houses were faintly recognisable, but overwhelmed with the architecture of nightmares.

"Laur?" Jen appealed somewhere behind me, her voice suddenly muted, awed.

"It's alright, pet," I heard Tom reassure, although I was sure I could hear the lie in his voice.

I turned on Sool, unaccountably angry at him for this atrocity. "How?"

"I explain. We see two universes," the odd little man separated his hands as if to represent the two universes. "Separate. One is yours, and is of

Matter. The other is Mind, and is of thought."

"Sool, I know all this."

Those odd grey eyes stared unblinking. "Yes, correct. The other Keeble affects the division, the… bridge. He weakens it. Your friends fell between at death, through a channel created by the other. They live on. Good consequence."

I cocked my head. Maybe.

He slammed his hands together. "When barrier fails, universes collapse together. Bad consequences are found."

"OK, let's run through this," I said. "This 'other Keeble', as you put it, is Peter, my brother, and he is doing something… bad?"

"He created his playground in pockets between the realms, but the emr is not so designed and cannot support. Thus began the collapse. Mind into Matter; Matter into Mind." He repeated his hand-clap. "Mind is not space-time, Matter is not thought-ether."

"But…" I began. "Why does the emr even have to exist? I don't get it, Sool!"

"You need only know this to be true," said Sool. "But remember how far I have come to you and know that this is not whim."

I ignored their pointless exchange of hostilities. "But – aren't our thoughts with us all the time? Why does it matter if this thought universe falls back into ours?"

"Thought is manifest."

Clearly, that was meant to answer everything.

I went to challenge him, but as I did so, brilliant light exploded around us, as though an atomic bomb had been detonated beyond the houses in front of us.

I drew a sharp intake of breath and, as I instinctively threw protective hands across my eyes I glimpsed the houses ahead of us melt into silhouette and lose all shape.

My whole body was gripped, the ground pulled away from beneath my feet; I tried to open my eyes and look but all I saw was the insanity of light and movement flashing past me, as if I were falling into a burning tunnel.

It was terrifying but familiar, resembling a more brutal version of my original jaunt out of the emr. This was another *transfer*.

Something solid slammed up under my feet, jarring my ankle and knee joints and sending a stab of bone-pain up through me.

Now I could open my eyes. A dark-grey tarmac road, solid sidewalls four-feet high and a great expanse of grey river coiling away beneath, away into the distance. The Thames; we were on London Bridge.

"Shit in my mouth," said Tom.

Not far from here stood my office, where I had wasted ten years of my life on a career that would turn out, in the end, to be all for nothing because the world wasn't going to end in a bang or a whimper, but a fat juicy splat. Evidence of the final splat was all around us. The surface of the road before us was cracked, split wide open in some places to create scary chasms that plummeted into the river below, if you were lucky; who-knew-where if you weren't.

It was dusk. Another time-shift. Thanks, Sool. The grey sky glowed with a melancholy light that cast faint ghostly shadows in the angles of everything and revealed in quasi-monochrome the crumbling buildings of this once-proud city – not an apocalyptic scene of devastation, but instead a rather sad sight showing that all the world's human caretakers were gone, and now their great metropolis was tumbling into neglect. The only smell, and that a faint one, was of dust. Even the river had lost its sour odour.

"Come," said Sool.

He led us across the deserted bridge and took us to where the road curved right and down towards the Monument, the echoes of his footfalls ringing flat in the dead air, as though the materials of the buildings around us were refusing to reflect the sound properly, keen perhaps to preserve the swollen silence.

"How far do we have to walk?" I called to the little man. "I'm pretty out of shape!"

I heard Jen humph. "When were you *in* shape?"

Bitch.

I caught up with Sool at the entrance to Monument Tube Station. "You can't be serious."

He aimed his dispassionate grey eyes at me.

"Sool, how far in the future are we?" I asked, knowing I didn't want to hear the answer.

He turned away from me, studied the forbidding, unlit lobby of the station. "This is a meaningless question. There is no more time. All laws have fallen into chaos."

"You can't be serious. That's not an answer."

Still not looking at me, he gave a small grimace. "The laws you cling to are no longer enforced. Physical, what is this? The air around is, because I have made it so. But for me, air becomes vacuum, stone becomes water; no stability for the merged realm. Hence Time is gone too."

He stepped into the abandoned, rubbish-strewn ticket hall.

I hesitated.

I was fairly certain I wasn't going to like whatever it was that he planned to show me, but as my companions edged closer I knew I had to at least *look* like I knew what I was doing. No way was Jen going to rub my nose in any more shit today.

"Come on," I muttered to them.

"In *there?*" Jen cried in protest.

I looked at her earnestly. "You can wait for us here if you're too scared, babe."

Oh, that felt sooo fucking good.

We followed Sool through the dirty ticket hall and to the automated ticket barriers. Sool pushed the turnstile pads apart with his hands, invoking a dry metallic groaning, after which we all filed through into an increasing darkness that obscured the escalators down into the tunnels.

I'd used this station back in my old life, so I had a vague idea where to step, but it was so utterly dark and stank so violently of dead rats that fear blurred my focus. I stumbled on something on the filthy floor but chose not to look, aware of my thudding heart and a vague acrid taste in my mouth.

My foot flew into space as I reached the escalator and I grabbed the rubber rail, sliding my hand down it as I stepped down onto the steep, solid, immobile steps.

It was too dark, oppressive, I couldn't see and the prospect of walking into spider webs or tripping on a dead commuter made my already-pounding heart fight to escape through my ribs.

"Any chance you can magic up some light for us?"

My foot hit the bottom and I teetered, clinging to the handrail as I levelled myself, but either Sool had heard me or there was light coming from somewhere because I could dimly see, now. I saw a turn in the wall ahead and followed it round, avoiding touching the walls in case there was something awful on them.

We were on the platform. Dead, silent, faint light with no apparent source revealed the curved ceiling and a litter-strewn concrete floor.

The stench was worse here and more cloying, the faint musty smell of dust and long-since-mummified rats and spiders curdling with a sharp metallic odour.

A flash of light blinded me for a moment but resolved itself into the beam of a big rubber torch in Sool's small hand. The beam picked out a yellow-and-green information banner. District and Circle Line. All around us hung great swollen shrouds of spiderweb, many the size of my entire body, hung from walls and ceiling, swaying in the air we had disturbed and looking ready to flop gracefully down upon us.

Finally I had a reason to be glad that everything was extinct now; it was a fair bet that the spiders that'd spun those webs had been some big juicy-bodied sorts of bastards.

"Shi-i-it," said Jen, her left cheek touching my right, both her tits squashed against my arm.

I eased her off me and handed her to Tom, and watched as Sool's torch revealed a tube train sat sentinel before us, tucked in close to the platform edge, its doors wedged open forever, the doorways draped with great sweeping curtains of more filthy web.

Inside the nearest carriage, the torchlight picked out shadowy, immobile figures seated in silence in there, as though they had dozed off during their journey and never been awoken.

The corpses of Armageddon.

"Why…?" I whispered. I cleared my throat, drew only as much of the fetid air into me as I needed to use to compose myself and then spoke then at normal volume. "Why are we here?"

My voice did not echo, muffled as it was by the drapery of webs, yet it still sounded massively too loud.

"Here, the last of humankind," said Sool. "Fallen to the wasting disease, the 'Atrophy'. Survivors, you say?"

"Survivors?" I stared at the grubby windows, trying to make out any detail. "They don't look like they survived anything to me, Sool."

He extended his open hand toward the carriage, indicating that I should go in. I looked from the hand to his face, sure he wasn't serious, but he held out the torch to me and gestured again.

I didn't want to. I really didn't.

I stared at the carriage, my dry mouth suddenly full of too much spit. "Why do I have to go in there? I can see what's in there, Sool; dead people."

He simply gestured again.

Tom touched my arm. "Just do it, Laur, it's not like they can hurt you, is it?"

Fuck. Sool had brought us here, it was up to him when and if we would ever leave, and he clearly had a point to make. I drew a huge breath that actually *tasted* of metal and piss and then, grabbing the rubber torch I took a hesitant step toward the carriage, then another and then ducked under the spiderweb curtains into the carriage, aiming the torch around in case of… anything.

I gulped more stale air into my lungs and looked around. There were bodies propped on many of the seats, slumped back against the carriage windows behind them, a few lain on the floor, curled up in a foetal end-of-life position, but all skeletal, their nude white skulls grinning sightlessly out into eternity.

"Who's there?"

"No," I murmured. "Ohh, no, no, no."

It had been a weak, hollow voice, trickling through my mind, trailing tendrils of its disease into my head – just the way the voices at the hospice had.

"Is someone there?" Another voice. I felt its decayed presence like a rotten trail across my consciousness.

"Please, please help us…"

So these were what Sool had meant by 'survivors'.

Mixed in with the voices, there was a hum, or buzz, that I had not noticed at the hospice. I couldn't tell what this extra noise in my mind might be.

"Help us, please…" "Hello?"

"Please! Help us…" "Can you help me, I can't move?" "Please?"

I swallowed a coarse fat wad of spit as more and more voices began to pile into my mind.

I lost count; ten, twenty, a hundred, every trapped mind on a packed commuter train at the end of the universe.

The voices poured into me as they'd done before, but that noise got stronger, too, and suddenly it made sense what I was hearing.

I groaned with a deeper misery than I would once have believed I could ever experience. These relics were far older than those I had encountered at the Relics' Hospice in the emr, had endured what might be decades, perhaps centuries of timeless isolation in helpless, immobile darkness. That buzzing noise was the babbling insanity of those driven mad by eternal nothingness, sealed into silent darkness without the hope even of death to free them.

I was hearing countless mindless minds humming nothing coherent as they waited out an oblivion that was never going to come. Whatever this atrophy was that had destroyed them, it had stopped when time itself came to an end.

"I can't," I said, foamy spit peppering my bottom lip. "I can't help you, I'm so, so sorry."

These insane wretches had once been mums and dads and daughters, now reduced to a dumb hum heard only by the mind of this pointless woman, me; their non-saviour, who had no power to help them whatsoever.

No power at all. Unless I could stop my brother back in the day, back when it counted; back when my gifts might have made a difference.

The voices swelled, calling to me, unable or unwilling to hear that I couldn't help them, whilst all the time the murmuring hum of the utterly ruined played a constant background to their plaintive cried.

"Please, stop!" I cried out, placing my hands, pointlessly and stupidly, over ears that were not *hearing* anything. "You're hurting me! I can't help you!"

I didn't know I had staggered until my back hit the floor-to-ceiling rail that marked the middle of the carriage and I realised that I had backed up the wrong way, adding distance back to the door and the relative safety of the platform. Disorientated, my thoughts jumbled in the mix of theirs, I was vaguely aware that I dropped the torch but it didn't matter because my eyes no longer saw anything that my brain could focus on.

The chaos in my head was shutting me down and there was no-one to save me from it.

"Focus your mind, Laura"

Sni Sool's voice wafted into my head like fresh air into a stale room and blew through the webby fat of the insane voices. It was distant and yet it was intimate, touching a deeper part of my mind than the relics could reach.

"You can control this"

"You must"

"Trust yourself..."

"Adapt to it…"

I strained to focus my eyes, to see through them into the absolute darkness instead of being pulled inward by the cries of the relics. I felt a nagging ache inside my eyeballs as they squeezed outward in a bid to see.

The voices faded back into the background hum and I began to regain a sense of the single layer of my self. I was doing it, stood still but fighting a full-blown war inside myself.

I fought to push the voices out and they swelled in response, increasing in their desperation to avoid abandonment once more to their oblivion.

I whimpered quietly to myself as I fought to focus my mind again. Suddenly, shockingly, the organ in my mind pulsed painfully against the base of my skull and my head filled with light.

Alarmed, I opened my eyes.

All I could see was blinding light. Nothing else. Overwhelming absolute luminescence every bit as all-pervading as the voices had been.

With a cry of uncomprehending fear, I threw a hand across my eyes. Blinding light and searing heat erupted before me, and the entire world exploded in my face.

-27-

Wrenched free of my dressing of meat and bone, emptied from my capsule of matter, I drifted formless without knowledge of the passing of time, unbound and free of any meaning or purpose.

But this had happened to me once before and I was prepared this time. I had been disrobed of my flesh once, seemingly a lifetime ago, and been drawn into Sam as he brutally murdered Susan Blake. That very visceral memory was part of my mind now; it helped me understand what I was experiencing, helped me grab control so that even though I was still far from my body, I was at least Laura Keeble in mind, at least.

I forced myself to focus on my physical 'where'.

It was a shabby room in which a bottle of whisky and a chipped, dumpy glass sat atop a cheap little chipwood table, beside a lumpy and damp-looking bed. Across the room, a gleaming new TV perched atop a rickety-looking low flat table surrounded by dusty piles of magazines, while a tangle of black cables crawled out in multiple directions like some steampunk tarantula to connect a decoder box and a games console.

There was one cheap veneered front door in and out of this scummy, depressing bedsit and it flew open brutally as if all it had been waiting for was me.

The distant noisy throng of drinkers and druggers partying swept in behind the lone figure as he slammed his door behind himself.

It was my brother, Peter. Well, now he saw himself as 'Alan', of course.

This was his life? I felt a momentary pang of sadness that this was all he had come to.

He screwed up his face as he twisted the lock into place, and I could feel disgust seeping from him as he momentarily considered those worthless people outside, forced to eke out their existence trapped in this ghastly world of the mundane and the pointless.

So, no. This was *not* his life. This was the thin facade of the man he had to be to live in my reality, in the universe of matter. He had his own Realms, whatever the cost for the rest of us, and was not bound to the dull trudge of life in the Matter realm.

His arrogance was palpable, yet I sort of got it. I was just beginning to understand for myself how much more I was than... everyone else.

He stepped toward the bed, unbuttoning his shirt, and stripped to his under-shorts before sitting on the edge of the bed.

His belly sagged over the pinching waistband of his shorts as he reached for the crusty glass tumbler on his bedside table. He grabbed the whisky bottle and spun the top off with an accustomed dexterity, dumped a shot of whisky into the glass and threw it into his throat with nonchalant skill.

He seemed so pathetic. Was this really the man who had engineered the massacre on the village green, had killed my parents, twice?

Re-filling the glass, he propped the bottle on the little table and eased himself backward into a reclined position on the bed, holding the sloshing whisky by the rim while his spare hand pulled up a pillow against which to prop his head.

His wavering gaze suddenly locked sharply onto *me*.

Incapable of feeling shock because I had no adrenaline, I was nonetheless aware of a reaction within me that might be called alarm, but he couldn't see me because there was nothing to see. His eyes were focused on the wall behind my point of view.

I tried to adjust my perspective, struggling because I had no physical parts to move, neither head nor eyes, but I succeeded with some difficulty and saw a long crack in the plaster of the wall 'behind' me, where a filthy old web hung bundled in the upper corner by the ceiling.

A fat, mottled black spider crouched in its vile trap of stickiness and dust. If I'd had skin it would've pimpled at the sight of that thing.

I felt power come out of Alan as a ripple passed 'through' me that was like nothing one could feel as a physical being, but it was somewhere between orgasmic and agonising in its intensity. The target of this power was not the spider, which Alan ignored in his characteristically non-Matter-sensitive way, but rather the greying plaster beneath.

As power hit the wall, the plaster and possibly the structure beneath began to ripple.

I had no potency, no influence on these events. I was a witness, not a participant nor even a bystander who might voice an opinion. I had a horrible sense of understanding, could feel the focus of his will, drawing minds that he had no right to touch into cohesion, assembling them from what he had stolen from their dying selves.

Faint outlines appeared on the wall and as Alan drove the force of his will against it, they swelled and began to bulge, the paint and plaster filling out to resolve into two faces, puckered way from the wall and made of its material.

I heard Alan pant with effort as the shapes swelled within the plaster, pulled away from the wall, became painfully three-dimensional – faces only, yet animate and real.

Having no flesh failed to entirely spare me from the painful pang of misery those faces inspired.

"Hallo, Mumma and Dadda," Alan greeted these monstrous animations breezily, swinging the whisky tumbler between thumb and forefinger.

The faces seemed to stretch and swell some more, fully formed yet only raised a few inches from the wall. They twisted in place, unable to break free, eyes and expressions contorted by the pain of this savage rebirth.

The stringy pale emulsion mouths peeled open and I glimpsed teeth, but then the deafening screams of my parents erupted sickeningly loud in the confined space of Alan's bedsit.

"*Enough!*" Alan roared, lurching and slopping whisky onto his narrow chest.

The forms jerked in response. I was unsure but possibly there was an extra push of mindforce in that command. Whatever the reason, the two emulsion faces fell silent.

My mother moaned softly.

"So," said Alan. "Here we are again."

He paused to catch a quick draught of whisky in his mouth and then slammed his glass down on the table.

He glared fiercely at Mother and Father with cold grey eyes. "Pay attention! I need information."

Father's emulsion eyelids opened, his glistening brown eyes far too real for the false face that held them captive. He peered out at his son from paint and the emulsion lips formed a grim half-smile. "You want to know about your sister, don't you, Peter?"

"Don't call me that. And, yes."

Father closed his eyes again, the faint smile still present. "You've killed us twice too often, little man. Do you really think we will help you hurt Laura?"

Alan smiled coldly. "I have the power here, *Daddy*. You'll do as I fucking say unless you want your bitch wife's screams to be the last thing you ever here."

Father's face was hard, but it was my Mother who spoke, opening her soft grey eyes for the first time. "Why do you enjoy hurting us, Peter?" she whispered. "You must know we love you."

Alan held the old bag's gaze.

Ouch. His thought, not mine. I had only love for her.

"You loved me, did you? Is that why you forced me to destroy my own family, to save myself from what you'd found out?"

"Peter, no, we would never–"

"Her powers," Alan said emphatically. "Tell me what I need to know and then you can go back to whatever place it is that nasty, hateful *cunts* go to when they die."

Her emulsion lips worked as she struggled to reply. "We... loved you, Peter. Gave you... everything... we had to give."

A thin drool of liquid emulsion paint escaped from the corner of her mouth. I could not feel mindforce but was sure he was doing something to Mother, to hurt her.

"Fucking *liar!*" Alan screamed, his face blooming into crimson. "I know Granny met you that day, you were all conspiring and I was just a little boy! Just a little..."

His voice caught, his eyes were wet.

He drew a breath, pursed his lips. Composed himself. "You and Granny planned to give me up to the sentinels. Those fuckers have haunted me ever since, that bastard Sool's been two steps behind me my whole fucking life." He aimed moist eyes at them, his glare harder, more earnest. "I've taken a few of them down over the years though. They ain't gonna put me under their fucking microscopes!"

He lowered his gaze, whilst Mother remained silent, her torture suspended momentarily, her cool grey eyes levelled on her son.

He looked up and smiled. "It was Grandpa Jack tipped me the wink. Didn't know that, did ya? He knew what you cunts were planning, he knew what was coming, you fucks, he made sure I was ready–"

"No, Peter," said Mother, softly. "You've got it all wrong. It was a family day out, that's all. We hadn't decided anything about you."

"Liar. That was going to be the day. Meet up with Granny, get her to call those bastard sentinels down on me."

"Is that really what you think?" She stared down at him from her prison wall. "I suppose you convinced yourself. That's why you..."

"Murdered us," Father finished for her.

"I had no choice after what Grandpa Jack told me. I did what I had to do."

Father's familiar rich laugh rang out. "Did you hear that, darling? Our little boy did what he *had* to do."

Alan's eyes were red and welling up with tears again. He stopped speaking for a moment, holding a hand up to let the facsimiles know he intended to continue.

"I had no-one." He swallowed hard. "From that day, I was alone in the world. I had no-one, you fuckers!"

"You killed your family," said Father, his voice colder than I had ever heard it. "You didn't deserve anyone."

"Why did you believe Granny? Why couldn't you have trusted me? I was your little *boy!*"

Slowly, a cold and ghastly smile peeled back his lips.

"You betrayed me, *Daddy.*"

I felt power erupt from Alan and pour through the place where my non-presence hung, hitting the patch of paint where Father's face protruded. As his face twisted under the onslaught I heard an almost inhuman howl of pain, saw eyeballs bulging out of the stretched emulsion sockets.

"Tell me what I need to know!"

Paint flecks showered the carpet beneath Father's effigy and his cries of pain grew more shrill and intense.

"Tell me!"

"Ronny!" Mother cried in anguish, her faceform twisted by her attempts to look at her husband. "Ronny, no! Peter! Stop it, please! Stop, just stop, we don't know, we never knew! Your grandmother has the gift, not us!"

The mindforce reduced, the distortion of that face lessened.

"Of course," Alan murmured. "Granny. I knew she had power, too; that's what brought them together!"

Father's eyes flitted toward his wife. "Darling, no!"

"It's alright, Ronny, he'd never dare pull her back from the dead, she'd fry him alive."

Alan smiled broadly. "You stupid old cunt, mother. Granny's not dead; she's still with us. Who d'you s'pose looked after poor little Laura, shielded her so I wouldn't find her after you two losers got your logins revoked? But Granny's sick and old, now; trapped in a senile mind. The fight to block me out took the last of her wits." He laughed. "She'll be easy now. This is gonna be fun!"

"Peter, please don't!" Mother cried desperately. "You're not a bad person, you were always a good boy!"

His eyes were glazed; he was already planning his journey. "I need to see what I can pick out of that witless old bitch's head. If nothing else, I'll enjoy paying her back for her fucking treachery."

"Peter!"

He leant forward, his belly squishing with the effort. "Well, it was lovely catching up, Mumma and Dadda, but I have what I need now."

"Peter, she's just an old woman, she can't hurt you now!"

That cold smile returned. He waved his hand and their faces crumpled instantly back into the wall. The paint and plaster oozed smoothly back into place so that there was no sign they had ever protruded from the plain flat wall.

Alan picked up his whisky glass and studied the last of the golden-brown liquid within. "I wish…"

He gulped the last of his whisky and slammed down the glass. "Nah, fuck it."

He clambered off the bed.

I felt the heat first. Having not realised that I was in the dark, I was surprised as light swelled into being around me, and as it did, I smelled the sweet and slightly scorched smell of milk warming in a saucepan.

Grandma poured the hot milk from her saucepan into a mug. The hand with which she picked up the mug trembled. She waited until she could steady it, and then set off for the stairs.

I was in the house I had shared with her.

She climbed the stairs. I drifted behind her, unsure if I had chosen to be here or had simply been pulled along in Alan's wake – although if that was the case, he was already here waiting for her.

Her shaky hand set the milk down on a small table beside her bed She straightened up, sighed, then went down the landing to Laura's room.

My room.

My thoughts and hers were entwined.

Her granddaughter's teddybear peered up at her from the floor. Grandma smiled. *Laura had loved that stupid worn-out thing ever since she was a tiny little dot.*

I had no smile of my own but I had empathy toward the sentiment. His name was Basil.

She bent down slowly and picked up the teddybear, before easing herself down on the edge of the bed.

"Dear, dear, Laura," she said, her voice a husky whisper, burdened by the toll of the long years as my unthanked protector.

Grandma! I failed to call, *Grandma, he's coming, you have to get out of here*

She looked straight at me. At where I was.

"I know, dear," she said simply.

Whoa. You can hear me?

Seated there on my yellow roses eiderdown, she sighed. "It was always so hard after Jack…." She paused. "I know you weren't fond of him, dear. After the war, after what he saw, what he had to do, he was always a deeply troubled man, but I wish you could have known him as I knew him, the gently kindness within him."

She glanced down at my bear and then returned her gaze to me. "It was the gift that brought us together, y'know," said Grandma, her pale eyes clearer than I could ever recall them being. "Your granddad showed me things I would never have seen, took me places I could never have gone to. We lived whole lifetimes in the blink of an eye."

She seemed so alive, her stare intense and a deep-seated intelligence behind it that had been missing for many, many years.

Since roughly when my brother would have been reaching puberty, I suddenly realised.

Her eyes, sharply alert, contrasted with the wistful smile playing at her lips as she kept her gaze fixed on the place where I existed. "The family never accepted us, of course. Never *forgave* us, as if we needed that from any of them. Silly. It's not as if we were brother and sister, after all. No-one bats an eyelid these days, but back then… oh. I've never forgotten the day I went to see my mother."

I hated the sadness in her voice.

She picked at a thread on the teddybear, my teddybear. "I'm sorry I couldn't be there in body for you, Laura dear," she said, "but I had to put everything into shielding you from your brother."

He's coming, Grandma, you have to get out of here

"Don't worry, dear, I won't be here when he arrives."

I was startled by her sudden movement as clambered painfully to her feet, but I followed as she shuffled back to her dark dusty room.

Grandma lay down on top of her bed and folded her hands under her tired breasts. "You should leave now, child. If I can sense your mind essence, he might, too."

Actually, he can't. Guess he's not as strong as he likes to think

She glanced at me. "Be careful you don't underestimate him."

I wanted to speak, wanted to tell her how much I loved her, but the sentiment was too elusive.

Grandma smiled softly. "Don't try to trap emotions, you've barely learned how to move or turn in mindform. You don't need words, child."

It's hard to mean it properly, but I do love you

"Oh, I love you, too, dear. No sadness, now, I know what I'm doing and it's my choice. You're a good, sweet girl and it has been my privilege to be your guardian in this world. My only regret is that I won't be there to shield you any more, but at least he isn't going to get any help from me."

There must be another way

She pursed her lips. "Nope. Be strong, now, Laura, and learn all you can. You need to understand what the emr is, why it's there. The battle you face isn't the one you think. Now, I have to do this before he reaches me. Goodbye, my sweet child."

Grandma's last mug of milk steamed silently away to itself, ignored by the woman who had made it.

She closed her eyes.

"Oh, I hope you're waiting for me, Jack."

Grandma...

I felt a swell of power in the room and then it was gone, sucking out Grandma with it and leaving her sudden, utter absence shockingly behind. I looked at the body that had grown old around her as she guarded me with her last ounce of will and saw its chest drop as its last, deep breath fled it.

All I had left of her was this corpse.

The sound of the doorbell downstairs was quickly followed by a crunch and tinkle as Alan broke in. I knew it was him, could feel him.

"Granny!" I heard him call cheerfully. "Oh, Granny! It's your little grandson, Petesy-baby! Come here 'n' give us a kiss! Come on, now! No hiding!"

There was the sound of his thudding and puffing up the stairs. "Come *out*, you senile old bitch, I know you're here!"

I heard the echoey drip-drip of the bathroom tap in a moment of silence. I'd been meaning to get that fixed, way back when I'd been just a career woman with few friends and fewer problems. One of those little jobs I'd promised Grandma... ouch.

Then, Alan burst into the bedroom. "Hello Granny. I've missed you sooo much. How *have* you been, you old...? Granny?"

He edged closer to the still figure on the bed, cautious of a surprise attack, I suppose; he was probably worried how much power she might still have.

"Oh, yeah," he was rambling as he edged forward, gaze watchful. "I've really missed you. Like a dog misses its shit."

I felt power surge in the room as he reached out cautious, probing tendrils.

"Oh, no. No way." He slumped down onto the edge of the bed beside her, hands in his lap. "I'm, er kind of impressed," he said, and laughed, his hand absently stroking Grandma's dry, papery cheek. "You gave up the last dry dregs of your tiny, worthless, wasted little life to protect little Laura."

He sighed. "Must be nice to be loved like that."

He moved so fast.

"Bitch!" A sharp crack.

"Fucking *bitch!*"

It took me a moment to comprehend what I was seeing, by which time it was far too late to ever un-see it.

Hot blood turning his face almost purple, he grabbed her left hand and twisted it viciously, cracking the wrist bone with a dry snap. He had snapped her right in that first explosive instant of rage.

Like a tiger mad with bloodlust he pounced onto the bed and straddled the body. He punched down once, twice, three times into the face beneath him and the nose crunched and folded, the false teeth sank back into the mouth as the jawbone creaked horribly and then, finally, Grandma's cheekbone folded inward under the onslaught.

There was blood, but it didn't flow from her. There was no pressure behind it.

He screamed abuse as he beat the defenceless body, blamed it for forcing his hand, leaving him with no choice but to kill me since he had no idea how developed my powers were – while Grandma's nightshirt rode up, her baggy white knickers slipped and then worked down her legs as he thudded into her again, again and again.

Finally, he clambered off the bed, panting for breath as he staggered out of the room, his eyes welling up with tears.

"Fuck!" he screamed. "Fuck, fuck, fuck!"

He stood panting for a few seconds. Then he snatched a large gulp of air and charged headlong at the head of the stairs, where he threw himself to his death, flying headlong into the floral-wallpapered abyss, body rushing down at the hallway floor below, stairs flying past beneath him and gaining on him, ready to toss and twist his remains.

He transferred.

Air wrenched inward behind him as he cut from the matter realm into the emr – unable to hold on to anything, I was sucked through the terrible maelstrom of light with him.

-28-

We stood (he stood, I hovered) in the desolate silence of a deserted country lane, where darkness clung between the silvery spatterings of moonlight poured through the trees all around.

Alan thrust his hands into his trouser pockets, gazed around studying the plump trees, kicked his foot against the tarmac beneath him and then peered up at the murky indigo sky above.

"Well, well, well," he said. "Quite an achievement for a bunch of no-brainers." A thin smile played across his lips. "Didn't fucking save any of you, though, did it?"

He had never been here before, had elected instead to send his minion to do his dirty work.

Yeah, look how that worked out for Sam. If you want him back, he's in a gooey pile in the relics' home

He set off into the night-time lane, unafraid, reaching the village green after a few minutes.

"Come here," he commanded.

A bulky, hunched figured lifted out of the charnel jumble of the green and stood, twisted and swaying, before giving a jerk and then lumber over toward Alan, its lopsided gait causing one arm to dangle close to the ground like an insanely creepy Quasimodo toy.

No way...

Sam had somehow survived the fight at the Relics' home. Did he not know the meaning of 'enough'?

Alan barked a sharp command at the creature. It either could or would not respond to him, lumbering closer with its thick heavy arms (one now ending in a pincer) swinging as though to build up for a big hit when it reached him.

"Sam!" he yelled, more sharply still, and just as I began to wonder if he might get torn into thin wet strips by his own monster, saving me the battle I had been promised, Sam heaved his bulk around and lumbered to a halt just short of his small yet impassive unafraid master.

He stood there, slightly shoulder-first, his one eye glaring at Alan. It was a tragically sickening sight – this once-magnificent man had been reduced by that last assault at the Relic's home to little more than a shell, his burst trunk emptied of its guts now, the split outer binding that had once contained his form now rent fully open to reveal the jumbled pot-pourri of his component parts.

A thin but very gory reddish drool oozed from the edge of his split mouth, and I saw Alan glance from that bloody spittle to the bodyparts that lay scattered across the green.

"Ohh, you didn't." Alan grimaced. "Ahh, Sam, that's disgusting, I raised you better than that!"

"Llyoooo," Sam slobbered through a ruined and twisted mouth, his jaw offset slightly to the left. "L-y-you did not help me, clloand me as-thyou once... did."

Bloody mucous pattered onto the muddy grass from his struggling mouth.

"Oh, you, you are utterly disgusting!" Alan cried. "You've been eating bodyparts off the green. They weren't even real people – ohh! Fuck me, Sam, I could take a liquid belch right on the spot, you filthy fucking bastard!"

"Llyou!" Sam snarled, his bulky off-centred form leering over Alan on uneven feet. "Llyou ha- habandoned me!· Can-cannot get full! Cannot, cannot get full! S-s-starving!"

"Idiot! You've got no stomach! The 'food' is just falling out onto the ground!"

"A- abandoned–"

"Enough!"

I felt Alan's will flex, felt it spill out of him to envelope the sad ruined creature that could do nothing but await its fate.

The heap of ruined meat stood and watched its master, teetering still.

My brother's expression altered, as if startled by something.

"What?" he asked his giant slave.

"Ylloooo... You..." Sam uttered, low and weak but forced out with determination as his single eye swivelled and his inhuman insectoid pincer gestured at the air. "You... made... me so."

Alan laughed but the sound seemed harsh, forced. "Are you... trying to resist me?"

"What... is this?" Sam gasped out, waving his sick alien pincer. "What... did... you... do... to me?"

Alan tried to look nonchalant, disinterested, but there was something alarmed, frightened, in the fluid glimmering of his eyes. There was another presence on the green with us, something weaker than either Alan or me but there nonetheless. A small mind, stirring from the slumber imposed when the Sam creature had been crafted - that day when whoever had owned the brain in Sam's head was pressed into slavery in this body.

"What... *am* I? What have you... done?"

Sam glared at Alan, but though his voice was the same the mind behind it was not. Fighting, resisting being pulled back into the harness of slavery despite the salvation from agony it must offer, this was the Sam who had, in a brief moment, peered through and shown us mercy in the shattered remains of Edward's house.

"I'll tell you what you are, Sam," Alan began, frowning in concentration as he fought to overwhelm this mind, this will, that had slept under his control for over two decades.

"I... am... *not* Sam!"

Alan's face hardened, his eyes narrowed. I'm pretty sure he farted, too.

"You are *mine*! I made you and you are *mine!*"

"Nlloo!" Sam howled, his already enfeebled body shuddering violently under the strain of resisting. "You stole me! Ugh, ugh! I was... never yours to take!"

Alan gritted his teeth with effort but his clenched-up mouth was formed into a grin. "You *died*, James! I found your mind, adrift in the emr! You're not you, James, you haven't existed in more than a century!"

"Liar!"

Alan emitted a shrill, maniacal laugh. "You fucking idiot! You really believed your puny mundane mind could match up to *me!*"

A huge mass of willpower crashed over Sam and that fledgeling mind collapsed into a fading glow as it was consumed.

The mind gone, the body remained. Sam swayed in front of Alan with loose red-streaked strings of phlegm still oozing from his twisted, gap-toothed mouth, silenced and stripped of any defence.

The ragged body and burnt face all pulled taut as Alan's mindforce gripped tighter.

"Dear, dear, dear," Alan sighed. "This won't do at all."

A wet ripping sound within the hollow body cavity was followed by a mewl of pain from the monster's ruined throat. A dull glow bathed the torn form and I saw a picture begin to form within, overlaying the ruin and pouring onto it. A pinkish gauze formed across Sam's tangled flesh and carapace and wove into and onto it, filling until a thick blanket of human-like flesh and sinew began to bind the carcass back together.

As he worked, I sensed a very odd emotion from Alan; nostalgia. I suppose he was recalling fondly the day he had first fashioned this façade, this surrogate body through which he could conduct all his evil little deeds. I wondered how many had suffered at those hands now re-forming in the birth-glow, how many had been violated, watched dispassionately by the new eye bubbling into existence in that empty socket, glutinous juice congealing and blistering, forming into a solid orb with a milky surface that cleared and resolved to a piercing blue eye once again.

With a wistful smile, Alan ceased for a moment. His mind quiesced as the human cloak of Sam fell into place complete and the broad, strong naked man stretched, shrugged his shoulders back and forth, lowered his hand to cup his heavy testicles and stroke his thick dangling penis, a contented smile on his newly-resolved face.

Flesh had been a minute's work. Clothes took but a few seconds. Alan chose smart jeans, trainers and a loose white long-sleeve shirt.

Alan appraised Sam before he spoke. "You know what to do."

"And the sibling?"

Sam's voice once again possessed that deep, rich timbre I remembered from our first meeting.

Alan shrugged. "I tried my best, Sam, but she's made her bed, now. She joins her friends on the death train. Get it done."

"And the protected one?"

He shook his head. "Not sure if we can make that work. I'll honour my promise if I can, but don't let it stay your hand if you get a clear shot. I'd rather waste an asset than lose the war."

None of that made any sense to me. Alan had some scheme in motion. I made a mental note. That, and the fact that Alan's hold over Sam might not be as solid as he would like.

Sam nodded curtly and walked past Alan, out toward the lane, resuming his mission, while my brother sighed, jammed his hands into his trouser pockets and stepped up to a severed limb, which he gave a nonchalant kick.

With a quick, ironic glance at the sky his former victims had made from their will to survive, he transferred to the street outside his rented hovel in the Matter universe.

And of course, I was dragged along with him.

-29-

Alan stood quite still in the middle of the road, oblivious to the dangers of traffic, and stared at the street around him.

The world had been transformed in his brief absence and he was shocked. I was aware of a sensation in myself that might be called dismay.

"Shit," he said. "Where's the fucking summer gone?"

Hard cold rain threw sheets of liquid across the streets, the stripes of rolling fluid lit by blinding flashes of lightning that whipped white across reality every few seconds. Distantly, the rolling rumbles of thunder echoed one after the other from the vault of the sky, ebbing and flowing yet never actually pausing.

The rain had already soaked his clothes when a sudden brilliant white flash lit the vast gothic towers looming over the street; twisted, epic forms with turreted rooftops and arched windows that had no place here at all.

He stared at the insane, precarious, almost impossible architecture. "The fuck?"

I felt his mind flex just as my own sensed something approaching.

We turned as one, he in flesh and me in ether, my control improving now, as a lone figure shambled along the street toward him, gesturing clumsily but urgently. He squinted through the rain, frowning, trying to understand what he was seeing.

The figure looked wrong, misshapen. Not Sam-misshapen, but somehow every bit as alarming.

Alan turned and hurried toward the steps leading up to his building entrance, hand frantically fumbling for his keys, water trailing from his sodden fringe. Behind him, the shambling creature on the street had reached the steps.

"Ahh, shit," he said as he turned to face this new peril.

The lightning flashlit the creature.

She stood less than three feet away, two steps beneath him.

She was a woman, or had been before dry grey fungus had eaten away most of her face, her weeping eyes apparently the only feature untouched by the terrible wasting disease that had torn into her. Her left ear was missing completely, the crusty open sore in its place drooling rainwater contaminated with thin blood and pus, that mixture drooling onto her neck and shoulders. Her scalp was bald and flaky, though the rain was patchily soaking it and turning the fungus into a porridge-like paste on her head; this also wept down her ruined face and drooled onto her thin summer tee-shirt, under which one breast protruded pert and firm, the nipple crinkled by the chill, whilst the other side was notable both by an absence of any protrusion but also by a dark stain where her breast had once been.

But her face. The forehead and cheeks were overrun by fungus, as if it were rampant acne, and her nose was crumpled at the end and grey, where the fungus was eating it from the inside. Her top lip was fleshy and red, but her lower lip was a grey horror full of sores that were so big I could see a tooth behind at least one of them.

And she recognised Alan.

I heard her whisper his name, although whether she could actually speak, or whether the thought was so intense I picked it up, I couldn't say. Regardless, the word sounded like an accusation, although surely she could not know that the decline of her world, much less her own misery, had all been caused by my selfish idiot brother.

Filled with rage and disgust by the sight of this decomposing woman, he spat a glistening black mass of thought energy at her. The thought knot hit her even as she threw her hands over her head, its glistening blackness enrobing and then scolding her, peeling her remaining meat to leave only bones.

He turned to his door once again and then paused.

Turning, he snapped his fingers and grinned at her as she slumped helplessly to her knees, engulfed in scorching fluid and in her final convulsions of death agony. "Of course! Cheryl! How have you been?"

Chuckling, he returned to the building's outer door and let himself in as her body was stilled by death.

Once inside his mouldery room, Alan sloshed gleaming amber whisky into his glass and dropped onto the edge of his bed, sipping as he pointed the remote toward his TV.

The number '1' appeared for a moment in the corner of the screen, bobbing in an ocean of static. He thumbed the decoder remote.

- no satellite signal is being received -

Alan leant forward, the whisky sloshing in his glass. "What the fuck?"

He stabbed at a button.

- no satellite signal is being received -

"Not having that." He lunged for his mobile phone, left perched on his bedside cabinet when he'd set out to torture Grandma. "fucking cancel my subscription you bastards."

He keyed a number from memory and pressed the phone to his ear. After a few seconds he frowned.

He held the phone out in front of him as if mentally daring it to fail again. Re-tried.

"Cunt."

He tossed the phone and it clattered away across the floor as he clambered up off the bed and carried his whisky to the window, where he peered out at the raging storm.

I was beside him and saw what he saw. From his second-floor vantage point, lit by the searing flashes from the dark grey vault of the sky, the storm was raging relentlessly across the whole of London, but although it *was* still London, it was not the London he or I knew so well.

He swigged whisky, trying to seem nonchalant, but I noticed the mild tremor in the hand holding his glass. His facade of confidence was so ingrained he had to maintain it even for himself.

Many of London's eternal landmarks were gone now, lost forever to be replaced by gothic monstrosities whose lines were beyond the power of the mind to properly comprehend, reaching up into the sky with twisted metal fingers, their wrought angular structures defying gravity by refusing to collapse under their own weight. St Pauls cathedral was still... recognisable? It was a vast brown easter egg nestling in a cradle of gold spikes and spines, these twisting upward like the dying limbs of a massive gilt octopus.

Alan farted but I had the advantage of not possessing a nose. He slugged more whisky and scratched absently at his balls.

Where Canary Wharf had been defined by proud towers, I now saw three lesser towers linked by masonry ramparts, but this was a sane conversion compared to other, more organic-looking, fleshy constructions that glowed with a green internal light.

Even the streetlights were wrong, alien, too ornate.

Alan gulped most of the whisky and then returned to his bed to top up.

"Cunt!" he shrieked, startling me. "Fucking piece of shit! Didn't I tell him? Wasn't I clear?" His hand shook as he slammed down the whisky tumbler down on his bedside table and drew in a slow, ragged breath to calm himself.

"Whore-son!"

What...

He flopped back and lay on his bed for a moment, eyes closed.

I heard him draw a deep breath.

I realised his mind had opened, I could see that he had touched Sam, presumably to see what his slave was doing. Clearly, not what Alan had expected him to be doing.

His hand fumbled blindly on the table for his whisky bottle and as he grabbed it he pulled himself upright, angry gaze fixed on the wall ahead of him, spindly legs and bulging belly both hanging over the edge of the bed.

He spun the cap off the whisky bottle, still staring. I followed his gaze, as best I could, and found my attention settling onto that fat and greasy-looking spider dangling hideous and swollen in its filthy fly-littered tangle of web.

I suppressed a shudder

Alan chuckled. "Come to Daddy then, long legs."

The spider twitched once and then crawled out of its web, its limited free will quelled by Alan's vastly greater mind. It crept a short way down the wall.

"Run for me," he told it.

I saw a small thought knot form in the air before it, a ball of death, perhaps, but maybe some proxy, a remote control. I wasn't sure. The spider darted down the wall, spindly legs obeying his orders utterly blindly.

Then, the little eight-legger halted and waited, quivering slightly, perhaps indignant of this change to the order of things.

Fascinated, Alan climbed off the bed and crossed to where the spindly-legged black bulb crouched, filthy and vile, exposed now amid the expanse of his wall.

"Oh, yes." He reached out a finger to stroke the spider, but his hand shook as it approached the bulbous little body and he withdrew without touching. "An army of beasties like you would serve me so much better than that *cunt* Sam. What d'you say, shall we put that oversized piece of shit out to pasture?"

Suddenly, Alan's hand darted forward and his fingertips pressed to the fat bulb of the spider's body. He held the fingertips there for a few seconds. *Touching* it. His will, it seemed, was strong enough to overcome even an ingrained phobia, which was kind of bad news for me, in the wider scheme of things.

He left the spider squatting there, bereft of new instructions, and went to change for bed, drawing the curtains before climbing in, so that he could not see the flashes of the storm outside as he slept.

I don't know how long he slept, but while he slept, I knew and felt nothing; I was bound to him, had no idea how to find my way back to my meat. Perhaps this was all part of Sool's plan – or perhaps I had fucked up so badly that my body lay dead in that tube train where I had left it.

When he awoke, I was aware again.

He stretched and sat up. It was still night. Lightning lit the curtains every few seconds and from far away came the growls of the thunder.

There was a knock at the door. There must have been a previous knock. That was what had awoken him.

He clambered upright in his bed. "Piss off!" he muttered irritably, but not loudly because he was already kicking off the bed to answer – which he did, gracelessly, still in his underpants.

Outside stood a young couple, a boy and girl, barely out of their teens.

He seemed momentarily angry, but then he relented, waved an arm at them to invite them into his home, and then crossed to a small cupboard beside his bed, and rummaged within it.

They hovered in his doorway, uncertain.

"We're collecting for–" the boy began, stepping hesitantly into the bedsit, his trepidation tempered by the fact that this occupant hadn't slammed the door on him the moment he saw the charity pamphlet.

"Gimme a sec!" Alan called, his head in the cupboard. "Close the bloody door, will ye? Thez a terr'ble draft!"

Why was he putting on a weird accent?

The girl nudged her by forward a step and pressed the door shut behind her, uncomfortable inside this stranger's grotty bedsit but aware I suspected that in this decreasingly charitable world, a giver was a giver.

"That yer girlfriend?" Alan asked over his shoulder, hand still in his cupboard.

The boy frowned. "Are you giving tonight, sir, coz we have a lot of people–"

"No you don't."

The boy cleared his throat, growing very wary now. "If you're not giving, sir, we'll be on our way."

He was so young. Had I ever been that young and stupid?

Alan stood up and turned to them. He was empty-handed, his cupboard rummage exposed as a charade. "Good pussy?" he asked casually.

"W-what?"

He pointed at the girl. "Good pussy. I mean, she looks a good fuck but some of them, you get down on it and it's like a ripped-out fireplace."

Before the boy could react, the rush of Alan's mind power flooded the room, rippling even through my incorporeal self.

The two collapsed instantly to the floor as if they had been unplugged.

"Guess I'll never know," I heard Alan say. "I mean, I could find out if I wanted, it's not like she can say no, but I'm not that kind of guy."

He took his time, grabbed each body under the arms and staggered to drag them both to his bed. Once he had, puffing and wheezing, deposited them on his bed, side by side, he straightened them out and placed their hands on their bellies.

Their eyes darted from side to side, the only sign of their fear as they lay paralysed and expressionless.

"Well," he said, "you're not much, but you'll do for now." He straightened up, turned to the wall...

Oh, no, I thought.

... to the wall where sat the fat spider he had toyed with earlier. *A willing slave.*

The world around me rippled; or perhaps I rippled. I felt myself pulled, hard, as though there was somewhere I had to be, but as I was taken from that place, I glimpsed a few final flashes of things that were being done...

A blackish knot of matter forming in the still laps of the two on the bed, initially resembling a thought knot but gradually coalescing into something more tangible, a dark bulb about half-a-foot across that started to sprout spindly legs….

Two black creatures the size of smallish cats crawling on eight spindle legs along the bodies beneath them…

Two sets of inhuman black scissor-like jaws attached to two fat spiders the size of a human head with legs….

The crunch as those spider jaws snipped through the defenceless necks of their victims….

Two discarded human heads abandoned on Alan's mattress as he formed two outsize black-visored helmets and placed them over the arachnid pilots embedded into the neck stumps of their steeds, a customised probe at the base of each abdomen hooking them into the exposed spinal cord….

And, as I was wrenched away, a glimpse of my brother's hard jutting penis oozing semen through his boxers as his hells-angel biker-teen monsters clambered to their feet.

-30-

I think that perhaps what I had witnessed had been so far beyond anything I could cope with, that I'd managed to throw myself away from it and, through a power beneath my consciousness, find my way 'home' – back to my own body.

There was no sensation at all as I folded seamlessly back into my flesh and my solid sense organs resumed their provision of my view of the world.

"Shit, Laur, you OK?"

I saw through meat-and-liquid eyeballs the worry-creased face of Tom Peters. The sky behind him was the fierce, dense grey of wintry rainclouds but it still dazzled me as I used my eyes again for the first time in a little while. It was daytime.

Other sensations intruded. Cold; I was really cold, my skin icy and soaked, with my shoes pinching my toes and a bra-strap cutting in and pinching my skin just under my arms. The patter-tap-tap of raindrops bouncing off the cupped hands of leaves above met the pungent tang of wet soil in the air drawn up into my nostrils as my breath wheezed and flopped tightly.

We were back in the country lane. The village reality.

I lay cradled in Tom's arms with rain splashing onto my eyes, causing my eyelids to flicker. I pulled at his wiry, strong arms to lever myself up and he lifted, getting me to a sitting position and then up onto my feet.

"How did we get back here?" I asked.

"Laur," said Jen. She stood just behind Tom, hands on her hips but at least a slight frown of concern on her face, I flatter myself to claim, while her overall appearance was of sodden misery, her hair and clothes pulled downward by the weight of rainwater, the chill causing her chin to judder.

She crossed her arms over her chilled breasts and cast a wary gaze back down the lane. "Laur, we need to get outta here, Sam, he's out there, he's gonna be coming for us."

I frowned at her. I knew that Sam had been restored. How did she?

She gestured along the lane. "We need to go!"

I walked cautiously in the direction she had indicated, to the spot, if I wasn't mistaken, where the portal ought to be.

I reached the place but nothing happened. I had been sure. Pretty sure.

I glanced back at them. "No portal."

"What does that mean?" he asked, his eyes narrowed.

I shrugged. "Either I've remembered it wrong or it's not there any more, which means something major has changed here. We should head back to the village, at least we can find some cover."

"Are you mad?" Jen threw her arms outward. "That fuckin' madman burnt the whole village down!"

I smiled at her. "Not the pub, he didn't."

Tom jogged enthusiastically as we made our way along the lane, possibly awakened by the 'p'-word. I was more cautious, however, and as we reached the green, I made sure he didn't blunder into his own death for the sake of a pint.

We skirted around the edge of the broken-doll carnage of the green to reach the pub, staying close to the burnt-out shells of the houses to avoid being caught way out in the open.

Finally reaching his objective, Tom eased the creaky pub door slowly open.

I'd been in this place a few times with both Edward and Tom, but at the time I had been paying attention to the company, not the place. Now, stepping inside with wary attention, I found the small, low-ceilinged space to be heavy with deathly silence, a few faint creaks of aged wood beneath our feet, a pungent whiff of stale cigars acrid in my nostrils from a mushed, chewed brown butt propped cold on the edge of an ashtray on the gleaming, polished hardwood bar. No smoking ban in the afterlife.

It was weird: though eternally silent and dead, this place was wistfully reminiscent of the cosy little country pub, my 'local', where Tom and I had gone for our one and only proper date.

Across the wood-panelled bar, the heavy, glazed hand pumps of a bygone age of drinking glinted under the yellowed light cast by small shaded lamps above the hanging beermugs , those cleaned and gleaming glasses winked at us from their overhanging hooks.

It was warm in here. It was part of the illusion, an innate cosiness engineered into this place, yet the reality of it was welcome after the chilled rainfall outside.

Tom eased the stiff door shut and then ducked and huddled low to peer out of one of the pub windows, studying the green.

"Well?" I asked him. "Anything?"

Tom straightened up, tee-shirt drawing tight across his athletic torso. He pursed his lips and shook his head, pushing his dainty spectacles up onto the bridge of his nose. "Nothing. No sign of matey."

An urgent pain begged me to excuse myself to visit the toilets, but this too was a feature engineered into this place to make the world seem more real, so I suppressed the urge.

Tom pressed a hand to my arm. "You, too, eh? Every time!"

I smiled for the first time in a while in response to his warm, open grin. But his face fell as he glanced over my shoulder.

"What?" he demanded.

I turned to see Jen's eyes glinting as she glared. "You two done making nicey-nice?"

"Come of it, Jen!"

"You come off it, Peters! You think I don't see how you look at that podgy bitch?"

Ouch.

"I'm right here," I reminded her.

"Shut up!" She strode right up to Tom, got in his face, fists clenched, lips drawn back from her teeth. "You think y'can treat me like a cunt, Peters? You think I'd fucking *let* you? I was good enough when you wanted to empty your nuts, but now you think you can crawl back to homey-girl here? Nah! Just fucking no!"

'Homey-girl'. I closed my eyes and drew a breath as anger welled up in me. As if it wasn't enough of a humiliation that Jen had snatched him out from under me in the first place.

I placed a hand on Jen's shoulder. "Tone it down, Jen."

She shrugged my arm off, gaze still fixed on Tom. Suddenly, her shoulders and face relaxed. "You're right," she said, much more softly. She laid a hand on his shoulder. "Hey. We gotta stick together now."

When she glanced at me, it was not to bring me into the group but to flash me a look of triumph.

Had she actually just staged that scene to get her claws back into him? Was she really that smart?

Tom looped an arm around her neck and she lay her head on his chest.

When he hurled her roughly away from him, she was as shocked as I was. She staggered, staring, expression confused and wide-mouthed, but Tom was gone, hurling himself bodily at the bar where he threw up the hatch and flew headlong into the serving area beyond.

Jen's face was close to being a swollen purple plum of rage. "Peters, you fuckin–!"

A piercing cry rang out from behind the bar. Tom was out of sight. Something was happening. The voice was young, squealy but just discernibly male. "Get *off!* Get the fuck *off* of me!"

There was a solid thud, a crash and then the tinkle of shattering glass. Tom re-appeared, lumbering out of the service area dragging a teenage boy by his twisted arm, the boy stumbling and pulling back feebly but clearly no match for a fit, toned adult male.

"Look what I found," said Tom. He flicked his arm and sent the boy reeling forward toward us, where he crashed to his knees a foot from me.

He clambered back up to his feet and rounded on Tom, chin jutting in a display of aggression that I strongly suspected he would not turn into action against the bigger man.

He was scruffy and young, practically a teenager and dressed like a scarecrow in a crumpled, dirty casual shirt, grimy-looking grey trousers and trainers that had probably once been white but were now grey, the ends of the laces tattered where they had been ripped.

I frowned at him. "Who the fuck are you?"

There was a sheen of sweat on his brow and a lankness to his long dark hair that suggested prolonged and desperate effort. He was terrified, but I suspected not of us. He stared at me but gave no answer.

Jen edged a step closer to him. "Hi," she greeted him, her voice deeper, husky compared to her shrieking rage of a moment earlier. "I'm Jen."

He stared, still panting lightly with fear but, now, strongly distracted by the front of Jen's soaking wet summer top, where the broad strawberries of her nipples protruded atop her full, round breasts.

He glanced up at her face, realising that there was a person operating those tits. He stared silently for a second, glanced back down to make sure her tits were still there and then gawped at Jen's face.

Tom clipped a hand across the back of the boy's head, causing him to stagger forward a pace. "They won't answer you, boy!" he barked. "Now answer the lady! What's your name?"

"Bob- Bobby."

"Nice to know you, Bob-Bobby," Jen simpered.

She subtly arched her back, effectively thrusting out her breasts for Bobby's benefit – not subtly, but he was too young to need subtlety. Even a frump like me, with brains instead of slut miles, could see that this display was perfectly designed to plunge into this teenage boy's heart. Well, I say 'heart'.

Vomitacelli.

I needed to know what her angle was with this boy. Was she merely flexing her predatory sexuality or was there an angle, did she maybe know something I didn't?

"So," she said, gesturing at a little table before flopping lazily into a wingback snug chair, "do tell us how you've managed to survive here all this time."

Tom and I grabbed a short stool each to join her at the table, each of us keen to see where she was taking this – although, perhaps, for very different reasons.

The boy perched on a stool, too, hanging on her silence.

"Bobby?"

His gaze diverted from breasts-legs-breasts for a moment and he frowned at her. "What?"

"Sam's still out there, Bobby. It's really important for us to know what made you different, how you survived when everyone else died."

"Me? You survived, too."

"What happened to us was a fluke, it won't save us again. That's why we need to understand what *you* did that let you survive." She leant forward and laid a hand on his thigh. "You might be able to save our lives. We need you, Bobby."

So that was her game. This boy had survived Sam's original attack somehow. In Jen's mind he must have some trick, something he had thought of that we hadn't.

He shrugged. "I was lucky too, I s'pose," he murmured, lowering himself onto a third stool. "I was out in the woods that day, went out at first light. M'Dad an' me used to go, but he went to the Hospice last moon cycle and I s'pose I just wanted–"

"Bobby!" Jen cried, too sharply. She hastily modified her tone. "We need to know about what you did that helped you survive, sweetie."

She flashed him a beautiful smile and I knew he wanted to earn it.

"But I, I didn't do anything. When I came back everyone was dead… and that… that *thing* was in the lane… He'd killed all of them." he trailed off, his eyes glazing as he remembered. "He was leaving, so I kept down and waited 'til he'd gone."

"No," said Jen, her brow furrowing now, "you *must* have done something to hide from him."

Bobby shrugged. "He was leaving, didn't even glance my way – I think he was hunting someone else. I haven't seen him since, but I've been pretty fucking scared! I went out to hide in the woods but I kept thinking I could hear something out there so I came back here."

"You're safe now," I said automatically, realising instantly what a stupid thing it was to say. No he wasn't, not even a little bit. He was alive through sheer dumb luck and so were we.

Jen lightly touched the boy's knee. My gaze followed and I saw a little protrusion swell up at the front of his grimy grey trousers. I quickly looked away.

Tom drummed his fingers on the table. "We can't just sit around here, that mad fucker's bound to figure out to look here sooner or later."

Jen cocked an eyebrow at Tom and then returned her loving gaze to the boy. "Bobby," she crooned. "How well d'you know this place?"

He started to give his customary shrug of a response, but she reached out and grabbed his hand. "I need you, Bobby! You're the only one."

She rubbed his thigh, held his hand, looked into eyes that could only stare at her breasts. "I don't know this place, Bobby, and that thing out there does! Help me? Please?"

Tom kicked away from the table, sending his stool crashing to the floor, and threw up his arms in disgust before stomping away across the room. Whether he was angry that Bobby couldn't help us, or disgusted by Jen's little whore show, I couldn't tell.

She barely seemed to notice her supposed lover as she studied the boy. "Bobby?" She was hanging off her chair, her body in close proximity to his, her rubbing hand quite a way up his thigh.

Poor little bastard probably didn't have enough blood going to his brain to think any more.

"Is there somewhere we can go, Bobby, somewhere we can hide?"

"W-well," he began. "I don't know the place th-that well." The bulge in is trousers pushed out more and slid upward. I'd never seen a penis harden like that before, not all the way from soft to erect. It was kind of hypnotic.

I looked away with a discrete shake of the head.

Jen pulled away from him. "What d'you mean, you don't know the place?"

His mouth worked for a moment before any words came out. "Dad came here before me, I ain't been here all that long."

It made sense. The boy was grimy and sweaty, but there were no signs of decay nor even a greying of his skin. He was a newbie, possibly newer even than we ourselves were.

"Dad took me everywhere, I never really went outside the village except when he took me. He was worried I might get lost or go through one of the windows."

Windows? Did he mean portals, because if so, that suggested that there was more than one.

"I'm sorry," he muttered. "I didn't mean to disappoint you."

"Fuck *me!*" She clambered off her chair and stomped away, heading for the bar.

Tom had crossed to the window, which I barely took in until I noticed him jerk upright and hastily whirl to mutter a panicked remark to Jen. She stiffened visibly but then held a finger to her lips.

Sam had found us.

Jen returned to her chair, her chest rising and falling rapidly but her tone even when she perched and leant to speak to Bobby. "Bobby, I'm so sorry, I shouldn't be upset with you. Listen, in case we need it, is there another way out of here? Out of the pub?"

"Erm, yeah, there's a back door, it's the only place in the village that's got one."

"Lovely." Jen aimed a very pointed stare at me. "Laur, will you go with Tom and check it out, in case we need it?"

"Yeah, OK, what...?"

I shut up, got up and crossed the bar room to Tom. "Is he...?"

Tom nodded. "Across the green."

We started toward the back, passing through the hatchway in the bar and into the back room behind it, but I paused and glanced back.

Jen was all over Bobby, her face to his, her thigh sliding between his legs while his hands grabbed frantically at her breasts.

Just as I was about to turn away, I saw he leg jerk up hard. Bobby emitted a shrill cry and hunched over.

Jen spun on her heel and ran at me. "Go!"

I knew what this meant. Bobby was stunned by the shock and pain of being kneed in his testicles, hunched over, hands pressed to his groin. Jen had found a use for the boy – as a distraction, a snack to leave out for Sam. With his bloodlust up, the giant would be unable to resist a victim standing right in his path.

I glanced once more at Bobby as he fell to his knees holding his balls, his eyes screwed shut, but then I willingly abandoned him to his fate and raced down the pub's back passageway after Jen.

It was cruel. Bobby was barely an adult and, thanks to us, he never would be, now – yet I also knew that he was already dead in the real world so I swallowed it as we reached the rear door and I heard Bobby's last desperate mewling cry of miserable protest behind us.

We burst through the door and out into a brick-walled yard in which I would have expected there to be beer barrels. If the pub had been a real pub in a real world.

I slowed, breathing hard, and saw a shabby wood gate cut into the brick wall before us. I gestured at it and Jen and I started off that way.

As we passed through the gate I heard a shrill scream emit from the pub. I could imagine that poor Bobby might just have managed to get to his feet in time to fall into Sam's merciless grasp.

We bolted down a narrow dirt pathway hemmed in by bushes as a rough ache in my lungs and a burning pain in my calf muscles warned me how badly I was running on empty.

The path opened onto the lane leading away from the village. I heard a long, high and horribly final-sounding scream, gurgling and hopeless, as we headed onto the lane. The scream cut off abruptly.

Bobby had done all he could, poor sap. We were back on borrowed time.

We fled up the lane, my breasts bouncing and slapping inside the tee-shirt and jumper I'd donned way back in Edward's attic bedroom, so that my nipples chafed horribly and added to my already bountiful woes.

The portal was gone, we needed another way out of the village reality.

"Wait," I puffed at Tom's back. "We need to—"

The sudden transfer was a bone-jarring shock. A flash of light and noise followed by a faint smell of cooking chicken and the pain of all my joints being stretched apart.

We stood in the Chadbury graveyard.

Again.

It was night, a faint silvery moon pouring through the skeletal fingertips of the treetops as a gentle breeze wafted lazily through the canopy.

Tom was looking for the lunar disc that ought to be above us. "Is this—?"

"No," I answered. "I don't think so."

"Hold on," said Tom. "How do you know? Last time, Sid Snail brought us back to our world."

I was sure. It was the first time I'd had such a feeling, but it came with such certainty that I barely questioned it.

"Trust me, this is still the emr. Something Bobby said about 'windows', I think there's more than one portal in each reality. Still, we shouldn't have ended up *here*. That grassland was the reality next to the village."

Jen grimaced. "Oh yeah, that fucking boat. I remember."

Tom pushed his spectacles up his nose. "You two wanna stand here nattering, or shall we run the fuck away before Frankenstein's less attractive brother catches up with us?"

He was right. We hurried toward the graveyard wall, but even as we reached it I heard a rushing sound behind us. Someone else had passed through the portal behind us.

I looked over my shoulder and stumbled over my own left foot as I gawped at our pursuer.

Sam had been repaired by his master and, now, his bulky muscular form thundered away from the portal, but even as he hastened to set those brutal hands to breaking bones and splitting flesh, I had to admire him. He really was a looker, despite what I knew about his construction.

We clambered frantically over the wall as heavy footfalls punched into the leaf-strewn earth of the boneyard behind us, fled up Tiler's Hill, which I quickly realised was a fucking stupid idea, fleeing uphill away from a stronger, faster pursuer.

"Tom!" I cried. "Tom!"

He slowed and turned back toward me.

I sagged in the middle, gasped for breath and gagged on something wet in my lungs. I gestured with an arm because my hand wasn't really working well enough to actually point.

"Th-*that* way!"

I caught sight of our hulking pursuer in the corner of my eye and straightened up with a gasp. Belly-gouging terror threatened to work with my fatigue to drive me to my knees but as that beautiful, ugly bastard lumbered ever close I felt a sudden surge of rage. Bastard had made my life a misery for so fucking long. No more!

I straightened up, ignoring a distant tearing pain in my lower belly. Glared downhill at Sam.

"Fuck you, Sam!"

"Laur?" said Tom.

I focussed, tried to channel all my rage and fear in his direction and felt a thrill of pleasure as power welled up at the back of my head and bathed my brain in warmth.

Sam was close now, mere feet away, he would be on us in a few seconds.

A ragged glistening black knot of thought energy formed before me and then flew at him, fast and lethal, aimed right at his head. He staggered to the right and hastily raised his orb, its energy field splitting my thought knot apart so that it sprayed harmlessly and failed to touch him.

He grinned and made a show of sauntering casually toward me, cock-sure of his victory, his newly perfect face smooth, handsome, yet full of carnal rage, his eyes metallic in the ghostly moonlight.

I had no time to re-group and fire a second burst and I felt a scold of adrenaline cut through my belly as I realised I'd stood still for too long and was far, far too close to his spiteful grasp.

"Sam, please…"

His eyes lit with joy and a genuine, white-toothed smile opened his face up as my begging words reached his ears. I remembered the tingling pleasure his body had rippled through into me when I'd last shared a kill through him, which turned me from cold-bellied terror to hot-faced humiliation and anger.

"Bastard!" I spat at him.

I raised a hand to smack him on the nose, give him a small bleed before he gave me a life-ending one, but we were interrupted as a female voice cried his name from across the road.

"Sam!"

We both looked, equally startled. I squinted and frowned. It was her; the woman from work, the one I'd watched him slaughter. The one I'd seen right here, I now realised, in a moment I had dismissed as a dream.

Susan Blake. Enraged and facing off against her murderer.

"Bastard!" she screamed at him, stealing my catchphrase, but as Sam's face split into an amused grin she must have realised how stupid she was being. I was hit by the breeze of his departure and then, with a shriek of panic and dread the woman fled down Tiler's Hill with the monster in pursuit.

Another sacrifice, another slice of escape time.

I hesitated.

Stupid time to grow a conscience, yet this would make two innocent lives sacrificed for me in the space of an hour. For all that I could tell myself they were already dead, that they were mere halflings, a part of me knew full well that all I was doing was justifying my own cowardice.

"Laura?" Jen called. "Laur, what are you – oh, no, don't be so fucking stupid!"

I turned toward the side road where Sam had pursued the screaming Susan Blake. It was quiet that way, now.

"Shit."

I humphed a breath, shot a shrug at Jen and Tom and then jogged across the road after Susan – aware of the insanity of being in pursuit of Sam, but certain this was a 'can you live with yourself' moment.

Hopefully I'd be too late and he'd be gone before I got there.

-31-

You know what; there's out of condition, there's pushing a cardiac and then there's me.

Never having been a gymnasium kind of girl, I already knew I was out of shape, but days and days, it seemed, of running and pushing and fighting, all told, had taken my poor soft squidgy body far beyond its limits.

I wrenched in a ragged breath which I cut short as I felt a sharp thin twang of pain over my heart, but driven by the need to *try* and save Susan I kept my scorched burning leg muscles pumping, while my feet pounded against the pavement of the false Tiler's Hill.

Rounding a corner, I flew headlong into a horribly familiar alleyway before my violently cramping legs could backpedal me to a halt.

I leant against the rough stone wall and puffed for air, feeling the cold jut of the uneven stones bedded into the rough concrete mix, while I bent and straightened my legs to ease the tightness of my so-called muscles.

This was the alleyway into which Sam had chased an old man and beaten him to death, treating me to a full-blown 3D experience of violence, bloodlust and intense shared agony. The sensations returned vivid and wet and I could taste tangy, sticky blood; feel the old man's broken pain.

I wanted to turn away, to run back to Tom, to avoid this. I'd been lying to myself. I wasn't up to this. Sam was so strong, so merciless and just too terrible to face. Maybe if he knew I'd let him have Susan he might be a little kinder towards me?

It was also, I was sure, the alleyway of many of the dreams that had dogged my old life.

Bordered by low stone walls on both sides and overlooked by the nude brown branches of eternally autumnal hedges, the alleyway was scantily lit by a few pools of light cast by weak street lamps and there was plenty of gloom for me to tremble at.

Back in the real world, a long time ago, that poor old man had been killed just a little way from where I stood now in this recreation of the same place. But not just *any* old man.

"Edward," I said softly.

I knew already that the old man I had seen Sam brutalize had been Edward, but the realisation hit me freshly raw in that moment, as if to provoke me deliberately. It worked. A rage tore through me at the recollection of that dear old man; of all that Sam had inflicted on him.

Driven now by a woken fury, I clenched my teeth and took a single step forward.

The place was made gloomy by the evergreen bushes that overhung the right-hand wall, causing a fracturing of the moonlight-glow from above that left a patch of deep shadow crouching by the base of the wall a few feet ahead of me – shadow that might harbour...

A scold of shock lanced my belly as a shrill, desperate howl of deep animal anguish split the air apart.

I gasped, my eyes welling with tears in instinctive sympathy with whatever had made that sound, my fingertips prickling, mouth dry and knees and bowels as loose as pebbles on a wet clifftop.

My rage now diluted with icy dread, it took every weeping drip of my courage to creep around the curve in the wall but as I reached it I lunged forward in a desperate act of courage spurred by my waning strength. My right knee cracked sharply in protest but my arse fell off when I took in the scene before me.

I Stopped. Stared. Gagged on a dry throat. My left knee tried to buckle beneath me.

Sam stood over Susan, who lay splay-legged on the ground. The dressing gown she had worn since arriving here was rucked up and I noticed with a stupid flash of envy that she had really nice legs, but this was an envy quickly wrenched away by the overwhelming horror of Sam, that sick, evil bastard, the front of his trousers distended as he held each of Susan's ankles, opening her legs.

I winced at the protracted, wet, crunching crack as Sam bore down and rotated his brutally strong arms, the biceps bulging so that Susan's legs twisted, crunched and thumped out of her hip sockets, wrenched free like juicy chicken legs. Her dressing gown fell completely away, exposing her naked body beneath. The skin on her hips stretched, split and then burst open in a crimson spurt, glistening white nude bone visible for a moment until the arterial gush drenched it before pouring in stripes down her inner thighs to smother the violently separated lips of her neatly trimmed vulva.

I gagged, my reflexes and my emotions shutting down in the face of a horror beyond understanding.

I squeezed my eyes shut.

Somehow her death seemed more awful than the deaths of the villagers, her homely dressing gown splayed around her violated corpse, her legs jutting out to the sides at an obscene angle, jagged shards of bone and ribbons of red meat hanging from her pelvis like a gory mockery of her brutally splayed vagina.

A small gout of deep dark fluid started to spurt in a narrow rhythmic jet from somewhere below her hip-bone, spattering the cool concrete pavement.

And then her eyes peeled lazily open, as if she were awakening from a deep, deep slumber. My mind rebelled at the horror of it, refused its truth.

She can't be alive like that

There was a long, protracted whine, but it didn't some from Susan and it didn't come from me.

Sam dropped to a crouch a few feet away, head cradled in his hands, his soft sobs pathetic in the silence.

I stared at him, kneeling in his incongruously clean and beautiful white shirt, looking suddenly very human-sized as he emitted soft sobs that were so... weak, so... broken?

Susan's head moved, her dull glazed eyes lost in unimaginable horrors.

"Pain," she murmured thickly. "Pain. No... more... pain."

Was a time when I would feign ignorance. Pretend I hadn't seen a beggar looking up at me in an appeal for help. Pretend that the starving millions were too far away and I couldn't help as I watched a charity appeal with a fat pizza on my lap.

Now, as I stared into those doomed, tormented eyes, I had nothing to hide behind. Her pain was beyond anything I could imagine as a great pool of her thick dark innerness wept free beneath her torn bottom.

There was no hope for her. Only release.

My eyes welled with tears but my mind served me and formed a thought knot in the air before me, the pulsing deep within my brain feeling familiar and mine, now.

There was a faint pop as the knot, fully formed, cut through the air at her and then a brief shrill cry from Susan, but then there was nothing but the last of the bubbling venom and the crisped black bones of Susan, steaming on the pathway.

The unbearably sweet cooked-bacon stink of her hit my nose.

I turned my fury on Sam, my mind organ fully aroused.

He sensed me and rolled back off his haunches to slump and sit on his backside on the pavement. His eyes were creased with pain. His mouth worked for a moment before any sound came out.

"Do it," he said thickly, his voice cracked and phlegmy.

I frowned, bewildered. I was sure he still had his orb.

"Not gonna fall for your shit, Sam."

The eyes that stared back at me were bloodshot and weepy. "He has abandoned me," he said weakly. "I have served my master as a slave without the will to question, let alone resist, but his power has left me. I am... *free*."

He said that last word with appalling disgust.

"That is just so sad." The sarcasm in my voice channelled a little of my rage, my hatred for this monster. The urge to kill him was stronger than any emotion I could ever recall feeling before.

He rubbed his temples. "They are in here with me, all of them. My master's final gift, to haunt me for the rest of this obscenity of a life."

I laughed. My gaze flitted to Susan's pile. "You have got to be fucking kidding me, Sam. You think that this bullshit is gonna save you?"

He rolled onto his knees and pulled himself up onto his feet, glaring defiantly at me as he straightened up. I fought the urge to back away.

He waited and I knew his defiant stare was a sham, an attempt to remind me of who, what he was. My mind organ pulsed. My hated enemy was at my mercy.

I controlled my power, held the thought knot back.

He shook his head. "No, Laura Keeble, you must not weaken now. You know what I am. The animal part of me is strong, mindless. If you let me live, I will weaken and it will take joy in a mindless rampage."

I held his gaze. "I don't doubt it."

His eyes were clearer, bluer and more beautiful, now. "Then kill me and be done with it."

I knew he was right. Even if not, he was still a vile and deadly monster that would never cease to be a threat to my, to my companions.

Except. Except...

Deep, deep down inside of me there was a scheming impassionate someone who knew that Sam was at a turning point. Killing him didn't hurt my brother, because he had his new henchmen now, in those awful spider-topped zombie things. Sam was powerful, deadly and lost. All he needed was a new master.

He must have seen something in my eyes, some doubt, because his eyes widened. "No, you *must* do this! You can't control the beast in me!"

He might have been a mere puppet before, but there was more than just animal behind that façade. Sam had been built around a real human mind. A mind that knew my brother far better than I did.

"No, Sam. You're going to start making up for what you've done."

He gaped at me. "Is this a joke?"

I shook my head once. "Your master made you kill for him. Now, you'll kill for me. You'll be on the right side in this war."

"What! No, Laura Keeble, no!"

"Sam, I've been fighting a losing battle and my shag-nasty so-called 'friends' are as much use as a condom in a convent. You, on the other hand, are a weapon I can use."

He glanced at the charred remains of Susan's broken corpse. "And if my master realises what you have done and seeks to control me one last time?"

"You're coming with me, Sam."

I turned and started back down the alleyway, averting my gaze from the corpse, sure he would follow but risking that he might pull his orb. Hell of a risk, but I had to be sure. I had a strong sense that I was right.

Still, my teeth started to chatter as I imagined I felt that orb aimed at my back, my legs quivering like the hind legs of a poodle taking a shit as I took my first few steps.

On my seventh painfully-counted step, Sam stepped up beside me.

"Thank you," I said, keeping my gaze firmly ahead.

"I have conditions," he said.

We reached Tiler's Hill, or the twisted mockery of it that dwelt in this realm, where it spiralled down in a dark grey tarmac ribbon toward the main town, which did not actually exist here.

I stared across the road to where the skeletal hands of the graveyard trees clawed at the bleak silvered sky. "I saw all of this end, Sam. If we don't stop your former master, my former brother, everything ends."

He humphed. "I would take some convincing before I could think that the loss of the emr would be a bad thing."

I looked up at him. "It's not just the emr. If the emr collapses, the whole of reality will unravel."

His eyes de-focused. "My time, my family, are long gone. Without my master I would have been dusty bones in a grave many years ago; and I *should* be. I want no part of your world."

I sighed, gazed down Tiler's Hill. "I remember."

He frowned at me and then pointed. "The exit from this pocket is that way. I presume that is where your friends have scurried away to."

We set off down the hill, heading back to the graveyard where no-one had ever been buried. A rumble of thunder rolled out from the horizon and startled me.

Sam halted for a moment and scanned the sky, a frown on his face. "That *is* curious," he said emotionlessly. "Thunder? Here?"

The ground beneath us jerked and seemed to roll as if the whole street were on a vast fairground ride. A wave of nausea was followed by a head-spinning throb of pain at my temples.

The pressure in my head wasn't from the storm because it was not a real storm. I pressed a hand to my temple and imagined what a glass of cold water would feel like as it sloshed around in my mouth.

Sam touched his forehead and winced. "Something is badly wrong here."

We hurried toward the graveyard but as we reached the low stone wall there was a brutal white-out flash of lightning that seemed to light the universe from one end to the other.

I staggered and jarred my right knee against the jagged cemented-in stones of the low graveyard wall but Sam grasped at my elbow. "We must move," he asserted.

As my vision cleared I stared in disbelief at the shocking vista before me.

"Fuck me," I murmured softly. "Right up the arse."

The treetops of the graveyard had become hard to focus upon, because their once-dense, solid forms were becoming... diluted.

It was not just the trees, I realised as I looked around. Everything was losing cohesion, becoming washed-out. The whites, greys and creams of the tombstones were as translucent as milk being washed off a glass, now, the trees around them now fading to nothing like erased pencil art to expose a distant horizon that was more a smear than a clear line as the moon-glow faded from the sky.

Sam clenched my arm painfully tight. "We must leave *now!*"

I wondered if my companions were still in this reality, but it was more important that I survive. They were dead anyway, whereas I had a war to fight.

I glanced one last time at Tiler's Hill, where the houses now succumbed to the explosive decomposition that was accelerating rapidly here, and then Sam and I clambered hastily over the graveyard wall and hurried between the pale melting ghosts of the gravestones until we fell against the portal and with a violent flash of cascading lights I shot out of the dying reality behind me and felt the solidity of a new world push up against my feet.

We were back on the country lane outside the village reality. It was night, eerie with moonlight from a non-existent moon and from utter, unending silence.

"Oh," I said.

Sam turned to me, an eyebrow raised in inquiry.

I gave a half-shrug. "Before, when you were... hunting us; this portal wasn't here any more."

"Perhaps you are right, that the emr is collapsing, as you said. Places exist, they vanish, but we don't understand how, so they may come back just as randomly."

Sam stood just ahead of me with the dark shadowy trees of the lane imposing gloom on his form. "We should avoid this portal until we know if the graveyard is gone forever."

He was right. "Agreed. Even if it's there sometimes, it's unstable."

We made our way to the village green, scene of one of Sam's greater atrocities, and he didn't need to tell me how the appalling aftermath of his massacre was affecting him as he stared aghast at this muddy, bloody pastiche of internal parts externalised. In the moonlight it was hard to tell the black of the churned mud from the black of the spilt blood.

"I'm not saying anything, Sam, except that needs must, and right now I need you more as an ally than I need some kind of revenge on you. Just so we're quite clear."

He halted and stared at the consequences of his own actions. "He stole me, Laura. Stole me from the last loving kiss my dear wife might have given me and he, he *twisted* me, forced me into this utter obscenity of a life to serve his vile will."

"I know he did," I said quietly. "I saw you die, Sam, and I saw you reborn."

"Yes." Sam turned his head to me, caught my eye. "That is why there is a link between us, I think. It's why I was drawn to you, even while I was under my master's control."

I studied him quizzically. "That first time at Leo's."

He shrugged and pursed his lips – an expression I had never seen on that smooth tanned face before. "A little of my will, a lot of my master's. He had been looking for you for a long time. When your mind began to awaken, you remained shielded from him, but his power was great. And, of course, he knew that there was an intruder visiting some of his realms."

"My 'dreams'. That first time in the office, he must've felt that ping I get around you and him." I rubbed the base of my skull, soothing a pain I was merely remembering.

He levelled his gaze down upon me once more. "All that matters to me is that you promise to destroy me when this fight is over. I have no desire to live on in this evil animated flesh."

I peered across the moonghosted green to where the village pub still stood. "I've got a feeling our friends are in there."

He didn't push me on my promise. "As have I."

"They must've doubled back here when the other reality… Sam, stop! Wait!"

He strode purposefully on long strong legs toward the pub and as much as I might have wanted to stop him, to get the chance to explain my madness to my friends, I was nowhere near catching up as he grabbed the door handle of the little wooden door. I hurried along the little pathway as fast as my tight, achy legs would allow.

-32-

I heard a cry of fear, a tinkling crash and two heavy thuds before Sam hurtled out of the pub backwards with Tom Peters, head down and back bent, gripping his pelvis in some rugby tackle sort of stupidity as he drove his bigger opponent out of the pub.

The two of them slammed down bodily onto the concrete fronting outside the pub, Tom atop Sam, but with one jerk of his massive arms, Sam hurled Tom off him as he rolled himself and gracefully regained his feet in a lithe inhuman movement that confused my eye and beat Tom to the punch.

But Sam did not punch; not this time. He just waited, wary gaze fixed on Tom.

Tom had hit the hard path on his knees and now he clambered up with a wince of pain, rubbing one kneecap, but his expression was hard as he re-acquired his enemy. He sprang and hurled a long hooked punch at the bigger man. As his knuckles crunched against the teeth of his opponent, Tom pivoted slightly on one foot so he could lift his knee and drive it hard into the giant's hard belly. There was a gut-wrenching thud.

Sam's expression remained unchanged.

I thought Tom might hesitate when that hefty blow had no effect whatsoever, but no. No, not *him*. He just swung his fist again.

This time, Sam ducked his head in an arc that brought him back facing Tom as soon as the fist passed by. Tom yanked his body back anti-clockwise to punch again but Sam twisted his legs and feet around as the fist came in, grabbed the fist as it got close and then use his momentum to pull Tom's arm through on its trajectory, taking him utterly off-balance. It was very graceful to watch.

Tom cried out in pain as he was forced to stop all his weight on his hurt leg. He probably would've fallen, but Sam still had hold of his wrist and now he twisted and pulled it back, bringing a screaming Tom violently back towards him.

I braced myself, ready to intervene, I hoped, if my mind would play ball, if Sam had lost control in this moment. Surprisingly, though, the big man let go of Tom's wrist as soon as he'd generated enough momentum to send his smaller opponent staggering back toward the pub.

Sam stood still. Waited.

Tom wasn't badly hurt at all. I knew what Sam could do to him if he wanted to, and so did Tom, except he was busy playing the twat and protecting his lady (ha!) from this great lumbering beast.

I had to intervene.

"Tom!" I yelled sharply, aware that a little spit escaped and hoping no-one noticed. Tom glanced, but his gaze was never really on me.

"Tom, stop! Please listen. He's not slaved to my brother any more."

Tom returned his attention to Sam and a grin spread over his face; malicious and cold. "So even that sick cunt of a master of yours can't stand you any more, eh, Sam? Tragic. Heart-breaking!"

Sam retained attention on Tom, but would not meet his gaze.

Tom lunged and slammed his hand against Sam's shoulder, rocking his bulk a little. "I'm talking to you!"

Still, Sam did not respond.

"I said I'm *talking* to you!" The hand slammed the shoulder again. "That sick cunt hates you too! You got *nothing*, you sack of shit!"

This was going to get out of hand. Sam could give in to his animal at any moment and it almost seemed as if that was what Tom actually wanted.

"Tom!" I snapped.

Nope. Too late.

Tom flew forward, aiming a punch at Sam's head. Sam spun on his heel and dropped into a crouch, so that he was out of the line of Tom's attack, and threw out his right fist at roughly belly height as Tom tipped past his balance point and windmilled past his target. Sam's extended fist thudded into his belly and I saw him spit out every drop of air and drip of spit as he staggered onto the little lawn and squelched to his knees on the mud-tacky grass.

Sam rose up and his shoulders lifted as he tensed, his glare feral, the brutal animal killer clawing up to the surface. Lost to his bloodlust.

But then, his shoulders uncoiled and he drew a huge barrel-chestful of air, turning his gaze to me.

"Oh, Sam," I said simply.

Tom wheezed, struggling feebly to get up off his knees whilst unable to breathe well enough to power his body. "Bastard...!" he gasped. "Fucking... kill you! Better... end this now, you... fucking...!"

"Sam," I repeated, and the giant's attention was all for me. I gestured at the pub. "Go inside."

Sam glanced at Tom.

I strode down the little path to the pub door and herded him without any resistance before me. "In. Now."

I turned to Tom and pointed a stiff jutting finger at him. "You, stay there and cool the fuck *off*."

In the half-light of the gloomy bar room, I was able to make out my former friend Jennifer Sullivan, seated at a table with a lit cigarette jutting between her pouting red lips. She seemed unaware that there was a red and white, glistening, jut-boned mulch of a corpse piled clumsily against the bar a few feet away from her, a red smear across the floor where someone, probably Tom, had tidied up. The remains of Bobby.

The tip of the cigarette glowed, she held in the smoke and then released a stream of blue-grey from between her pursed lips.

I bit down on my lip to help me resist the reflexive urge to vomit at the sight of Bobby's remains. I'd been a willing participant to the monstrous act committed against that poor boy.

"Jenny?" said Sam.

She turned her head and glared at him.

I saw his Adam's apple bob as he tried to swallow. "Jenny, I need you to understand, I'm not as I was. Not any longer."

She raised an eyebrow, withdrew the cigarette from the pert caress of her lips and held it out between her fingers. Then, she flicked ash onto the floor and flicked her eyes in the direction of the pulped corpse of Bobby, before returning them to Sam. "But I bet you still like your *sport*, though, right, Sam? Still got that *uurge*." She squeezed her eyes into a tight squint and she emphasised the word.

Sam looked at the remains, his gaze lingering. A few hours ago, that gory stinking pile would have made him salivate. Now, he was trying to take control, rein in the animal, and Jen *really* wasn't fucking helping one little bit.

She protruded her red lips to full extension to take a puff on her cigarette. "Barely done being a boy, poor thing."

Sam glared at her and I was startled to feel the heat of his rage. It was a hot, intimate sensation, like accidentally brushing a hand against a man's groin and finding him unexpectedly erect.

"Enough, Jen," I cautioned.

"Just a boy," she repeated, returning the cigarette to her pursing lips.

"Jen," I repeated, risking a glance at Sam to find him studying the seated smoker calmly. "You should be glad no-one's looking too closely at how poor Bobby was left helpless to cover our retreat."

Jen stared at me, now, and her gaze was hellishly cold.

Sam's lips twitched but I couldn't read his expression. "It seems we were both doing what we do best in this case, Jennifer," he said calmly.

The smug aloofness dell away and Jen's cheap, nasty veneer was exposed as her lip curled into a snarl.

Tom chose that exact moment to lumber into the pub. Of course he did.

"What you fucking say to her, you oversized chunk of shit?"

He grabbed a chair by the back and flung it roughly aside, the glaring eyes in his dark red face locked on Sam.

"Enough, now," I said, catching Tom's eye. "I brought Sam here."

"You *what?* Are you completely...?"

A sudden spike of malice pressed out from behind my eyes. "I thought it'd be nice to have a man with some loyalty in my life for a change."

I saw something move behind his eyes. Not sure what it was but it must have been either remorse or outrage.

Too harsh. However bad I had felt, I was supposed to be the one calming the situation, here.

"Sorry," I said hastily. "I'm sorry, Tom. That was cheap, nasty. Unfair."

Regardless of how shitty it had been to say it, saying it had done a power of good for calming Tom down. His gaze dropped to the floor.

I sighed. "Look, he didn't follow me here, I brought him because we need him. My brother's let go, so his human mind is in control for the first time since..."

I glanced at Jen but she avoided me.

Tom laughed harshly. "Silly me, yeah it's that simple! Your puppet."

What was he saying?

"Like brother, like sister, eh?"

"Tom, it's not like that," I insisted. "I've got more reason to hate him than you have. He killed my parents in the village, in case you've forgotten! I wanted this bastard dead, Tom, fucked if I don't *still*, but he's forgotten more about my brother than we'll ever learn!"

Tom's eyes cast chilly light on me. "Now there's the fucking truth. It's all about your little *war*."

"*My* war?"

He glared at me. That hearth was definitely cold now where I was concerned. "*Your* war, Laura. It certainly ain't mine or Jen's, because thanks to someone, we're dead. Or did you forget?"

"Thanks to someone, Tom?" I challenged, getting angry now. "You're blaming *me*?"

"No!" He jabbed a finger toward Sam. "Him, you silly fucking bitch! Him!"

Shit; of course. I reached out to touch him but he shrugged me off and slouched away with a hang-dog glance in my direction, moving to a low table where an ornate-handled pewter beer mug awaited him. He scooped it up and took a swig and then crossed to Jen and perched on the edge of her table, beer mug hung in his hand.

"Just go, Laur. Take your nice new friend and jus' fuckin' sling your hook."

"Tom, you can't stay here," I told him.

He perched on the edge of the table, his backside inches from Jen's face. "We'll be fine."

"No you won't. The emr isn't stable any more."

He lurched off the edge of the table and slammed his tankard down as he did so, glaring hard at me. "Look, we're staying. That's an end to–"

"No," Sam uttered bluntly. "No, you are not."

"You fucking telling–"

I held a hand up sharply. I had felt something.

Tom's eyes widened as saw that something had changed in us.

It was hard to fully grasp what I could feel but it was clear Sam had picked it up, too. My mind had flexed without my meaning it to and I had felt a presence in the shadows way back beyond the bar, back where the rear entrance was. The rear entrance we'd fled through after Bobby.

The rear entrance that was definitely not locked.

I'd never felt a presence so strongly, except for Sam, but this was far colder and much more malevolent than Sam had ever been, its presence leaving a chilled trail across the ridges of my brain as it poured into me. Violated me with chill sliminess that drooled across my mind.

Shit. I'd just walked in, just assumed this place was safe. With Sam no longer a threat I'd dropped my guard.

I cursed my own stupidity.

"Everyone get out!"

My mind lashed out to block a thought knot that snapped out of the recesses behind the bar and flew burning and shrieking straight at my face. My mind organ was way ahead of me on that one, too. Conscious me was coming a poor second as my mind flexed and swatted at the lethal mass hurtling at me.

The thought knot spun away from me and smashed into the front window of the pub, destroying glass and frame and punching out a jagged chunk of wall the size of a bicycle.

"Where!" I heard Sam cry, but the word made no sense. I distantly felt him grasp my arm, but I was still in mind mode. "Where did it come from, Laura!"

I was jolted back inside my own meat. Staring at Sam I realised that my mind had reacted by reflex, I had no idea where that fucking missile had come from! Our enemy was going to hold that advantage for as long as this ambush held.

"Out!" I screamed again.

Jen was past me like a shot, doing self-preservation almost as well as she used to do pornographic evening wear. I stumbled for the door and was also overtaken by Tom, but Sam waited at the doorway for me, his orb back in his hand, providing cover as best he could.

We threw ourselves outside almost as one, and as we did I finally considered the idea that maybe the ambush inside had been *intended* to herd us outside.

Too slow again, Keeble

A thought knot flashed across the green at me. My mind was too slow but Sam thrust his orb up and the second knot darted off on a sharply curved tangent as he focussed and drove it away through the lens of that strange black ball. The knot hit the garden wall of a scorched neighbouring house, sending bricks and wood chunks flying up in a great geyser before igniting the materials and reducing the fence to the same state as the house it had once bordered.

I spotted movement in the shadowy bushes across the green, in the direction of the lane.

"They've cut us off!"

This was so obviously a coordinated attack that I was left feeling dog-fucked and sucker-punched by my own stupidity.

I glimpsed a white sliver of reflected moonlight glint as something smooth and dark moved forward in those bushes.

I heard Tom blubbing somewhere outside the limits of my interest. "What we do? What the *fuck* do we–!"

His high, broken voice cut off as I spun on my heel to face an intense malevolence that only a mind like mine could feel. My mind pushed and I saw Tom fly back away from the edge of my vision, pushed aside as a smallish figure stepped out of the pub.

About the size of a fifteen-year-old boy, it was visible only in silhouette and from the angle I was looking, its head seemed monstrously oversized.

It stayed in shadow and I felt, rather than saw, another thought knot snap into existence deep inside the misshapen head.

"Down!" I screamed, and hit Sam hard with the flats of both hands. He must have been responding to my scream rather than the blow, because he spun off his feet in a way I could never have made him do and rolled across the grass.

Tom was already down, felled by whatever force I'd hit him with, and Jen... well, I didn't care, so maybe I'm a bad person.

I stayed on my feet, opened my mind as best as I could and sought the knot. *There.* I saw it with my mind just before I saw it with my eyes as it raced at me, aiming for my face so that my body screamed for me to run, flee, anything but stay still! Yet I knew full well that if I did any of those things I would die right here, right now because no human body could outmanoeuvre one of those evil fucking things.

I held my ground. Focussed.

There was a sharp pain in the back of my head and the flying hulk of venom suddenly slowed. Shockingly, it came to a halt and hung in the air about five feet away from my face, twirling and shimmering, its light composed of blacks and silvers that were hard for the eye to focus on, as though they were made of matter not meant to be seen by human eyes or perceived by a human brain.

My mind organ throbbed. It was a shockingly visceral sensation, feeling almost exactly as if I had a pulsing heart thudding away inside my skull. It hurt a bit, but it was keeping me alive. My mind held the knot steady, spinning and twisting in the air as if it were fighting to break free.

Exactly what the hell I would do if one of the other figures out there fired a *second* knot... well, there was no time to worry about that.

"Inside... the... house," I gasped, breathing hard as my mind drew on the resources of my body to hold the knot still. Sweat was teased from my skin and a chill crawled along my spine.

"Which house?" I heard someone ask.

My lungs burned, my head ached.

"Does it... fucking... *matter?*"

"We'll be trapped!" Tom protested.

I was sure the knot was starting to creep closer to me as the pain in my head intensified, as my lungs pumped air and my heart rattled in my chest as it tried to keep pace.

At least I was going to lose a bit of weight before I died.

What was Tom bitching about?

"Tom, that's... the least of our worries," I said between puffs of air, my vision blurred by tears as I stared fixedly at the knot. "Too exposed here. Go!"

"Move!" Sam barked from somewhere to my left, and then he stepped up beside me and aimed the orb.

As we backed away there was a bit less pressure on my head. Combining backward movement with holding the knot was helping.

I felt rather than saw the movement of the assassins as they began to move out of the shadows toward us. Another shot at us would probably finish the job they had started. I was unsure why they would bother to stalk us – like prey rather than an enemy.

I now had a dull ache at the back of my skull and two jagged streaks of much sharper pain in both temples, but I kept my aching eyes locked onto that sick black thing as we backed up. It rolled, shimmered and crept along, never any closer to my retreating face but never much further away, either.

Distantly it occurred to me that I was struggling because my mind was suppressing their ability to fire – I was not just holding off one thought knot.

"Sam," I murmured fearfully. "I don't know how long."

"I'm here with you, Laura."

We hit a door with our backs, it was pulled open from within and we tumbled through, off-balance, but this worked in our favour because Tom had suddenly started using his brain and he slammed the door just as I felt the slimy evil knot slip free of my mind.

There was a bang and a black smudge spread on the inside wood of the heavy front door as the knot found a victim. There was a weird gurgling noise like a woodsaw cutting underwater and then a brutal-fast shower of jagged splinters erupted at us in a sharp shower.

I threw myself back and shielded my face, but when I dared look up a moment later I saw that the door had held, sustaining a scorched area about the size of Medusa's mane, which was peppered with tiny holes.

"That was too close," I said. Fuck, my head was sore.

Sam rounded on Tom. "You might have killed us! We fell through that door when you opened it!"

"Ahh, shut up," Tom retorted sagely.

"Sam," I said. "Leave it. He did his best and it worked."

I gazed up at Sam and he gazed down at me, the two of us pleased with our night's work so far.

I smiled at him. "I think we need to–"

My smile vanished as I heard a rustle to my right. I tried to swallow to moisten my crunchy-dry throat but I had no spit at all. There was something in here with us.

There was bluish moonlight intruding into the gloomy house through windows and a few holes in the walls, this being one of the least damaged homes left in the village; but it was not enough to ease the nightmare terror of being trapped in the dark with an unseen something, its form creaking, rustling and cracking; the sound of a crab trapped in a bucket.

I sensed rather than saw motion to my right. I flashed a thought to Sam and hoped he'd pick it up, as if our minds had some sort of bluetooth. If so, his bluetooth was on, because Sam reacted to my thought without a sound or a hesitation, stepping fast across me to cover our rear as I reached out and unceremoniously shoved the starstruck lovers toward the front door they'd just come through.

~ *Ready?* ~

I jolted. The thought was almost like one of my own but *not*. It was flavoured like Sam. I replied with a thought of my own.

Yes

I could ponder whether I liked this new thing later.

~ *Now!* ~

We both lunged just as a thunderous bark of noise split the air apart and the wall beside Sam's head erupted just as he cleared it on his way forward, a shower of plaster and black energy pouring out and then collapsing back in on itself, the thought matter at once brighter darken than the gloom of the hallway.

A few splashes of overshot thought matter spattered the opposite wall and ignited the wallpaper in little curls of fire. It burned into the switch cluster and shorted it so that suddenly the hall light flared into life and we were blinded by the sudden glare.

Oh, look. The lights still work

Sam's mind did not reply. Apparently only I could see the funny side of our imminent demise.

A figure stepped out into the newly-bright hall. A slightly-built girl in jeans and tee-shirt, slim-hipped and with small, unfettered breasts, mostly nipple, jutting through the smudged greyish fabric, she wore a hugely oversized motorcycle helmet, supported on two sides by thick metal struts welded to the helmet and resting on pads that sat on her shoulders. It was weird, ridiculous and it should have been laughable but it wasn't, because I knew what kind of Frankenstein horror lay concealed beneath.

Tom backed away from the small form with its gleaming babyhead, while all I could focus on was the faint yet belly-chilling malevolence exuding from behind that impenetrable black visor, reflecting us all in the electric glare of the hallway.

The body rotated, turning that smooth blank stare on to Jen as a viscous black thought-knot burst from the very glass of the visor, shooting toward where my friend stood. In that instant, before Jenny could even realise her fate, Sam hurled himself into the path of the knot. I lunged at it with my mind and was able to deflect it in a curve away from his stupid self-sacrificing chest with a microsecond to spare.

The knot dispersed in the air as though it had never been, harming no-one, but my frantic lunge at it had cost me badly.

Sam help

Jagged shards of light zagged across my vision and a vice clamped my skull and *squeeezed*.

I sagged against the stairway wall with violent head pain gouging out the meat of my brain as it smeared clumps of cortex against the inside of my skull.

I grabbed my head and heard a scream that was probably mine – more in frustration than pain as I fought to stay in the fight, my eyes dim and my thoughts dispersing like migrating geese.

If Sam didn't back me up, we were all dead.

I felt sick with pain and the room was lurching dizzily in front of me. Sprawled against the wall, I forced my eyes open only to have them forced shut by searing pain somewhere at the back of those balls.

There was a loud bang and a thud. Something bumped my shoulder, something else hit the floor with a thud, and then something wispy trailed momentarily across my face. I bit my lower lip and drove my eyelids up, revealing a blurred scene that it took me a moment to resolve.

With a feral roar, Sam hurled his bulk at the biker girl just as she rotated to aim her dark visor at its next target. There was a flare of heat as a poorly-formed thought-knot erupted from the helmet but discharged explosively in mid-air as her body was whumped sideways by the eighteen-or-more stones of Sam's mass.

A deadly assassin she might well be, but she still had the effective fighting weight of a skinny girl, and as Sam's bulk drove her into the wall I heard the wishbone crunch of bones, probably ribs, breaking under her clothes. Lost in the bloodlust he had allowed to overtake him, Sam's massive hands gouged and tore at the assassin, while it frantically fought to twist free, get a hand onto him, but it was pinned.

Its physical body was useless. Its mind weapon was not.

I felt a new thought knot forming and tried to act, but my mind was still rice pudding.

I spotted Sam's black orb on the floor to my right, just out of reach. He must have dropped it protecting me while I was down – he had no defence against a thought knot.

Sam didn't need my help, though; not on this one. He gripped her right arm and left hip and used his bulk and musculature to lever her completely off her feet and up over his head like a crash-test dummy.

I could feel the new thought knot coming to malevolent life, but Sam was too quick and with a roar of naked rage he hurled the body the length of the hall. It slammed into the already-scorched front door and burst through in a spray of charred and splintered wood chips, dust, cloth and blood.

I wondered if damaging its human host would stop the evil pilot inside that helmet.

Either way, I used the brief respite to close my eyes, gather myself, swallow and focus. There was a gnawing ache in my temples and everything was still spinning, but as I opened my eyes again I focused through it, took three deep breaths.

Sam glanced my way. "It knew I would protect Jennifer."

I clambered up, my head pinging like a bastard. "They know what Peter knows."

"Whoa!" To cried out. "The bitch is back!"

She was looking tatty. Framed in the doorless doorway, her visor was cracked, something jutted up through the tee-shirt on her left shoulder and that arm hung awkwardly at an odd angle. Being thrown through a doorway is bad for you, kids. One leg was twisted inward and the hip on that side showed a hideous jagged bulge against her jeans. Most of all, though, there was a stream of arterial blood spurting from a wound under her left breast, soaking her tee-shirt and jeans and pattering onto the hall carpet.

I clambered hastily to my feet, sensed the black flare of a new thought-knot filling her visor.

"Down!" I screamed.

Sam dropped fast but the other two were not too shoddy either.

I grabbed the thought knot before the creature could launch it, trying to shove it back into its helmet and take that hideous arachnid pilot off the web once and for all.

Its mind fought frantically, aware that I was trying to pot-roast it. The mind I faced was not bright but it was strong, bolstered no doubt by my brother's proxy influence.

I would not be able to hold on for very long. I needed to use my superior intelligence to win this fight.

I pushed harder on the knot, felt the resistance swell and then immediately relaxed. The creature inside that helmet thrust hard and, as it did, I pushed again and threw the knot over her shoulder as soon as it emerged, the force needed to curve it far less than that needed to hold it still.

The knot exploded against the wall beside the front door, punching a hole as it flew out into the night at speed.

I hadn't killed it, but I'd forced it to sacrifice its attack. Felt pretty damn good, actually.

Sam sprang up and again threw himself headlong at the girl. She'd been no match for his bulk before and once more she was like a rag doll that folded under his locomotive charge, folding gracelessly as he rammed her out through the front door and into the garden.

I flew after him.

He rolled off the assassin and her good leg snapped up, her toecap thudding against his testicles, a blow that would have felled a human male, but Sam dismissed the pain instantly and, as she kicked again at the same target, he kicked her under the thigh like a footballer taking a penalty. Her leg snapped back and there was a dry-twig crack.

She tried to use her arms to lever herself back and out of range but she had only one working arm and so she folded onto her back. More than the time Sam needed to kick her in the ribs. There was a nasty crunch that inconveniently reminded me of Susan Blake.

I had no idea if she could feel pain but she was stunned long enough for Sam to step back, lunge an throw a deadweight kick full into her visor. Well, *through* her visor. It shattered in a spray of glinting glass and the helmet spun in a move that would have broken her neck had there been a neck left under there.

The body lifted off the ground in a graceful arc as the helmet lifted free of the shoulder braces slightly to expose the grisly cut flesh of the girl's neck.

The female host body jerked as its pilot's control was severed. It slumped and lay still.

Sam edged closer, cautiously.

"Sam," I warned.

I seriously doubted we'd killed what I knew was inside that helmet.

Sam's foot was an inch from the girl's shoulder. He suddenly drew back. "What on Earth?"

The gaping hole where the shattered visor had been was filled by a mass of glinting black jewels peering at us from a flat stone face that caught the ghostly moonlight at jagged angles.

"Shit in my mouth," I heard Tom say behind me as spindly black legs tipped with fierce pincers lashed out of the smashed visor like streamers trapped by a high-speed fan. The helmet tumbled off the girl's shoulders, completely disconnected now, before a huge, heavy-jawed spider clambered free of its prison, perched as it had been on the girl's neck stump.

Somewhere behind us in the cowards' gallery, Jenny let out a gargling scream of horror.

The monster thrashed on the ground as though to force its feet to re-acclimatise to the earth, and then it scuttled around in a circle on the grass before us, so that the gleaming jewels of its soulless black eyes could fix on me.

I shuddered involuntarily. I faced, for real, a horrid, bristly black spider the size of a fat cat on eight lightning-fast legs. Ohh, you bastard; if we lost this fight, this vile thing was going to fucking *eat* me. Beneath its several night-black gems of eyes was a short expanse of bristly blackness that passed for a face, and then below this hung two razor-sharp fangs the size of tusks, protruding from fleshy pouches, these two objects rubbing each other furiously as though aroused by the desire to splice human flesh.

Was I going to have to *touch* this hideous thing?

If Sam shared any of my fear or revulsion, his built-in animal rage suppressed it. I felt his rage as a wave of emotion that splashed me, wetting me with strength in its wake momentarily.

"Shit," I muttered.

Sam, your orb is still in the house

He patted himself and glanced back at the house, working out a path to get the orb, but the spider was carrying an orb of its own, attached to the bristling hairs on its front-most left leg. It had been holding an orb while it was inside the crash helmet, which explained how it could churn out thought knots.

~ Can you cover me? ~

The creature turned to face the door, aware that something was going on, possibly aware of Sam's orb through its own.

Go, I'll keep it busy

I could focus a thought knot at the creature, but it might get a shot out of that orb before it died. No, I would have to kill two bugs with one shoe.

As Sam threw himself headlong at the front door of the house, I fixed my mind's focus on the spider's orb, seeking to grab control and turn it on its owner.

I felt myself enter the orb but, as feeble as its mind was, the creature was already embedded and in control. My mind-self flailed helplessly to gain a purchase.

I failed completely.

The spider's mind commanded and the orb spat a thought knot that flew past Sam's hip as he lunged for his orb. Inches from his grasp, it burst apart in a devastating explosion that would have blinded him but for the snip-fast reflexes that had him dive into a room off the hallway.

I exited the orb, having seen enough, my head filled with jagged cracks of pain. The spider scurried toward me and I cried out with revulsion as I frantically sought to bite down on my fear and focus my mind, my only weapon against this bristly horror; but the creature scuttled off to the side.

I was not its target. It saw Sam as the greater threat, but without his orb Sam was just muscle and bone.

A cruel joy curled my lips into a smile. "Wrong call, bitch!"

With its focus on rushing at Sam, I found far less resistance in the orb as I drove my mind into it, my vision filling with its weird, 360-degree world view rolling and pivoting. Despite my pain I wrenched at it, *pulled at* it and watched through it as the spider lurched to a halt, ceasing its planned attack on Sam as it perceived a new and greater threat.

I had a third eye. Seeing through the orb I watched Sam, myself, even Jen cowering over the way with Tom.

And I could feel the orb's desire to be used, a deep hunger that filled me.

The spider scurried to the left, its leg joints clacking horribly, feinting, but Sam was not fooled and he reacted with equal speed, his body a closer match now I'd taken the orb out of the fight.

The creature lunged forward and suddenly, with a hideous inhuman scream of rage, Sam threw himself into the air, over its back, twisting in mid-air to grab at the hard bodyshell between its first and second legs to pull himself down onto its back.

He was riding on its *back*, for fuck's sake.

The monster shuddered as though repulsed by the feel of him. It scurried to left and to right on rapidly-scurrying legs, jerked rapidly forward and then back, its joints clacking in that faintly metallic way as it strained to tip him off so it could bring those venomous fangs in for a single stab that would reduce even Sam's durable body to a liquified bag of blood and pus.

The creature's conversion from small to giant had not compromised it; it had the relative strength of a real spider, so it was incredibly strong for its size — but Sam was far, far more than a man and he clung to the creature, kneeling on its back like a schlock-horror rodeo cowboy.

There was little I could do. I had seized control of the orb, but I couldn't fire it without hitting my ally.

And then Sam lowered his face and rammed his open mouth onto the monster's hard hairy carapace. He bit it.

He *bit* it. It was a shame I had nothing to vomit up.

The spider reared up on its backmost legs, the front pair flailing in the air, but as it did Sam threw his legs back and got his feet on the ground behind the thing's bulb-like abdomen. With a cry of strain he straightened his legs. His boots dug deep into the still-muddy earth as he levered with his all the strength of his inhuman musculature and lifted the spider aloft.

Its spiny legs lashed frantically and tipped Sam off-balance. He tumbled forward, still gripping the beast as if his life depended on it. Which it did.

He sprawled facedown in the mud, arms out straight over his head and fingers embedded in the thing's body. The spider was pulled down at the back by his weight but those eight legs thrashed, the bulb-like abdomen jerked and I could see that in a moment it would pull free and then turn to drop its tusk-like fangs deep into his meat.

Sam, stay low!

I drove my entire mind into the orb and submitted to the urge to inflict destruction. The targeting system was indiscriminate; it did not care *who* it killed, but I fought to gain focus. Sam, Tom, Sam, the spider.

Gotcha!

I lashed wildly with my mind in the vain hope that I would hit the trigger mechanism and

… I was thrown from the orb. With a gasp, I collapsed onto my behind on the wet ground as a ghastly hole in my mind popped wetly shut.

I grabbed my pulsing head. "Uuuh, fuck!"

The spider pulled free of Sam's failing grip and turned, reared up over him with yellow venom dripping from its fangs as its jaws pulled apart to strike deep into his body, and I knew I'd failed him.

-33-

I watched those razor-tusk spider fangs sink toward Sam as if in slow motion; as if time itself had decided to torture me with the pleasure of my new ally's destruction.

Then, however, there was a pop in the back of my head and a really ghastly, deep, heavy *plop!* out there in the world as the spider's fat body burst open at its fattest bulge, spraying white, yellow and red pulp across the lawn. Its legs ceased thrashing instantly and it collapsed, smoke wisping from its blown-open shell as it fell onto Sam in a spray of internal juices.

Its jointy limbs twitching in uncoordinated jolts.

~ *Well done, Laura* ~

Sam thrust the corpse off himself and clambered to his feet, wiping spider sauce off his dress shirt. "Lobster surprise, anyone?" He grinned at me..

Tom ejected a fountain of spew somewhere behind me. Wanker.

"You owe me an orb," Sam told the arachnid corpse. Reaching down, he pulled its weapon from the split and dead front leg still clinging by a twisted joint to that fat black bulb of a body.

He began to rub off the remnants of spider juice still gunked onto the orb, but suddenly stopped, started and looked up at me, expression alarmed.

~ *Another one!* ~

A single image from the orb came with his words in my head, the first thing he had seen as he took control of it: a second helmeted assassin creeping through the house.

I suppose my brother had wanted to test one of his assassins before committing more, but now there was a sneak attack in progress.

Fuck me!

Sam had reached my side. "Buy me dinner first."

I glanced up at him and smiled. He returned the smile momentarily but we both knew we had an urgent task in hand.

Fear was a squeeze on my bladder and there was a tightness in my chest. "Come on," I told my huge companion before my resolve could dissolve completely.

We separated instinctively, striding purposefully toward the house in an arc to create a sixty-degree kill-zone and two targets for our enemy.

The second helmeted assassin, this one apparently male based on the crotch-bulge at its jeans and its flatter chest, emerged from the burning hall and stepped into the house's tiny front garden.

Unprepared for the scene on the lawn, it rotated its body smoothly and tried to decipher the meaning of its dead partner, the man and woman huddled shuddering a short way off, yet still alive; and Sam and me, waiting patiently for it.

"Too slow, eight-leg."

Sam fired his new orb. Once. Again. Once more. The black venom of the mind energy discharges seemed brightly black in the moonlight.

I opened my mind and unleashed the force it contained.

Sam's thought knots thumped a hole in the centre of the assassin's chest and then widened it with successive hits, whilst I had focussed my mindforce on the thing's helmet, forming a thought knot at distance for the first time – inside that rounded chamber.

As the host body started to collapse from the impact and burning hunger of Sam's thought knots, I detonated my mind energy inside the assassin's helmet and was at once violated by a hideous, shrill, inhuman scream inside my head as fragments of helmet, visor and thrashy-legged burning spider corpse blasted up into the air and formed a glorious arc that spattered the house walls and pattered down onto the little garden.

~ *Are you OK?* ~
You heard that scream too?
~ *Yes. Satisfying* ~
I nodded and studied our handiwork.

The headless corpse had been reduced to a skeleton by knot venom, a few random sheaths of scorched biker leather clinging to the tips of a few ribs. More helpfully, across the small garden and just over the low picket fence lay a twisted tangle of scorched black legs curled inward around a shrivelled black bulb of a body.

I'd given the spider pilot the ultimate baked potato experience inside that helmet. It was short by a few legs and there was no sign of life there whatsoever.

I crossed to Sam. "That was effective. "We make a good team, see?"

His jaw was taut. "My master will know his ambush failed. He will escalate his attack, now."

I pouted, disappointed by a truth I already knew. "Can't we be smug for a few minutes?"

He smiled at me, his blue eyes so beautiful. "I wish we could, but I served him for a long time, I know how he thinks." He forced the orb into his left jeans pocket, creating a ridiculous bulge as he peered out toward the lane. "We have to leave here while we still can. Who knows how many of those things he might have made?"

I nodded and stepped forward onto the green but Sam didn't follow. I turned back to see him stumble, one leg buckling beneath him.

"Sam?"

He would have gone down but, to my utter amazement, he was grabbed and held up by Tom, who must have noticed what I had not; that the giant had been injured fighting that last assassin. My former boyfriend's arm hugged Sam's back as he ducked under his arm and propped him, standing up straight to take up his weight.

"I gotcha, big fella," Tom muttered gruffly.

I caught Sam's eye. "You're hurt?"

"It changes nothing," he said. "We must leave this emr now."

I scurried back and ducked under Sam's other arm, doing my best to prop him despite being a full three inches too short to usefully take his weight.

Tom gestured to Jen with an irritated jerk of the head and we set off along a non-yellow and distinctly brickless road, with no hope of a smart-arse wizard at the end of it to bail us out of the shit we were rapidly sinking into as my brother prepared his next happy little trick for us.

-34-

Exiting the village, Sam propped between Tom and me like a slaughtered pig, an arm over each of our shoulders, I was hit by a horrible realisation.

I slowed to a halt. "Shit."

By stopping I had forced Tom to pull up and re-position our bulky passenger's arm.

My gaze moved from the lane ahead toward that darker, forbidding second lane that we had always avoided.

Tom could see where I was looking. "Not a fucking chance, Laur," he said.

I huffed a breath. "I think we have to."

"Come off it! Why?"

There was a tremor to his voice and I understood perfectly why. That alternative lane inspired a cold dread in us, had done from our very first day in the village reality; a dread that was deeper than the foreboding appearance of that road, gloomily resistant to the night's moonglow, could really justify.

"We can't use the portal, Tom. The reality beyond it is, well, it's fucked."

On the far side of Sam's barrel chest from me, Tom shook his head. "What about the woods?"

"You think my brother hasn't already sent his spiderbastards up there to lie in wait for us?"

"He might not—"

"Face it, Tom, we don't know what's down that other lane, but I *do* know that my brother is going to pick our eyes out and fuck our skulls if he finds us, and he'll find us *seriously* fast if we're stupid enough to run the way we went last time."

Tom hoisted Sam's arm more securely over his shoulder. "Fuck!"

He knew I was right; he was just voicing the same argument I'd already had with myself. We moved toward the darker lane.

Fear began to build in me as we approached. It began with a deepening pressure in my head, but rapidly swelled to a chill that made my heart thud and my legs turn heavy – and then we crossed whatever passed for a threshold onto the lane and the growing panic in me immediately began to subside.

I puffed my cheeks and blew air hard, the effort of breathing out calming me a little. "See?" I said, "it's not that bad."

"Seriously, Laur?" Tom's tone was exasperated but I heard him chuckle.

"Thanks for jinxing us, you fucking pilchard!"

I felt the very welcome twitch of a smirk pull on my lips. "Shut up, Tom."

I'd missed our banter since things had soured between us.

The gloom on this road was caused by vast behemoth trees whose thick boughs twined each other intimately far above us. Even with their winter deficit of leaves, there was still enough of a mass to the clasping lovers' limbs above to cut out most of the moonglow.

"Weird how the fear vanished," I said. "I wonder if it was a barrier or something?"

"Protecting what, though?" said Jen, looking warily from right to left at the dark, surrounding woodland.

The road ahead sloped away from us downhill. We stepped up our pace but stayed watchful, both for foot-snagging groundroots and for anything that might lurk in the forest around us.

As we reached the bottom of the hill, the road levelled out. "Jelly legs break!" I declared.

Tom and I manoeuvred Sam to a nice spot at the roadside and propped him between the fat, surfaced roots of an ancient tree. We slumped down on the cool, damp earth either side of the big man to catch our breath.

Jen glared at me, pouting. There was no room for her in our knotty crook. I resisted the temptation to smirk. She glared a moment longer, huffed and then flounced across to a foot-high tree stump a few feet away, where she perched her pert bottom.

I touched Sam's arm. "How bad?"

He angled his head up to look at me, his eyes alert again, now. "Your kind help gave me the time I needed to heal my injuries, I will be back to strength in a few minutes, now."

I smiled. "Built-in puncture repair kit, eh?"

He smiled back at me, his eyes lit and his teeth shiny and fresh. "Something like that. Where are we?"

"You don't remember?"

He shrugged. "My body heals but I can still lose consciousness. I was drifting in and out."

I fidgeted as coldness penetrated the seat of my jeans from the damp earth beneath me. "We're on the *other* fork."

He frowned. "The other...? Really? Remarkable. Even my master... your brother, was wary of this path. He could sense the barrier, I know he was curious about who had created it but he never sent me here. It was not as if any of the villagers try to flee this..."

I rubbed his arm. "I know you blame yourself, but that wasn't you, Sam. He was controlling you; you had no choice."

The big man was silent, but he offered me a weak smile.

Tom let out a long sigh. "What I wouldn't give for a nice cup of tea."

"Phwoar, yeah," Jen cried, and I glanced and saw her wriggle her bottom on the stump she was seated on, apparently with the sheer pleasure of the thought.

I smiled ruefully at the admission of such a joyfully mundane pleasure. "Now *that* would be something."

"We can't stay here," Jen suddenly piped up. "That fucking maniac ain't gonna take too long to figure out where we went, he's not stupid."

The chilly dampness from the rooty ground had seeped through the seat of my jeans and onto my bottom, so I was getting pretty uncomfortable anyway. "You're right, let's get moving."

I clambered up but as I did so there was a brief but potent vibration at the base of my skull.

"Oww. Sam...?"

My skull was hit by a jarring thud. It began to vibrate.

~*Yes*~ Sam sent. ~*I felt it too*~

"Anyone else hearing that?" Tom asked, eyes flitting wildly around to seek the source of what was, in fact, a physical as well as a thought-based sound.

whump-whump- whump-whump

It was strong and brutal, earthquake hard and heartbeat steady.

whump-whump- whump-whump

And it was getting louder. Closer.

Sam sprang up effortlessly and Jen clambered off her stump. We closed together at this new threat.

"Shit my mother's knickers," Tom cried. "Look at *that* bastard!"

Up the lane, back the way we had come and obscuring everything from earth to sky, was a wall of dense impenetrable blackness that was pulsing closer an inch at a time, cutting through thick branches with a woody crunch, clawing up earth hungrily into its maw.

~*thought energy* ~

Sam was right, the wall's surface was hard to focus on, seeming to suck light *from* the eye due to the same anti-luminous glow as the thought knots that had so quickly become an accepted feature of my life.

A tree suddenly split and splintered clean in half down its heavy ancient trunk and that was enough to prompt us into action – but then an area of moonlight-and-indigo sky exposed by the eaten behemoth swirled, peeled free and was slurped into the maw, a chocolate milkshake of the heavens impossibly fed into the oblivion of the thing.

"Run!" I screamed at the others. I had cramp everywhere but adrenaline was in charge of my body for now and we fled along the road.

The relentless *whump-whump* joined the rhythm of blood pounding through the middle of both my eyes as my feet pounded the ground. Up ahead there was a bend in the road. I slowed to take it.

Then I staggered to a halt with a muted cry of despair.

Jen stopped, cried out, too and wrapped herself in Tom's arms.

A dense thicket completely blocked the roadway ahead, dark and oppressive in the gloom.

So the barrier of fear I had imagined might guard a deeper treasure here was, in fact, a complete red herring. This wasn't even a road to anywhere.

"A dead end?"

I felt suddenly very cold and exposed, out in the woods in the dead of night, my enemy closing in on me.

"Oh dear," said Sam with masterful understatement.

Tom looked ready to join Jen in her despair when he spoke. "What the fucking fuck do we do now?"

"I'll tell you what we can't do," I said. "We can't risk crawling into that, look how thick it is, we'll get tangled and trapped."

"Agreed," said Sam. "The unbinding force behind us is slow, but if we become immobilised in there, its speed will not matter."

I turned to him. "What did you call it?"

He frowned as if caught in the act somehow. "An unbinding force. It's not a wall, Laura, it's the limit of this reality. My master is collapsing this emr pocket by unbinding its condensate matter to revert it to freeform energy. He knows we can't use the exit portal, so all he has to do is collapse the world with us still trapped inside it."

A tremor shook the ground beneath our feet. Jen whimpered and Tom hugged her closer.

"Can't you do something?" he asked, his cheek resting on top of the blonde head. "Can't you, I dunno, make a portal of your own?"

I glanced at Sam, but he was lost in contemplation. "You can't make a portal," he said, as much to himself as to me.

"Helpful, Sam. Really helpful."

-35-

"Laur?" Tom said meekly, his hand cupping the back of Jen's head as if she were some innocent child who needed to be shielded from this horror. "Now would be a great time to come up with a Class-A idea."

I sighed and aimed a rueful look at him. "Sorry, Tom."

He pursed his lips and frowned at me. "A completely shit idea would do as a work-in-progress?"

"I wish, Tom. I don't think–"

Sam interrupted. "You can't make a portal, Laura, but–"

I glared at him. "Heard you the first time, thanks, it didn't help then and it isn't helpful now."

The pulsing worldquake sounded terribly close now, the vibrations in our ears and beneath our feet.

"No," the big man insisted, his fierce blue eyes alight as he stared at me. "You misunderstand – you can't make a *portal*, but you don't need to. All you need to do is create an exit."

"Oh, is that all?" I had tears in my eyes and I suddenly understood why people want their mothers in times of crisis; not that I really had that option anyway.

"No, no; you only need to punch a hole through the skin of this emr. Assuming the pockets are pressed together, we should be able to step through into the adjacent one."

"That's a big if," I said.

Sam smiled. "Tom, we have that completely shit idea you ordered!"

I laughed despite our terrible plight. "Well, a shit idea is better than a kick in the tits."

"I'll take your word for it," the big man replied. "I was never much of one for deep philosophy."

I turned from him and studied the area between us and the thicket. Open air. Not actually air, of course, any more than the thicket was really thicket. What did he call it? Condensed... fuck knows.

"So how do we do this?"

Sam had his orb in his hand. "We must assume that my master is only deleting this reality, of course, because this plan relies on the next reality being stable and safe."

"Do me a favour, Sam. Stop calling him your master, you sound ridiculous."

He cast me a sideways glance and held up his orb. "We focus our energy on a single point in space. You sight it and share it with me. I will fire the orb at the same spot just after you fire, to ensure we are hitting exactly the same place."

"OK." I opened my mind and focused on a single spot in the air dead ahead, tuning into Sam's mind to share that spot with him.

As soon as I felt our weak yet intrusive symbiosis in my head I pushed with my mind and, as pressure swelled inside my skull there erupted a focused translucent black jet that sprayed from just before my face out the few feet onto that spot in the air, but rather than passing through to the bushes beyond, the jet sparked and spattered at that place.

After the briefest of pauses, Sam fired his orb straight into the centre of the place where my jet was sparking.

I don't know what it looked like to the others. It felt like a universe ending inside my head as I sensed rather than saw a tiny flaw in reality, a pinprick that wasn't quite right any more; most similar to a faulty pixel on a computer screen, I guess.

But this pixel had serious testes.

My mindforce, spent, coiled back into me

Tom staggered and grabbed onto Jen. It took me a second to realise what was happening; they were closer to the fault and suddenly their heads stretch away from them like a stream of meat, spooling toward the broken pixel, elongating and growing thinner as they went.

They both shrieked but their shrieks were hoarse and horribly distorted.

Their bodies, too, elongated into long, thin, bobbly strings of human spaghetti. Then there was a *plop!* and their ghastly cries were cut off as they vanished.

"Ouch," I murmured. "I hope we didn't just kill them."

Sam grabbed my arm. "Tight for time as we are, let's assume it worked, shall we?"

He shoved me at the tiny whistling hole and sprang forward himself.

Sam spag'd and popped through the hole fast, but I held back, opened my mind to resist the suction for just a scant second so I could turn back, my curiosity awakened now that my immediate death had been postponed.

That wall of gouging, chewing destruction was very close now. There were no more than eighteen inches between my nose and the black maw of it, I felt the pull of it on my skin. Clearly, it was accelerating.

It tore up a tree in front of me and swallowed it whole.

The sinkhole behind me pulled one way, the greedy maw before me pulled the other.

I wondered briefly if the greedy thing I had made was any better than the greedy thing my brother had made. Mine had a better motive, but I'd had no time to work out details. A hole that lets you out of a mineshaft is great, but a hole that pulls you out of a plane in mid-air; not so much.

With a dry crunch the whole bulk of the doomed tree trunk and the mop of its branches crunched in a spray of wood chips into the maw and was gone.

I felt a terrible, beautiful thrill in my belly as I resisted the pull of my own escape route so I could indulge the wonder I felt at the sight of that vast force before me, the sensation of its pounding presence thrusting against my mind. I wanted to *know* it, to grasp the power of that force pulling hungrily at me. The fabric of reality peeled apart before me like wallpaint under a flame, the tattered remnants picking free and tumbling into its oblivion but I was enraptured, caught in the wonder of it.

Pain. Pain cutting through everything. Agony clawing strips off the crinkled surface of my brain, agony beyond anything I could have imagined in my old, tiny, mundane life.

Pain, yes. But suspended in that moment before death, so very very alive.

My mind opened out of its own accord and stretched wafer thin to taste the whole of that great mass, the entirety of the dying emr sector it was consuming, so that I glimpsed the convolution of structures webbed together like congealed ejaculate to form the knotty reality of the village emr.

It was astounding.

I was so... big.

To grasp within my essence an entire reality and, more, the very structures beneath that had been used to build it, as they were unravelled before me.

I was so lost in the glorious sensations, as I opened wide and held the realm and its glorious destroyer within my own boundary, that I barely noticed as the emr succumbed, crumbling away like a hollow pastry in the tightening grip of a hungry child.

I no longer had a reality for my physical body to stand in.

Oops

I pulled back violently and was poured back into my meat and bone in time to see with my liquid eyes the blackness pressed close to my nose, yet no longer progressing in its inexorable way – as if waiting because in fact it dared not try and take *me*.

In that moment I was so great a force that even this behemoth hesitated before me. By comparison, even my lifetime-best orgasm was a faint itch.

With my mind, I flicked casually away from the waiting wall and accepted the embrace of the sinkhole I had made.

My only physical memory is of having my tits squashed together. Then light. Dazzling light and...

Tumbling....

Passing; sounds, smells....

Faster, falling now, faster....

Then a violent jolt jarred me as a cool rough solidness spread across my back and solid ground pressed up against my feet once more.

A feeling of warmth seeped into me as if sunlight were bathing my skin. My eyes were assailed by light and my nose by a seriously bad stink.

I kept my eyes shut a moment longer.

Daytime. Hot sunshine blazed onto my cheeks. Its seductive warmth was ruined in a second by the reek of old banana skins, though, and the stink of previously-enjoyed baked beans and liquifying vegetables hit my nose a moment later.

Decay. Dirty old bins.

I hesitantly eased my eyelids off my eyes and squinted until I could see in the glare of sunlight.

It was a tiled patio with a cool brick wall against which my back had come to rest; an open created by two worn, greening wooden walls abutted against the brick of the building behind me.

To my left were two large, cylindrical metal bins, weathered to a dull chalkboard-rough grey, from which the rich brown aromas were no doubt arising.

Ahead of me, the open side of the little bin enclosure revealed a rather pretty and ornate stone patio spreading away to left and right.

I went to call out, but stopped myself because I was getting too smart to do an obviously stupid thing like that.

I stepped out of the bin enclosure and peered into the distance. Beyond the patio, a vast lawn sprawled downhill for at least half a mile and then levelled out onto a sun-baked yellow-green meadow…

The smile I had barely notice sneak onto my face now slipped off.

The glorious summer-blooming meadow ought to have rolled away to the horizon, but it didn't. It stopped bluntly at a deep, dense, dark forest that filled the rest of the visible world, ominous and forbidding.

"What is it with brooding forests?" I muttered to myself. "Is this a special emr fetish I don't know about?"

As the word 'fetish' passed my lips, who should appear around the corner of the building but Jen, Tom following puppy-style.

Sam, apparently, was around the corner, investigating, so as much as I loved spending time with the star-fucked lovers, I set off to find the more useful of my companions.

The building was boring brick on the first two sides I had seen, at least seven or eight storeys high, the patio an even width all the way around, surrounded by lawn and, in the near-distance, the forest too.

On the next side, it became clear what this place was. In the middle of the brickwork, at ground level, there was a great yellow-and-red canopy shielding a crescent-shaped burgundy welcoming rug onto a large glass revolving door.

It was a hotel.

Sam was close to the revolving door, so with a glance and a nod we went through together into a deeply rich sprawl of red-velvet lobby, its wave of passionate crimson sweeping out across a broad circular space overborne by a glorious crystal chandelier hanging imperiously some dozen feet above us.

In the middle of the gloriously luxuriant carpet sat a circular hardwood dais supporting a huge spray of vivid flowers in a china vase bigger than a teenager, the dais itself surrounded by a great circular seat of swollen scarlet cushions pouring off the edges of a matching hardwood seat-base.

A few guests milled around, crossing here and going there.

The pungent creamy tang of wood polish reached my nose as a lone porter, dressed in beige coveralls, put down his spray-can and yellow duster to stoop and pluck at the dense seat cushions.

"Now *that* is interior decorating," said Tom with no discernible irony as he joined us. "Do you think we're safe here?"

Idiot. "Get a grip, Tom. My brother made this, we're not safe anywhere that's got his grubby fingerprints on it."

The porter straightened up from the seat cushions, an invisible piece of fluff pinched between a finger and thumb, his hand held out before him as though what he had found were a miniscule yet hideous alien. A moment later he had disposed of the item and collected his polish to improve the already shiny wooden tabletops scattered about here and there around the great lobby.

Tom was still arguing. "You can't be sure your brother made this place, he didn't make the village."

The pungent creamy tang of wood polish reached my nose again as the porter sprayed the central dais again, then put down his spray-can and yellow duster to stoop and pluck at the dense seat cushions. Again; in the same place.

"Wait," I said. "Did you see that?"

Tom stared blankly back at me. "What?"

"I saw it," said Sam. "He's repeating precisely the same task."

The porter was carrying the non-existent piece of fluff away for disposal again.

There was no way to be sure, but...

"Everyone stay still, just watch," I suggested.

We stayed where we were and waited. The porter wandered away from the dais, armed with polish and a cloth, to tend to the tables. About a minute later, just as I began to think I'd been mistaken, he reappeared at the central dais, accompanied by the tang of polish, to pick once again at that long-since removed piece of fluff.

"I was right."

There had been no transition, I hadn't seen the moment when he vanished from near the tables nor the moment when he reappeared at the dais.

It was physically impossible.

"Laura was right," said Sam. "He isn't real; just... window dressing."

I felt a moment of pity for my brother. What kind of life had he known, where he had to create his own play-world and populate it with fake people?

Sam glanced at Tom, lending him sympathy he hadn't earned. "Perhaps my... Alan, thinks he destroyed us when he purged the village emr. It could be a while before he has any reason to come looking for us."

I wanted to believe that. "Of course he'll look for us, Sam."

"Right away?" Sam offered.

I sighed. I really wanted to believe he could be right. "OK, fine. We need a break and a hotel isn't the worst place for it. If we even can stay here, we'll take a night – but we stay alert. Never forget this is *his* world."

Tom grinned.

"Let's go and try this out. There may not actually be any real rooms; remember Edward's 'kitchen' back in the village?"

Jen coiled onto Tom's arm and he leant in to let her whisper to him. Whatever she said made him smirk and the pair of them scampered off across the lobby, arm in arm. How nice.

I went to follow, but Sam touched my arm. As I turned back to him, he wore a strained expression. "Can we talk for a moment?"

"About what?"

I was pinned by that huge earnest blue stare. ""I want to help, Laura, to ensure we will win this fight and save your world."

"Good to know. And?"

Those piercing eyes seemed to dilute. "The world we are saving is *your* world, Laura, not mine. I am long past my time, I have no right nor desire to continue this mockery of a life any longer than I have to."

I touched his arm. "I don't want to make you a stupid promise, Sam, we may all be dead soon."

"But if not – I don't know if this body would ever die naturally."

"If we survive, if I'm still in any state to do anything, I'll use whatever power I have left to send you on your way."

A half-promise of murder was all I could offer him. We crossed the lobby to the curved, ornate, leather-topped reception desk.

Jen was pretending to read some leaflet at the far end of the desk, with Tom lapdogging beside her as usual.

There was a little push-button bell on the desk. I leant on the leather desktop and rang it and the staff door at the rear of the reception area snapped open immediately to release a small ugly troll of a man upon us.

Shocked, I reacted on instinct. My normal senses receded into background as my mind opened up, ready to defend or attack as my brother emerged through that door.

With the clarity of my mind organ I saw the walls of the hotel, I saw the swirling mind energy that had been coalesced to form those walls, and I felt the power of my mind organ waiting impatiently to cut into my beloved, hated enemy as he crossed the space between the door and the desk front.

But then I saw something else – the swirling mind energy that had been coalesced to form the little man in front of us.

It's not him I sent to Sam.

The clone approached us and held my gaze lightly with blank doll eyes, lids unblinking, corneas dull and unreflective.

My mind coiled itself part way back into me, still ready to be opened up if I needed it, but the danger had diminished. This was an empty, dead facsimile, a vanity, perhaps, but surely not a threat despite the weirdness of its existence.

~ Do you think it's linked to him? ~

I glanced at Sam.

We'll soon find out

"Good afternoon, Madam."

He didn't really sound all that much like him. A deeper, much richer and more manly voice. A vanity toy, then, as I'd suspected.

He waited patiently as I stared at him.

"A room, please," I finally said. "No. Make that two."

I didn't think through the sleeping arrangements, if I'm honest. I should have asked for twin beds.

The fake Peter (Alan, I had to remind myself) sprang into action, flouncing to the little peg rack where the keys dangled expectantly, before returning to lay them on the leather counter-top.

"We hope you enjoy your stay."

Apparently there was no cash or card payment involved, because the little clone seemed to see that as the end of the transaction as he stood and smiled faintly at me.

Snatching up the keys we set off toward the hotel's broad ornate white staircase, Sam bringing up the rear and glancing back frequently at the copy of my brother, unconvinced I suppose that it could really be as benign as it wanted us to believe.

Sam bounded up the stairs to catch me up. "It might yet call out to its creator," he warned gravely.

I focused on lifting one foot, then the other. Shit a cooked pig, my legs ached. "My mind is still open in background, I'd feel it if that thing used any kind of power – you know, the head pinging thing?"

His blank look revealed that he didn't experience the same accompanying pain when he sensed trouble, but he got the point.

Upstairs, we found the first of our rooms. Tom took a key off me, opened the door and led Jen inside. I was surprised to find that this didn't hurt me as much as I would have expected.

Jen glanced back and flashed me a sneer. "Nightie night," she muttered pointedly.

"You can't just go to sleep, Jen!" I protested. "We need to stay alert for at least a little while, we don't know how safe this place is!"

Jen shrugged. "You keep lookout, then. Anyway, who said we're gonna be sleeping?"

She flashed me a smile then slammed the door. Fucking bitch.

"Fucking bitch," I said.

Sam and I moved a little way down the corridor, where we found 'our' room, but on entering I realised the error of my cock-up as I saw the cream eiderdown draped across the one double bed, bathed in the twin pools of pink light cast by bedside lamps whose job seemed to be to make the bed look even more alluring, soft and ready for hugs and love and sexytime.

I caught Sam smirking. "Don't even think about it."

He shrugged but kept his smirk on. "I have no need of a bed, Laura." A glint made his piercing blue eyes even sharper. "Take the bed, I promise to be the *perfect* gentleman while you sleep."

I leant him a wary gaze. "Just remember who you're dealing with. I cooked your nuts once – "

He laughed and held up placating hands. "I'm hardly likely to forget!"

Seeing that I was reassured, he leant on the room door until it clicked shut, and I was accosted by the faint but realistic aromas of old coffee, bathroom mildew and ingrained carpet dust. This really was a hotel room.

I flumped down on the edge of the bed, sinking and bouncing for just a moment as I took in the remainder of the room: a worn and over-stuffed armchair, a small table and the coffee-making facilities; all little sachets and a titchy kettle.

Coffee. It seemed like *forever* since I'd savoured a strong, sweet coffee. Even the shit coffee from the office machines of yester-ever-ago seemed like nectar to my wistful mind's eye.

Sam landed hard in the armchair.

I lay back on the bed and felt the deep soft comfort of pillows and I wondered if I ought to shower, I was sure I must be getting tangy-ripe under my tee-shirt and sweater, but then I wondered if I'd be able to actually sleep and then I realised my thoughts were cascading and thinking was getting very, very difficult – and then I wasn't looking at anything because my eyes were closed and then I was asleep.

I dreamt.

An office. Brightly lit, the air conditioning whooshing discreetly behind the busy sounds being generated by the milling people.

"Lonely in here without the ladies, don't you think?" The man asked.

"What? I... what?" Sam stammered, casting his gaze about wildly.

He was seated in an office chair, in the middle of a brilliantly-lit office, and the man before him, whom he could not recall having ever met, was somehow familiar. This was Laura's boss. *My* boss. Have to hold on to myself...

My boss. Ben.

Ben swivelled his chair gently left to right and back again, smiling and holding Sam's gaze as if they were old friends. "I quite miss Laura being around, although..." he leant forward in his chair, smirking. "You know, I really can't say the same about Jennifer, in all honesty."

Sam frowned at him.

"She needs to mature. She's just so... frivolous." I could feel Ben warming to his subject. He listened to the silence for a moment and then frowned. "What d'you mean, 'not a little girl'?" he asked, staring at Sam's chair.

Sam stared back, baffled.

Not as baffled as me, though. I wanted to cry out, to demand an explanation of what the hell was going on, but I had no voice. This was a dream, I was sure of that; it lacked the harsh clarity of the mind-links I'd shared with Sam at various times and, besides, the giant seemed as bewildered as me this time around. Was this the real Sam, pulled into the dream realm along with me?

Ben seemed to have scented gossip. He leant forward in his chair, eyebrows raised and lips extended in a rather feminine pout of pleasure. "I think I could hazard a guess, hmm? That little lady can certainly be, er..." He paused and smirked. "Persuasive, shall we say?"

Sam turned his back on him and studied the desk at which he sat. A computer, a notepad and a closed pen; a half-finished cup of coffee. A picture of his family. No, of James's family; the family of the man from whom Sam's mind had first been constructed, snatched from his deathbed and pulled through realities.

This was Sam's dream. How could I know what his family looked like? The woman looked faintly familiar, though she was younger than she had been when she had been tending her dying husband, witnessed by my disembodied presence. How could I be in Sam's dream...?

I felt the longing within the man, the need to pull free of the false life imposed by artificial flesh so he could become James once more, even if only in death.

Ben's telephone rang. Lifting the receiver, Ben stated his name mechanically and then listened. "Really? Are you…? Oh. I see. Yes, of course." He hesitated for a moment. "Thank you for letting me know."

Sensing Ben's gaze, Sam brought his chair around to face the thin man and whoever he represented in this scenario must have spoken, because Ben responded, tight-faced. "Well. Apparently," he said, swallowing what appeared to be a very dry and painful wad of spit, "the Police have found Jennifer dead in her flat after a complaint from a neighbour. She seems to have been that way for a few days." He paused, again presumably listening to a half of conversation that was not being shared with Sam and me. "Yes, the whole weekend." "What? No. He didn't say."

There was a pause during which Ben's gaze grew unfocussed. His mind was elsewhere.

His eyes sharpened very suddenly and fixed on Sam. "*You* killed her, didn't you, mister St Vincent…"

Sam jolted.

"Hello killer."

An elderly gentleman sat in the armchair to the right of a sealed fireplace in a small back room. His chair faced casement doors onto a neat garden in summertime, his chair angled so that with a turn of the head its occupant could look out at the garden or into the room. The elderly gentleman held a brown, discoloured brier pipe in his left hand, from which narrow trails of blue-grey smoke curled lazily upward into the air.

The gent smiled at Sam, pressed the pipe between his lips and sucked so that his cheeks momentarily collapsed inward like a parchment bellows. Smoke poured from his nostrils and the corner of his mouth and almost immediately, a sickly-sweet cloying odour reached Sam's nostrils. I felt the smell, the taste of it as Sam experienced those things, which was taking passive smoking to a whole new level.

The old chap drew the pipe gently from his mouth, a thin string of saliva pulling free and hanging between pipe and lip for a moment before peeling away.

His wrinkle-wrapped eyes flicked in what seemed to be my direction, though what he said was clearly not meant for me.

"Well, *obviously*," he growled in his course, gravelly voice at his intended recipient. "It is clear *now* that the division was a colossal mistake."

He seemed to listen to a side of some conversation that I was not privy to.

"No, it should not have happened, you're quite right. It should not even have been possible." The old man's tone was sharp, reproving, but his voice weakened as it thickened with phlegm. "Sometimes, the laws of the universe simply do not work."

Sam towered over the seated figure. "Who are you?"

The old man's pale watery eyes drifted to Sam. "Call me *Jack*."

Fuck!

A coldness that would have made my real flesh shudder at the realisation was more a disembodied disquiet in this dream.

How had I not recognised him? That cold, cold stare; that harsh abrasive voice. Good old grandpa Jack. Jack Esagen, the evil old bastard.

"What the hell is going on?" Sam cried, bewildered.

Jack puffed his pipe contentedly, his throat flexing like that of a croaking frog as he drew in the smoke.

He pulled the pipe free from between his thin lips and leant forward whip-quick, his eyes suddenly ice-sharp and glinting in the stream of sunlight entering the old room through the casement doors. "Mister St Vincent, this point cannot be over-emphasised!"

Sam started and took a half-step back.

"It is crucial that they reach union. *Crucial*, mister St Vincent. The sentinels have turned! Do you understand? The bounds of the realms are threatened, their dominion is incompatible with ours."

Sam was visibly struggling to get his act together, to ask the right question, but abruptly the old man slumped back in his armchair and sighed, exhausted and resigned. "Oh, too bad, too bad. I wish we had more time, mister St Vincent, but Bobby is ready for you now. Take what I have shared and do as you are able. I must return to death, now."

"Bobby? What?" Frowning, Sam turned to see…

… Bobby slipped out of the house while his family were occupied with their preparations. Where were they going? – Escaping. Escaping from Sam.

Bobby grabbed his raincoat, holding it over his head as he ran across the green to the village pub.

(old Edward's meetings were pretty unbearable unless you got yourself on the outside of a few beers!)

He pushed the little door open, stepping into the pub. As he turned to close the door, he thought he saw a figure approaching through the drizzle, but he was unsure; the light was bad today. Shrugging, he pushed the door shut and crossed to the bar, thinking that he might take it on himself to install some decent lighting in here. This was more his pub than anyone else's, since he used it the most. So why shouldn't he change it from this stupid 'Olde Worlde' place into something a bit more modern?

Lifting the hatch on the bar, Bobby slipped through and set about pulling himself a pint, only to find that the pump was off. He crouched down behind the bar, probing around for a clue as to why there was no beer; this wasn't a real pub, so it shouldn't really run out of beer.

Suddenly there was a dull whump of noise and then the orange bloom of fire outside.

The noise repeated and then an explosion rocked the pub. Bobby threw himself down and cowered under the bar.

He stayed concealed, waited.

The violence outside went on forever but then stopped as sharply as it had begun. Bobby waited, too afraid to move.

Alone in utter silence, he must have dozed off because suddenly there were voices.

"Jen, it ain't like–"

"Fuck off! Just keep the fuck away from me, OK?"

"Aw, come on, Jen!"

We had arrived. Jen, Tom and me.

Sam lunged forward, trying to grab at the boy and save him, but he was not here any more than I was, and whether we liked it or not, events played out as they had before and Bobby was soon on his knees just as before, clutching the testicles Jen had devastated with her knee, and all too soon the then-version of Sam would be arriving.

We heard a creak as someone opened the pub door. This was it.

It was over so quickly.

Bobby tried to clamber up off his knees but his body failed him. Sam lumbered straight at him, grabbed his head and wrenched the boy up until he was virtually dangling on his tiptoes. The giant stabbed his straightened fingers full force into Bobby's exposed throat and let him go so he could stagger back on bowing legs. Sam swung a leg and kicked up hard between the boy's legs, his boot crunching against the testicles Jen had already traumatised.

The boy would have collapsed, but Sam grabbed him by the hair.

Driven by the mindless rage of his animal self, Sam threw the boy against the bar, grabbed a heavy glass ashtray, struck it on the bar-top to break it and stabbed the jagged edge into Bobby's throat.

The Sam of then turned and left Bobby clutching his throat, gagging, falling to his knees as the pub door slammed shut and he struggled to breathe through the thick lump in his throat, a large jagged chunk of apple stuck in there that he would never again get his breath past.

The Sam sharing the dream experience with me was left to watch the consequences of his former actions.

I felt it. Felt the ghastly, choking, suffocating death that this boy was enduring. I guess Sam must have felt it too, experiencing first-hand the agony he had inflicted whilst under my brother's thrall.

Hands clawing at his throat, feeling two loose wet flaps of flesh, he struggled to draw breath as his own blood bubbled in his windpipe. He turned his eyes up suddenly to Sam. The Sam of now, the one dreaming all this.

"I'm sorry," Sam whispered to the dying boy, his voice constricted by the grief of remorse. He staggered back, stumbled, fell …

… and landed in a comfy office chair. He turned quickly, expecting to see Ben again, but he was alone in a work pod, a different pod.

The sound of footfalls approaching along the corridor. Female feet; heels. He waited to see who it would be.

He watched her walk past in the corridor, turning his head to follow her as she went into the coffee area. He cast eyes over her entire body…

My body. My fucking body!

…her breasts, her full hips and those big, strong thighs.

Bastard!

Sam teased himself for a furtive moment, his penis pounding, his balls crawling with sick delight. But, no. Not Sam's balls.

No, not Sam's, and I had a bad feeling I knew who it was who was lusting after me. I felt Sam's unfamiliarity with the balls at his fingertips, the penis pulsing with anticipation. This was someone else's fantasy, someone else's lust for me, although that didn't make it any less real to Sam; I felt the blood pounding through that erection and I knew that Sam felt the same lust, the same twisted and sick desire…

…and then began a yearning of the spirit that was much more potent than mere lust, but which hid itself behind his lust and thus remained concealed. Imagining the deeply secret things that he would do with her, the pain in her eyes, the blood on his hands, and the tears that would drip to deepen the crimson of the floor …

Shit!

Laura kicked the strewn clothes aside to make a space on her bedroom floor.

Hey! Look at me, star of my own show!

OK, this was fucking weird.

Her blouse fluttered to the floor, followed by her bra. Her skirt dropped around her feet and she stepped out of it, her panties still hooked around one ankle, trailing.

*Er, **my** panties. Hey, Put your fucking clothes back on you silly bitch! Sam's getting a full-frontal view here!*

"No!" Sam cried, and lurched a step toward her. Me.

Laura looked up, straight at him, eyes wide and terrified, backing away as he began to approach her.

"This was never – it didn't happen!" He protested, and I had to agree.

She backed away, naked, wide-eyed and helpless, with a thin drool of saliva oozing from her gaping mouth, the stark blend of naked tits and naked terror arousing Sam's base nature even as he protested against it.

Yeah, fucking right this never happened, and as for you, you dozy bitch, will you for fuck's sake cover up our fanny!

He reached out a hand toward her, his groan seeming half protest and half tortured lust. She screamed and staggered back, but then Sam heard the thump of footsteps on the stairs beyond her door and suddenly Tom Peters crashed through the door.

Sam was released from the grip of whatever force had driven him to act out his part, and he staggered away from the pair, panting and clasping the hand he had tried to molest her – me – with.

"Oh, Tom, it was horrible," she sobbed, sounding lame and pathetic…

I needed a voice to protest. This was the bullshit icing on a bullshit-flavoured cake with real pieces of bullshit in it. I was *never* once *that* weak in my entire fucking life! Was I?

Was this an alternative day, one I hadn't remembered yet? Surely not, I'd remembered the other splits in reality…

Tom came to her, folding his arms about her body. He was solid and heavy and smelled pleasantly of spicy soap.

Ohh, shit, I could taste that scent on my tongue, remember the pressure of his body that one time in the bathroom at Grandma's house…

He shifted awkwardly, trying to place his hands on neutral skin, so she pushed against his body, forcing him to feel the heat of her flesh, and as she did she felt him respond, at first hesitantly, but then in a moment his hands were mobile. He ran them down the curve of her back, down, down, until he pressed them into her buttocks. She gasped, pressing herself against him harder.

Great! Now I'm a porn star! What the actual fuck?

Tom's hands came around onto her belly, then moved up her body. She drew her head back to look at his face, but his eyes were cold and he just stared at her, his hands dead on her skin.

"Hey, don't stop," She whispered, the tingle of his hands on her skin filling her with an unaccustomed and overwhelming sexiness. Now she moved her hands onto his buttocks, gazing into his eyes and moving her head closer, lips parting to kiss him.

But now, suddenly, Tom's eyes looked dead…

He was dead. His skin was dry, his eyes wilted and half-collapsed, his lips withered. Tom was a corpse and he was still touching me.

We woke together at that moment.

Sam jolted awake and his buttocks lifted from the padding of the armchair, his arms flailing outwards in reflex, his wide eyes reflecting more panic than I would have thought possible on that face.

His breathing was hot and thudding and the after-echo of his aching lust drew into me the recollection of the physical pressure of his throbbing hard-on. None of which helped to ease my horrible sense of having just played the porn star for him.

"What the *fuck* was that?" I panted.

It was gloomy in the room but not so dark we couldn't catch each other's eyes with enough clarity to both recoil and look away. Outside the little window, night had fallen.

I pursed my lips, trying to suppress an irrational anger toward Sam. "I assume from your juddering boner that we just shared that bunch of messed-up dream-porn."

He kept his gaze on the window. "How long did we sleep?"

I saw, revealed to me, the motion of the muscles that created that expression – the fake ones I was supposed to see and the real, actual manufactured workings beneath; the inhuman, botched-together materials that made up Sam's workings, laid bare by my keen mind's eye.

He lowered his hand and gingerly touched himself and I watched the motion of his muscles, human-looking but driven by a hotch-potch of animal mechanisms, yet still, as his hand moved to his groin and I recalled the tingling ache of *his* erection between *my* legs; I drew a sharp intake of breath at the shockingly vivid arousal I felt.

His or mine?

The image was only slightly tainted by the spattered spider goo that was now a dry residue across the front of his prettyboy dress shirt.

He glanced at me sharply and I realised he was still linked to me. "Sorry," I said. "It's very confusing for both of us."

He grunted and I heard the chair creak as he laid his weight back into it. Because we were in an artificial place, because there was no wildlife outside nor any real guests apart from our two friends down the corridor, there was a deeply hollow silence in the room.

"Our link," I started, suddenly keen to justify myself. "It makes me share your, well your animal feelings."

His brow creased. "He created me so he could experience things without placing himself in harm's way. I was a puppet, but also a proxy. I do a thing, he gets to experience it."

There was an awkward silence. My brain raced but I had nothing to say that wouldn't sound patronising or lame.

At last, Sam spoke. "I suppose it's a good thing. The way he made me, as a conduit for his mind, has made our link possible." He turned his head to look at me. "And we fight well together that way."

I sat up, fumbled for the switch for the wall lights beside the headboard and flicked on the little shaded lamps on the wall either side of the bed. "Guess we're through with sleeping for the night."

He held up his hands and stared at them. "So much blood." He drew a deep breath that swelled his chest massively. "But at least for the last part of this war I get to fight at your side, not his. That's why I came looking for you; I think maybe this is all my fault. When I found you, my proximity must have triggered something in you that started all of this happening."

He wouldn't look at me, now. He seemed to forlorn.

I smiled at him. "No, Sam. My brother worked in the same office as me. Not a coincidence. All our lives we've been unconsciously drawn toward each other; him more than me, but I can feel the pull of it when I'm with him. It's like we were meant to find each other. I don't think you can blame yourself."

He shared a half-smile wit the floor, thought for a moment and the looked earnestly at me. "Who is Jack Esagen?"

"What?" The question startled me, caught me completely off-guard. I bit my lip.

"He seemed important in my dream. I wondered if you knew who he was."

I rubbed my calf muscles, which were tight from the position I'd held whilst sleeping, although better than they had been in the last – what? Hours? Days? How long had we been on the run, now?

"He was my grandfather," I told him. "Jack was my grandfather. Mine and Peter's."

"I wonder why you dreamt of him; were you close?"

I laughed coldly and shook my head. "I hated him, Sam. The only tears I shed for him were tears of joy when he died, knowing I'd never be under that old bastard's cold scrutiny ever again. No way was that *my* dream."

"Well, then that begs a question, does it not?"

"I think he had our power; I mean, maybe our power, mine and Peter's, comes from him. Wait. What question?"

He spread his hands. "Where did all those images come from?" He arose from his chair in a single fluid movement that defied physics and the natural fatigue of muscles.

"Coffee?"

Grey light began to bloom into a wintry morning glow outside as Sam busied himself with the little white plastic kettle and the sachets. I stretched my arms up and let loose a great yawn, feeling jaw and spine crack under the strain of these movements.

-36-

After a rather unpleasant cup of cheap instant coffee and faux milk, I decided to take a shower before we ventured out to find the other two.

In the bathroom I kicked off my shoes, dropped my jumper and jeans on the towel rail to keep them dry and then peeled off my sweaty tee-shirt. As I was about to drop the rag into the bathroom bin, a thought occurred. Hastily pulling my jumper back over me, I opened the door a crack.

"Sam?"

"I'm here."

I tossed the stinky tee-shirt around the gap in the door. "Put this on. Stinks a bit but at least it's not covered in spider goo!"

I slammed the door and finished undressing. My panties would be unfit even to wipe up spider goo, so those I binned.

I caught a glimpse of myself in the mirror and was snared by my image. I stared into my own eyes and met myself staring back.

It was so strange. I had barely given it a thought but suddenly, seeing myself, the me I had always been, the me I had been before all of... *this*; reality hit me cold and hard.

I was going to have to fight my brother, the self-styled 'Alan', and whichever way I looked at it I was going to be changed forever. I would either live but as a survivor in whatever world was left to us – or, more likely, I would die.

I had been holding my breath and now I blew a ragged breath out and gasped a new one in. The reality of it. My life was over already. And very soon there was a very good chance I was actually going to be dead. I wondered how anyone could cope with this knowledge, the idea of death approaching. How could they be brave in the face of their ending?

I was falling. Tumbling down into darkness. My legs were trembling and I felt cold, alone and really scared.

"Damn," I murmured. Dragged myself away from the mirror and tried to put it out of my mind as best I could even as it was very clear to me that this revelation of my terrible future was going to haunt me every time I paused for breath.

The shower needed time to heat up so the initial cold slap of water against my skin hit me as a painful yet welcome shock, invigorating me even as it made me shudder, pimpling skin and puckering nipples. It warmed quickly enough, though, becoming hot as it spattered across my skin and prickled against nerve-endings.

I soaped my body slowly, pressing fingers into my neck, arms, breasts and belly. The sensations grew intensely pleasurable and I realised, too late to stop myself, how low my fingers had ventured, how deeply they were massaging.

The dread of mere minutes ago abated – or perhaps was the catalyst for this sudden need for distraction, relief.

Thoughts of the feral beast in the other room intruded into my mind, the possibility he might burst through that flimsy bathroom door at any moment.

Thoughts of Sam's power, his bulk filled my head and teased me in an ever-upward crescendo of sensation as I worked my fingers, imagining his primal response to my nakedness, picturing his vast hard cock, his broad strong rampant unstoppable body naked as he gave in to his animal and was consumed by lust, took my helpless naked body to him and imposed his manhood upon my yielding, willing flesh.

As the fantasy grew more base and vile, so the warm waves of pleasure grew hot, scolding and consuming me completely; eyes shut, the world beyond my fantasy washed away as my Sam fell to the brutal aching of his inhuman manhood and... and...

My last frantic cry fled my lips as I crashed against the mind-numbing final sensations, but I didn't care if he heard me, I wanted him to know, to come and find me and make it happen, oh make it happen right fucking *now!*

Climax over. Just the shower.

I glanced at the door, suddenly aware with a thrill of humiliating dread that he might have come in, might even now be watching me strum one off for him.

The door was closed.

Sam called from behind the closed door, though. Checking that I was OK.

"Ohhh…"

"Laura?"

"Fuck," I murmured. "I'm fine, Sam!" I called out.

He might not believe me, might burst in and find me clutching my fanny like it had fallen off and wouldn't re-attach. I slumped back against the cold tiled wall and forced myself to let go down there, ending the last of the afterglow.

I cleaned myself properly this time, used the shower for its intended purpose, then clambered out, scraped myself dry with a classic hotel towel and checked my remaining clothes.

The jumper I'd acquired at Edward's place was OK, the tee-shirt had borne all of my stink, so I pulled it on without bra or tee-shirt, and then the jeans with no panties. Full commando – I was practically a hooker.

I pulled the flat pumps on, ignoring whether or not they smelled of feet because I knew they did but there was no useful choice in it.

When I left the bathroom I breezed past Sam and casually suggested that we should go rouse the others, before leaving without waiting to see if he would actually follow.

As we passed along the hotel corridor, I was careful to drop my heels a little harder than usual, enjoying the way the jolts made my breasts flubber under the jumper, the nipples rubbing in a wonderfully intimate way. I'd never done it before and it felt really nice.

I only knocked once on Tom's door before he answered, peering out with dull, dark-ringed eyes.

"Breakfast?" I offered cheerily, smiling sweetly.

"It can't be morning already," he moaned thickly. He looked shocking, as if he hadn't had a minute's sleep.

"Look out the window, lazy bones," I advised cheerily, loving the chance to give him some of the shit I felt I owed him for chivving me for Jen.

He grunted. "Yeah. Who needs sleep?"

serves you fucking right

~*really, Laura?*~

I glanced at Sam. I'd forgotten that he could hear me if I pushed my thoughts out too forcefully.

A moment later, Tom re-emerged in his blue jeans and white tee-shirt, followed by Jenny in her tight black skirt and that tight white summer top through which her podgy, crinkly brown nipples protruded and gyrated with the rock and swell of the fleshy mounds they rode so boldly upon. She flashed me a smug smile and brushed past Tom like the cat-who-got-the-cream.

We went downstairs in silence.

I was struck by how fresh Jen looked; fresher than she'd looked for days, now; and how that contrasted so sharply with Tom's weary bedraggled face. They had both been looking a little grey but now Jen suddenly looked fucking *blazing*, when she ought to look how I felt – exhausted, bedraggled.

There really was no justice.

-37-

Downstairs in the restaurant a few people were already taking breakfast, eating in silence. These were virtual diners, of course, just raw meat characters engineered to make the place seem real, sketched but not completed, their faces faintly similar to each other and their actions repetitive – spoon the flakes, butter the toast, sip the coffee.

Sam and I did a raised-arms rumba between the tables and caught up with Jen and Tom as they claimed the prime spot; a round table in the bow of the large bay window overlooking the hotel lawns.

I shuffled my bum onto a chair and drew it in toward the table, just as a vicious arc of lightning spiked across the dark grey sky outside and snatched my attention, a ghostly silhouette of the distant forest burnt onto my retinas.

"Ouch," I protested weakly.

"Oh, very imaginative," Jenny said disinterestedly. "Another storm."

Unable to dismiss that blinding streak as readily as Jen had, I peered out across the gloomy lawns, down toward the bleak black forest sitting in its own private storm beneath glowering grey clouds. She was right, another storm was hardly the last word in originality in the emr.

Sam sat down smoothly, displaying his fake body's easy grace. "The storm is not part of this reality, it belongs to the wider chaos closing in on us."

I glanced at him, wondering how bad the world we had left behind was going to be, when or if we ever returned to it. "Thanks, Sam. Any other cheery thoughts?"

A big if. I was probably never going to go home.

The weirdly blank clone of my brother approached us, a small pad and pencil in his hand.

I avoided the thing's gaze, finding it too eerie to look at those tragically soulless eyes in that now very familiar face.

"Good morning!" he cried with a queer false cheer in his voice. "May I take your order, please?"

I glanced at Sam and he looked back at me, his brow furrowed. This absurdly cheerful clone was halfway between hilariously funny and horribly sick, but it was probably even more disturbing for Sam than it was for me.

We ordered breakfast from it and the clone walked away. As we waited, I pushed damp hair back behind my ears, drawing a sharp breath as my naked nipples scraped the rough interior of my jumper. A shudder shimmered down my spine and I realised I was looking at Sam just as I realised how intense my gaze would be as I once again indulged a grossly predatory urge towards his penis.

"I don't know how much more of this I can stand," Jenny murmured quietly to Tom. Whether she'd seen my flirty eyes on Sam or whether she just meant this whole situation, I didn't know. Or much care.

Tom slipped an arm around her shoulders.

Before I could react to Love's Labia Lost, the organ of my mind sprang sharply from background to foreground, seizing control of my motor functions and turning my inner eye, followed by my actual eyes, toward the restaurant entrance.

Sam's head snapped up too, his gaze fixed upon me. Our link was still there, passive in the background but now beginning to spike.

Two leather-clad men had just strode into the restaurant area, their oversized motorcycle crash helmets glinting menacingly off the glare of the old-fashioned bulbs hanging from the ceiling. Caught off-guard by the unexpectedly potent activation of my mind, it took me a moment to grasp the sight before me.

"Shit!"

Sam grunted. "So much for our respite." He rose smoothly to his feet and I clambered up to join him, my pulse quickening as a fresh chance to die violently presented itself for my consideration.

A fork clattered to the floor with a melodic chime.

The Alan-waiter swung his hips left and right as he manoeuvred between his seated patrons and hurried across to the waiting figures, the consummate host intent on greeting the new arrivals. The nearer biker swiped him with the back of its hand and the little man was hurled flailing across a table and out of sight.

Guess the Alan clone doesn't get master's privileges over the slaves, I thought in a moment of spiteful glee that was instantly wiped away.

My thoughts collapsed to a far-off pinprick as I felt a dark and malevolent something touch my mind.

One of the spiders. I felt it probe at my mind, exploring me. Seeking a weakness.

Distracting me.

Cunt.

I snapped focus away just in time to sense thought knot forming before the visor of the second creature's impassive visor. It snapped across the room at me with a harsh bark of sound. I aimed my mind at it. Pushed. My mindforce diverted the knot and it snapped across the room to burst apart, sizzling and burning, against the far wall of the dining room. I smelled and tasted the acrid tang of scorching materials as a slab of wall fell in on itself and spouted grey dust at the nearby diners.

The 'people' at the tables seemed blissfully unaware, chatting and clinking cutlery, too stupid or basic to sense or care about the danger to themselves.

I sensed another thought knot. It flew at me but my mind pushed and it looped away from me, but somehow this one had some spin on it, because it curled in an arc and clipped a diner off to the side of me.

A middle-aged man in a vaguely grey suit, he began to scream and thrash around as a smear of knot venom blossomed on his arm and scorched its way into him. So, the dummies here could feel pain. Oh dear. It seemed a harsh and unnecessary feature. He staggered screaming into a small family party at the next table, spreading the hungry venom and bringing their screams into the party.

I edged around a table, the assassins my only focus as the rest of the virtual diners finally realised their peril and kicked free from their tables in screaming panic.

Another thought knot shot at me and I swiped at this one too, but this one slowed before my mind could grasp it; it drew back, dodged my defence, twisted itself so it could swerve back at me for a second bite.

"Fu-uck!" I cried as that evil mass came at my face.

Blistering heat on my face, my eyes, I pushed out frantically with a cry of panic, but in my hasty defence I exerted a lot of mindforce and managed to throw the knot straight off into a cluster of fleeing diners, incinerating them in a spray of black filth.

Sam, where the fuck are you!

The rich cloying stench of burning flesh hit my nose and I heard the pop of frying skin as their remains were incinerated.

I had no time to experience the horror of killing what little life they had as I felt another knot forming.

I was getting a serious cuntpunting. I just wasn't ready. Sam and I had been lucky when we faced these sick spider-piloted assassins before, but this time, no, this time I was barely defending myself —I hadn't even tried to fight back yet.

I staggered away from them as my mind organ felt the pinging ache of a new thought knot forming behind one of those visors. My vision was blurred, my head ached. The terrifying possibility hit home that I might faint – only to awaken on fire in the gore of knot venom that these bastards planned to dump on me.

Sam...

He had abandoned me. Stupid, stupid Laura. I should have known.

My head throbbed and my vision swam in a lazy loop of dizziness. Closing down, losing focus, I caught my leg on an upturned chair and flailed, just managing to keep my balance, but then one of the assassins unleashed its deadly black venom upon me.

Still staggering I struggled to focus my mind as the lethal black mass flashed toward me but I had no chance, my mind literally wasn't with it.

I slumped, fell and landed hard on my backside on the cold, unforgiving floor of the restaurant.

I think I whimpered as my mind quiesced for the last time.

The brief few seconds that the black mass took to slash through the air across the room seemed to slow, to stretch out into an eternity.

-38-

Two things happened at more or less the same time: the thought knot burst apart – and my mind cut back into sharp focus at a familiar presence in my head.

~ *get up, Laura* ~

I heard a whimper and knew it was me. Oh, the shame of it. I found my strength through the sheer humiliation and clambered to my feet, mind opening out to feel the room.

you took your fucking time I sent to him with a smirk.

Sam ignored my 'wit' but my focus had shifted anyway as I zoomed in on the nearer of the two assassins. I sent it some unwanted mindmail. Full force – its visor exploded outward, the jagged hole left in the black crash helmet welling up and bubbling over with the scolding venom of my volcanic fury.

A hideous alien scream echoed through my mind as the shrivelled, steaming tangle of a fat, burning spider plopped out onto the floor.

Sam hurtled past me, orb already raised and targeting the remaining assailant.

A thought knot erupted from the orb, flying at the second assassin, but this creature anticipated the attack and deflected Sam's knot with its own orb-derived mindforce, sending the venom veering in a wild arc across the room, while the creature instantly targeted Sam and returned at what was now virtually point-blank range.

Sam only had time to stagger back a pace but he was never in danger.

No, no. Sam had all the cover he needed.

the bitch is back! I sent to him as I grasped the thought knot and crushed it with the rage-fuelled torque of my mind. Almost at the same instant, I threw out a blast of mental energy, yet this time what emerged from me was quite unlike a thought knot; pinkish, translucent, a streaming ribbon of mindforce that rippled across the gulf between me and the assassin with timeless ease and grace like a vast tentacle.

No-one was more surprised than me at what I had created.

In that millionth of a second, I had all the time imaginable to study this beautiful tendril, glimmering, ethereal yet strangely organic as it rode the push of my will straight out across the room, toward the assassin.

I felt my enemy's instinctive, mindless fear at this new and unknown thing. I *liked* that fear.

And I decided to touch with my new limb, to use it; to kill with it.

It moved like a tentacle but it was lightning-fast and it covered the space between us, my enemy and me, in less than a breath.

The leather-clad body burst open like a ripe soft fruit dropped on concrete. It was an utterly silent death as pilot and host instantly ruptured so completely that there was not even blood in the vapour of their detonation.

Its work done, the cord furled itself back into me and was gone.

Sam was staring at me. I wondered what he had seen.

With a quizzical tilt of his eyebrow he dismissed the moment and led the way out of the breakfast room to check for further hostiles.

The hotel lobby was empty. The porter with his polish was nowhere to be seen.

My mind opened out but sensing nothing. Nothing to see or sense, nor any pinging pains in my head warning of trouble.

nothing I sent to Sam

~ *no, just those two, it would seem* ~

As we turned from the lobby to re-join our pointless companions, I saw out of the corner of my eye that the porter was suddenly back, his yellow cloth calmly and evenly caressing the central plinth and creating that warm, deep, homely aroma of furniture polish.

The porter had been 'turned back on'. This reality was resetting itself.

Back in the dining room, I saw the carnage with eyes now that my mind was furled.

Jen still sat at the table across by the window, gazing at her cutlery as if she were simply awaiting her breakfast.

Tom was kneeling between the upended tables. He looked for a moment as if he were having a crafty wank, but as I drew nearer I saw that he was tending one of the fake people, a man who had been seared across the belly and legs by the black venom but had somehow survived being consumed.

The structure of the room looked ready to collapse in on itself. There was scorched brickwork and plaster exposed on many parts of the walls, most of the tables were upended, some had legs sheared off in splintered stumps. Chairs, too, lay in various states of ruin – and amongst this wreckage were bodies.

They were not real people, of course, but they looked real and that made it hard to look at their burnt, twisted forms, many missing limbs and all very definitely dead. Including, I now saw, the one that Tom had been trying to tend.

"Jen," I said as we reached the table. "You OK?"

She didn't answer.

Tom moped over, looking all forlorn. He sat carefully beside Jen and took her hand, although she remained wide-eyed and strangely disinterested... or perhaps just distant.

I would have asked my former friend what was wrong, but at that moment there was a ping at the base of my skull. Not a big one, not painful, but it made me turn and scope the room and I spotted the Alan clone, our dumb waiter, returning.

Not him; that shallow drone could not be the source of the warning. I opened my mind to address the urgent need to trace the location of whatever new enemy we faced.

Sam, do you see it? where is it?

~ *he's here he's here he's here* ~

Sam's thoughts were jumbled, frantic; I could not recall him ever falling apart like this. It made no sense.

A moment later I felt a scold of adrenaline flood my belly as I caught up with Sam and realised the enormity of the threat.

My brother stopped a few feet from me and smiled. His potent mind flicked at mine. How could I have thought this was the fake Alan-cum-waiter?

My mind was already open, I was ready for him; but then his eyes vanished.

What? No.

Impossible as it was, in that instant they were gone, the sockets empty, a corpse gaze from a still-living face.

My rational mind reasoned that this must be a side-effect of mindforce, but seeing bluish veins in the smear of red meat at the back of those bone sockets, I felt bile swell into my throat and I staggered away from him I wild dread.

Faced with my enemy and my beloved brother at such immediate proximity, shocked and sickened by his ghastly display, it was all I could do to extend a defensive layer of thought energy across myself and my companions before he could fire on us.

To my right, Sam twitched and stood still. He was even more stunned than I was as the will to act battled the inertia of paralysing fear in the face of his former master. His orb hand hung uselessly at his side.

Two bolts of thought matter swelled into existence in those cadaverous sockets. My body let out a guttural cry but my mind was more lithe and it grabbed at the lethal matter, pulled it from him and hurled it away.

His thought energy was a hundred times stronger than the energy from one of the orbs. I did it, hurled it away, but it was like lifting a wardrobe and realising someone's been using it to store their anvils. It tore every muscle in my mind.

A vicious dagger of pain split my brain in half and threw lit fireworks across my vision. There was a rapid rush of air through my ears and, straight afterward, darkness and then a bang in my head.

A dazzling flash of tumbling images. The restaurant walls / defend Sam / defend Tom / push Alan back / the restaurant ceiling / new attack coming. I had already fallen into unconsciousness and everything was dark, yet my mind organ was somehow still fighting my brother in my absence and I was still hooked I enough to experience the battle as a sequence of disjointed moments.

There were bangs, cries of pain, or maybe rage.

I had a sudden sense of Alan's mind; strong and focused, but then fading, a defensive wall of mindforce shielding it as it moved off and vanished.

-39-

"She's sleeping,"

A whispered voice intruded into the black silence.

I heard movements that I recognised from earlier. Sam was taking the little kettle into the bathroom to fill it.

Other voices. *"We're in deep shit, Jen. Just look at her!"*

"Keep it down, she might hear you." A woman's voice. Jen.

"Nah, she's out for the count." The man's voice again. Tom. It seemed to drift nearer and further, as though its volume were being deliberately altered. *"Look at her. That fuckin' brother of hers barely broke a sweat and look at her!"*

"Did you see his eyes, Tom?" A note of fear made the female voice waver.

A pause. *"Course I did."*

A smear of light I'd barely been aware of suddenly spread out before me and coalesced into a field of vision encapsulating the ceiling of my room and, peripherally, two figures watching over me. I felt the bed, at my back now, then I glimpsed movement on the other side of the bed and turned my head to watch Sam click the kettle on, rip open a sachet of coffee far too forcefully so that its brownish granules scattered all over the little table, and then glance at my nervous friends.

"You are both weak. Even as an enemy I could respect Laura. She at least had some little courage, even when facing her fears and shortcomings."

Ouch. Damned by faint praise. I was still detached from the room, too distant to really feel angry or upset.

Tom bit back. *"Good for her, but who's caught in the cross-fire, Sam? We ain't all got fucking orbs, you know."*

There was a clink as Sam dropped a spoon into a cup. *"Oh, you are right on so many levels with that remark, Tom. No orbs. That very succinctly sums you up."*

I flinched and opened my eyes but the ceiling above me was dancing and my stomach was trying to join in. I winced as a sickening ache pulsed through my head.

"It was much nicer being unconscious," I muttered.

"Welcome back," said Sam. "What do you remember?" Sam asked.

"Shit!" Panic trumped nausea and I tried to wedge my elbows under me to get up but there was a sudden lack of certainty concerning up and down and I slumped back with a whump onto the pillow. "Where is he? Help me up! Where is he?"

Sam laid a hand on my shoulder. "We are safe for a moment. You fought him off, Laura, forced him to retreat."

"I did?" That made no sense. "How?"

He shrugged and smiled. "All that matters is that you did it. I saw that strange, well, tentacle that came out of your head when you detonated the second assassin. You fell down and I thought that it was over, yet even as you fell, your tentacle lashed at him."

"I was unconscious for the whole thing, Sam."

He smiled. "That perhaps explains the ferocity of it. He was clearly overwhelmed and made a fairly hasty retreat, I suspect he was shocked by such a brutal assault."

I laughed although I felt bitter and hopeless. "Shocked, yes. He wasn't expecting such a pathetic opponent to bite back at all!"

"*How* is unimportant, Laura. What matters is that he'll think twice before coming at you head-on like that again."

"No, Sam, it does matter how. So we can win every time as long as I'm unconscious?"

He rubbed my shoulder and stepped away from the bed. "You just need to practice, Laura; train yourself to be able to call on the full power of your gift at your conscious command."

I felt the hotness of tears boil up out of the corners of my eyes.

i can't do this....

I missed my house, I missed my car, I missed Basil the Bear... a wistful image hit me hard; of sitting in front of the TV in our parlour, just me and Grandma, slurping tea and watching one of 'our' programmes. Hers, really, but it was still our time. Soaps, tacky quiz shows, occasional wildlife documentaries. It hurt to remember. I wanted to go home, I was never ever going to win this fight.

Sam was at the coffee-making facility table. "Would you like some coffee?" he asked me.

His words reached my ears as his thoughts hit my mind.

~ be strong for the others, Laura, you did hurt him, it's still a victory, however small ~

He turned his ultraviolet gaze on me. Clearly he had been tuned in to my self-pitying moment of doubt. I think that this had more of an effect on me than his rallying thoughts ever could. The power of shame to motivate.

I smiled half-heartedly at him. "Coffee would be nice."

The four of us perched on the edge of my bed and sipped the coffees that Sam had made for us. It was cheap awful shit; not even that, it was an approximation of cheap awful shit; but it was hot and almost like an actual cup of coffee and it helped.

I glanced at Tom, hoping he could at least be civil to me, now. "Not quite that cup of tea you talked about in the woods, but something; right?"

He humphed and nodded.

~ he does not deserve your time or your regret, Laura ~
tell me about it

"Could do with a biscuit," Tom suddenly offered, so that I glanced his way. He flashed me a quick wink and I couldn't help but smile back.

Chugging the last of his coffee, Tom got to his feet and crossed to the room's little window. I could see daylight outside, which suggested I hadn't been unconscious all day. Well, that or I'd been unconscious a day and a half!

It was daylight outside, but gloomy. The 'boutique' carriage-lamps on the wall were switched on, as were the bedside lamps, to push back the oppressive gloom. It had been a blinding summer's day when we arrived a day ago, I thought wistfully.

Tom leant on the windowsill and peered outside. "We're never going to be safe, are we?"

"Nope," Jen contributed. "I'm beginning to think we're on the wrong side."

I rounded on her but she was smirking straight at me. "Kidding you soppy cow!"

I doubted her sincerity, somehow. "We won't be safe until we stop my brother."

"Fat chance," Jen pouted out.

I was about to tell the bitch her fortune, when the lights in the room – all of them, carriage lamps and bedside – flickered and dimmed.

"Whoa," Jen uttered.

The lights came back up.

Sam arose swiftly off the bed. "Something is happening."

Jen peered up at him and pulled a face. "No shit, professor."

The lights ebbed away a second time and I glimpsed, over Tom's shoulder, that the light outside the window also grew dull. The *day*light.

"Get away from the window, Tom!" I snapped.

He pushed away from the sill and turned to me. "Fuck's going on?"

Outside the window, the world beyond was pulsing from grey and stormy day to ebony night in perfect synchronisation with the lights in the room. There was more going on than some weird effect of the light.

"It's him!" I declared. "He's going to erase this reality!"

When the light next faded it did not well back up, but rather it diminished into deeper gloom, absolute absence of light, and stayed there. As the seconds passed my eyes did not adapt and I felt panic rise in me at the realisation that this was utter darkness. We were blind.

Utterly defenceless without my eyesight, not even a glint anywhere to orient myself by, I felt panic billow up through me as my heart thudded violently against my ribs.

are you still there? I sent out to Sam, but to be honest to anyone who might help – and I was suddenly, horribly reminded of the terrible, hopeless appealing voices of the relics.

The darkness stayed, pressing against my eyes, leaving me helpless and alone in the dark. No reply to my mind send, while I dared not actually call out with my voice because that primordial fear whispered its fear and dread deep into me.

I drew in a huge gulp of air and held it in for a moment, teeth gritted as I determined that, if this was really it, I was not willing to go out as a cliché my grandfather could sell to his mates, of a helpless female weeping in the dark. Fuck that with a big rubber dick.

Sam had been right. Why should my brother risk another face-to-face with me when he could simply collapse the realm I was in, from far away?

And yet...

On the one occasion when I had successfully interacted with the emr village realm, I had done so by wrapping my mind presence around it – so did that apply to Alan, too? Was at least part of his mind self in contact with this realm?

It seemed reasonable.

Purpose percolated my fear and panic down to steely resolve; determination.

My mind self pushed outward and, as it did I was no longer blind as my 'other' sense took in the realm around me and billowed outward, seeking my brother.

Suddenly I touched an ethereal presence, a thin tissue that even a mind organ might easily miss, more like a name whispered softly in a distant room than the presence of the person themselves, yet in that instant I knew.

Gotcha!

We each knew the other and our extruded minds wormed and looped around each other, seeking purchase, progress, pushing at each other across earth and air and sky and then onward to the upper threshold of the realm, where the coalescence of this universe came to an end and the nullness of the emr was reasserted.

We touched and recoiled again and again, the sharp sting of contact not painful as such, but rather... unwelcome.

Momentarily in a lull after our unsuccessful attacks, our mind selves rolled in the bath of the reality in which we floated, slid along each other, in as much as non-physical things can, but that lighter contact revealed something shocking to me.

I saw my brother, Peter; not the corruption of him that still lived but the loving boy he had once been. His mind relaxed against mine and I sensed that he saw my purer form too, perhaps the sister who had shared those brief best years with him.

We both relaxed. And bled into each other.

Our selves shed all concept of a boundary of self and we lost our uniqueness, our distinctiveness as we... merged.

It was at once the most terrifying and the most wondrous feeling I had ever experienced, like an orgasm in the middle of a heart attack. Free of our lifelong binding of flesh and its self-imposed physical limits, we surged into each other and coalesced.

I became aware, again, of Alan, while he, again, recognised me rather than the child I had been.

We both reacted, both *pushed*. Still entangled, though, our combined energies had nowhere to go.

Blinding light and heat engulfed me.

It was shocking to feel sensation suddenly after being disembodied for however many timeless moments but these sensations were definitely of the body as well as of the mind.

Something terrible had happened.

I felt pain; real pain, and still blinding light everywhere. Had I killed myself? Did I at least take him with me?

-40-

I had eyes again and, realising they were shut, I opened them.

I was back in my meat, but the hotel room no longer surrounded it. There were no walls, no carriage lamps, no comfortably tatty bed, not even the storm – it was a bright summer's day.

Far too bright. And I wasn't alone.

Three feet in front of me under the glare of a brutal white sun stood my brother; once Peter, now Alan. Once a little boy I had loved with all my heart, now a monster I was going to quite enjoy killing.

My mind organ already knew my rage-fuelled need. A mass of mind energy formed before my face, rippling with deadly intent.

He saw, put up a defensive wall, but weak – far too weak, as if he had only a little to give.

"No! Sis, wait!" he cried.

I felt a thrill at the realisation that it was finally his turn to beg *me*. I had no idea why he was suddenly so weak and nor did I care. Finally, I had him. Game over, bastard.

"Wait," he was bleating. "Please, sis, just stop! Look around you, something's changed, something's happened to us!"

A little stink of truth undermined my determination. The mindforce I had been extruding relaxed back into me a little. Just a little. The urge was potently seductive.

"We might be each other's only chance," he finished weakly.

I hated the idea that he might be right and wanted to ignore the truth, to sate my urges, but I couldn't ignore the fact that something bizarre *had* happened to us. Our fight had released a blast of energy far greater than anything I'd ever felt before and now I was... where? We had been blasted out of the emr, but we could be anywhere.

And this place was totally alien.

I furled my mindforce further back into me but kept a defensive layer in place.

"OK," I said. "Truce. Just for now."

He was going to smirk, I knew, so I fixed him with a cold look. "Don't," I warned him. "You push me and we go toe to toe, so start talking. What's going on, where are we?"

His glinting grey eyes held fast to me. "Look around you."

"Why?"

"You'll soon see."

He was still so sly, so scheming. No way would I ever be stupid enough to let my guard down, but I also sensed that something bigger than either of us had happened.

We were standing on a roadway of smooth, flat, even white slabs in the middle of a deserted street of pure white buildings, shockingly stark and blank in the brutal glare of a fierce white sun that cut x-ray sharp through everything.

The road was level where we stood, but it tumbled steeply downhill a few yards from us, the two rows of white windowless block buildings facing off all the way to the bottom, but...

I frowned.

Glare bounced off the multitude of flat white surfaces and created a sickening, dizzying dazzle where there was nowhere comfortable to look, but even so, I could see it was no trick of the light; the houses bowed in at the top, leaning toward each other, closer and closer going down the slope, until their tops finally met at the bottom of the hill so that there was an enclosed... I suppose a tunnel would be the right description.

That tunnel was oppressively dark, but what was really odd was that I could see right into it.

"That's ridiculous," I said.

I was at the top of the hill, perhaps twenty or thirty feet above the bottom where that tunnel began, yet I could see into it, could pick out the grimy curves of its walls disappearing into the gloom.

I raised my gaze a little, dazzled by the glare of the sky, but I could also discern that it was impossible to see over the tops of the houses, as hard as I stared, I couldn't see over the rooftops of the houses.

I turned to Alan. "How can that be?"

I couldn't see over them at all, in the same way it's impossible to stop seeing an optical illusion, even when you know your eyes are being deceived.

"You can't break the illusion, sis, coz it's not an illusion."

"Rubbish!"

He rubbed the back of his neck under glanced away under the full beam of my glare. "Trust me, sis. Only you and me could even survive here. We're... oh, what? Extra-dimensional? The laws of physics as we know them don't apply here. There are more and different dimensions here, than just the three of space and one of time we know."

"How the fuck do you know all this?" I asked, but as I did, another thought struck me. "Did you said only *we* can survive here?"

"I know all this because I've lived in the creases between the realms all my life, sis, while you had your warm happy family time with Nanny. And yes, only we can survive here. The Sentinels, too, although they can't linger here any more than they can stay in our universe too long. But me and you; we can see and think in Mind dimensions."

"So that means that... is this the Mind universe?"

"Top of the class, sis!" He gave a crooked grin but it faltered, suggesting that he was getting scared, now, just like me. "I think our little spat back in the emr caused a surge of mind energy, enough to trigger an expulsion that pushed us out into this universe."

I hated being on the back foot with this arrogant prick, but I had a shit-ton of questions and my life might well depend on understanding this.

"Why would a surge of mind energy do that?" I asked, determining to try and make sense of whatever he said next so I could look at least 50 mils smarter than a total bimbo.

"What?" He gaped at me open-mouthed, genuinely taken aback or exaggerating for my greater humiliation. "You really don't know what the Mind realm is, do you, sis? You and Sool never had 'the talk', then?"

His lip twitched as he said that and I was sure he was mocking me.

He must have sensed my rising anger, though, because he held a hand up. "OK, sorry, but to understand what happened, you need to understand why there's a Mind universe in the first place."

I was pissing sweat from every crease and crevice. "OK, fine, but can we move into the shade, first?"

He nodded. "Good shout. I can show you what I mean about the dimensions being different. Focus on the entrance to the tunnel down there."

I did. Once again, despite our elevation, I was able to peer straight into the tunnel.

"Now," said Alan, "walk into the tunnel."

I glanced at him. "That's stupid."

"Trust me." He shrugged. "This one time."

I returned my gaze to the tunnel, tried to ignore being about a hundred feet away and some twenty feet above it, and stepped... into a waterslide sensation and was in the mouth of the tunnel.

"Shit," I murmured.

Glancing around, I saw Alan smear into place beside me as he too used the weird dimensional quirk.

"OK smart-arse, you win. That's a nice trick. Now, why don't you tell me why there's a Mind universe."

I was still fighting the urge to blast his smug face with mindforce, but if he and I could survive here, it had implications. What would happen to us if, as I'd been warned, the universes collapsed into each other? Would everyone else die? Would I be adrift in a world of nonsense dimensions, alone and scared until the madness of my reality finally drove me insane?

He gave a quick smirk, clearly having read that thought as it passed through my mind. "You really don't like me, do you?"

"No," I answered flatly. "So get on with it before I call an end to our already-flagging truce."

He giggled.

He actually giggled. "Fair enough. But you're right, as far as I know. We probably would survive a collapse; so would Sool and his lot, coz they're also... I don't like the term, but let's go with 'extra-dimensional' for now."

"So you're still reading my thoughts, then?"

He pulled a mock-pout. "Is that what's important here sis? Come on. Now then. The Mind Universe, or '*What Sool Should Have Told You*'. So, there's the universe we know, right, and once upon a time that's all there was, see? Then at some point, sentient life appeared and started to generate thought energy. It was new and somehow... well, outside the laws of reality. Y'know, physics or kinetics or some shit."

"Sounds unlikely," I said. "But tell on."

"Unlikely? Why? What's the limit to a thought, or a dream? They can span a day, an idea or a summer holiday! You know what thought can do when it's wielded – from, oh, I don't know, our last couple of fights?"

"Yes, but we're *special*, Peter."

I meant the word to be ironic, but I heard myself and cringed.

He didn't pick up on it. "Please don't call me that, sis, I stopped being 'Peter' a long time ago. Anyone can dream a whole world, recall the dead, visit far-off places from childhood, jump a thousand feet straight up. In a universe with a fixed amount of mass, there was suddenly all this potent energy that could make and destroy whole worlds in the twitch of an eyelid."

"I dunno," I said. "It's all a bit Doctor Who."

He sighed. "After all you've seen, sis, really? Trust me, thought energy is real and, more importantly, it's created each time there's a thought, breaking that rule of physics, what is it? *Constipation of energy*?"

It was funny how little I knew about physics. "I think I've got about the same amount of the science gene as you. I sort of know what you mean, though, about energy not being created or destroyed."

He gave me an odd, amused frown. "Yeah, that one. So the universe had to adapt. Somehow the thought energy extruded out and got syphoned off into a pocket universe. That law of energy was protected in the Matter realm and meanwhile the Mind Realm was born as a dump for all the thought energy."

As he talked, Alan moved closer to a tunnel wall, fading a little into the gloom a little as he did so.

"Hey!" I called, wary of being left alone. As I took a step I realised that my footfall created no echo whatsoever. "Shit, don't leave me alone, this place is all kinds of fucked!"

"Only here, sis, don't panic!" He called back to me.

"Let me catch up!" I waddled warily into the gloom after him, my footsteps a flat whump as they failed to bounce off the tunnel walls, each placed carefully in case of trip hazards as the weak light fell closer to absence.

He had resumed his smart-arse monologue, his voice seeming terribly far away now. "I guess you'd say that the emr is the neck of the bottle, pinching it off so that thought energy can trickle in when it builds up enough but can't get back out."

"Right, I said, squinting into the gloom in a desperate attempt to locate him. "That's what happened to us. Our fight caused a flare-up of energy and we got sucked in."

"Yeah, sometimes the Sentinels have to intervene, do a spot of housekeeping but the process normally starts itself up, like it did with us when– *FUCK!*"

I gasped and staggered, my swollen heart trying to kick my tits off my chest. I drew a ragged breath. "Al... Alan?"

He had gone silent.

"You OK?"

There was silence and gloom.

I edged into the dark, suddenly alone and vulnerable. "P-Peter?"

I stepped up my pace into the tunnel because being completely alone was scarier than facing whatever had snared my brother.

I bumped into him in the gloom and damn near laid a fresh one in my jeans.

I grabbed his arm. "Fuck, Peter!" I held onto his arm, starting to make out his features as my eyes adjusted to the gloom. "Are you OK?"

"Seriously, don't call me that," he said, his tone pissy. "Yes, I'm fine, just tripped on something is all, sprawled across the tunnel. Something that should definitely *not* be down here. Take a look."

Discernible in the weak light reaching us from the tunnel entrance, there was a human body sprawled against the curved tunnel wall, propped with its legs sticking out straight across the floor, motionless.

I crept cautiously toward it, hunching over instinctively. "Is that..." I said. "Wait. What?"

Had the tunnel been a little darker, I might have been fooled into accepting the corpse as human. It was not. Dead, humanoid; but not human.

Dull insectoid eyes bulged blank either side of a sharp downswept beak like that of a parrot, roughly where its nose ought to be. Thin lips, a narrow slit in the gloom beneath that terrible beak, drooled a drying trail of greyish phlegm onto its mottled grey-green chin.

"Your dreams were never dreams," Alan said. "You get that now, don't you, sis?"

I swallowed reflexively and it hurt because I had no spit to swallow. "A thing like this attacked me in the alleyway." I turned to look at him. "Not a dream?"

He shook his head. "You proved to be a late bloomer, sis, slipping into my emr sub-realms and alerting the sentinels. That's why I sent Sam for you. I'd been closing on you for a while."

"The alleyway," I said.

"What I believe you called the 'False Chadbury', sis. You started visiting my realms, so I visited yours."

"My office."

He nodded.

Then, he kicked the inert, booted foot of the thing on the ground. "*This* thing shouldn't be here, Laura. You're looking at the native state, the true form, of all the realm sentinels including your so-called friend Sool."

Oh. I had known that the human face Sool had shown to me was not his real one – not least because the mere effort of trying to smile sent him into a paroxysm of muscle spasms that made a strangling rattlesnake look serene.

"Is this him?" I asked. "Sool, I mean?"

I was curious but dispassionate. In that moment I didn't care if it was Sool, I'd shed no tears for him. He'd hardly been straight with me.

Alan peered at the alien deathmask at our feet. "One of his kind, but they all look the same." he said. "Hard to be sure."

I frowned at him. "I'm sure that still counts as racism."

He grinned without looking at me. "No, they really do, I've seen a few there's literally no difference. But it shouldn't be here. Still, I can confirm that it's as dead as yer nanny's ovaries."

I shared a special look with him. "You're really pissing on your chips going there, after what you did to Grandma's body."

He winced and took a half step away from e. "Oh, you saw that, did you? Not my finest hour."

Suddenly, his mind swelled into the space within the tunnel – but not hostile; simply probing. "It's not Sool," he stated.

"Oh, Peter; euch! You touched it with your mind!"

He straightened up and grinned at me. "Had to know for sure."

Alan sniffed. "Let's get out of here."

He stepped carefully over the corpse and faded into the gloom.

"You're going the wrong... fuck." I stepped over the splayed legs of the dead sentinel and was instantly hit by a shockingly ferocious flash of white light.

Alan caught me by the arm as I staggered, hands over my eyes. "Easy, sis."

I blinked streaming tears out of my eyes while I regained my balance and a little of my dignity.

We were outside again. Obviously.

"I hate this fucking place," I complained. "No warning, just bang! Welcome to outdoors!"

The smile he gave me contained a little too much contempt. "Extra dimensions, remember? Forward isn't just forward here."

We were outside the place where we had been; a great white city within curved walls, the whole thing resembling a vast white featureless igloo.

The city sat in the same white sand that pressed soft and grainy beneath my pumps – a huge desert of white under a blinding sky of white that was a far more terrifying place to find myself than the city street had been.

I drew in a breath of hot, dry air.

My brother's brow was deeply furrowed, his ferret eyes buried under his brows. "This is all wrong, sis."

"You're telling me." I squinted and tried to sight the white-on-white intersection of desert and sky that would signify the relative sanity of a horizon.

"No, sis," he was saying. "Not this place; that thing in the tunnel."

"The Sentinel?"

He reached behind his back and tucked the rear flap of his white shirt into his rather baggy grey trousers. "Fucking shirt; cunt. Yes," he snapped, glaring at me as though his shirt issues were my fault. "Of course the Sentinel!"

I wasn't sure if it was the shirt that was the cunt, or me. Still. "OK, what's wrong with the Sentinel?" I asked him.

The shirt refused to go in straight, so he gave up with a pout and fixed his grey eyes on mine. "I've butted heads with the Sentinels a few times, Laura. No-one knows them better than me and I don't know much. They live in some hidden layer of the emr that even I can't find, and their whole reason for existing is to oversee the process of thought energy syphoning – or to 'protect the realms' if you listen to that pompous stiff-neck Sool, but either way they're the universe's bin-men!"

"They must love you," I said, "pissing around with the emr and damaging the barrier."

He laughed. "Yeah alright, sis, stick fucking pins in me! Come on, it's fucking hot out here."

He stepped forward and smeared away from sight along that mysterious dimension he seemed so proud to know about.

"Bugger," I muttered and stepped forward. Nothing changed for me, though. The blazing sun continued to make my crevices weep sweat.

"Fuck." I recalled the rule Alan had given me and chose to see the tunnel as I took another step. It went dark and my whole body tensed as my foot nudged something. The corpse. *Step over, that's it...*

Alan's tone was soft in the gloom. "Well done, sis, you're a pretty fast learner."

"Don't patronise me," I muttered, but it was a wry rebuke, almost said in jest. "You were saying?"

"Oh, yeah. The sentinels don't belong to the Mind *or* the Matter universes, any more than we belong in the emr. They exist in a specialised layer, half-Mind and half-Matter, the laws of 'physics' a hybrid of our universe and this one. Prolonged exposure to the realms is deadly to them. So, what could make our dead friend so desperate that it would stay here long enough that it actually died!"

"Peter," I began.

"Come on. It's Alan. We've been lambing as buddies for a while now."

"Alan," I corrected for him, unsure that 'lambing' was even a thing. "As much as I give a shit about all this Sentinel stuff, what are *we* going to do?"

He shrugged, just visible now as my eyes adjusted to the gloom once more. "I've already tried to transfer back. Have you?"

I stared at him. "No. When did you...?"

"Soon as we got here. Just as you decided to unload yer mindforce on me."

He grinned.

Dick. That was why his defence had seemed lacklustre.

He studied my face, sighed and then smiled. "OK, give it a try. Just in case this is one thing you can do that, y'know, I can't."

I smiled at him. "You won't live it down if I can."

I opened my mind and forced an image of the hotel room into my mind, drawing up images of familiar things that were there such as Sam's stupid little kettle, the carriage lamps, anything that could form an anchor.

I closed my eyes and pushed out.

Pushed *out* with my mind, reaching for that sensation I'd felt when I'd reached out in the village emr, as the blackness approached; of the tangible edges of something intangible, of grasping the reality around me; but my mind slipped off the smoothness of an intangible barrier and gained no purchase on the edges of this unfathomable universe.

I let out a breath I hadn't realised I was holding, opened my eyes. I was dazzled once again by the brutal glare reflecting off the vast curve of the white city's wall. I had shifted myself out onto the city's street once again.

"Fuck it."

Alan smeared into place beside me. "Fly in a jam jar, right?" he said. "Worth a try but I didn't think it'd work. Come on, let's see if there's anything here can help us."

He started up the hill toward where we had first arrived and, with a sigh that came from right down in my shoes, I followed.

-41-

The city was big and very, very dead.

Walking up the street we passed a seemingly endless parade of featureless buildings, which for all they looked like houses showed no sign whatsoever of any life. If I had to guess, I'd say we walked about a mile along this unchanging path until, unexpectedly, the street opened out into a vast, empty, white-paved town square.

Stopping, I ran a tongue over my lips expecting dryness, but found that they were as perky and cherubic, ahem, as always. I wasn't particularly thirsty at all, in fact, which considering the lethal glaring white sky and my sweaty moistness, was rather surprising.

"Well," my brother said with a cocking of his left eyebrow, "How about that?"

The square was huge, the buildings on the far side seeming at least a mile away and those to the sides of us looping away to create a similar distance.

In the centre of this otherwise blank white-paved space, stood what looked like a bandstand, only much bigger; probably the size of a football pitch, that I guessed was intended as some sort of central plaza. Its tiered white roof was held up by ornately bevelled marble pillars, each some fifty feet high, I'd guesstimate.

"Shall we, then?" I suggested.

He frowned at me. "Really?"

I punched his arm – gently, mind, since I wasn't trying to start a war. "Oh, come on! We'll never find our way home if we don't investigate, Al!"

He rubbed his arm, although it can't have hurt. "Will you stop calling me that, and yes, you're probably right."

I could *hear* how much that admission had chapped his arse.

We moved cautiously across the open square. I glanced up at the buildings around us, half expecting to get Lee-Harveyed at any second, but we reached the central structure without incident.

My brother held out a hand. "After you, I insist."

I gave him a special look, focused on the bandstand, stepped and

I was upside down!

I was standing on the inside of the pavilion roof. Looking up I could see Alan 'above' me on the ground below, watched him step forward and flip into place beside me.

"Another Mind dimension?" I suggested.

"Errr, sis..." He pointed.

We were no longer alone. Now, rotated into this new perspective, we were aligned with whatever plane it was in which the dwellers of this realm existed.

At first all I saw were rapid blurs of movement, indistinct and momentary, that flicked across the floor of this place, but slowly they took shape.

A woman, holding a basket. A man and a boy, happy to be together; I could feel that emotion so distinctly, as if the man had lost the boy once and was clinging to the... memory of him.

"Shit!"

That man was a person in our universe; maybe still alive, maybe long dead, but this was the thought, the memory of time with the son he had lost, played out as a single, permanently joined and living being here.

A great vista coalesced into semi-solid existence, white mind stuff becoming the vivid colours and smells of a market place, wheeled wooden stalls set out everywhere with foods and clothes and toys under heavy green canvas canopies.

I took a step closer and a viciously sharp pain cut across my belly.

Laura!

He was pulling insistently at my arm.

Whether it was his hand or his mind, Alan pulled me back and, as he did, I saw the source of my sudden pain. My legs and pelvis stood a clear foot away in front of me, the top cut in a straight line, my meat showing inside and a single reddish-purple rope of intestine snaking from the top to join with the rest of me.

"Oh, fuck!" I cried. "Help me, Peter, fuck what, what, what...!"

My pelvis and legs slammed back into place as he pulled me to safety and I turned and fell into his arms sobbing, my need to be strong lost in the aftershock of being ripped in half.

"The, the fuck!" I sobbed into his shoulder.

He stroked my hair. "We're adapted to cope with some of this but we're not Mind beings, sis. I guess there are dimensions here even we can't handle. We have to get home before we hit an *m*-dimension that turns us inside out."

I nodded, sobbed a final sob then had a word with myself and pulled my shit into a neat pile, sucked in a ragged breath and stepped only slightly back from him. "Do you trust me?" I asked.

"Eh?"

I cocked him a look. *Really?*

His lip twitched. "Within the constraints of our current dilemma, yes."

"OK." I placed my hands on his shoulders and stared into his ferrety grey eyes. "Focus on me, mind open."

I felt his mind swirling around near mine. I too opened up.

"Now," I said, "focus on the emr as I do the same."

"There's no reason why this should be any different – oh."

We both felt a surge of our mindforce, reaching out from the plane of our current existence, feeling for the emr, somehow sure-footed in seeking it, our combined minds enough to pierce the barrier containing this bizarre reality and finding the way into the 'neck of the bottle'.

There was a pulse – not light but bright, not sound but loud and as the link that had bound us was severed I fell into existence on my bed in the hotel.

-42-

I sat up, suppressed a cry of pain as my head pinged out a sharp pain, immediately accompanied by a violent cramping in my belly to which I sent frantic rubbing hands.

The cramp eased off and I glanced around. It was day outside the little hotel window, the daylight drab and grey but daytime nonetheless. Still, the wall lamps were on and the bathroom light, too, had been left beaming, sending a shard of light searing across the threadbare carpet. As if the occupant of the room didn't trust the daylight.

I saw Sam. He sat immobile in a chair at the foot of my bed. He had not reacted to my return at all.

I was tired. I wanted to sleep.

Sam arose in a single smooth movement to make me a coffee. He had felt me need and had responded.

This all felt very, very peculiar – even by the standards of *my* life.

Having put a sachet of coffee, a sachet of sugar and a little plastic potlet of so-called milk into a toddler-sized hotel mug, he crossed to the window while I awaited the sound of boiling from the kettle.

"Where...?" I started to ask.

"Out searching for you," he answered, peering out of the window.

I went to speak but he went on, straight across me. "I assume that your return to us indicates a successful outcome?"

So, I had taken my physical body with me. I'd thought so but it was good to cross that particular 'T'.

"So," I said. "I guess you know where I went."

He did not turn around. "I gave the other two an explanation sufficient to persuade them to go looking for you in this place, said I should stay here in case you reappeared where you'd vanished from."

"And they were fine with that?"

He shrugged, still showing me the back of his head. "Jennifer seemed more interested in the details of our link than where you might have gone. Tom... well, I think his head is poached. He didn't take much in."

"Sam, I... wait, what d'you mean, Jen was interested in our link?"

"She seemed to have a surprising number of questions about it. For her."

"You gonna look at me, Sam?"

He turned as the kettle clicked and finally I caught his gaze, his sharp blue eyes cool but not icy as he finally looked at me. "We should talk later. When you feel a little better."

Lightning flash-lit the window behind him and damn near blew my retinas out through the back of my head.

"Fuck!" I clapped my hands to my eyes.

An after-image of Sam's ghost played across my blinded eyes.

"Tea or coffee?" Sam asked when I opened my eyes, dabbing tears.

I couldn't shake the feeling that it was chilly in the room with him.

-43-

I perched on a high stool at the hotel bar and studied the me that was reflected in the mirror back there behind the drinks optics.

I looked tired. I still *felt* tired.

Still, at least I was clean and fresh. I'd showered, but more importantly I'd gone foraging and had found a clean white tee-shirt in a drawer in a nearby room. I was stuck with the same jeans I'd worn, well, for*ever*, and bereft of underwear to separate the rough denim from my... front porch. Also, I had only the one pair of sweated-in-and-re-dried pumps, which I couldn't smell but everyone else was probably dying from.

And yet. At least I was swinging my tits in a clean top. Amazing how much that helps. And I'd finally been able to dump that sweltering jumper I'd acquired at Edward's house.

The thought of Edward brought the memory of him back sharply for a moment. His decayed face, his dried-out, clicky eyes. His kindness, his friendship and our time together. I snatched a breath and it tried to go ragged, like a sob.

I pursed my lips and banged a hand on the bar top, catching the attention of the bartender; another, or possible the same, Alan-clone.

"Vodka," I ordered flatly.

Alan.

I stared at the mirror as his pale reflection brought me my drink.

I had missed him for such a very long time and now, back here with my friends, well; companions.... whatever, but back here again, I was forced to wonder why I hadn't taken my chance to end all this. Was my longing for that little boy I had lost so very great that I would let the monster he had become walk free?

No. We had needed each other out there in the Mind realm.

And yet... he had hurt so many people, including my friends, work colleagues, a smattering of bystanders. And me.

I took a sip of vodka, the sharp antiseptic aroma flooding my nose and throat as the heat of it hit my stomach.

They were playing jazz in the hotel bar. No idea who 'they' were, but the tinkling piano and pulsing bass created a mellow bar-room experience, enhanced by the tang of alcohol on the air and the faint under-smell of permanently booze-damp carpet.

A smirk replaced the sad troubled look on my reflected face. The hotel drinks lounge was a joke, a fantasy creation of my brother's making that stood for no place that had ever existed.

The patrons here were of course the usual clichéd automata: a crinkle-jowled old crony at a corner table huddled over his crystal drink glass, a cigarette smouldering between the yellowed fingers of the hand on which his temple rested; a nestling couple on high stools at the far side of the curved bar; he middle-aged, she younger, cheaper and easier to open than a first-birthday present.

I glanced away. There were other filler people that flitted in and then back out of here, all of them mere caricatures, weakly-sketched animated dummies whose sole purpose was to create the illusion that this hotel actually had people staying in it. None of them deserved my attention.

My reverie was interrupted when the Alan clone sidled up to me on his side of the bar, neatly dressed in a black suit and white shirt cliché, a tea-towel draped over one arm.

I grimaced and necked the remainder of my drink, ice cubes clacking against my teeth, then slammed the glass down hard on the bar. "Another. No ice this time."

I took a big chug of the next vodka and nearly choked as it scalded my throat. I barely had time to pull my composure up as the magnificent form of Sam entered the bar, a clear head taller than any of the fake patrons, his strong body enrobed in a flowy white dress shirt, newly-found or possibly laundered, and his tight jeans wrapped closely around his legs.

I tipped my glass at him when he reached me.

"May I?" Sam asked, gesturing at the stool beside my own.

I nodded, waved my glass at it and watched as he perched pertly on the dainty bar stool and gestured sharply at the Alan clone, seeming to enjoy having a version of my brother that he could push around.

I downed my vodka, avoiding the choking hazard this time.

"Brandy." He pointed to my glass. "And another for the lady."

His voice sounded different when he said 'Brandy'; older somehow, more... sophisticated. Maybe I was imagining things. Perhaps a little of his original persona was trapped within the idea of his old, old tipple.

He nodded a curt thanks to the 'barman' as our drinks were placed before us on little paper discs on the polished bar.

"You owe me a chat," he said.

I tapped my empty glass down on the bar and picked up the newly-delivered drink. It chinked, perhaps because the barman had forgotten, or possibly because he knew the ice would slow me down.

"Fire away," I said. I sipped my vodka. Acrid, medicinal, warming.

"You lied to us earlier."

Stark and to the point, he caught me off guard. I dug in for some composure and shielded my immediately defensive thoughts. "Oh☐"

His reflection looked straight at mine. "Your story was flawed, Laura. You said you were in this other reality only a short time yet your absence was far from brief. Perhaps time works differently there...?"

He left space for me to volunteer information but I stared at our reflections, dressed on all sides by hanging drinks bottles.

"Are you with him, Laura?"

I rounded on him, shocked by the accusation. "The fuck? You playing the jealous ex now, Sam?"

He held my gaze, his resolve undiminished by my attempt at shaming him. "It's completely understandable, Laura, he was your brother once."

Anger welled up in me and I felt pressure building behind my eyes, but even as the words emerged I realised that anger had made me give myself away.

"He still is!"

My fingers pressed down hard onto the polished surface of the bar, my gaze dropping there to avoid facing the man beside me while my brain raced frantically for the words that would cancel out my admission of guilt.

Suddenly, one of Sam's huge spade hands laid itself gently over the top of mine, caressing but not grabbing. "It's completely understandable that you would have a conflict, Laura. No-one is blaming you."

I slid my hand out from under his and he let me, which left me free to grab the vodka he had ordered for me. I bolted it and ice tumbled into my throat, forcing me to hastily gag and spit it back into the glass.

Classy. Fuck it.

I let the acidic vodka coil its scolding path downwards into me.

"I understand, Laura, even if the others do not. You and he have a bond. Still, if you let him weaken you..."

I snorted resentfully into my empty glass.

"Laura," he rebuked, leaning on the bar and brining his face closer to mine, "You can't trust him; as soon as he realises his mind games have worked, he'll make his move and it will be over before you even know it."

I suspected he was right but I had shared a moment with my beloved brother in the Mind universe and it was hard to accept that it had not been sincere, both ways. Despite evidence to that fact.

I flicked the glass and it teetered across the slippery bar before halting without upending. My gaze turned on Sam, along with my resentment, as if my brother's betrayal were his fault – since he had pointed it out to me.

"So now what?" I demanded coldly.

He overlooked the unfairness of my hostility. "Are you able to find him again?"

"Find him…? Oh, with my mind organ."

I tried to recall to foreground memory that potent sense of him that I'd experienced at each of our encounters. It came back readily and made the base of my skull tingle. "I think I can, yes," I answered Sam with a hint of surprise that it was true.

He swirled the brandy in his glass, then brought it up to his lips to sip. "So," he said. "That's what."

He slugged the alcohol.

Find Alan, face him, with no other intent than to fight him, to *kill* him? A scold of adrenalin cut across my belly and my head felt dark with the apprehension.

"Will you come with me?" I asked him.

He lowered his glass, touched his tongue to his top lip. "You know how dangerous I would be to you, Laura. He might still be able to regain control of me, turn me on you at a critical moment."

I felt sick. I was safe and I was pleasantly drunk in a bar-room yet my heart was pumping like a randy rabbit's cock. I told him that I was scared, both of having to do it and also, having determined to do it, of finding myself wanting at a crucial moment.

He sipped more brandy from his glass and said nothing.

~ perhaps it is too much for her ~

I smiled at our reflected selves behind the bar optics. "I heard that, arsehole."

A smile flicked at the corners of his mouth for a moment. Of course he had meant for me to pick up that rogue thought. Bastard.

I just need some time

He shook his head. "He knows we're here and we are rapidly running out of places to run to in the emr. There is no time."

Another horrible thought hit me. What if Alan realised my intent, could sense me as I crossed between the realms? What if he could then simply reach out with his mind and shred me as I tumbled through the maelstrom we must traverse?

Could I die like that? Would it hurt?

Panic swelled like bile from within me at how fucking real this had all just become but at that moment Jen flounced into the bar, all blonde hair and bouncing tits, a pack of smokes clasped in one crimson-taloned claw but her once-customary mobile now absent, her spare hand swaying with graceful indifference at her side.

Where the fuck had she found cigarettes?

"Dinner, people!" she declared flouncily. "I'm famished!"

Sam and I exchanged a glance and slid off our stools.

~ there is no time for such trivia, Laura ~

agreed, we need to act before I lose my nerve once and for all

We made our excuses to Jen.

At the time I thought she took our rejection with her usual pouty ill-grace, but later I'd have cause to reflect that it may have been more than that. My once-attractive friend was edgy and fearful, favouring one side of her face, refusing to look at either of us face-on while she anxiously patted at the side that she kept angled away from us. I snatched a brief glimpse of her reflection in the bar's mirror and saw, just for an instant, what looked like a patch of dry, crusty grey skin forming on her lower left cheek.

My thoughts were too focused on my own troubles at that time, though, as Sam and I left her at the bar, trapped in her own personal nightmare. She faded from sight and my interest as I braced myself and fought to mentally prepare for the impossible task ahead.

-44-

"Err, no!" I declared. "Not a fucking *chance*."

The wardrobe door in our little shared room hung open and Sam stood holding up a ghastly bastard for my perusal.

He peeled it off its hangar. "You may need a coat, Laura, you don't know where you are going."

It really was a nasty piece of shit; heavy, quilted, shapeless – none of the qualities one looked for in a fashion accessory.

I snatched it from him with a pout. "I hate you. Stop being right."

With the quilted horror draped over my arm, we departed our room and returned down the corridor.

"Will you tell the others where I am?" I asked the big man at my side. "I don't want them thinking... y'know, that I've run out on them."

He smiled and continued to stare along the way we were walking. "You're worried they'll think you've turned coats?"

I was irritated but I wanted to laugh. I settled for faint praise. "Very amusing."

It was raining outside the hotel. Lighting bounced off the glass of the entrance doors and flung water against the hotel's entire frontage as I pulled the ghastly coat on.

Sam smiled and touched my arm.

I flashed him a weak smile. "I'm scared, Sam."

His expression, his eyes, were sympathetically warm but there was little comfort for me there. "Do you see another way to end this?" he asked me flatly.

I pulled in a hard breath and zipped up the front of my poxy quilted coat. "Be seeing ya, James."

His smile faltered at the use of his real name but I didn't wait for a response, vanishing into the wettening maelstrom.

As harsh water slashed at my face I closed off my senses and opened my mind, seeking the familiar presence of my brother until, with a ping, the rush of the transfer pulled my body from the emr to meet him once again.

-45-

Sometimes, people surprise you. Other times, they really fucking don't.

The transfer had dropped me onto an eerily deserted version of London Bridge; the one in the real world. London, Earth, the Matter realm, but a version whose once-firm ground had been contaminated by the insane physics of the Mind realm.

There was no echo from my first or any subsequent footstep, each a flat whump of noise that cut off in the deathly silence of the vacated city, as had happened in the white city in the Mind realm, although there was no sign of the fierce sun of that place – it was gloomy here, as a weak watery sun fought to weep through the dense grey clouds crowding out the sky above me.

I'd stepped along the bridge a few paces but I came to a halt and stared across the bridge at the shocking wreckage of a London skyline that had always grown and changed, yet had still been a steady stalwart throughout my life.

Until now.

London had been washed away by the new physics, the incomprehensible dimensions. A few buildings sat amongst the madness seemingly unaltered, but the rest had been twisted beyond recognition by the architecture of imagination; from the vast back marble ice-cream swirly, at least forty feet high, that had replaced the dome of St Paul's Cathedral, to the twisted turrets and gables of the surrounding buildings that joined to the granite swirly via wrought-iron gantries. Along the river, the Tower of London remained untouched, as did its matching bridge, but all around it, futuristic metal and glass spires and buildings were skewered by fluidic tendrils not unlike tree roots, punching through apparently solid materials and coiling up towards the sky.

As for the river – I gave a shudder. The winding shape cutting through the city was unchanged but the flat, unmoving, tepid water was black and as vacuous as death itself. It looked sick, as if the rot of every fish lay beneath its dull surface.

Of course, with the state of the river, the whole area should have reeked of sick water, of boats and fish; perhaps blended with the stench of human bodies, which had to be around here somewhere.

Yet no.

The smell of none of those things pervaded the air; just a vaguely musty smell, a mummified waft of cloying museum neglect that had no place on an open street.

"Enough," I muttered to myself.

I had come here for a reason.

I hurried across the bridge and plodded heavy-footed yet silently past backdrop buildings that were unchanged, yet seemed as flattened as backdrop buildings in a video game, until I reached the vast wrought-iron archway in the straw-yellow brick of Hays Galleria, a former warehouse and dock for merchant ships that was converted years back into a semi-enclosed, arch-roofed shopping mall opening onto the river front.

This place, too, seemed unchanged by the invading universe. Perhaps the change was creeping across the face of the world. What an awful prospect.

I passed through the first arch into the galleria, crossed a service road and stepped onto faux-rustic cobbles as I passed through a second, almost identical archway into the main shopping cloister of the galleria, where I slowed and softened my pace.

He was here. I could feel him.

I glanced up, stupidly, at the great wrought-iron-and-glass vault of the ceiling far above me.

he isn't fucking spiderman... my own inner voice rebuked.

My mind spasmed just a little but enough to prompt me to duck behind an ornately-carved concrete support pillar, the rough flaky feel of it matched by that omnipresent dusty pong.

Two figures flitted into view some twenty feet ahead of me, emerging very suddenly from an unlit walkway onto the great central court of the galleria.

One was a man. Short, dressed in a long black coat, his features mostly concealed but his lank brown hair and pot-bellied scrawniness as recognisable as a top hat and a neon name tag. The real mystery was the other figure; a thinnish woman draped on his arm; about my height but nimbler, perhaps younger than me.

The pair flounced away and skitted into a covered walkway on the far side of the galleria. I risked leaning out a little further from behind my concrete cover to get a better look as they stood before a glass shop front.

After saying something cunt-stupid like *'Open Sesame';* hard to tell from the distance to my hiding place; Alan opened his arms out dramatically like a magician. I felt a potent twang at the back of my head in response to what he was doing and then the glass of the window in front of him rippled, wobbled, and bowed inward.

With a subdued ping the glass exceeded its stretch capacity and the whole window came apart with a pop followed by a crystalline rush of noise as a million shards sprayed deep into the shop.

The chorus of tinkling subsided too quickly, robbed as it was of any echo, while all the bits of glass settled into their final resting places and the former sound was replaced, now, by the equally jarring (in my opinion) latter sound of the woman's delighted squeal.

That squeal. I went to swallow but found I had lost my spit. The recognition, but mostly its implications, was devastating.

no

Alan grabbed her hand and they jumped into the shop, kicking glass away and rummaging joyfully through their spoils as they laughed and plunged and vanished from sight deeper into the gloom of the shop, like two newlyweds on an acid trip.

I ducked back behind my protective cover.

Unfortunately, the joy of their little jaunt had attracted some unwanted attention. London was not as barren as it had seemed.

A broad ugly man was lumbering across the galleria toward them, his left leg dragging slightly, his straining face edged with a mottled grey fungal roughness that I had seen before, more than once. He was closely followed by a mismatched pair of lumbering apes who were far more noticeably deformed than their leader.

The first companion's face was mis-shapen on the left side, a crusty grey lesion distorting his jawline that had crawled up onto his cheek and split it open in a ragged, vaginal moue whose fungal edge seemed to be creeping hungrily both up and down towards his eye and his top lip.

The second companion seemed less deformed at first.

Then he turned his head.

As he glanced back over his shoulder, I fought to suppress a cry that would have rendered my hiding place pointless as he revealed a nose that had only one side. Past the centre line of his face, that same grey fungus had eaten away his entire cheek, exposing a white shard of cheekbone and some red shit I chose not notice; yet worse, the whole side of his nose was gone, leaving a ragged hole lined with a wetter, mulchy-looking mix of grey fungus and yellowish crust.

Yikes. Fungus and congealed mucus. Even I would have to think seriously about whether I'd be willing to date that.

His glare moved dangerously close to pointing my way and I saw that one of his eyes was milky, a section of the lower eyelid already crusty grey as the infection below journeyed upward.

I ducked back to avoid being seen by his one good eye.

He would not get to keep that other eye much longer, but I was unconvinced that this made him any less dangerous in the here and now.

The trio of apprentice relics reached the shop-front just as the newlyweds emerged, still smirking. I finally got to see the female's face and felt a thrill of horror as my worst suspicions were confirmed.

Some people just have to play to type.

Standing beside my brother, her arm looped through his, willingly at his side and looking more vibrant and alive than I would have believed possible, was my former friend Jennifer Sullivan.

The same Jen I thought I had left back in the emr with Tom and Sam. Which led to an even more urgent concern...

I wondered at my own stupidity. My brother was smart, he'd had years of practice in manipulating dumb human cattle like Jen; she must've been an utter piece of piss to seduce. With his powers he could sweep away the atrophy she was doomed to and restore her looks. Frankly, that's all that my selfish bitch friend would need to sell the rest of us out.

She had betrayed me – us. Obviously. I was surprised I was surprised.

I squinted at the version of Jen over there with Alan and discreetly snuck a peek with my mind, too. She was definitely the real Jen, which meant that the one I had left at the hotel was... what? A copy, no doubt, just like the Alan-clone, but was there an ulterior motive? Was she also a diversion or, worse, an assassin?

I had to get back to the emr, to my dwindling band of allies.

I quickly appraised the galleria, the exposed open spaces without cover, looking for a way to leave my hiding place and get out without being seen. I was too close to Alan's line of sight to try and transfer. That was a fucksure way to find out if he actually could attack me mid-transfer and jelly my bones; the boys needed me but I would be no use to them if I got myself killed mid-escape.

Across the stone floor, one of the zombie crew barked something at Alan and pulled my attention back to that scene. One of the thugs had edged around behind my brother.

Alan stood still and smug, cocksure of his own power over these crumbling men. Before he even knew he'd fucked up he was clubbed on the back of the head by a hefty fist that sent him staggering against a support pillar, where he sagged, hands on the stone and gaze far from here.

Jen was left to confront a big, ugly assailant. I noticed the patchwork of wet and dry brown patches at the rear of his well-soiled jeans and didn't envy her the pleasure of his ripe and pungent intimacy. How she wasn't retching...

"Fuck away from me, you pig!"

The other two men were either side of her, pincering her. Her head flicked left and right in a desperate bid for an escape route.

She wasn't my problem. It was time to transfer out of here while Alan was out of action, to get back to the emr and help my friends.

I opened my mind.

It was just as the first swell of the transfer lapped up over me that I heard Jen's piercing scream as she was grabbed.

In that instant I knew, I just *knew*, that despite her betrayal I couldn't just leave her to be raped and slaughtered by those monsters. It didn't matter that I hated her, it was enough that I *knew* her; maybe not even that.

Perhaps even a stranger in that situation...

I let go of the transfer and let my body slump back into reality; re-focused my mind as I edged free of my cover and crept, knees bent in a nervous half-crouch, across the galleria floor until I reached a pillar nearest to Jen.

She was making a fight of it. She gouged at the big man's eyes but he clasped her wrists and crushed her hands together. She jabbed her knee at his groin but he turned his hips and pulled his knees together so that his meaty thighs blocked her.

She screamed and cried out my brother's name, but the big man released her wrists and swung a stunning slap all in a single motion. It was kind of impressive. She staggered from the hammer blow, eyes wide and dazed. He pulled her close and I saw a bulge in his filthy trousers that made it clear to me that, for him, the violence was part of the appeal.

Alan glanced her way but remained slumped against the pillar just down from me, to Jen's left, on his feet but his knees still bent, his face blank and dazed.

The big thug raised his hand to hit her again.

This was about to unravel so I opened my mind.

Mindforce erupted from me but the reality of a cold-blooded kill against a fellow human, however degenerate, weakened my attack. The two thugs behind him were blasted down hard onto the concrete floor like discarded dolls, but their leader remained completely untouched.

fuck!

I pushed again and felt the satisfying impact of my mind against his meat as he grunted and rocked on his heels for a moment. He flicked Jen away and turned towards me.

Jen staggered, turned and saw me, her expression a hilarious cocktail of shock and disbelief. *You? You saved me?*

The zombie crew leader glanced and saw his prone companions-in-crime lying on their backs, their breathing shallow, their eyes shut and blood bubbling up out of their mouths.

"Betch!" he snarled at me.

I braced for the next attack suddenly the sack of shit squaring up to me emitted a startled, strangled cry as his body jerked violently and he was lifted up onto tip-toes by an unseen force.

I felt a ping at the back of my head.

Alan stepped forward with a rabid glare aimed at the thug, while his mind held that big, filthy body in a vice of unwavering mind energy. His winter greatcoat billowed impressively as he strode purposefully toward the immobilised thug, who seemed limited to a few strangled gurgling sounds, his head angled back, eyes bulging and body stretched taut as if hanging from wires.

Jen stepped up close to my brother. "Alan, honey," she simpered, touching my brother's shoulder. "Just wait a moment, would you, sweetie?"

I frowned. Jen? Growing a conscience and stilling the hand of her monster Rottweiler?

My surprise was of course quite misplaced. She stepped up to the thug while he hung helpless in the grip of my brother's will. Stood before him. Stroked his chest. Reached down to the front of his soiled jeans.

"Jen..." I heard my voice say, although I had no idea what I was going to follow that with.

"Well," she crooned to the helpless thug. "You did want some action downstairs, right?"

I heard the rasp of his zipper and knew I didn't want to see at the same moment that I knew I'd never be able to look away. Jen's hand slipped into the opening in the front of his jeans. He moaned deep from within his paralysed throat, his head lolling back within its constraint as she touched something sensitive.

Then I saw Jen's arm muscles tense and the thug's neck muscles went taut in the same instant. His mouth formed a huge 'O' and his eyes widened into saucers of shock and pain.

Alan laughed softly nearby.

I tried not to hear the wet gristle noises as Jen's merciless fingers crunched deep into his testes, but what surprised me was how silent he remained in what must have been a moment of unendurable pain.

Piss sprayed out of the opening in his jeans and Jen leapt back, releasing whatever organs he had left and shaking her yellow-splashed hand as his flaccid penis lolled free and continued to patter piss onto the stone floor.

At the same moment, I felt a ping in my head as Alan let go with his mind.

The former zombie crew leader slammed to the ground, the last of his urine spurting between his clasping fingers as he finally got to clutch his balls – well, not that they would be *balls* as such, any more, but y'know. He got to hold what was left of them one last time.

A black mass shot past me and burst against the thug's face, his eyeballs instantly popping like dropped eggs and his skin peeling away in bacon strips from his bare skull.

That bolt of energy, so close to the side of my head, should have galvanised me to get the fuck out of there, but instead I watched fascinated as the venom seethed across the rest of zombie top-dog's body, stripping skin and flesh and nerves and glands. He was a gutter-turd of a man, but still I really hoped he was unconscious for those last few seconds. I couldn't wish that level of suffering on anyone, although I found that I simply *had* to watch him burn.

-46-

I turned away from the bubbling mass of black venom as it collapsed and lost all semblance of a human shape, a single intact arm protruding sideways from it as an incongruous insult, the skin mottled raw red and black. As the mass sank to the ground the hand patted weakly on the ground as though he were still in there and wanted to submit.

I felt a swell of bile at the back of my throat. I swallowed hard and turned away.

An amused smirk twisted my brother's already-ugly face, while at his side, Jen dipped her head and flashed me a coquettish smile as she shifted her slight weight from foot to foot. I couldn't hold her gaze; I'd seen too much of the rotten core of her.

My gaze snapped to Alan, instead, to that smug fucking face of his. "I know it seems like I saved you," I said. "Trust me, I didn't mean to, I'm as baffled as you are."

He cocked an eyebrow and held my gaze, his smirk, I felt sure, slipping slightly.

I fought to summon my rage, to conjure the image of my parents, of Grandma, of the entire life I had lost, all without tipping him off by showing a coherent intent. I stoked a little coal of anger until it swelled hot within me, so that as I focused on Alan and opened my mind it was running hot and he, I hoped, had no idea that I was about to fulfil my mission objective.

He realised just a second too late. I felt the ping, saw his smiling mouth sag and his eyes turn cold, sharp.

Far, far too late at the speed a mind battle is fought. Hours too late.

I pushed and thought energy burst from me with a satisfying *thump*, arced across the space between us and slammed into him.

His body burst apart in a sickening orgasm of spurting, billowing blood and curling ribbons of meaty gore, followed by the clattering of tattered bones as they hit the solid floor.

I stared at my handiwork, bile in my throat and an equivalent warmth blossoming between my legs.

"Shit in my mouth," I murmured.

I glanced at Jen.

"Bitch," she gasped, staring at me beetle-eyed. "Fucking... fuh. Bitch..."

A red-taloned hand clasped her mouth and she backed a step away from me; then another and another.

Still loaded on adrenaline and a simmering blood-orgasm, I bolted the few paces to her and slapped her full-palm on the temple, grabbed her by the arms and glared into her dazed eyes. "Your meal ticket's been *punched*, you treacherous fucking *bitch!*"

"N-no, wait, Laur, please. For all the years we–"

I flung her away from me in disgust, my buzz dampened by an unwelcome streak of morality. "If I ever lay eyes on you again, I'll fucking *kill* you where you stand!"

She stared at me as tears streamed from her eyes, mostly from the slap but I hoped also a few for shame. "Laur, no..."

I turned away in disgust and strode across the Galleria, heading for the exit arch as I started deep breathing to calm myself for the transfer back to the emr. It would not do to be angry for the transfer – I had no idea what effect that might have.

I reached the first archway out of the main galleria, but with my foot in mid-air, I felt it; a heavily oppressive, alien weight on my mind, a faint ghost headache that evoked a familiar flavour behind my senses.

Familiar. Very, very familiar.

"The fuck?" I turned on my heel.

The scene I was returning to had changed. Jen sat sprawled on the ground, face visible at this angle so I could see her glazed expression of bewildered horror, as if something even more awful than Alan's gory demise had unfolded before her.

I drew close and saw that the patch of floor where Alan's gory remains had splashed down was now so clean it seemed certain that an itinerant vacuum salesman must have given Jen a demo.

Except, of course, that was nowhere near the truth.

"Little Laura," crooned a familiar voice.

That feeling, the familiar presence in my mind, was simply the re-filling of the space he had left there when he died.

My brother stepped out from the far side of the nearest pillar, rested his hand on the stone of it as he leant casually, smiling at me serenely as though posing for a snapshot on a lazy summer's afternoon.

"Hey, don't be too hard on yourself, little sis," he said. "You weren't to know; how could you?"

"W-what?" I said stupidly.

He scraped a hand down his newly-made cheek. "I bet you thought I'd created copies of myself out of some sort of vanity, right?"

I thought I had experienced misery until that moment of realisation opened my eyes to how low it was possible to sink.

"They're backups," I murmured with dumb resignation.

Fuck. How many partitions had he created in the emr?

"Oh, yes indeedy, sis." He cocked his head to one side. "There might be quite a few little Alans lurking around in the emr."

How could I not have seen this coming? I worked in I.T, for fuck's sake.

The first rule of computing. Always keep a backup. He had copies of himself, living pointless pre-programmed lives in the emr, as templates from which he could rebuild himself.

I had to know more. Curiosity beat overwhelming horror for a moment.

"How does that even work?" I asked him. "I mean, if you're dead, you can't exactly trigger a recovery, can you?"

He pushed up off the pillar. "I'm not going to tell you how I do it, sis, I'm not a fucking divvy! So, are you done now? Can we stop this pointless war and talk about how I'm going to be persuaded to forgive–?"

I fired at him, mind energy pumped out as easily as a fart.

He swiped my attack aside with a defensive flex and fired back at me.

"That was just rude, Laura," he chided. "You interrupted me–"

I swiped at it with my mind but he blocked and we locked together once again. Pinned by the pushing forces, I couldn't expel any more mindforce, but apparently neither could he because there was a stillness to our entwined mindforce extrusions.

Stalemate.

Suddenly I felt pain. A sharp pain in my ribs. Then in my groin. Another fierce burst crushing my right breast.

Jen, the fucking bitch!

I pulled back enough focus to see with my eyes and my entire field of vision was filled with Jen's hateful face as she violated my body with punches, kicks and knees.

She was now also, stupidly, ideally placed for me to divert mindforce for just a moment and spray her like a housefly.

She drew a fist back.

I diverted my line of fire for just a moment, like flicking the garden hose up off the roses to drench Daddy, instantly pushing it back into Alan's stream of energy before it could gain much more than three inches toward me, but more than enough to punch a hole in reality where Jen had been standing.

She didn't even have time to scream before she burst apart like dropped ripe fruit to spatter on the cold floor.

Without consciously agreeing it, Alan and I both ceased fire and our mindforce battle was placed on hold.

"Laura, that was low, even for you," my brother said with a frown as he took in the mess of gore, blood and bones that was the remains of Jen.

He seemed less upset than I would have expected – which should have told me something.

Still, I was done being the class dunce when the mess of Jen twitched and rippled.

There was a copy of Jen in the emr, too...

As I stood opposite my indestructible brother and watched the scorched twigs of Jen's bones begin to twitch and dance, I couldn't help feeling that Sool had fucked me over. How had he not known about this?

A halo formed the pool of my friend and slowly stretched up into the air over the mulch to shape her outline.

"I do not want to see this!" I muttered.

"C'mon, sis, this is the best bit. I never get to see this, normally."

Information in case I survived the next ten minutes – someone had killed Alan before I came along, since otherwise his remark made no sense.

Her bones leapt up into their allotted places in the frame created by the halo. Then, glistening red and pink meat began to peel up into place onto the re-forming frame to create a raw, naked and skinless mockery of my former friend.

My brother casually extended a hand and a thought knot flew at me.

"Fu–!"

I threw myself at the ground whilst my mind pushed out a blocking force. I distantly felt a crunch of pain as my elbow hit the ground.

Sprawled on the ground, I got double the good fortune on that one, because my elbow saved my head from clacking against the hard floor as I landed, while my deflection force sent the knot sailing through the galleria and out across the still, silent, river Thames.

I rolled and clambered to my feet, body sluggish like old lard but my mind razor sharp and on a hair trigger.

I ignored the naked and skinless Jennifer Sullivan trembling to my left, her wobbling breasts a mess of crimson flesh and pale yellow fat and focused on holding up a guard against Alan as I backed away across the galleria.

I couldn't win against Alan while he had such a huge advantage. All I could do was survive long enough to re-group. I had to get far enough away that he couldn't easily ambush me when I transferred away.

He seemed more interested in nursing Jen, his mind focused on cradling her re-forming body with a tenderness that was, in its own perverted way, rather sweet.

Once out of his line of sight, I turned and ran out through the Galleria archways.

There was an agonised howl as Jen's mind was re-integrated with her still-forming body. Good. Bitch.

I kept up a steady jog along Tooley Street, mind open to detect the faintest ping if Alan decided to try to give chase and shoot me in the back.

I ran and ran, my legs an agony of aching and my lungs ragged and torn from breathing too hard for too long but convinced that distance was my best friend; distance from Alan, so that he would find it harder to reach out and snatch me mid-transfer – although for all I knew the distance made no difference to mind powers. I just wasn't enough of an expert yet.

I was heading the wrong way – moving away from London Bridge, where I had first arrived, heading toward Tower Bridge where the More London riverside complexes had vanished and been replaced, again I suspected, with run-down and ancient-looking buildings.

London was too hard to deal with in this hybrid, half-emr state.

I staggered onto the pathway onto Tower Bridge and stopped to grab air to cool my seared lungs. Exercise, I believe I have mentioned, is one of my major allergies. I rested my hands on my knees beneath the watchful iron structure spanning out across the Thames which, thankfully, seemed to have retained an unchanged façade.

Only as my breath levelled off and my eyes could focus did I properly take in the scene before me on the bridge.

Now I knew where at least some of the cars had gone.

On the bridge before me, all the way across as far as I could tell, was a vast multi-car pile-up blocking the entire road with its rent-iron wreckage. Cars lay at all angles and in all states, some even sprawled across the walkways.

My gaze brushed the nearest vehicle and I saw a figure inside, dead I was sure, slumped across the steering wheel. I was sure I didn't need to go get a medical degree to confirm that she was dead.

Every car seemed to be occupied. All dead. No decay, though, which meant that this was recent, or the laws of nature were already completely fucked by the steady collapsing of reality.

My reverie was shattered as I sensed Alan behind me.

A hot scold blossomed in my belly and I hastily turned.

Jen's fist blotted out my view and then struck my left eyebrow, sending a shard of pain into my skull.

"Bitch is back," she spat.

I'd have been happy to agree, except she wasn't bitch enough to earn it.

You see, Jen was no fighter; not really. She could pull a woman's hair, kick a man in his happy place, but what she couldn't do, with her talon-like nails and anorexic arms, was clench a proper fist or put any useful power into a punch.

She had not hurt me badly *enough*, but she had given me the chance to gain an advantage – assuming my brother still had aspirations to recruit me that would make him reluctant to kill me if he didn't have to.

I clapped my hands to my face and hunched over, which allowed me to seem stunned whilst allowing me to peer through my fingers and assess both her and Alan.

She was now in some pain from the bone-on-bone impact which had probably hurt her hand more than it had hurt my head, so she was not focussing on me at all.

Alan, however, had me in his sights. Fucking stupid plan, all I had done was given him time to line me up. Oops. Bugger.

What a way to punch out! Cause of death: being a brass-plated fucking idiot.

But he did not fire. In fact, his gaze had already drifted off me by the time I started cursing my own stupidity. No, he was staring at the wreckage of cars.

"What... what *is* this?" he asked, dumbfounded.

It was so odd I gave up my feint and straightened up. "What?"

I could not understand why he was so shocked about a car wreck while the whole world was folding into chaos around us, falling to bits on a global scale.

"Wait," I said with sudden realisation. "Did you not know how bad the world was? Are you telling me this is a shock to you?"

"I knew it was changing," he said, staring out across the bridge.

His daytrip had probably begun when he transferred himself and his floozy straight onto the concrete flooring of the Galleria, without ever seeing the rest of London, with its silent, twisted gothic ruination. Maybe he'd seen glimpses of his own street, too, but now, suddenly, he was confronted by a whole cityscape.

oh, this is priceless

I regretted the unguarded thought but he seemed to be too distracted to read me properly, his gaze flitting to me momentarily before floating away to the scene before us.

He approached a nearby car and Jen followed him, her painted face still wincing as she shook her punching hand. With a bit of luck the bitch had broken a knuckle.

I went after my brother, thinking to press my advantage and tip him fully off-kilter. "Look what's become of our world, Peter! Look what you've done!"

Inside each car and, in many cases, spilling out of open doors to sprawl dead on the ground, were corpses. Victims of whatever accident had happened here, or victims of looters; but victims, in every single case, of their fellow man.

This was the world Alan had helped create, but not in the way I had originally thought. The collapse of reality wasn't the cause here. This had been caused by the panicked selfishness of the human herd, reacting to their oncoming doom.

With a sharp scraping sound, Alan picked up the blade of a garden spade that lay on the road. It's handle had splintered off very violently.

Nearby, inside a Mini Cooper, lay slumped the body of a woman who had clearly died by the very spade in Alan's hand. The top of her head had been split open by a single blow, as if her assailant had planned to plant potatoes and had rammed the spade in, ready to dig, before realising that he had forgotten to bring the vegetables themselves.

The amount of blood was shocking. Her black hair was parted a full two inches by a crevice that opened gorily into a mottled cavity, the soft parts of her brain not visible in there, while her face was caked with dry blood that had clearly poured like a waterfall when the wound was first made, before subsiding and drying. One eye was buried under dry blood. The other had been popped from its socket by the blow and lay on its side in the blood river on her cheek.

My brother dropped the spade, seeming numb and far away.

I saw an arc of spew before I heard Jenny call for Ralph and Hugh. A moment later I caught the rich, acid-fart stench of vomit on the still air and heard the last liquid pattering onto the tarmac as she finished up. Classy.

I approached Alan. Not too close, of course.. "This is what you've brought down on us, just the way Sool warned."

"No," he insisted, catching my eye and giving a single, assertive shake of his head. "No, that's not right, can't be right. Can it? I mean, Sool... No."

His appealing eyes held my gaze as if seeking some comfort there.

"Oh, Peter," I said. "Do you see, now? This was always going to be the price of your little games in the emr. Now look at what you've done. The whole world's gone. *My* fucking world is gone!"

The feral depth of my anger shocked me even as I fired at him and he was blasted into the air, his blackened, crisping corpse looping over the wrecked vehicles and passing over the side of the bridge.

He would not stay dead. Time to go.

I squinted and pictured a swirling disc against a dazzling blue sky, bringing the image into sharp focus in my mind's eye and seeing the patio outside the hotel in that disc. It just seemed to be the easiest way.

The sky above smeared, the clouds melted into each other and the ornate metal of the bridge sagged and rolled away, accelerating as it coiled past me and joined a spinning vortex of colour and mixed noises...

... and I felt the solidity of the patio well up beneath my feet as the hotel peeled up from the newly-formed ground and solidified to stand before me.

Sensation returned. Rain slashed violently across the back of my coat and my hair was instantly drenched and caked flat against my head. A blinding flash of lightning splintered against the brickwork of the hotel, bright enough to dazzle my eyes.

I ducked my head and scuttled close to the building, where I hugged the rough brickwork and fumbled my way, blinking out raindrops that wanted to flood my eyes, until I reached the entrance.

As I fell through the revolving door into the warm, familiar, red-velour lobby, I was immediately blanketed in heat.

Time to lose wonder-coat. I tugged at and hastily unfastened the bastard thing tugged it off, dragging it behind me like a dead badger as I strode purposefully past the eternally on-duty porter and into the dining room.

My instincts were spot on. My friends were seated at our accustomed table in the bay window.

As I approached, drenched and wild-eyed no doubt, Sam glanced up at me and Tom followed suit, both starting at the sight of me. Tom lowered the china teacup he had been nursing and it clicked as it docked into its saucer, a thin coil of steam rising into the air.

It was a moment before Jen looked up.

I dismissively tossed wondercoat over a chair.

I stared at her. It. Tom was probably still alive only because the whore-clone hadn't managed to get him away from Sam yet. Still plying its part. My heart thudded and my head ached as I held the cold aching rage caged behind my eyes.

The pleasant smile she'd planned to fake for me died stillborn and her gaze turned cold. "Oh, is my little secret out, then, *little* Laura?"

Tom started to rise from his chair, but Sam laid a hand on his shoulder and pressed him back down into his seat, gaze never leaving Jen as he discreetly reached into his pocket for his orb.

Jen snorted contemptuously. "Oh, who do you think you are, you fat little cunt?"

I loved the cold feel of the smile on my face.

"I want you to know how much I'm going to enjoy killing you, Jen."

"Stupid cunt, you underestimate my master if you think for one second you can poss—"

I blasted her with enough mind energy to shred a city and her last word stank of burnt pork as an orgasm of relieved pressure coursed through my body.

-47-

A thick white dust drifted across the dining room and began to settle on chairs, tables and condiments.

There was nothing left resembling Jen's body. Tom made a small strange sound in his throat.

I leant on the table to face them. "The Alan clone is a backup. I think there's one in each of his emr creations, and if you kill the real one it's restored from one of the backups; probably from *any* of them."

Sam pulled a face. "Makes sense."

"Yep," I said. "We have to destroy all of them all before I can even think about fighting the real him. Questions?"

"Shit, Laur," said Tom. "He ain't gonna just let us wipe them out if they're that important to him.

I pursed my lips and frowned at him. I had let that weakling fuck me, once. Once too often. "What should we do, Tom? Throw ourselves on his mercy?"

He had no answer for that, of course.

I grabbed my coat off the chair, spraying a little water around. "Come on."

I threw on the poxy coat as armour, or a cape of courage, as I headed for the doorway.

The lobby was empty as we exited the restaurant, the reception desk unmanned.

I glanced at Sam. "We start here."

He nodded and indicated a door at the back of the reception desk area. "I would suggest our quarry has taken cover through there."

We crossed to the desk, where Sam flipped up the hatch to let me through in his strangely gentlemanly way and I crossed to the door at the back.

As I reached for the heavily scratched brass ball doorknob, a violent bang hit my ears and pushed all my blood out of my arsehole. I turned sharply with a gasped and shuddering breath.

"Sorry," said Sam, stroking the desk hatch that he had just allowed to slam down.

I wanted to call him names but I had too little breath. A glare would have to suffice.

I turned my back on him and grabbed the doorknob.

The door was not locked. It opened onto a dark narrow enclosure that ended, after three or four feet, in a wood staircase that descended beneath the hotel.

"Oh, a cellar," said Tom. "This'll end well."

I turned a smirk on Tom. "It could be worse. At least there's a light on down there."

He peered past me and saw what I had already seen; a weak yellowy glow coming up from below to taint the walls a pissy straw colour.

"Oh, epic!" He held out a hand, palm up. "After you, then."

I felt a little mirth at that. "You're too kind."

Sam wanted to go first but I dismissed him because I was less than half his weight and would have a chance at getting down there silently, so it was me who descended the wooden stairs, hearing every creak and crack from the old steps in full-spectrum. So much for discretion; I could maybe have signalled our approach more clearly by sending the Alan clone a text; but I doubted it.

At the bottom of the stairs was a narrow corridor made even more claustrophobic because its walls were panelled with six-by-four slices of varnished wood, making the place feel like a nineteenth century mineshaft; an effect exacerbated by the row of naked bulbs hanging from filthy yellowed wires from the wood-clad ceiling.

About twenty feet from us, the corridor turned sharply to the right so we could not see what awaited us.

I felt prickly sweat on the back of my neck as the walls seemed to lean in toward me.

"Phwoar, what's that smell?" Tom exclaimed as he joined me.

As I drew a deep breath to quell my claustrophobia I was hit by the rank stink Tom had picked up. Beneath the dry sawdust-and-dust tang of the corridor lurked a cloying, acrid, musky smell halfway between meat and sweat.

Suddenly my quilted coat was too heavy and an oppressive and I regretted putting it on as armour. It didn't make me strong, it just made sweat crawl under my clothes and across my skin. Even so, its cloying mitt was at least a layer between me and whatever horrors awaited us around the turn in the corridor.

Sam touched my arm, causing a violent jolt of shock that made my heart thump.

~ *do you sense it?* ~

don't fucking do that, Sam! Sense what?

~*something up ahead. Something... unpleasant*~

I shrugged.

come on

I realised Tom couldn't 'hear' us. "Come on," I repeated out loud.

One step, two step... I still felt nauseous and chilly-scared, which was only exacerbated when I glanced back to see Tom clinging to the staircase and resolutely *not* following us.

Sam, protect Tom
~fuck Tom~
I wish I could say I argued.

We hit the corner and passed into line of sight of what awaited us and words completely failed me.

Sam gripped my hand urgently and turned me to face him. "I swear to you, Laura, that I had no part in this, even in the thrall of my master."

I nodded and laid my other hand over his large hand. I wasn't sure I entirely believed it of that it mattered; he had definitely done terrible things back then but he was someone new now.

This was certainly a horror show of the kind that Sam in his previous guise would have got off on – brutal, violent, sexual and utterly devoid of any compassion or respect for the human victims brought here to this degradation and misery.

The corridor opened out onto a large wood-floored area, probably forty feet by forty feet. Against the walls to the left, the right and at the end furthest from us stood large slatted cages, each large enough for maybe two or three reasonably-sized adults. And they were all occupied.

Inside every cage there were bodies, all in varying states of dismemberment, some with limbs missing, some with glistening purple ribbons of bowels protruding from slits in their bellies. Some partly skinned, their crimson muscles exposed to the air.

And they were all alive.

They made no sound, none at all, as if they had been made to understand the terrible and much worse price of making any; but their eyes looked toward us, devoid of hope, expecting more horror and violation from us as we took a step forward, because that was all that was left for them in their lives.

The old-coins-and-lard stink of bloodied meat was unbearable here, which made sense because the girl in the cage nearest to us was missing her left arm and right leg, but the stumps were roughly stitched with thick black thread that allowed clotting blood to ooze out, along with bright yellow pus from a ravaging infection.

And yet she was not the most pitiful of the victims here.

My nose and mouth felt full of the blocked-drains-and-old-food smell of faeces where many of the victims had lost the last hint of self-respect or hope and had simply spilled their shit down their legs (or stumps) and sat, hopeless and ruined, in the resultant mulch. Many had sores that were infected, ragged and open sores on thighs, bellies and even breasts, ruined and rent open by this devastation.

"Why?" I uttered, my mouth full of drool as my body prepared to vomit anything that might be lurking in my stomach.

Sam cast his gaze about. "Well, since they are all female, I would hazard

345

a guess that they were brought here by my master for what he would consider... romance."

"*Romance!*" I cried in protesting disbelief.

"Not this, no," he replied. "He would have... tried to impress them, woo them, but faced with the reality that even in his own private universe, he was hopelessly unappealing..."

"He did this to them out of spite."

Sam's sharp blue eyes glimmered with suppressed tears. "I was a part of this, Laura. Many of his victims got here because I brought them."

I reached out and touched his arm, because even in the midst of this charnel revelation, I knew that *my* Sam had not done any of those things.

A sudden hot scold of vomit burgeoned up my throat and ejaculated from my mouth, mostly stomach acid based on how much it burned. Sam danced delicately aside as the spurt pattered onto the wooden floor of this nightmare prison.

I wiped my mouth and checked the front of my coat, tears streaming from my eyes at the sudden violent retch. "Fuck, sorry Sam."

He didn't reply but he accepted my apology. Then, he pursed his lips. "I know what you are going to ask me next," he said. "Trust me. Don't."

I frowned up at him. "There's nothing I want to know about this, Sam."

"Good," he said, his expression relaxing. "Then we need to decide–"

"Except..."

"Laura, no."

I shrugged. "I have to know. Why would my brother keep them alive in this state? I mean, torture them, kill them – it's horrible but I get why someone as sick as he is might do it. But *this?*"

He leant down and aimed his blue-crystal gaze into me earnestly. "You do *not* want to know."

I stared back at him. "But do you know why?"

He sighed and straightened up. "Yes, Laura. I know your brother far better than you do. And, please forgive me, because you *will* regret knowing this. He enjoys the act of desecrating the flesh of those who emotionally betray him, even to the point of sexual penetration of their open wounds."

My belly cramped. "Ohh, get me the fuck out of here!" I cried. "Now, Sam, now; the clones not down here."

He hunched over so he could loop an arm around my waist and we went back around the turn in the corridor, where Tom was still waiting for us at the foot of the wooden staircase. "Hey, any luck down there?" he asked.

I didn't answer him as Sam helped me onto the staircase and up out of the hell beneath my brother's hotel, but I glanced up at my stronger companion. "We have to bring this whole fucking place down, Sam."

-48-

My brother had proven that he understood the emr better than me, that he was stronger than me and, oh yes, that he was far, far more brutal than me. But in one respect he had failed to be top dog; he had made the error of underestimating me.

I had figured out the weakness of this particular clone of his, and it was all to do with the design of the little hell hotel itself.

Sam helped with some of the details, having been here consistently for far longer than I had, but I had the basics. The whole reality ran on a cycle that he was able to confirm ran for about eighteen hours, within which some of the backdrop characters, such as the porter, exhibited even shorter cycles, looping round in minutes or hours. The clone was not a background character, but to protect the sanity of even his tiny mind, he was locked into the main cycle and got reset every eighteen hours along with his pocket universe.

All we had to do was lay low until the end of the day's cycle. The clone would forget that he was supposed to be keeping his head down.

Sam, Tom and I went to the room I had shared with Sam and relaxed. Kicked back, as they say. Well, as far as I know that's what they say. We had coffee and tea, a deck of cards that Tom retrieved from his room. Hell, we even went down to the hotel lounge and found a scrabble board with most of the letters and wasted a scary amount of time spelling words wrong and finding it hilarious. And most of all, we talked a plan into shape.

Night fell outside the hotel and then, a few hours later, the whole of reality reset itself and morning sprang into being out there.

The boys went outside, by prior agreement, to wait on the rear patio for me. The portal out there didn't lead anywhere any more, with the village realm gone, but being near a portal, even a dead one, seemed likely to be helpful when it came to needing to transfer us out of here, which I was going to need to do pretty soon if everything went to plan.

And I had made it clear to the boys that I wanted to do this next bit alone. This was *personal*.

I crossed the hotel lobby toward where the copy of my brother stood behind the main desk, carefully and slowly writing notes in a large red-leather book. As I approached him, he suddenly paused and lowered his pen. The writing implement, a bespoke ballpen of some brand or other, clicked as it met the desk.

I closed the distance on him more rapidly, passing the porter who, poorly-drawn character as he was, ignored me completely.

The clone gave me a short, insincere hotel smile. "May I help you, madam?"

"Yes," I said. "You can die for me."

He frowned. "I beg your–"

I fired.

He burst apart as the mindforce slammed into him, through him and punched through the wall behind him in a shower of concrete dust and masonry fragments.

The wreckage of the non-man was still tumbling to the ground when the porter cried out. Without thought or hesitation I span instantly on my heel and fired, depriving him of the very little existence he had ever possessed. He puffed apart like dust, as something that had barely been there to begin with.

As I turned back, I saw, as expected, that the gory remnants of the clone were twitching under the influence of an unseen force as they began their re-animation, so I hurried out of the hotel as fast as my pathetic muscles would allow and was punched in the eyes by brilliant blazing daylight as I walked into a brilliantly sunny day. The storm of the previous day cycle had apparently abated.

"Well?" Sam asked, when I reached the bin area at the rear of the hotel.

"It's like we thought," I told him. "The backups are backed up."

~you know what you have to do~

I stared at him, suddenly confronted by the moment of truth.

"I don't know, Sam."

Tom looked from Sam and back to me, having not, of course, heard the thought our companion had sent me. "Don't know what, Laur?"

~trust yourself, Laura. You are strong, as strong as your brother~

I disregarded Tom and focused on Sam. Nodded once as much to tell myself yes as accept his trust in me.

I drew a breath. "Right, when the moment comes you need to grab me, my physical body, anywhere and any way. Miss the moment and it'll be the last thing you ever do."

"Yeah, we know, Laur."

I turned my back on the hotel and faced out toward the world beyond, to allow myself to focus on the first step. Expansion.

There was still an echo of the storm that had been raging when I returned here, distant and affecting only the forest in the distance. Violent punches of electrical light that my slowly opening mind sensed were an incursion of the Mind realm into this reality. A feature of the collapse taking hold across the universe. Universes.

I pushed out and my mind self extruded outwards from my body, widening as I accelerated outward and passed over grass and tree and hotel. I almost panicked as I expanded across the sweeping lawns, the cold, dark forest and the bricky chunk of the hotel, as all things here in this emr pocket were encompassed within the boundaries of my greater self. I held my nerve, the cold dispassionate power of the stronger me within taking over from the frightened girl who had run the show for so much of my life.

The cool formless chaos of shadowed silence at the perimeters of this micro-realm were my confirmation that I had it all within my grasp. I could feel and see every inch, every particle, every mile of it, all at once.

I pulled inward. Felt a sharp pain in the thing that was, somewhere down there inside me, my own head. And then it happened.

now

I sent the thought and hoped Sam could hear me from out here, could tell Tom with his flesh voice as my wrenching grasp pulled reality in toward me, peeling it off the emr like an old poster coming grudgingly off a wall.

Everything warped, buckled and then the sky folded downward, the lawns rolled upward, the ashen trunks of the trees split, cracked and shattered into kindling before hurtling inward at me, at my core.

One tendril of my mind sought and found the boys hanging off my meat form and I steadied them ready for the transfer as the material of this reality became a formless, swirling maelstrom coiling down into an infinitesimal point.

The hotel was gone and along with it the clone. Brick and meat had become dust and that dust mere particles in a freeform soup that sprawled outward into the unfocused abyss.

I focussed my mind and transferred us.

The chaotic multi-coloured rush of the transfer washed us away just before the hotel's realm ceased to have any reference point to anchor to, and we landed in fierce heat.

-49-

We stood in a desert. Not as fierce or bright as the Mind realm had been, but enough that heat from the scorching sand began to bake the soles of my shoes. As we settled into place we were hit by a fierce, fast and scolding hot wind that hurled sheet after sheet of cutting sand at our faces, our eyes.

"Nice choice!" I heard Tom shout over the whoosh of the sandstorm.

"I didn't have time to be fussy!" I yelled back.

I then slammed my mouth shut as vicious, razor-sharp sand particles intruded onto my tongue. I glanced at Sam.

maybe we should transfer again

~ no, there is something ahead — we are where we need to be ~

I frowned up at him inquisitively but was forced to clamp my eyes shut as another blast of hot sand spattered my cheeks and lashes. his strong arm pulled me in against his thick trunk.

Apparently unaffected by the vicious sandstorm, Sam led us step by trudging step, steering us until, suddenly, my foot kicked a wooden step. I stepped up and felt another step. Took it.

Sam let me go.

The storm was gone. I opened my eyes. Shook my head and blinked hard to clear my eyes of any rogue sand before dusting the last few particles off wondercoat.

Sam had helped Tom onto this veranda, too. He glanced around in wonder. "How did you see this place?"

Sam had finished dusting sand off his dress shirt. "One of the very few advantages of this body is that I feel almost no pain and can withstand a great deal of damage. You two could barely open your eyes, I knew you hadn't seen it."

We stood on a wooden veranda built at the front of a pale wooden shack, a place which stood alone and incongruous in the middle of this insane and barren sandstorm world. The floor beneath us was pine or something similar, while a waist-high wood walling enclosed this open area – and beyond these otherwise open sides to our shelter's frame, the storm howled and bared its sharp sand teeth as if peeved at our escape. Yet it did not venture through the entirely open upper two thirds of the sides of the veranda; a tiger pacing inside its cage. Well, outside in this case, which was even stranger.

I drew a breath. "Clearly we can assume that this is another of my brother's little toyboxes. I guess we don't need to look any further."

I gathered myself and started to open my mind, ready to tear this reality down without bothering to meet its resident – the clones were really not much of a threat in themselves.

Except that, as I opened my mind, I felt a huge warning pulse and hastily closed my mindself off to shield it.

fuck

~what is it~

this one is stronger, Sam. we're going to have to deal with it before we can tear down this place

I quickly explained to Tom and we crossed the freshly-new, ochre-coloured timber floor to a wooden entrance door with a ball-shaped brass knob.

Sam grabbed the doorknob without hesitation and pushed it open to the tooth-nagging grinding noise of rusty hinges scraping metal-on-metal across each other.

Inside, the shack was warm and homely, so many rugs in browns, deep greens and dull yellows scattered and piled together that the wood floor beneath was barely visible, while the light in here had a subdued warmth, supplied as it was by a window in the far wall with pale yellowy cream curtains drawn across it.

It was warm. Felt safe. I was not fooled.

To our right stood a cabinet in a darker wood than the shack walls, a tray on top containing a cut-glass decanter and whisky tumblers. One tumbler missing.

careful

I sent to Sam.

~ I saw.. the missing glass ~

The space between the window and the cabinet was no longer empty, because into existence had come a wide, round wicker chair and, embedded deeply within the bulky, floppy, dark green cushion wrapped into its curves, sat my brother. Well, a copy of him, at least.

I glanced at Sam.

The clone crossed his scrawny white legs and raised the missing whisky tumbler to me, while the hem of his red silk robe fell away for a moment to reveal a hint of penis.

Straightening his robe, he gulped a throatful of amber liquid and then tilted the glass towards the drinks cabinet. "Have a drink, why don't you? Relax. Trust me, you won't get three feet toward that door if you turn you back on me, *sis.*"

That word made me shudder. It had felt jarring coming from the real Alan, but from this pervy-looking wretch it was like vomited semen.

He adjusted himself in the wicker chair, causing it to creak and pop but mercifully concealing little Alan's pointy bell-tip, while in the same moment he swung the whisky glass at his lips, caught the rim in the same movement and gulped a little more of the fierce fluid through his wet, pursed lips.

"What is it, *sis?*" He grinned as I glared at him, my anger building at his deliberate repetition of that word – as he had surely intended that it should.

"Don't fucking *read* me!" I snapped.

He held up a hand. "Hey, take it easy! What's brought this on? Surely you're not still mad over dear, treacherous Jennifer?"

~ he is deliberately provoking you, Laura, do not let him make you react emotionally ~

i don't care, Sam, he's going to get...

~ no, Laura! he is goading you because he is smarter than the last copy, he is thinking strategically and he wants ~

Our moment was interrupted by Alan's harsh bark of laughter. "How *lovely!* Do you lovebirds always chat amongst yourselves like this?" he turned sharply to Tom, but his expression softened. "Do they leave you out like this a lot, my poor boy?"

I took a step closer to the clone, rage bubbling and just about held down by my lid. "I guess you're the *drone* who got all of Alan's perceptiveness, aren't you?"

He gave a casual shrug that caused the robe to slip slightly off one shoulder, revealing his flat toneless chest a bit too much, but his eyes sharpened as they came back to look at me – I'd chosen the word 'drone' quite deliberately and it had worked.

The copy slugged the last of his whisky, smacked his lips and smiled up at me from his nest of cushions, his eyes glinting but a hint of a tear in the corner of one, from suppressed rage, I liked to think. "Fuck what you think, Laura. Stuff your opinions up your big, fat arse."

He let his tumbler drop onto the wooden floor as emphasis for the word 'fat'.

"Ouch!" I exclaimed with a laugh of genuine amusement.

He had been aiming squarely at my body paranoia, but actually he'd shown his hand, with such a playground jibe and, of course, in showing me that I had managed to sneak under his skin, even if only a little.

I smiled calmly at him, which flipped his piss/off switch. He grabbed at the wicker arms to lever himself up. "Fuck you! Fuck... *you!*"

As he wrenched himself free of the chair I was ready, focussed on him, and I opened my mind.

Before I could fire there was a blur of movement to my right and I had no time to react before a slight figure shot across the shack and slammed an object in its hand against Tom's head. My friend staggered headlong in front of me before slumping against the wall.

My aim had been thrown completely and, still distracted, I watched Sam rush at the figure to stop it going after Tom again.

Jen.

Fucking bitch was becoming a real overhead, now; I was going to have to deal with her.

I stared in disbelief as she melted completely away into formlessness, leaving Sam grasping at empty air, also off-balance.

But she had served her purpose…

Those few seconds were all that the clone needed. I opened my mind and pushed out defensive mindforce, but his blast of mind energy still hurled me off my feet and sent me slamming against the far wall – a jolt of pain spiked through my back at a jagged angle and I distantly felt myself toppling forward toward the floor.

stay conscious!

I struggled to aim my unfocussed eyes or my unfocussed mind – anything – at the copy of my brother, but I could not enforce any kind of cohesion on myself.

I knew I had to stay conscious. If I passed out now, I was done. *Take thy rest and sleep forever, chubby princess.*

Alan sauntered across the shack as the bulky mass of Sam tumbled forward, felled by something I had not seen. Sam now on all fours, whilst I was on my knees and half-slumped against the cool shack wall.

"Wait," I murmured weakly. I wanted to cry but also to laugh because why say such a stupid thing, had that ever worked, my drifting mind wondered pointlessly. *I know you plan to do this, but just wait, would you, for no specific reason…*

He glared down at me, his eye sockets empty holes in his head; terrifying but just a side effect of focussing mind energy.

None of which affected how fucked I was as thick black venom spat from his eyes and I watched in disbelief, helpless, as the lethal charge slammed toward my face.

-50-

I stared, body frozen and powers quiesced, as the glistening blackness seethed inches from my face, seeming frustrated that it could not close the distance and bring me to a terrible end.

Honestly, I was as puzzled as I was grateful that the clone was choosing to hold it back; he just stood staring at the knot while I huddled, a useless sack of bones in sauce with a fuddled mind, terrified and yet also baffled at his expression of anguished concentration.

He was toying with me.

Suddenly he was swiped from my field of vision as Sam slammed bodily into him, although that of course did nothing to disperse the thought knot that still hung in the air ready to sear the meat from my bones.

Anger spiked through me. I was the biggest threat to him, yet the little bastard was toying with me; he seemed to be favouring the males with greater respect. Fuck *that*. Enraged and indignant, my vision came sharply back into focus and my mind instantly crushed the thought knot it had been holding back.

In that moment, the immobilised knot and the clone's almost agonised level of focus made sense. My subconscious mind-self had held back the deadly burning filth, continued to fight for me while I played in soft grass with the cuckoos.

I felt better about myself.

The glistening black cluster crumpled inward to a tiny white point and I turned my attention to the ongoing battle, where to my left, Sam lay sprawled on top of the clone after his body-slam attack, seemingly trapping it.

Sam, get out of there

Before the big man could respond I felt a power build-up from our enemy through the bones of my skull and, an instant later, Sam was punched bodily up into the air with enough force to clear the clone but not enough to do any real damage. He slammed to the floor with a dust-spattering whump.

The little shit turned that socket-eyed face on me as he rose to his feet. He was smiling. He had reserved the main force of his power for me.

I felt a smile within myself, unsure if it showed on my actual face, but I was where I belonged – at the heart of the fight.

As he fired, I grasped his knot, plucked it apart and flung it away but, as it scattered into fading, harmless beads, his mind flexed to fire again.

~ *I'm coming, Laura* ~

Sam rolled rapidly onto his feet and hurtled at the clone, while Tom, seeming to anticipate Sam's needs, dropped onto all fours behind old no-eyes.

I felt a smile escape onto my lips.

nice

The giant slammed bodily into the clone and threw fists at him to drive him back. Alan allowed himself to roll with the impact, accelerating backwards away from Sam but unaware of the crouching form behind him. His legs hit Tom's shoulder and he was upended, spindly legs flailing free from under his robe as he was flipped. He fought desperately to twist in mid-air so he could focus a defence in my direction, but *oh, no you don't.*

I blasted him with mindforce and his still-tumbling body burst apart in a glorious display, thick ribbons of blood looping outward and upward as gore and gristle coiled free and bones clattered across the wooden floor.

I clambered upright and limped across to my male companions, several joints aching and pinging after the knocks of the battle.

"Go, team," I declared with a grimace.

Sam pulled what looked like the wrong half of a smile. "You could say that. Perhaps now would be a good time to tear down this rather nasty reality before our friend is able to... heal."

"Not quite," I said, indicating the patch of floor where the disassembled mulch of our enemy was already beginning to squidge into a single collective pile shape under an unseen force. "He gets his shit together too soon and I'll have him coming up behind me while I'm focused on doing the deed."

"Ah." Sam rubbed his chin. "Yes, I see the problem. Still, I don't see how we can stop him re-forming. That's what he is designed to do, after all. In fact it's fairly much the only point of his existence."

There was a ghastly slurp when several dollops of crimson muck were sucked into the swelling central mass of a torso. A moment later, in a vile organic implosion, a limbless trunk formed and began to dress itself with clumps of shreds of meat and glistening white bone.

Tom coughed wetly. "Excuse me," he muttered, then bolted for the shack door.

"Weak stomach," I murmured.

"Weak everything," Sam stated.

I didn't want to agree, but I kind of did. I looked up at him. "You're right about one thing, Sam; we can't stop the process of re-forming."

He pulled his gaze off our resurrecting enemy, his blue eyes glinting at me. "I know."

"OK, so what happens when a creature that can't die fights a force that won't quit until he does?"

His eyebrows shot up. "Oh, I like that!"

I kept my smugness in check and turned to the mulchy form before us, its shape already resembling a human body.

here we go, then

I fired a hard pulse of mindforce at the almost-complete clone. It was sufficiently alive again to put up a defence and easily presented a forcewall that held my attacking energy away from itself.

It was going to crush my mindforce attack with relative ease, of course, but that was the point; I needed to give it something to do, to keep it distracted.

Within myself, I drew all my resources together and packed the forefront of my mind with all of the rage, resentment and jealousy my mellow-bland life had afforded me and formed a dense, black, glistening thought that hung in the air right in front of my face.

The thought knot had long been the weapon of choice for my brother, being effective and horribly cruel. It seemed strange that he would not have seen the danger it posed to his backup system.

Before the clone could finish disabling my fake attack, I launched the knot hard and fast. It shot across the short distance to its target.

My body sagging as all my strength left me, but Sam, having anticipated, grabbed my arm and supported my lower back, keeping me on my feet.

The clone finished dispersing the first mindforce wave and its still shiny-red face sought me in gloating triumph, but that triumph was instantly shattered as it saw, too late, the lethal horror I had thrown at it.

I felt rather than heard its enraged, terrified shriek and then the knot engulfed it. Its mind swatted at it frantically but far, *far* too late. My feint had worked. The black mass spread out, sprawled hungrily across his form in a violent, burning rampage.

His eyes bulged with shock and pain as the clingy, glutinous venom peeled away his meat, pouring into his mouth as if to deny him the right to scream his agonised outrage at this violation and, after less than five seconds, dissolved his body to the point of collapse.

What was left hit the floor.

I opened my mind a little so I could indulge in the raw, slicing pain, the exquisite horror of eyeballs popping and lungs flooding and scolding. It was a sensation that I felt warmly, viscerally, sexually.

However, the frantic terror of his suffocation quickly became overwhelming so I pulled back, my breaths sharp and ragged, skin prickling from the intensity of the sensations.

"Are you finished?" Sam asked me.

I glanced and saw a wry expression that I suspected harboured some level of disapproval, but before I could challenge him on it, the blackened, skeletal legs of our enemy kicked one last time and, as death descended, two thing happened at once: the thought mass began to quiesce, its victim consumed, but, also, the resurrection process immediately kicked in, trying to pile flesh back on even as the knot mass retracted.

The process was automatic, innate, unstoppable; a fact of the clone's existence. He could no more control it than I could choose to stop breathing. His body began to re-form, still engulfed within its steaming liquorice prison.

The knot matter bubbled back into searing, hateful life, raging across the re-forming flesh in a feral rage. The birthing, undulating body spasmed violently as it was ripped from life once again.

"It's working," Sam murmured.

The process was all a blur now, the knot shredding flesh and the reforming of that same flesh happening almost in parallel, so that the clone remained broken, seared and trapped in the moment between life and death.

I briefly hoped that there was not time for him to become conscious, but I had to close my mind because opening it even a little exposed me to a tortured, keening, unending mind-scream like nothing I could have dreamt up in my worst nightmares.

"Come on," I said, my voice husky.

Outside on the calm, quiet wooden veranda, where the sandstorm raged silently a few feet away, we found Tom hunched over, wiping flecks of vomit from his chops. There was a pavement pizza drying on the decking between his knees.

"You OK, soppy-bollocks?" I asked. "Come on, it's time to end this little party."

Both men took hold of one of my arms.

I relaxed. I was tentative at first, worried that opening my mind would let the howling clone's agony in, but once I realised that I could not sense him from out here, I fully opened up, expanded my entire self and hurtled outward, bound for the far horizons of this reality.

Body left far behind, vast expanses of desert and the great vault of the sky came to be within my boundary. I touched the cold edges of reality, the edges whose outsides were exposed to the formless desolation of the null realm.

She held fast to the corners and bore down, pulled inward, drew herself back into me. Ripped down reality like old, unwanted wallpaper.

The collapse became a cascade, a self-sustaining inward-spiralling vortex. I focused on the transfer and pushed my body and theirs through the chaos between the realms.

We were dumped onto solid ground and a sky lit up above us, a familiar sound repeating in my ears; a distant *tock, tock, tock* and, somewhere nearby, the tinkling of a stream of water.

Tom cried out. "Oh, *really*? Fucksake, Laur, not again!"

What a dick.

-51-

Still disorientated by the transfer, I became aware of the rough tickle of coarse grass against my face and realised I had landed facedown. The cloying, dry, earthy musk of soil and withering grass filled and tickled my nose and throat.

I raised my head. We were in the middle of a familiar wild grassland that waved and whispered in the warm, pre-summer breeze. The *tock, tock* sound came from a line tapping against a mast in a row of such masts in what I recalled was a deserted boatyard just a few yards from us.

I clambered to my feet and glanced at my companions. "How is this place still here?" I wondered aloud.

Tom glanced at me disdainfully as he finished dusting himself down. "I think the better question is why the fuck you dragged us back here in the first place, Laur?"

"What? No, I didn't mean to. I mean, the fake Tiler's Hill was about to collapse last time we were there, right, Sam, so how can this place still be here?"

The big man opened his mouth but, before he could answer, my charming ex cut across him. "Whole place is like a nerd's wank palace. Maybe time works different here, maybe we'll meet ourselves from last time! Fuck me."

I blew air through pursed lips to release the angry heat flooding my face. "you're not helping, Tom." I cast him a smile. "Perhaps you could, I don't know, shut the fuck up?"

"Charming."

Sam finally saw his chance to get a word in edgeways between us. "I suggest that we do not linger. You're right, Laura, it's highly unlikely that this region is stable."

I nodded assent. "Grab onto an arm, boys!"

Tom huffed but he joined Sam and they latched on. I focused on the transfer.

Extruded my mind self. Tried to.

Nothing happened.

"Erm, Laur?" I heard Tom say. "Everything alright, babe?"

I strained to open my mind but it was as if I had simply imagined ever being able to do it – I simply couldn't, I was as mundane as everyone else, now.

I let out a sound that was horribly, embarrassingly desperate. "It… It's *gone*," I murmured, a tremor in my voice. "There's… nothing there."

My companions reluctantly let go of my arms but Sam's large hand came to land heavily but tenderly on my shoulder. "You're just tired, Laura. Give yourself a moment."

"A moment?" Tom cried. "What if we haven't got a fucking…"

He fell silent under Sam's withering gaze.

I looked out across the wild, rippling grasslands, to conceal the tears of frustration welling hot from my eyes but also to avoid seeing their faces. Sam's kindness was almost worse than Tom's panicked outrage – I had failed them and the big man knew it.

"Tom's right, Sam, we are fucked. If my powers have quit on me we have no way of fighting Alan, and you *know* he's coming."

Saying it made it so much more real. My brother was coming and there would be no mercy.

"Well," Tom suddenly chimed, bright as a button, "if we're shanksing it, we should get a move on. Tiler's Hill, anyone?"

"What?" I looked at him, bewilderment momentarily replacing my despair. "Shanksing…?"

He frowned at me, looking defensive. "Shanksing. Walking. Don't give me that, Keeble, you grew up where I did!"

"Yes, but not in the same 1930's cockney district you did, apparently."

He pouted but it was lain over a chuckle. "Yeah, alright, I'll give you that one."

"What's with your change of mood, Tom?" I asked with genuine curiosity. "A minute ago you looked like you wanted to stab me in the eyes."

He grinned at me. "Yeah, sorry. Sam's right, though, you've prob'ly got a touch of burn-out. Let's find somewhere to lay low for a bit, re-charge the old brain batteries."

Without warning, a thunderclap more violent than a frying pan to the side of the head shuddered through reality and shook the ground beneath our feet. It was so violent that I saw little showers of soil up sly up between the tall blades of grass, the world seeming to tilt like a mad fairground ride.

Tom ducked and swore, while Sam and I turned to seek the source.

A huge wall of blackness had smashed down onto the grassland, cutting deep into the earth. Now it began to edge forward, slow yet relentless and malevolent, delighting in pulverising this reality an inch at a time as it swallowed earth and air and sky.

~ *did you get any warning?* ~

I glanced at Sam.

none

My usual early warning ping had simply been absent.

oh, shit… Sam, it's coming straight for us!

~ *i suppose this confirms it. you didn't bring us here – we were brought* ~

"That bastard." I fought the heavy tug of despair trying to buckle my knees. "He's been one step ahead of me the whole time. He set it up so I'd end up here!"

"Hang on," said Tom. "You don't know that."

I rounded on him. "Wake *up*, Tom! Something made me choose this place, my brother must've planted something to draw me here, he's too smart for me, I can't–"

"Laura!" Sam snapped. He grabbed my arms and pulled me to him, his face lowered to within an inch of mine. "Snap out of it, we have to run!"

For the first time ever, I think, I could hear panic in his voice.

I nodded hastily. I had no power to fight and none to transfer. We had one option.

We ran *hard*. Through the long leg-snagging grass, battling for balance on uneven ground beneath, hurtling towards…

"Now what?" Tom cried, as we stumbled out of grassland and onto the grey-brown muddy sludge of the riverbank.

"We have to cross!" I yelled. The wind sang loud as though to shout over me. The river was wide but the wall behind us was as wide as reality. We would be in its maw before we got to a shallow part. "Where's the fucking boat?"

The men looked at each other, at the water, then at me. Sam pointed.

The little boat was bobbing amidst the reeds on the far side of the river, where Jen, Tom and I had left it so, so long ago, at the start of everything, when we'd crossed this river for the first time.

I wedged my hands on my hips, my despair threatening to tip off into hysteria. "I just don't believe this!"

I'd landed us on the same side as we'd started on last time, so we were crossing the same way, which meant we'd left the boat the wrong side for it to be of any use now.

I edged down the bank, placing each foot into increasingly pliant mud and terrified of slipping and twisting an ankle, my arms outstretched to gain some level of balance.

Tom joined me close to the water's edge and squinted across at the boat. He had no spectacles. I wondered for an instant if he'd lost them, but that was a question for a time when we were not about to be gulped down whole by a merciless abyss.

Suddenly, he reached into his front jeans pocket and pulled out the little wire constructs, popping them onto his nose and pushing them up the bridge. "Guess we should've seen that coming, eh?"

Sam joined us and his quick, panicky glance back told me all I needed to know about the urgency of the situation.

"Laura," he cried urgently into my ear, gripping my shoulder tightly but not painfully. "We will have to swim."

I glanced at that expanse of water and then dared to take a glance back up onto the grassland. The blackness of the wall seemed to be only feet away. "You might make it," I told the big man, "but Tom and I will never swim fast enough!"

"Ahh, shit," Tom said, his voice brittle. "Can we get *around* the water?"

I'd already considered that possibility. "It goes at least half a mile each way, we'd be abyss-food long before we managed to get around."

Sam puffed air out. "Then you *must* bring the boat across to us."

"How?" I cried in exasperation. "I'm burnt out, Sam! For fuck's sake we had this conversation–"

"Try!" he yelled, his eyes flaring wide. "Laura, you must try! If you have even a little of your power back, it would be enough."

I drew a deep breath. I couldn't transfer us, I didn't have the strength, but maybe my powers were like a phone battery. Leave it a while… no, that was bullshit, of course, that's not how *anything* works.

I glanced back. Nope, no sudden change of fortune, we still had only minutes to live.

"Oh, well. In for a penny…"

I tried to summon a little anger, a little of my former urgent desire to survive; anything to give myself a spark.

My mind opened a little and I felt the rough dampness of that little bobbing bow of wood.

"Gotcha!"

I grasped the curved wooden slats of its structure and drew it toward me. It popped free from the reeds and glided through the water, gathering speed and slewing water in a foamy delta until it reached the bank near my feet and hurled the last of its bow wake at us, wetting our clothes.

I locked back into my body as the boat bumped onto the bank with a final slosh of water and a cloying pong of marsh mud.

"Show-off," said Tom, but his eyes were smiling when I turned my watery gaze his way.

There was a rhythmic thrumming behind us as the destruction force pounded ever closer, consuming reality as it came. With no time to waste we clambered into the boat, the wind lifting the potent grey veggie stench of old, stagnant water and wet, rotted river weeds. I was startled by the smell, because emrs didn't tend to allow for smell or taste.

"Fuck my life, Laur!" Tom cried. I'd managed to kick the oars out of their hoops when I'd pulled the boat to us.

"Well, that's to be expected on any day in *my* life," I muttered. Opening my mind a little, I cupped myself around the boat and us, pushed out some of the little power I had started to recover and pushed us away from the other bank and out into the water.

I'd recovered more than I realised and, as a result, I loaded a bit too much power into pushing the boat. As a result we thundered through the water, a wave of shit-smelling mucky water boiling up either side of the bow as the boat tipped back.

"Whoa! Fucksake!" Tom cried as we all grabbed the wooden rim to keep ourselves in place on the slatted benches.

Worryingly, a little water was seeping in through the sealed joins at the bottom of the boat, creating moats beneath our feet, but this was not an issue because I had barely noticed this before the crunchy, stony grind of the bank vibrated through our feet.

"Out!" I yelled superfluously as the men climbed free and left me sitting there like a tit.

Sam glanced back and noticeably relaxed his shoulders as he noticed that Chompy The Wall of Death had apparently halted on the far side of the bank.

I shrugged at him. "Perhaps it doesn't like water," I quipped; gallows humour, given what we had faced a moment earlier.

Sam's smile was as watery of Carvery wine. "Where now?"

"Tiler's Hill," I said. "Sool used the portal in the graveyard to jump us out of the emr, I'm hoping that perhaps that means it's more stable than the rest of the Chadbury sub-realm."

Sam agreed that this was a reasonable assumption in lieu of anything better, but Tom was still unhappy. This was far from my biggest concern, however.

My ex suddenly leant in close to my ear and touched my arm with his fingertips. "If the worst comes to the worst, transfer us to, y'know, the *real* world."

I looked into his eyes. I'd forgotten the sad beauty of them and I felt a twinge of loss. "Tom, even if I could do that, you don't have a matter form anymore. You'd just… disperse in the Matter realm."

He stepped away from me, lips pursed. "Better that than spending the tail-end of my life running from one emr to the next from your fucking brother. I'll take my chances."

We set off across the last of the grassland and, after a wade through long grass that probably lasted ten minutes but felt like an hour, we reached the jutting edge of concrete, three feet thick and jagged with metal barbs and protruding cables, that signalled the buttress between this reality and the false Chadbury.

The sky in the adjoining reality was a shock, mostly dark greys and blacks but with raw red rips that resembled fresh lava, glowing ominously up in the vault and casting a bloody gloom over the hedges and houses up there.

The men hesitated but I strode forward and grabbed a steel spike, hauling myself up and carefully avoiding the wickedly sharp-looking edges of the concrete as I clambered up to stand once more on Tiler's Hill.

It was quiet and the air was still warm and summery, but the smell here was wrong. Acrid, like the stink of a kettle that has boiled dry – the heat was coming from the volcanic sky and it brought with it an ominous smell.

Sam stepped onto the tarmac beside me.

~ *not very promising* ~

I began to feel heat seeping through my hair and onto my scalp.

A vicious white streak of lightning sliced across the red-and-black maelstrom above us and the lava-like red pools rippled and sprawled wider, consuming more of the sky.

"State of that," Tom grumbled pointlessly at my side. "Follow the yellow brick road, eh?"

We climbed the hill, staying in the middle of the road, but as we reached the top I sensed something. My recovering mind-organ suddenly pinged the base of my skull, shooting out sharp pains into my neck and eyes.

A fiercely-glowing ball of, well, lava, it seemed, was hanging in the air a few yards from us – specifically, between us and the graveyard wall.

"Forget the graveyard!" I screamed. "Go to my house!"

I bolted. They followed.

~ *Laura* ~

Each breath scraped gravel around in my already hot lungs, but we reached the garden gate and Tom kicked it open without hesitation.

~ *Laura* ~

yes, Sam

~ *it feels like we are being herded* ~

There were no good ideas on the table and we couldn't just stand here and wait to see what the lava bomb might do, so I shooed him forward.

With Sam's bulk applied to it, the front door never stood a chance and we were into the hallway in seconds.

The house was dark and creepy, a relic of a terrible time when my grandfather had prowled this hall, these rooms, his taut and timeworn face always frowning, his eyes cold, his voice always sharp, harsh.

Except at story time.

Story time?

I stumbled on a corner of the hall mat and came to a halt, but I would have faltered anyway as the memory peeled open within me.

"He told me *stories,*" I uttered in amazement, more to myself than to the men.

One of the men spoke, said "What?" or something similar, but I barely registered it.

Memories were blossoming within me now, moments long-buried that had been hidden from me for so long. The dampness of the mildewy wallpaper seeped into my skin as I steadied myself with a hand against the wall.

I glanced at Tom, lost in recollection. "My grandfather," I said.

"You say he told you stories? I thought he was supposed to be a grouchy old bastard."

"He was, or at least that's how I've always remembered him, but now I… I remember… No. He did. He told me stories at bedtime, Tom. How did I forget that?"

Tom made a muted, disinterested noise. "So not wishing to go all Chicken Dickens on you, but the sky's falling in out there, remember?"

"I don't think it's Chicken Dickens, Tom" I heard Sam point out, still disconnected from their conversation and its setting.

I saw that old face in my mind's eye, and suddenly I saw it clearly – not through the shroud of hatred and resentment I'd allowed myself to drape over it ever since his death, but rather, as it had really been. Scowling at my defiant disobedience, yet the eyes alight with joyful pride… pride in me. And the stories, the childish stories that were the last refuge for a heart grown cold by a burden carried too long.

Tears were stinging my eyes.

There was a ping at the base of my skull that cut into my reverie and drew my suddenly sharpened focus to the living room door.

the door

~ what do you feel there? ~

I was much more alert, now, could recognise the danger of being ambushed.

we need to seize the initiative

Sam snapped forward and I was close behind as he grabbed the handle and burst the door open in a single, blindingly fast movement.

I threw myself forward so I could be at his side, mind opening to respond to whatever faced us.

A cold, gloomy chamber greeted us, decorated with damp-looking grey floral wallpaper that was more grey than flowery, a fetid stench of wet rot hitting my senses and distracting me.

This house had always been meant for this purpose. I had been drawn here more than once now and it was so painfully obvious that it was a trap, purpose-built for me, exposing the rawest nerves and something that only my own brother could possibly have the foreknowledge to exploit.

I felt Sam's orb awaken as his hand sought it, stashed in his pocket.

~ Laura, are you alright ~

he's overplayed his hand, Sam - I remember the love now, Grandpa Jack wasn't the ogre Alan thinks he was

(game over, sis)

The intrusion into my mind was so shocking that I hesitated as I spotted Alan leaning on the fireplace, that treacherous bitch still at his side, all painted nails and slut lips.

My *friend*. How sour that word felt now.

Even as my gaze fixed on my brother, Tom launched headlong past me, inadvertently stabbing a hard elbow into my ribs that sent me staggering, as he charged hard at my brother.

I gasped and the pain broke my concentration.

He crashed into the weakling meat of my brother, unopposed by Alan's spindly, unconditioned frame, and clamped his hands around the scrawny throat.

He must have squeezed hard because Alan's face reddened instantly.

I felt the fully-expected pressure well up at the back of my head as my brother prepared to blast the life out of Tom, so I focused hard on the mid-point between Alan's crimson face and Tom.

Alan fired.

I felt pressure as his mindforce slammed against the wall I had placed in its way, hoping desperately that my powers had fully recharged – if not, this was going to be a humiliatingly short fight.

I dampened the blast, able to see a ripple effect where my defensive wall had dissipated the deadly blast my brother had launched, but some of his energy punched through and Tom was shoved three steps backwards, albeit, mercifully, still in one piece.

Alan rounded on me, glaring coldly as he disregarded the insignificant enemy that Tom had proven to be.

Careful, brother dearest...

I poured into his head, avenging his earlier intrusion

...your advantage is gone   your copies are all... **gone**

His face split into a feral grin, but I felt his mind go out, seeking, checking on his precious backups in the desperate hope that I was lying.

"I think we're alone now?" I mocked.

This might be the moment when he unleashed everything he had on me, but I knew that, for the first time ever, we had a level playing field. I suspected his cowardice would win out.

His grin melted, his glare faded. "Fair enough," he said calmly.

His mood change caught me off guard. "What?"

He shrugged. "Does any of it matter, now?"

~ *what is he doing?* ~

A good question.

Alan opened out his arms, palms face-up. "What are we really fighting about? Is anything gonna change if you kill me, now? Neither of us can stop the atrophy that's killing our world, any more than we can roll back time and undo the damage already done."

"Damage caused by you," I pointed out sharply.

He lowered his arms. "If killing your own flesh and blood for *nothing* will make you feel better, little Laura..."

366

~ he is trying to get into your head, Laura ~

perhaps, Sam, but is he wrong?

All this time, we had all been so busy fighting that none of us, not even Alan, had considered if it was a fight worth having. Why kill him when the damage was done? Revenge for the world?

"Thatta girl," Alan smiled.

My brother blinked out of existence, as did Jen.

"What?" I cried.

~ I tried to warn you ~

I glanced at Sam. "Not helpful."

Sam was gazing warily around the room. "He steered us here. It's a kill-zone."

Tom laughed. "Of course! Why risk himself when he can make spider-babies to do it for him?"

As if it had awaited its queue, a black glass visor appeared in the doorway. Holding up the enlarged crash helmet was a body dressed in a smart business suit, a clumpy splashing of mud spattered up one side of the suit trousers and a liberal drool of blood congealing on the shirt collars.

I pinged Sam and he turned and brought his orb up in a single smooth movement. The helmeted assassin fired and I threw mindforce out in a wall ahead of Sam to absorb it as my large companion completed his movement. The blast was castrated but it still knocked Sam backwards, his attack defeated.

Suddenly, it was as if a new part of my mind had awoken. Perhaps my re-charge had done more than I had realised, or maybe that momentary scenting of victory against my brother had changed me.

Either way, I had a new focus. A new level of strength to me.

I sensed the energy buildup of the assassin's next volley and I reached behind its visor and held it there. I didn't stop it – I held it in, trapping the buildup inside the visor. Malevolent energy with only once desire. To consume flesh.

There was a shriek inside my head as the compressed thought knot tore through the spider pilot, emptying the helmet. Then, still unsated, it poured from the bottom of the helmet and engulfed the body, burning suit, shirt, trousers and shoes to charred embers.

The torso folded in on itself as meat was peeled and guts were boiled away. The helmet tumbled off and hit the floor, the visor shattered in a spray of black glass and the ash body collapsed behind it in a gush of yellowed steam.

Tom stamped out miniature fires on the hessian rug while Sam flashed me a grin. I returned the smile, feeling strong again and pleased to have won.

We turned our attention to the door to wait for the next attack.

Nothing came. Grandma's old mantle clock wasn't ticking but I felt the seconds creep by.

"Is that *it?*" I asked aloud, incredulous.

Tom laughed. "Don't complain, Laur!"

"Complain?" I managed a grim smirk, still focused on that doorway. "I'm fucking furious!"

He pouted and shot me a frown. "How's that?"

I ignored him and turned to my battle partner. "Just one assassin, Sam. One! Is that all my brother thinks of me?"

Hurt pride is an ugly thing, but it really chapped my arse that my brother would think I could be stopped so easily. "Well, fuck him! He should know better, by now!"

Sam had not reacted to my rant and, glancing at him, I saw a distracted glaze to his eyes.

~ *it was a decoy, Laura* ~

I glanced back at the doorway.

~ *he wanted to keep us here just long enough* ~

fuck

"Are you two fucking thinkmailing again?" Tom demanded. "What? What is it?"

Sam smirked.

I decided to try and be less mean to my ex, so on this occasion I actually bothered to answer him. "It was a decoy, Tom; a way of keeping us here."

"Oh." His eyes widened. "Oh!"

I nodded. "See? He was keeping us here, in a world that's about to turn super-volcanic on us."

Outside the window of Grandma's parlour, the lava had spread and now the air itself seemed to be stained red.

"Easier than losing more henchmen, I s'pose," said Tom. "But here's a thought, Laur; why are we still standing here talking about it?"

"Grab onto me," I told them both.

Tom held back. "Where to, Laur?"

"Does it matter?"

He took a short step closer to me. "Yes. You need to go for the real world. I'll take my chances, but it's the last thing matey-boy will be expecting when he knows I'm travelling with you. Gives you a chance to dodge whatever traps he's set."

I held his gaze. Bless him, he was trying to help. "Tom, *we* might have a chance. You'd have none, you don't have a Matter form any more."

He shrugged, looking older now than I'd ever seen him before; smaller, hunched inward. "I'd rather fade away watching a final sunset in the real world where I belong," he said, his voice heavy with gloom, "than end up at the mercy of your sick-as-shit brother."

Poor Tom. This was it for him. There was heat in my eyes as I held out an arm to him, but he and Sam made physical contact and I opened my mind as I pictured my office building back in the matter realm.

There was a sense of a being pulled, swirled, and then the transfer kicked in.

A force like nothing I'd ever felt wrenched at my mind and my body, hurting both in such radically different ways that I was momentarily paralysed. The snare that Alan had prepared for me.

Pain stretched me like pizza dough and then squashed me so hard I was sure my kidneys had fused with my ovaries. My body fought to gasp for breath while my mind lost all focus and dislodged, separating from my meat. Whatever was left of me tried to claw at whatever had hold of me but still, I tumbled in fragments and lost all sense of where, of when, of what.

A moment of peace, oblivion.

Then, fierce light punched my eyes. They wept, stinging and I knew I was reassembled and physical once again.

Opening my eyes, I saw that I once again stood in the middle of a stark white street paved with smooth, flat, even white slabs - the Mind universe.

To either side of the street stood silent, bright, blank buildings, as perfectly uniform as I remembered them from before; windowless, lifeless.

The boys were not with me. I recalled that Alan had told me that only he and I could survive here and the idea that I'd just got my companions killed gave me a cold thrill of dread. I went to call out for Sam, but remembered the weird beings that lived here, coiled up in the extra dimensions of this universe.

No – Stay *quiet*.

Besides, there was the weird physics here that would flatten my voice and prevent it travelling.

I was alone and I had no idea if I my friends were alive here somewhere – or dead. And… I was *alone* here.

"Don't *panic*," I muttered to myself as I felt panic boil up in my belly.

Deep breaths, Keeble. Deep breaths.

A moment later I gasped and my body dumped eight pumps of scolding hot adrenaline into my guts as a humanoid figure emerged from between two buildings quite close to where I stood.

Heart kicking my tits like a bastard, I was ready to bolt, to run up the hill or down it or anywhere that was not here.

It staggered back two steps, teetering as if it was going to tumble down the white stone hill, whereupon I saw its face in the dazzling sunlight.

"Sool!"

I hurried toward him as he flailed his arms and regained his balance. He didn't look well at all, his face horribly drawn and pale, reminding me that the last one of his kind I'd seen had died here because this universe was lethal to them.

"Sool!" I cried. "You have to get out of here, this place will kill–"

He saved me finishing my sentence by collapsing to the bright white ground.

-52-

I rushed to him, knelt and lifted his head and shoulders carefully into my arms. His dead grey eyes sought me, apparently struggling to focus. He had never looked like a healthy person, but now he seemed positively poxy with disease; more pale and sickly than a living person ever should.

"The realms..." he murmured, mouth clogged with stringy old spit and his murky gaze failing to properly find me. "Realms collapsing; my kind, all... dying, now."

"Oh, Sool."

He felt like a bag of oddly-assorted doll parts, too light and hollow to be a man.

"Did you bring me here?" I asked him.

His lips puckered out and parted, a murky purple tongue lolling between his teeth. "Dying now, LauraKeeble. Had to pull you here, somewhere the other... would not follow."

"What about my friends?" I demanded, alarmed that my part-time ally in this war might have killed my actual companions in it.

"All dying, LauraKeeble."

"What? Sam and Tom—a"

I felt rather than saw his attempt to give a shake of his head. "My... people. Dying. Too... late for me, now." His eyes locked onto mine for an instant, washed-out and grey. "Help them... please."

His eyelids were descending like the final curtain at the end of a play. I gave him a gentle shake. "Sool, how? I can't stop the collapse now, it's too late!"

His eyelids raised a little, but the eyes beneath were dull, dry, dead. "Stop the other."

He tried to swallow but the effort made him wince.

Now, at the end, he suddenly seemed so very human. There was, after all, a bleak parity between our species in the pathetic frailty of death. His little weight was fully on my arms yet my arms didn't ache at all.

"Oh, Sool, I'm sorry. It's over – I failed. Even if I could stop him, it's too late to stop the collapse."

His eyelids fluttered very slightly. "Must finish... what you began."

I tried to contain my frustration, knowing that he was dying. "Why? What's the point?"

"Master the dimensions," he murmured.

"W-what?" I blustered, my frustration at this one-sided conversation boiling over.

"Strength fails me, LauraKeeble. To return to your realm... master the dimensions. This skill… is the final lesson you need."

"Sool, you need to listen, I don't know what to do! You have to send me back before you - Sool?"

His last breath had fled him and I was holding a limp, dead thing.

I laid him down as I silently contemplated my fate, trapped here in an alien universe full of alien beings who hated me and weird otherworldly dimensions that made no… sense?

"Well fucking *duh*," I autodissed.

Standing up straight, I looked down at Sool's limp body. "See you in the next place," I told him.

Opening my mind, I reached tentatively outward from my body, allowing my self to ripple across the twisting superhighway of dimensional layers looped and curled around each other. I let my mindself take on their contours, shape itself to resemble them, and then I started to picture where I wanted to be – the Matter realm, my old office in London. I saw the dry old carpeting, recalled the dusty smell of the place, masked with sweet furniture polish.

I felt the place, as if I was already there.

The ground melted away from under my feet and, as a sharp, painful pulse hit the base of my skull a harsh, hard surface slammed up against my backside and I sat on a cool and unyielding floor.

"Whoa," I muttered.

I lowered a hand to steady myself and there was an incongruous softness to that surface beneath me. A hard floor, but thinly carpeted.

A faint smell of polish. Also, something metallic.

"There she is! Thank fuck."

Tom's voice.

"Laura? Can you hear me?"

Sam's voice.

I knew I should be able to see but I wasn't yet looking through my eyes. Pushing myself back into my meat I found my head and gave it a gentle shake.

Sam's face came into focus, frowning at me.

My friends were alive, at least.

I was sitting on the carpeted floor of an elevator. On the wall panel behind Sam, the number 4 button was lit. I murmured words but my brain was misfiring so I probably made little sense.

I concentrated, swallowed hard, closed my mouth then re-opened it to try again. "Where…?"

Tom held out a hand to help me up. "You should know, Laur; you did it! We're back. Even me, apparently."

I frowned at him. He seemed to be suggesting that we were in the Matter realm.

Sam was frowning and exploring my face, like a mother looking for dirt smudges. "Did something happen, Laura? When we appeared here without you, we assumed the worst."

Tom was still holding out a hand. I grabbed it and he pulled, helping me to my feet.

"I got detoured," I told them. "I was in the Mind realm again."

Sam's left eyebrow lifted. "Your brother?"

"No, I thought so at first, but it was Sool. Last stab at getting me to finish the mission."

Tom folded his arms. "Bastard, putting you at risk like that."

I started to explain what Sool had been trying to do, but at that moment there was a light bump and the elevator stopped. I hadn't properly registered that it had even been moving.

The number '4' light winked off and the doors slid open.

Tom unfolded his arms and squinted, trying to focus on what lay outside. "With our track-record for galloping headlong into the shit…" he said, "maybe a touch of caution is called for."

The space outside the lift seemed innocuous enough to me, but I felt the corners of my mouth twitch at his dry assessment of our standard tendency toward feet-first fuckery.

"Put your glasses on, Peters," I said with a smirk. "If you think that looks scary, then whatever comes next will make you fill yer pants."

He humphed out a rough laugh.

Just a carpet-tiled lobby. Moreover, a place that had once been a very, very familiar feature of my life.

Floor 4. My floor; my office.

From a life I no longer owned.

Except that, of course, it had to be a trick, another of my brother's jolly emr deathtraps. I would've lost control of the transfer the moment Sool snatched me away, so now all I could do was deal with whatever fight lay just around the next corner.

Sam took the lead. He stepped out of the lift and, after a discreet and hopefully indiscernible pause to ensure he didn't get instantly vapourised, I followed.

Tom joined me, craning his neck and squinting past me along the corridor. "Is this…?" he asked in an awed, whispery voice.

I laid a hand on his arm. "Sorry, Tom. If this were the Matter realm you'd have winked out of existence, remember?"

Tom scratched his stubbly chin. "Yeah, but… you *sure*? It just *feels* right. Feels like the real world."

"Nope," I asserted, more calmly than I felt. "It may be a good fake, but it's definitely another facsimile designed to bring us all kinds of uh-uh. Good enough to fool us, except we know that you can't exist in the Matter realm."

He looked so sad.

I rubbed his arm. "I wish I could lie to you, but I'm afraid we've fallen balls-first into the exact trap we were trying to avoid."

He started and pulled his arm free of me as the elevator door slid shut behind us with a *ping!*

He chuckled nervously. "No choice now, eh?"

Silly sod. "In my experience, Tom, you can usually call a lift back; you soppy tit."

"Come on," I said decisively, striding at the double doors with a confidence made entirely from bullshit and bravado, my heart starting to accelerate as I opened my mind defensively.

Pushing through those heavy doors, we were assailed by the potent, musty smell of old grime and uncleaned carpets, but, other than that, the computer centre was silent and dead; a *Marie Celeste* lit in clinical white.

The backup generators were still going, I realised – until I remembered that this was a false reality.

I glanced at the windows and saw that it was night-time here, blackness pressing against the glass. Perhaps my brother had only created an interior for this little mock-up.

I pointed a thought at Sam, who took out his orb and pushed himself into it, using it as a scanner. Fuck knows what I expected to find, it was all a bit Star Trek but, in the moment, it kind of seemed like a smart move.

Tom passed me on his way to the office windows. "I'd kill for a fag."

My intake of breath at those words was an involuntary reaction to their implications, but as the air entered me it confirmed my shocking realisation because it carried with it the acrid reek of his pungent body odour, of many days' accumulation of stale sweat, cloying my nostrils and making me gag.

It seemed so impossible, enough to justify my wide-eyed stupification.

"I am a twat," I stated.

My one-time lover grinned over his shoulder. "No argument here."

Sam turned and cocked an eyebrow at me, lowering his orb hand as he sensed something in my tone.

"Tom was right, Sam. We're in the Matter realm!"

The big man didn't seem convinced. "Why so sure?"

"Tom has a body odour."

Tom was leaning against the sill of one of the large, black-glassed windows across the room from us. He turned to me. "Charming, Laur! You can go off people, you know."

"No, no," I said, hand held out in my urgency. "I mean, we probably all do, but it's just that you *can't* have a smell – you don't have a body, remember? I mean, what did *anything* smell like in the emr?"

"No, hang on. Nah." He frowned. "I'm sure I smelled the flowers, or maybe the grass…?"

"Did you, though?"

He didn't answer.

"Also, you just said you need a fag. You're craving a smoke, now?"

Sam pulled a doubtful face. "That doesn't prove much, Laura."

"True," I said, turning back to Tom, "but didn't I see you squinting out there in the corridor?"

Tom gave a small head-shake. "So?"

"You need your glasses again, right?"

He looked a little offended for some reason. "I've worn specs since I was a kid, Laur. I wore them in the emr."

"But you didn't *need* them when you were there!" I glanced from one to the other of them. Come on, some back-up here, guys. "Come on, Tom, half the time, you even forgot to keep them in existence when we were in the emr!"

I felt Sam's reaction – the mental equivalent of an eye-widening self-arse-kicking, except only felt in my mind. He *had* smelled our companion, but unlike me he hadn't quite made the connection.

I was distracted by the sudden, worrying thought that perhaps Sam could smell *me*, too.

Tom gave a dismissive shake of his head and turned to peer out of the window, but immediately he had, he called us over.

"What?" I asked.

"You gotta see this, Laur!"

Sam and I crossed to the window, just past the orange chair at what used to be the Environment Manager's desk, where our backlit reflections mirrored our shock.

A bleak and horrific ruination had replaced London. The Mind realm had utterly subjugated reality, an abomination of a world under a black lamenting sky that glowed white in places where the dark vault had been split open in jagged slices, as if lightning had been captured and frozen in place up there.

"Ahh," I murmured, recognising the fulfilment of the changes that I had seen when I was last here in the Matter realm, in pursuit of my brother.

The change had seriously accelerated during my brief absence. Now, vast grey gothic castles stood buttressed against gangly futuristic towers, the buildings they had replaced lost forever, presumably; crushed or erased by these unphysical, top-heavy and convoluted unstructures, many of which were crowned with great balls and spires of a dark, glinting glass-like substance.

Worse, these invaders had not finished their overthrow of 'my' London. Many of the hideous creations were, even now, writhing and twisting themselves as if trying to settle into a comfy chair as great masses of ironwork latticework cut and pushed into and between them.

Suddenly they seemed more like desperate refugees from the Mind realm, rather than invaders.

Tom made a strange sound. "Tell me this isn't our world, Laur," he appealed in a small, soft voice.

"I wish I could, but I've seen this before; at least the start of it. This is what we were fighting to prevent."

He made that odd sound again and I realised it was a small sob. "We fucking failed, then, didn't we?"

He was *crying?* What kind of a reaction was that?

I nodded. "I suppose we did. On the up side, though, that's probably how you can survive here. You're probably more real than Sam or me now, because this realm is more like an emr than the world we knew before."

My former lover let out a juddering breath. "My mum's buried over there, 'bout three miles over. What's happened to her grave? What about my kids, Laur, to my sister and *her* kids?"

Out of the corner of my eye, I saw Sam lower his gaze. Even he had shown a more human reaction to Tom than I had. I hadn't even considered the people we had left behind to go and fight in the emr. Tom had far more invested in this world he had left behind than I had ever had. Hell, Sam had more... his wife and family would be buried somewhere out there.

A blinding flash whited out the scene ended the discussion as it flash-froze my eyes.

I blinked blurry tears away and turned from the window. When the jagged imprint faded and I could see, I looked again and saw a new glowing gash in the sky to the west where the lightning had gone off.

Sam stepped away from the window. "I suppose that means that this is not really lightning."

"No, I suppose it isn't," I answered, still studying our broken Earth with a gallows-fascination.

There were still streetlights casting their weak amber glow in places down at ground-level, although even these stalwarts were remade in a new image now, transformed into great glass bowls hung from twisting black wrought-iron posts, looking for all the world as if they were lighting the way for Jack the Ripper's walk into the fires of hell. Many of them flickered almost constantly, as if they held fire rather than electric light.

I finally pulled myself away and back into the room.

Tom stared at me, his wet, despondent eyes seeming emptied of everything of him.

"I'm sorry, Tom. Even my brother can't have wanted *this*."

His eyes narrowed, then. "So fucking *what?*"

"I have to agree," Sam added; rather sheepishly, I like to think. "You give him too much credit, Laura. At any time, he could have stopped this."

I glanced out the window, struck by an incongruity. "Hey," I said to them. "If my brother's responsible for the end of *everything*, how come the Mind realm hasn't changed?"

Tom let out a cry of exasperation. "Aw, come on, Laur! You'll cling to any fucking straw to defend that bastard brother of yours!"

"No, I'm serious! I was in the Mind realm just minutes ago and it was *exactly* the same as the first time I went there!"

Sam's frown seemed to carry disappointment, maybe even an accusation. "It's a different universe, Laura."

"*Yes*, Sam!" I snapped back. "But. If we're seeing Mind-sorta things appearing here, why aren't there Matter kind of things appearing over there? Why hasn't it changed at all?"

"I fail to see…" Sam's objection died in-flight and his eyes widened.

"Maybe we're *all* wrong about what's really happening. Us, the Sentinels, maybe even my brother!"

"Bollocks," Tom concluded decisively.

It was clear that Tom needed someone to blame and Alan was the obvious choice. Mainly because, even with my sudden doubt, he was clearly to blame for at least some of this. Just… maybe not all of it?

There was a faint sound that I might have ignored, except that I saw Sam's eyes narrow and his shoulders tense.

The big man pressed a finger to his lips, pointed at the double doors back to the lift lobby and then glided with a surprisingly silent grace back across the office space, orb in hand.

I followed, allowing my mind to open in readiness.

We scanned beyond the door, he with the orb and me with my… me. We sensed nothing, so we edged through as small an opening between the wood behemoths as possible.

The lift lobby was as deserted as ever, but we both sensed something lurking in the coffee room. We edged toward that door. Tom brushed my shoulder, still reeking of body odour and yet slightly reassuring for it.

Reminded me of our one and only sexytime.

In a dizzying blur of movement, Sam burst through the coffee room door hard and fast.

"Fuck!" I cried and bolted in after him, mind flaring like a Jedi on amphetamines.

The dimness in the room, lit only by the feeble glow from the two big coffee vending machines, was irrelevant. Sam and I both locked onto a form cowering behind the square, plush sofa chairs clustered around low wood-block tables.

"You!" Sam barked. "Show yourself!"

I'd stopped noticing Sam's powerful and richly deep voice, but that sudden shock of it booming into the silence was enough to scare the most determined assassin. Perhaps they were more scared of me than I was of them.

Or was that just spiders?

There was a whimper from somewhere in the room. We were locked on and ready. Whoever and whatever was lurking there was fucked if it tried anything.

I felt a ping at the base of my skull as Sam prepared to fire the orb.

"Final warning!"

At the last moment before both of us let rip, a thin male figure in a suit uncoiled from behind a chair near the window, reedy and tense, his face obscured by the gloom. His hands wavered as he held them up, level with his shoulders, in surrender.

"Don't shoot!" he cried. "I'm harmless!"

And in that moment blinding light whited the room out.

"Fuck!" I cried.

I like to think Sam swore to, but probably not. He was such a cool fucker since he got out from under my brother.

With my heart in my mouth and my arsehole round my ankles, I rounded furiously on Tom, realising the dumb cunt had flicked the lights on.

"Fuck me, Tom, what was that, I nearly shat a kidney!"

The moment had been interrupted but I knew the voice I'd heard when the intruder had stood up.

My former boss, a man who had held such power over my life – my hopes for a glorious career that hadn't mattered at all in the end – was like the ghost of a man who'd died locked in a box with no food for six months. Hideously gaunt, his eyes were shrivelled into his skull, the tatty mess of what had once been a tailored grey pinstripe suit hanging baggy off his ghastly wireframe of a body, he looked forlorn and, frankly, pathetic.

"Please," he whined, his palms held out in appeal. Then a frown creased his brow. "Loh… Laura?"

He had aged a dozen years since I had last seen him and had obviously not shaved, the scraggly whiskers coiled off his chin peppered with white, the power he had once seemed to own drained completely away to leave… this husk..

I smiled sadly. "Hello, Ben."

"You… you came back! " A small weak sob escaped him. "You came back for me! To save me. Is, is it over now? Can, can I go, go *home?*"

His lips pursed into an achingly sad smile as he drew out the 'mmm' in 'home'.

Poor, sad bastard, there was nothing left of him. Whatever he had been through had utterly destroyed him. I had once dreamt of standing triumphant before this man, of finally feeling *better* than him, superior; but there was no triumph in *this*. All I felt was an empty sickness.

He stood there in our coffee room and wept. Tears seeped from his eyes and trailed clean lines through the layers of grey grime painted onto his dusk-weary cheeks.

"Ben," I said as gently as I could, "Ben, can you tell us what's been happening?"

"What?" His eyes were unfocused, seeing me and yet not seeing me at all.

I held out an arm to gesture at the window behind him. "The world out there, Ben; the lightning."

His dazed gazed snapped into a painfully intense focus that stared through me into a world I couldn't see. "The lightning! Oh, Laura, the lightning!"

He reached out a hand to touch my arm and Sam surged toward him in response, quelling Ben's momentary urge for human contact.

The broken man edged back but held my gaze. "You have, you have to know, Laura! It's not *lightning*, at all. No, not… not lightning, It's not. It's *alive!* It *looks* for you, Laura, it seeks you out – it finds us all in the end!"

OK, so he couldn't help me. Poor bastard was riding his own tits to pixieland.

"I swear, Laura!" he took a step toward me in his desperation but was driving back by Sam's looming presence.

"I've survived in here," Ben's wavering arm flailed in a gesture towards the window. "Hidden from it; seen from this window, Laura; it *hunts* people, it never stops, once it's picked you out it never stops, it, it snaps and snaps until you, until it…"

"Ben," I said softly. "It's OK."

He studied me for a moment and then his shoulders sagged. He edged back and slumped down onto one of the coffee room couches, eyes open but mind far from here.

There was a blinding flash that whited out the room and overpowered our eyes. The whole building shuddered violently, but then seemed to continue juddering, as if something powerful had grasped it by its foundations and was determined to shake the contents free.

"Fuck was *that?*" Tom cried.

that was close

Sam glanced at me and nodded sharply, once.

The windows rattled and the lights flickered. A fine powder trickled down from the ceiling.

I gestured at the door without speaking and my two companions moved with me towards it.

I glanced back at the slumped form of Ben. "Coming?"

Behind him, outside the windows, a brutal punch of lightning flashlit the world beyond that thin layer of glass and revealed the sight of the sky itself rippled with waves, buckling as if something was peeling it off the world from above – alarmingly like the way the skies had peeled away in the emr realities I had collapsed.

"Laura!"

My arm was grabbed in a painful vice and I realised I had stopped retreating. I resisted Sam for a moment, staring at the dying sky as it tore open with vast gory wounds, so that huge, glowing-hot chunks of thought mass pulled loose and tumbled the miles and miles down to burst apart on the London streets, destroying and slaughtering without discrimination or mercy.

"Damn," I muttered to myself, suddenly very numb. "Looks like Chicken Little was right, after all."

A giggle wanted to escape me but I was sure that it was the only thing corking up my hysteria.

"Laura!"

The coffee room lights flickered once and then gave up, fading away to leave us in darkness. Outside, new jagged holes in the sky pulsed a savagely alien red every few seconds and spat more and more frequent barbs of lightning through to decimate our universe.

I was sure I felt the ferocious heat from them.

The floor beneath my feet now felt like the deck of a ship in a storm, rolling and shuddering. The only light was the glow of doomed matter beyond the window.

I looked up expectantly at Sam. "Oh, Sam, it's all over, isn't it?"

His usually intense blue eyes appeared soft brown in the reddish light of our dying world. "We will never make it out of here before the building fails, Laura. You have to transfer us."

I nodded.

Sam turned his head. "Tom!"

Tom flew back in, hassled and puffing. "What happened to the fucking lights... Oh!" As his gaze took in the nightmare outside the windows, his hand flailed until it found my shoulder. "Say no more, transfer time, right?"

I opened my mind.

The floor gave a brutal, sickening lurch and I felt plaster dust raining down on my head as Ben shrieked like a castrated lamb and ran from the window, straight at us.

I was painfully aware that this might well be my last transfer, ever – *if* it even worked.

The presence that was my mind peeled away from my body and expanded outward across the dying landscape, rippling across the splits and tears in its fabric as I sought the one thing left to find – another presence like me. My brother.

I sought his mind and the transfer began almost unbidden, as if it had been waiting for me to do the right thing and did not plan to let me change my mind and shy away from whatever came next.

Reality fell away as we took our final trip.

-53-

I felt a slump in my chest as I realised we were still in the same building. We'd shifted through space, alright – straight downstairs into the basement.

I was about to list my five favourite swear-words when Sam hastily pressed a finger to his pursed lips.

~ *this was no accident nor your fault laura* ~

I frowned up at him and he gestured toward the double doors into the computer room, visible in the gloom of the few sparse emergency bulbs that still cut into the dense, cold-bricked gloom of the basement.

I nodded at him.

i feel it too

I could. The basement was dim, cold and damp, with shadows everywhere, and yet there was definitely a deeper menace beyond those double doors, pressing dread upon me, a malevolence that only Sam and I would be aware of through our heightened minds; hateful, strong, and ready.

we have to go in there, sam

~ *you understand that this is a trap* ~

Of course I did and he knew I did, but our world, our options, had been shrinking for a while, now. The trap was indeed set, but there was no other direction to head into, any more.

I stared up at my loyal companion.

let's just get it done

We edged up to those dark doors and I was comforted; falsely, I knew; by my companion's bulky presence.

get a grip, keeble

Sam glanced at me, puzzled.

ignore me

come on

My mind pushed outward, tasting the fabric of the reality before me, while Sam's orb pulsed softly at the periphery of my awareness.

He pushed through the doors and we were hit by blue-white light like the summer sky.

The computer room was still lit dazzling bright by sharp bluish-white LCDs that glared boldly, sustained for now, and maybe forever, by a non-interruptible power source. Those fuckers would be lighting this basement long after the last human that might need them was a pile of dust.

Which was, of course, pretty much nowish.

Brightly lit, the room offered very little shadow to hide in, but its design, with long bland white banks of computer cabinets laid out like some arcane library of digital wisdom, ensured our view was obscured at every turn.

Whatever was here was hidden amongst the hard kit laid out in here, some cabinets as tall as me, so even as our bodies edged toward the main aisle between the banks I decided to make use of the extra-material dimensions I had recently been shown.

Extruding my mind led to a deep delight at the sensation of self rippling outward along a plane unbounded by light or time, where I passed through every point in the room in a half-instant.

there, Sam

A small bulge extruded into the matter realm, invisible to eyes but visible to the extra sense of my mind – a swelling mass that was pushing in from outside of our plane of existence, still half-formed.

Sam was ready with his orb.

Alan pressed into existence but Sam was already firing. My brother parried the orb attack but, by diverting it, he hurled the lethal mass straight into the black-visored face of one of his own assassins, also emerging to attack us but now suddenly and finally diverted into the joy of its own agonising death.

Its dying screech was still bouncing off the inside of my skull when my head pinged.

Another assassin, in a pincer attack – my brother's standard snare.

As I turned to face it, I realised that Alan had, for perhaps the very first time, really fucked up on his battle plan.

The dark figure hurled itself at me as soon as he transferred it in, but while it was on a perfect line of attack against me, it was also running straight across Alan's line of returning fire against Sam.

The mindforce my brother meant as a gift for Sam hit the creature, punching a hole through its chest and shaving off its entire left shoulder. I hit it with a blast of my own to make sure, but I didn't hit it hard enough, spinning it as I smugly enjoying a gloat at Alan's error, only to allow the spider-jockeyed bitch to carry on its momentum toward me even as its body disintegrated.

A great swinging arc brought its remaining arm chopping down toward my head, and although my desperate lunge to the right saved my questionable brains, it exposed my left shoulder.

That limb, the last of the creature not tangled in scorching tar, tumbled, bounced off my tits and flumped to the floor at my feet, but the damage was done.

A searing shard of pain sliced down from the impact point at my shoulder and cut deep into my chest, the force of it driving me down to feel the twin impacts of the hard floor against my knees.

"Fu-uck," I heard my hoarse voice cry as the room fell away and all that remained was pain.

~ *laura* ~

~ *laura are you hurt* ~

I squeezed my eyes shut and fought myself to draw a breath against the raking pain in my ribs.

I had to get up before I was attacked again, but all I could manage for now was to find my mind organ and throw up a defensive wall of mindforce between my useless meat and my hateful brother.

The part of me that could remain rational made a quick assessment.

My body was in crisis, sucking hard to drag air into its distressed self and failing. Slow down, do *not* panic, but instead *ease* air back into myself. I was only winded, but my animal wanted to pull every lever in its desperation to protect itself, making the situation worse. On my knees with only the blindly-extruded mindforce to protect me, my mind had to rule over events and ensure I acted right.

No second chances.

~ *laura* ~

I had to ignore him for now, to focus on getting myself working again.

An oily malevolence touched the edges of my expanded mind as Sam's orb focused on my defence. He had me. I focused on breathing and healing.

As my aching lungs finally caught some air and the wrenching pain in my shoulder settled into a sick ache, I finally managed to look up.

Nearby, a smoking, leather-clad corpse showed that Sam had felled another assassin. Its helmet had flown off and I could see the charred, jagged spider legs jutting out from the pilot's last desperate bid to save itself.

Now, Sam meant to launch a lethal black lash straight at Alan – but he had reckoned without Jen.

The treacherous bitch stepped into sight, placed herself between the two men and cried out Sam's name in a perfectly pitiful feminine key designed to play on his long emotional weakness for her.

That rancid little snatch placed a high value on her slut hide and I *really* hoped that Sam had grown enough to see through her disgusting ruse.

Fat fucking chance.

The big lump hesitated, but a moment later I was grateful for his distraction, because another assassin dropped into existence close to me. I wasn't ready, and if Jen hadn't broken up Sam's attack, he would not have seen this threat.

The orb fired. The shrieking helmeted figure staggered back, boiling and disintegrating.

Thanks, Jen; you worthless twat.

Alan took advantage of the moment Jen had bought him and launched a blast so full of his hateful rage that it sent a headache all the way back to my childhood.

The mindforce flew straight at Sam's head.

Still on my knees, mind tied-in to holding up a mindforce shield to protect myself, I was unable to react in my companion's defence and could only watch with my liquid eyes as he was hit, since Sam, too, was unable to react fast enough and failed to re-focus the orb to deflect the attack.

The impact sang out a resounding boom and there was an ugly bright black flash that broke across its victim and flung his dying remains into the air in a messy spinning geyser of bright crimson juice.

His corpse was thrown across the computer room to slam against a white machine cabinet which it spattered with dark reddish gore released from multiple exit wounds.

The clean floor and shiny white machines down the aisle were now juicy with spattered red, purple and brown guts, while his burst body lay still, one limb lying separated and lonely on the floor a few feet away from it, completing the impression of a ghastly broken doll.

I heaved my trembling body off the floor and aimed my hating gaze at Alan and Jen. I saw my former friend's eyes widen as she saw me, for the first time, in full fighting form.

Distantly I wondered if she saw me as I'd seen Alan – with my eyes missing, hidden by mindforce.

I fucking hoped so.

I fired death at her bitch face.

It was a rage-fuelled blast of mindforce and it was actually aimed at both of them, fulfilling my reptile need for vengeance, although Alan instantly pulled himself and Jen to safety, thwarting me.

Faint annoyance that I'd failed to kill either of them. A problem for soon but not now, as Sam laid a hand on my shoulder.

"Go to him, Laura. I will guard against their return."

I glanced at him. "What?"

"You only have a moment. Go to him."

I moved across the white floor toward the non-white smeary area where Tom lay, ruined and broken, in an incomprehensible horror of his own scattered parts and darkly wept fluids, a coil of smoke rising still from his chest.

It came into focus for me as the whole of my reality became that ruined human form, a passenger who had finally paid the price for no greater a crime than having loved Jen and me.

We got him into this.

Nope. Not us. It was *me*; I had got him into this.

Got him… killed.

I'd hardly given Tom a thought since we had walked into the computer room; he had been so far in the background of my concern or my interest.

I'd failed to protect him, and yet when it really counted, he had stepped up and thrown himself in the way to save Sam, my stronger and better ally. To give me a chance.

Kneeling beside him, careful to avoid his spilt fluids, I was forced to take in the scarlet mess of him, in which cloth and flesh were indistinguishable, mulched into reds and purples, while an open black cavity had replaced much of the athletic solidity of his strong, warm chest.

It was too much.

The steaming wreckage of him, the salted-pennies tang of blood a strong flavour on my tongue.

"Tom."

The impact had ripped off his right arm and rent open the whole right-hand side of his chest. A broken rib jutted out in sharp shards at a right angle from his body cavity, a tatter of either cloth or skin, too reddened to tell, still tagged to the end of it.

I started as he made a weak sound.

His eyes flickered and opened.

"Tom, can... can you hear me?"

I reached out a hand but could find nowhere to touch him that wasn't... internal. The hand hovered out from me in anticipation but I never did touch him again.

His face was splashed with smeary red and brown goo and as his mouth opened it drooled thick, dark blood, his tongue and teeth stained crimson. A mouth I had once kissed, now resembling the world's clumsiest autopsy.

I still wanted to touch him. Still didn't.

His mouth worked, his eyes flitted up at me.

"Roll..." he gasped, voice wet and accompanied by a whistling wheeze from his burst chest.

"Why, Tom? Why did you do that? We could have, might have, we... You didn't have to die."

Even as I said it I knew it was nonsense. Tom's sacrifice had been the only way to save Sam and, hence, give me even a slim chance of holding out in the imminent fight against Alan.

Tom pulled a face that might have been meant as a smile but just turned out as a grimace of pain. He made a desperate, ragged, wet attempt at a breath so he could speak.

He repeated that word.

Roll.

"What, Tom? What are you...?"

I leant over him, closer to his face to ensure I heard his reply, seeing a glint in his eye as his gory mouth twitched and he focused on me for the briefest moment.

"Roll me... a fag, would you, Laur?"

I pulled my head back and stared at him. "The fuck…?"

His mouth twitched again. "Heh-heh…"

Then, a thin wheeze of air pushed red bubbles up out of his mouth, his eyes widened momentarily and then he stopped completely still as if time no longer applied to him.

The moist gleam of life fell back from his eyes and he became that unreal thing that people become when they die.

"Tom?" I cried, aware of an ache in my chest and a hot wetness on my cheeks. "Oh, Tom."

I wanted to tell him something. I wanted to touch him. I wanted to do all the things that I had left for a few seconds too long and could never now change.

It wasn't fair.

Then, shockingly, the gory remains of the man who had mocked and grumbled his way through our journey together began to fade before my eyes.

I clambered up onto my feet and staggered back. "No! Oh, no, no, no!"

His spilt blood turned pale and faded off all the surfaces it had spattered onto, as the head, chest and legs that had shed such liquid also become insubstantial and melted away to nothing.

In a moment, the computer cabinets and the floor were clean and white once again.

Tom was completely gone.

I stared.

Just a clean white floor and the even cleaner white computer cabinets; a pure white mockery of a whole person who, without true matter to bind him to reality, had simply ceased to be anything at all.

Tom's real physical remains had been collected from the library long, long ago, and had been buried, or cremated, or some other mundane human thing. What had been living on as my companion was a mind echo of the real man, so in death he had simply flitted away like an errant thought.

It was a bitter tasting truth, though.

My mind organ pinged and I felt a gentle, gentle breeze brush my cheek as something moved into existence and pushed air from its new place in the universe.

"Can't say I didn't give you time to grieve, sis."

I turned fast, adrenaline burning white with hate. I threw out thought energy that blistered with all of that potent hatred, too quick for Alan to react to.

Well, no; *almost* too quickly.

Sadly, he was able to hastily throw himself through the Transfer to escape my wrath once again.

"Fuck!" I wiped my wet cheeks with my forearm and glanced at Sam, who gave me a nod that might have meant many things.

And Alan was behind us.

Shit! I needed to read Sam's cues better, for fuck's sake!

I turned fast, but Sam was physically faster so he was able to spin and fire from the hip.

There was the weird sensation of a sideways swipe of mind energy and the pop of Alan winking instantly out of existence, to be replaced by something else that he had elected to throw into the path of Sam's weaponsfire.

Another figure now stood exactly where my brother had been, a sheep in the path of the oncoming thought knot.

I heard my voice cry out but it was too late to do anything.

Poor, broken-headed Ben stood there in Alan's place, too dazed and helpless to even be scared as the thought knot burst across his face.

Sam and I stared open-mouthed as the flesh was instantly scorched clean off his skull in a single shrieking peel.

My former boss's grinning, bald white skull dropped free and tumbled as the lethal venom seared away the body beneath it, hungrily devouring skin and muscle in blistering ribbons.

The head was ash before it hit the floor.

Ben...?

Had I transferred him with us in the haste of our flight and just not noticed he was with us the whole time, or had Alan found him after I left him behind?

I realised I had no idea. Didn't matter now, anyway.

Two for none: I had left both of my most helpless companions completely unprotected and now my brother had used them both to show me how badly outclassed I really was – and perhaps more devastatingly, he had forced Sam to commit murder for him once again.

I turned to the big man and saw the devastation in his eyes.

Even as the frame of Ben's body collapsed within the mass, Alan appeared right in front of us, his mouth twisted in a malicious grin and his eye sockets hollow, that wonderfully ghastly illusion created by the weight of mindforce that swelled behind and through them.

Sam failed to react to him at all as he wallowed in his gloom.

"Not your fault, Sam!" I cried as a reminder and a call to arms.

"I know," Sam murmured, but I could feel his chin sinking, the re-awakening of the horrors in his memory, his sudden despondent recognition of how easily he could be turned back into the monster my brother had forced him to be.

He was going to hesitate, now.

OK, then. It was all on me.

Alan chuckled, his mirth rendered hideous by that eyeless face where oil-on-water mindforce swirled vortices in his emptied sockets.

Studying my predicament, I made an instantaneous decision.

He had me cold. Already locked firmly in his dark mind's eye, I was never going to summon my power without him sensing it. Also, he had locked a vice of mindforce around the despondent Sam, binding him to the spot in case he had a sudden re-awakening.

"Peter, wait. I'm not your enemy."

A new strategy; maybe a shit one, but he cocked his head at me, curious no doubt at my sheer audacity.

He made a ghastly sound that might have been a laugh. "Is that the best you can do, sis? Really? Oh, I'm not really your enemy?"

"Please, Peter, just talk to me," I appealed, playing on his need to gloat and be the big man in charge. "I think maybe we're both being played. Just hear me out. Come on, you owe me that much."

His head tilted a little. "Do I?"

"Peter…"

"See, sis, I think I've been more than fair. I could have taken out both you and that big lump of pity while you knelt weeping over poor, dead Petey-weters. But I was *kind*, see?"

The k-word sounded alien on his tongue and came laced with sarcasm.

I held his gaze, clinging to my inner meek and burying my rage and contempt where he'd never sense it.

He sighed and the swirling mindforce coming from him abated slightly. "But if you're really starting to realise that this isn't all black and white like some old movie, I guess that's progress. Go on then, sis. Talk. Fast."

I fought to keep my helpless resignation at the forefront of my perceivable mind while I fought frantically behind that façade for a way to keep him talking.

And I realised that I actually did have a genuine question for him.

I took a breath. "OK. I always knew we were coming to this and I kind of knew I didn't stand much of a chance, but you had *way* more time to prepare than you should have had. Time to lay traps, pull me down here for an ambush – so you knew I'd landed back in the Matter realm the moment I touched down. How?"

"Oh, poor sis!" he made that horrible laughing sound again. "You really don't know?"

I shook my head slowly and swallowed the indignant feelings climbing up my throat. "Tell me. Your last chance to gloat in this lifetime, brother dearest."

I could see his eyes dimly in the swirl of mindforce now. He was enjoying our little talk, bless him. The tactic was working.

Reign in the smugness, Keeble. Keep it tight.

"Look, sis, you can move between the emrs and flick back to the Matter realm as much as you like, and you make such tiny waves a person needs to be *really* looking to even notice. But you, fuck me. That last time you transferred, you went 'bang!' from the Mind realm *straight* into the Matter! Fuck me, girl, you made a bow-wave so big you tipped granny and gramps out of their grotty little coffins."

"Hold, on," I said. "You mean that was what left me exposed?"

Suddenly, my ruse of a conspiracy, that we were being played, didn't seem so far-fetched at all. I'd only needed to make that final transfer because Sool died and left me no option. Had he made a terrible mistake at the end, or was someone else working behind the scenes to throw me into Alan's path?

I felt his mocking mirth as an insipid prickling in my mind. "Bitch, you could certainly use a shot of whatever power Sool lent you right now!"

My brother was right.

And at the same time, he was terribly, terribly wrong.

Sool was already dead when I made my escape from the Mind realm. He had forced me into a position where I had to escape by myself, unassisted, and in my desperation I had generated enough power to throw myself all the way across to the Matter realm.

I only knew I was smiling when I saw a shift in Alan's expression.

"Oh, dearest brother. I actually *do* have that kind of power."

Suddenly panicked, he fired mindforce in an almost desperate reflex and I watched, unconcerned, as it rather failed to come at me much at all.

Ohh yes; I had a new toy.

The mindforce he was firing was still happening but very, very slowly. It billowed into existence between us, moment to moment. My brother, too, was moving incredibly slowly, each blink of his eyes a slow sultry gesture taking several moments to happen.

I knew what was happening but it was hard to conceive of – I had initially wondered if my mind had slowed down time but of course that's ridiculous.

No. My mind was just running so fast that my perception of time had been completely altered.

The mindforce my brother was still in the process of launching at me sat half-formed in the air before him. I swiped it away, almost casually.

I'd woken something in myself. Something I should probably package and sell to the masses.

His face was slowly beginning to register shock as I fired along a plane that made use of my new-found ability to look beyond normal dimensions. Even in slow motion, his move to throw out a wall of mindforce to protect himself hinted at desperation.

The utter haste of his response was shockingly uncharacteristic. I had taken him by complete surprise.

Poke my anus, I'd taken *myself* by surprise!

He scarcely had time to recognise that my attack was coming along an alternate dimension, reacting at the last instant in a way that reminded me of… well; me, a few days earlier, when *he* still held all the cards.

Oh, how things were changing now! What's that saying? The worm has turned? Fuck does that mean anyway?

Regardless, I was stronger now, which coupled with his loss of backup clones meant that this was a very, very different fight right now – perhaps our very first even match.

My brother, of course, had the same ability as me – I guess he just hadn't ever needed to use it much before. As we synchronised to each other's speed, our mind forces thrashed at each other.

A pressure point formed between us where our forcewalls met.

I guess he didn't fancy the fight so much anymore, because he suddenly snapped away from the Matter plane in a defensive transfer.

"Oh no you fucking *don't!*"

Sleek with power and the lust for the hunt, I opened my mind and threw out tendrils into the soupy mess of reality.

Finding a trail I lashed out and grabbed at my companions to pull them with me into the transfer, before realising that there was no longer a plural.

Pursuing him now sam

I grabbed him and launched us both after Alan. He might be planning to loop back around and hit me from behind, but now that I was looping back around behind *him*, it would be his arse that would get the razordick up it, not mine.

I didn't give a second's thought to whether I even *could* make the transfer, and perhaps that single-minded thinking worked in my favour, because instantly we cut through the buckling mulch of reality in a swirl of light and sound.

Facing my enemy, I was outdoors and in the midst of some new insanity.

It was a good news and bad news kind of situation.

The good news: Alan hadn't been planning to loop back on me, he had actually made a break for the border. I had finally pushed him onto the back foot.

The bad news: it was doubtful that my brother and I even needed to help each other out of our skins. The whole world was fucked beyond recognition.

Alan stood a few yards ahead of me, staring open-mouthed at the world as we had found it. I wanted to kill him. I didn't want to pity him. Yet, all of a sudden, in that moment, he looked so weak, so small, so like the little boy I had lost so long ago.

I decided to bide my time before veal-crating him; maybe I didn't need to any more, now.

We were no longer in the city and, impossibly, it was daytime. Perhaps it had been daytime in London, too; it was hard to say for sure when the decimation had stolen the sky. Who could really say if it was night or day there, really?

Above us, the sky was a vast and ominous grey vault, while out at the horizon there was a hint of crimson where the sunset ought to be, busily smearing burnt apricot light between the distant trees of a pleasant green copse.

We stood in the small garden of a quaint little cottage just big enough for an elderly couple to potter about in while they awaited the reaper, and beyond its neat drystone wall a twisting, pebbled country lane wound downhill to meet the warm, weary heft of nature's meadows in the afternoon glow.

All this, I could see. None of this was what lay before us, though, since although I could see what this place had once been I was confronted by the carnage of what it had become. Blotting out that idyllic world was the truth of what this place was now.

The once-carefully tended garden would have tipped my imaginary old couple over the edge. The lawn was shredded, the earth piled up in churned heaps against the low drystone garden wall, with the last protesting and splintered stems of rosebushes reaching desperately up from the mess as if trying to rise from the dead.

I felt myself teeter and glanced down in alarm.

The ground beneath our feet was evidently also quite far from stable.

A deep rumble juddered beneath my feet and set my leg muscles trembling, while the last of the little garden's paving stones vibrated, cracked and wept down into the earth, consumed.

The stones actually *vanished* into the mire of the earth before me!

"Sis!" Alan cried, voice shrill as he lunged at me and grabbed my arm. "Sis, we have to transfer away *now!*"

I shook free of his oily touch, ready to blast him if this was some new, sick tactic. Looking at his panicky face, however, I was quickly reassured that he was no longer a threat to me.

A distant bellowing roar building in my ears heralded a fearsome and clamorous assault on my senses and, as I stepped past Alan and squinted out into the distance, I was hit full in the eyes by a blinding white flash from beyond the far treeline.

Lightning punched free from the sky with a shriek and slammed into the earth where it burst five trees apart in a shower of splinters. A vast eruption of soil and rock was hurled into the air like a volcano of shit.

I threw my hands to my eyes as a blinding jagged after-image cut through my vision and whited it out but, even as my eyesight was quiesced, my mind pulsed and reacted as it sensed the incoming blastfront.

Force pushed out from within me, a shield around my frail collection of meat.

My brother did the same, reinforcing my wall with his own; the two walls knitting together.

Fierce hot wind punched at our defences, a little warm residual breeze seeping through to whip lightly across our faces.

We let our forcewalls unentwine and fold back into ourselves while I rubbed at my eyes and waited for the flash-blindness to subside, drawing a breath of warm damp air that reeked of eggy sulphur and the pungent smell of scorching.

As my eyesight normalised I was confronted by my brother's wild-eyed stare, right before me.

"Sis!" he bleated.

I pulled free from another despicable touch of my arm, his second, with my face hot and my belly boiling with rage.

"What?" I snapped at him. "You still wanna transfer, right? Well, sorry, but where the *fuck* do you suggest we transfer *to?*"

I was shocked at the venom boiling up out of me and heating my face.

Also stunned by my reaction, he gaped at me. "The emr, Laura. We can hide in the emr."

"You fucking idiot!"

I paused, grabbed a breath. I needed to get a hold of my rage.

I leant in toward his face. "This is happening everywhere, *Alan*, don't you get that even now? This realm is fucked! The Mind realm is fucked! The emr…"

He took a half step back and held up placating hands. "OK, sis, OK."

He had never looked quite so lost, so helpless. Nor quite so much of a little bitch.

I drew a ragged breath because I had emptied my lungs pouring venom onto him. Let it out as a sigh.

"Look at the sky if you don't believe me, *Alan*."

I saw a little fire return to his eyes at my repeated sarcasm in using his chosen name. But still, he looked up.

Above us, the lightning strike that had so blinded us had also ripped a vast gaping hole deep into the fabric of the grey-blue sky, a livid rip that now wept roiling red magma like a volcanic flesh wound. Fierce heat scorched our heads as, above us, a fluffy white cloud got too close to the infernal gash and shimmered and evaporated in an instant, while clots of magma drooled and threatened to drop onto the earth to sear it.

My brother looked at me, the ghost of what he has seen alive in his gaze.

"What the fuck we going to do, sis?"

I don't know what answer I would have given him but whatever it was, it was lost and forgotten as a shrill grinding shriek overshadowed all sound or thought and we both turned in alarm to see a new insanity unleashed.

With the merciless screech of hard stone clawing across glass, a shiny pure white building, all smooth angles and swirls of iridescent colour, birthed itself violently into existence right precisely where the little cottage stood.

The little English structure crumpled and burst apart in a spray of shattered stone, plaster and roofing.

We reflexively pushed out forcewalls to deflect the hurtling debris.

Sam came back into my field of view as he ducked close to me to take advantage of my protection.

I stared, empty-hearted, as the shiny new Mind building punched solidly into place and took up residence, vast and gleaming as it snuggled down atop the matchsticks and brick dust of the devastated cottage.

I squinted up at it.

It was similar to the structures we had seen in the white city of the Mind realm, but bigger, more elaborate, at least forty feet high with ornate loops and whirls carved into its flat, angular white façade, each swirling with embedded, iridescent pinks and greens that seemed to suggest flowing liquids beneath the surface. It was hard to focus on it, as if the matter comprising it were somehow not... real.

Of course, the building's matter wasn't real; it had no place in our universe.

Sam, already off-balance from diving behind my forcewall, slumped down onto his backside and decided to stay on the ground, his knees half-up and his hands dangling off them as he stared despondently up.

I guess even undead henchmen have their limits.

Alan reached a hand toward me again, with greater desperation. "Fuck, we can't stay here, Laura! Without the laws of physics, even the air we breathe...!"

I felt myself relaxing, shedding the immediacy of my own fear at the pleasure of witnessing his. "The Air We Breathe, eh? That's an old song!"

He looked at me, aghast. "How can you joke about it? How are you not scared of dying?"

I so wanted to slap him. "And how is it that you don't get that dying is the *least* of our worries? Think about it! Imagine your body losing all substance, falling apart, setting your consciousness adrift, undying, forever – like the Relics."

"Like the...?" His eyes widened at the realisation. "Oh."

I felt so full of myself. "Exactly."

He stared despondently but not, I now realised, at me.

"Oi. Alan."

He was staring back at where the cottage had been and I could feel immense despair from him, a deep, aching sense of loss; so deep, so intensely personal to him that I was now certain he had chosen this place for a reason.

"Peter?"

He was barely shielding his mind, which allowed me to skim his feelings, even his thoughts to a degree, so I could say with certainty that he'd dragged us all here because there had been something he had fully expected to find.

Something personal, familiar, comforting; but not a thing; rather, a person. He knew the former occupant of the little cottage.

I glimpsed a dull suit, the smell of tobacco; oldness; a name.

"Peter," I said. "Who's Graham?"

His eyes snapped over to meet my gaze. "What?"

"Graham," I repeated flatly.

His gaze darted free of mine. "No-one."

"Liar."

He sighed and his shoulders slumped a little. "It really doesn't matter any more, sis. He… He's no-one any more. I thought he might have been able to help me, but…" He shrugged. "He's gone, I can't even feel an after-echo."

I stared at him, waiting for more.

I think I was giving him the same look that Grandma always used to give me when I forgot to do my chores. Now, Alan was the one being a naughty girl, which made me – oh dear. They do say we all turn into our parents.

Alan huffed but resumed. "He was my… when I was a lost little kid, alone, after the accident–"

"After you killed our parents, you mean."

His expression hardened. "You want to hear this or not?"

I shrugged. "Sorry."

"Graham… helped me when I was a kid alone in a world that I was sure rejected me for what I was. He understood, he… like I say, he helped me."

"You can't seriously think I'm going to let you play the poor boy all alone in the… wait. You said he understood what you were; Peter, was he like us?"

He shrugged, despondent and useless. "Doesn't matter, he's gone."

I grabbed his arm. "Was he like *us?* Did he have our powers? Peter!"

"Yes, yes he did! Fuck, sis!" He shrugged free of me.

"Peter, wake the fuck up! He's our one small chance in a world of giant fuck! Show him to me!"

His stupid face frowned at me. "*Show* him to…?"

I tapped a finger on my temple with the vigour of irritation. "Share your mindview, penis!"

He gave a brief, embarrassed chuckle. "Oh, yeah. Sorry."

The briefest touch of our minds showed me a rough, grey old man, tall and gaunt, his face blank, expressionless and yet full of intensity.

It was familiar, it seemed to be a face I knew.

"I know him," I murmured. I looked to my brother. "Why do I know that face?"

"You don't," he asserted. "You can't."

I had a moment where I almost grasped that loose thread of recognition, but then I was distracted by the return of a most unexpected presence, crossing the fields.

-54-

A short and slender human form was approaching us.

I felt a build-up of power from my brother as he prepared to attack and hastily threw out a hand, palm-out. "Wait," I urged. "Just a second!"

"What!" he snapped, irritated, his righteous rage burning hot like his mindforce. "That fucking–"

I touched my brother's arm. "Trust me; we're not enemies on this one."

His gaze touched mine and he felt my truthfulness.

Sni Sool's flat, blank face was aimed at me alone as he walked calmly toward us.

"Edward," said the little man.

A random and rather incongruous word, it nonetheless pulled forth the memory of that gentle, crumbling old man, such that my thoughts turned to a vivid recollection of his terrible end at Sam's hand; at Alan's hand. My brother, somewhat aware of my thoughts even as he held his mindforce in check at my request, felt apprehensive and angry to me as he sensed what Sool was doing.

The Realm Sentinel, still approaching us, continued to reel off names.

"James William St Vincent. Cheryl Ann Donahue, Susan Marie Blake."

There was a ping at the base of my skull as Alan's mindforce threatened to spill over alongside his hateful rage of Sool.

"Please, Peter," I appealed, "Don't let him manipulate either of us again!"

"Ronald Martin Quaid," the Sentinel continued. "Dorothy Judith Esagen, Jennifer May Sullivan, Thomas Lionel Peters."

"Enough, Sool!" I barked at him, surprised by the venom in my tone. "My brother wants to unleash hell on you, and right now, I'm not sure if I want to stop him."

My own mindforce began to build, throttling up to match the pent-up output from my brother.

Sool paused in his approach. "You hear the names of the most recent to die by the Other's hand, LauraKeeble, yet you turn your anger to me?"

I wrestled control of my emotions, pushed down the lethal extremes of my power, but left a residual level of mindforce bubbling in reserve for now. "I don't like being manipulated," I told him.

"This so." Sool cocked his head. "And the latest to die… the one you called Tom."

It seemed as if he wanted to piss me off.

"I've warned you about manipulating me, Sool – I won't fucking have it! And you're wrong, so get your fucking facts straight. It was *Ben* who died last, not Tom!"

"Of little matter," the small man said airily. "Merely, I call out only the extent of the Other's—"

Alan barked a harsh laugh. "You hear that, sis? Of little matter, the life of a human being; now who's the bastard?"

I glanced at him. "The jury is still out."

"Is your mission forgotten, LauraKeeble? Might you imagine the Other will not destroy *you*?"

Alan cocked an eyebrow at me. "Gotta wonder, eh, sis?"

I did have cause to wonder, in that moment, as it was clear that Sool was desperate that I destroy Alan whether there was anything left to fight for or not, which led me to wonder how much else had been manipulation on Sool's part.

I returned my attention to the Realm Sentinel.

"Tell me," I demanded. "Who is Graham?"

Without waiting for Sool to answer I turned to my brother and spoke at the same time as I sent him a low-intensity thought that would fall, I hoped, beneath Sool's notice.

"Here's the thing, Peter. Sool has lied about a lot of things to me, but I think, now, that maybe he deceived you even more."

I sent a thought.

It was Graham's face, the same image that Alan had shared with me; except this time I overlaid it with an image of Sni Sool Techkatha in his fake human form, let the two false faces blend, to show my brother that they were the same lie, told twice with a little cosmetic tweaking.

"No," Alan breathed.

"As soon as you showed me Graham, I could see it, Peter. The only reason I can think why you haven't seen it yourself, is that the Sentinels somehow blocked you from noticing. They gave you a mentor just when you needed one, and they've been pulling your strings ever since."

He floundered at this revelation. "No, sis, that... no."

And then, without word or gesture, I sent him another image; of he and I slowly edging apart and creating a pincer movement around Sool, placing the Sentinel in a kill zone should we need it.

Alan flashed me a look that I took as assent.

To distract the Sentinel as we opened out, one step at a time, to each side of him, I feigned an outburst that was only partly put on, to be honest.

"You manipulated us *both*, Sool!" I yelled at him, stepping slowly away from my brother but focusing hard on my words so the Sentinel would not read our intent. "Why? *Why* did you do it? Why set Peter up to destroy the universe and then set me up to destroy *him*?"

And as fake as my outburst had begun, it led to a shocking epiphany.

I stopped dead and stared at the Sentinel.

"The same reason you faked your own death in the Mind realm, forcing that clumsy-arsed transfer that flagged me up to him! You don't need *me* to destroy *him*. You needed us to destroy *each other*."

Manipulated from the outset, everything I had fought for, watched friends die for, turned into a lie, I could contain myself no longer.

My boiling seething rage exploded from me in a lashing whip of mindforce that engulfed Sool completely. Had he been a human, or one of Alan's slaves, he would have been annihilated, but Sool was made of stronger stuff and had his own defences.

There was a savage flash of white light laced with glistening black veins, as he pushed my force away but I pushed back hard and he remained engulfed, unharmed but trapped immobile in a vice-tight web of crackling mind energy; invisible but for the occasional spark as our opposing powers bristled against each other.

"Release me *now*, Laura Keeble!" He cried. "This has only futility!"

He was right, I could not hold him like this for long, but the idea of just setting him free…? No, he had taken everything from me, and all for his self-serving agenda, his lies and half-truths.

His bland alien face really did show an expression now, as his pinned body and quiesced mind struggled beneath the density of my snare. An expression of rage, causing his unaccustomed facial muscles to dance around his narrowed eyes. He continued to push against his bonds, but they held – for now.

My head was starting to ache. He was too strong!

Suddenly, the pressure on my head decreased and yet the power of the prison holding Sool increased. Reinforced, it shut him down; immobile, his mindpowers quiesced. I let out a gasp and wiped sweat off my eyebrow, only now aware that I had started to perspire.

Alan glanced at me. "I got your back, sis."

"Go team," I muttered drily.

"Look, we're in this together, now. Whatever our lying beak-faced friend might've told you, it was Graham who encouraged me to go play in the realms; I don't know I'd have ever done it without him."

Sool was immobile and looked as furious as his relatively expressionless face permitted. "Release me and–"

I shook my head. "Talk first. If Graham was the reason my brother started playing in the emr, then you must've wanted it – but then you decided to use me to stop him; well, to kill him, which is much the same thing. So, what changed?"

He held my gaze for a moment. "You know, LauraKeeble, that there are two universes. Matter came first, at the start, but with sentient life came a new energy, a force unknown, of thought. Thought defies the physics, fails to conform, creates chaos. We emerged as Sentinels. We forced thought into a… bottle."

I nodded. "I know. The Mind universe."

He tried to nod and the invisible prison around him glowed and crackled for a moment. Instead he spoke. "Yes correct."

"Not hearing anything new, Sool," said Alan, sighing. "It's a pocket universe. Big whoop."

"Bottle is better word," Sool replied with a little seasoning of disdain. "Thought energy pours in through the neck and stays in, can be contained, only accessed when needed. Dreams, so to say."

"The emr," I said. "But why encourage Peter to damage it?"

Sool hesitated, fell silent.

"Sool?"

"We Sentinels protect the realms but we can only live outside them, in the interstice, there is a… local guardian for each realm. The Esagen was that which enacts our will in the Matter realm, but he was… damaged by a human war and slowly failed. The Keeble woman had some power and she conceived, so we expected the power to pass on."

"To Mumma," Alan murmured.

"We found no Keeble descendants, but meanwhile the Esagen's failing mind intruded on our realm, damaged the interstice, we halted him but… too late."

"Wait," said Alan. "Found no Keeble descendants? You think that's our family name?"

I sighed. "That's why he keeps calling you 'the other Keeble'. Grandpa made me change my name when they adopted me, but I hated him so I changed to Grandma's maiden name; but, Sool, other than that, there were no members of our family with that name for years."

"Yes correct. We lost the existence of a whole generation but finally, a power surge and we found the Other, who had concealed his name."

Alan laughed. "I was using my real name, you idiot."

The power surge that had led them to him had to be my brother's first major use of his powers, to create the accident that killed our parents.

I suspected Sool was dragging his story out to distract us, because I could feel him trying to discreetly build up mindforce beneath our shroud, so, glancing over at Alan, I pushed out with a little more force to block him, hoping my brother would take the hint to do likewise. He did.

I made no reference to it, choosing to simply proceed with the interrogation of my treacherous new enemy.

"And once you found Peter, you put him to work to destroy the emr. Why the hell would you do that? How does that protect the realms?"

"No, no, no," said Alan. "Don't you see? Their agenda had already changed."

I felt irritated; Sool and my brother were playing that annoying game, now, the one that always boiled my piss. The 'we know something you don't know' game.

"Explain, please," I snapped.

Alan sighed. "Grandpa lost control of his powers, he damaged the interstice realm; the realm they live in, which is a juncture state formed from fused aspects of all the realms. They live there, and they breed there."

"So?"

"In a place where the laws of its nature are a fusion of Mind and Matter. A merge-state universe."

Oh, fuck.

"Like what's going to be left after this is over…"

I stared up for a moment at the burgeoning red maelstrom of the sky, took in the countryside where, even now, trees and fields were being rolled up and replaced wholesale by weird structures that did not belong here.

I rounded on Sool. "Is that what this is all about? Destroy the emr, collapse the realms together and you get a whole new reality to live and breed in?"

Sool thrashed against us and I felt a hard ping at the base of my skull. Alan's mind chocked up against mine again and a solid wavefront pushed through me and locked our little alien friend into place even more tightly than before.

We were not going to be able to hold him forever, though.

He fixed his beady little faux-human eyes on me. "You understand nothing," he stated in a far colder and more clinical voice than I had ever heard him use before. "Our reality was unravelling, our hatchings failed, our kind began to die in the only universe we could thrive within. Did I owe my allegiance to a species who had caused this, or to my own kind? Answer that, LauraKeeble!"

I was aghast. I suspect my mouth hung open before I spoke. "You're murdering *all* life to save yourselves?"

"It is *survival!*" he hissed at me.

"You used me, Sool!"

I was sickened to feel hot tears well up in my eyes, like some soppy schoolgirl who got dumped at the dance, so I bit my own tongue angrily and drew a harsh breath. "You used me, manipulated me to… wait. Why did you need me?"

I need to structure this to reflect the two key facts: they are half the power each,

It was my brother who answered me. "We come from Grandpa, but we're half each, sis, the power got split between us, but I reckon they realised that if we ever joined up, merged our powers together…"

With a mind-shriek worse than a thousand distorting guitars, Sool threw a huge weight of mindforce against the prison we'd constructed.

It crumpled. He burst free.

The Sentinel lunged forward, his diminutive human form peeling away to allow his vastly taller, beaked, grey-green, reptilian form to erupt, its weird yellow downswept beak stretched open, the bulging, insectoid fly eyes either side of the beak catching the red light of the dying sky as it erupted first from its humanlike pupa, before shattering our mindforce barrier.

My brother and I both pushed power out and, as we did he offered more of himself and I let that greater amount of him flow into me, a thrill of terror running through me at the thought that I might lose myself in this merging and yet sure that this was the only way to face the Realm Sentinel that we now knew wanted only our destruction.

I heard my meat voice cry out as something new and deeply fundamental seized control of me.

I was becoming... *we* were becoming... something new.

Sool closed on us fast, his screech of alien rage hideous in our mind. Sam, however, came from nowhere and swiped the Sentinel with a big, solid arm. The reptilian staggered back but brute force was surely no weapon against it.

Peter...

I hear you sis

We entwined ever tighter even as our meat bodies locked immobile and useless and fell into irrelevance behind us as we pushed into each other and began to become a single other thing.

Beyond the core of our union self, we had already begun to generate an energy field that was us and yet separate from us – our merged mindself creating a gloriously potent level of thought energy that built into something dreadfully beautiful.

we have to stop the atrophy

My mind.

I felt him agree, from somewhere within us.

would stopping them take all this back?

His mind? I struggled to tell whose thought was whose.

Sam was swiped away from us by mindforce emanating from the reptilian Sentinel who now reared up ready to take us on for the final time, but even as that threat solidified for us, we saw a new and greater challenge.

A blinding white slice of light had split the universe open a few yards from us, clawing itself into being, pushing wider and brighter. Pulsing out from either side of it marched a dense wall of blackness that tore up earth and ripped down sky as they pushed hungrily out across our world, our universe.

But back within that dazzling rip I saw, faintly against the incandescence, a glimpse of many, many jostling humanoid shadows, flaky against the blinding glare but moving inexorably nearer and growing more solid with every passing second as they crossed over from their side of the aperture.

Sool's beaked kin, the Sentinels, were coming to claim their new home. All of them, by the look of it.

-55-

I felt the orb re-ignite as Sam rolled back up onto his feet. Sool sensed him and spun but was too slow. A wicked black thought knot slammed into the Sentinel and engulfed him. The force of it slapped the beaked creature clean off his feet and he hit the ground, dust puffing up around him. He lay writhing as the mass engulfed him, hissing and bubbling.

No matter.

Individuals would live or die. I no longer cared.

The mass of tall, slender figures squirmed and pressed against the thin membrane between their swirling corridor of light and our universe; they would soon finish emerging from that shimmering haze to take this world, this entire universe, once and for all time, so that, now, finally, the moment had come to step up or fall.

It was now or never.

are we sure about this?

My brother's thought. I shared his doubt but could not risk admitting it for fear that it would simply overwhelm me.

I think we have to

are you afraid?

I was aware of seeing, for perhaps the last time, our meat bodies standing close to each other, but I was no longer that thing – the me that I identified with, the me that mattered, was not that flesh.

It was strange. I was aware of being afraid without really *feeling* it, as if it were someone else's fear, or the fear one might affect for a character in a book or a game.

Fear no longer mattered.

we won't survive by running away Peter

I say we go down fighting

So certain, now, so ready for this fight; had I ever really just been plain old Laura, with her career and her dreams of falling in love and living a vanilla life until death came to move her across the board for the last time?

This panoply of thoughts, of doubts, of to-and-from with my brother, had taken but a second. Now, Sool's vast hoard, wave after wave of beaked creatures, were erupting from the white fissure to thump down onto the crumbled earth, still just inside the fiery whiteness of the rift's perimeter, still trapped inside but only just as they reached into the physical world, just beyond its boundary.

will stopping them really change anything?… our world is gone now

His thought. Doubt, fear; I understood it but I no longer felt it.

I hope it does … but honestly I'll settle for taking some of them with us if not

Blinding white light, as dazzling as the rift itself, snapped from glowing discs on several of the emerging beaked creatures' chests, cutting through the membrane into our realm and snapping out in sizzling arcs that cut the air all around Sam, forcing him to dive for cover in a small crater behind an already-scorched but solid tree.

The energy arcs from the discs met the rough hard bark and sent a flare full of sparks, heat and splinters outwards. More energy discharges joined and pulse after pulse punched through the wood, rapidly shredding the tree to get to Sam.

While some of the beaked creatures continued this attack, a number of others suddenly disregarded Sam and turned their attention onto their real targets – Alan and me.

let's do this then, sis

His reassurance that we were now in this together was welcome but changed nothing. I opened my mind and, just as I did, saw Sool rising to his feet just a short distance from us.

I folded into my brother's welcoming embrace, our mind selves coalescing, and was faintly aware of our meat bodies doing the same.

The Sentinel had defeated Sam's thought knot, perhaps because such weapons could not really harm his kind, or perhaps because the laws of physics were dying and this was now becoming his realm. Regardless, although his long body seemed more twisted, his bland clothing scorched here and there by orb energy, he showed no sign of faltering in his resolve as his sharp, downswept beak parted I heard a shrill alien shriek much like a war-cry.

His glinting insectoid eyes seemed flooded with contemptuous hatred for us, although perhaps this was the last vestige of my human emotional self projecting even as it withered from me and I felt my brother's mind swirling within mine, mine within his as we extruded, blended, left our meat bodies far behind to become this new thing.

And then the disc on Sool's chest flare bright.

Our meat bodies, which had stood vacant as we hung formless just beyond our enemies' perception, still stood in an embrace that weakly mirrored the wondrous merging of our mind selves. Bodies that were instantly incinerated, standing silent and proud for a moment, as searing power snapped from Sool and cut away their flesh to strip them instantly back to bone, then to marrow, then to ash.

My body collapsed first, then his, the remains reduced to a pitifully small amount of powder.

With the threat we presented removed, Sool issued another cry and joined his emerging kin in eliminating Sam.

The big man had seen our demise, but now, as every Sentinel pumped energy at the pathetic remnants of his cover, he gritted his teeth and tried to find his feet, rolling from his crater to dive for new cover. Sool's disc coiled out a fierce scolding beam that snapped forth and burst the orb in his hand, blasting the big man off his feet, the stench of cooking meat in the air as he tumbled back into the little crater that he had just tried to flee.

At least Sam's miserable, unwanted second life would now come to an end.

The Sentinels had misjudged the situation, however, by assuming our eradication. Although we had been deprived forever of our flesh, our way back to human existence, we were far from powerless. Our minds existed bodiless, now entirely unconstrained by our meat selves and the weaknesses and corruptions inherent within such forms. Fear was of the flesh; the dread of pain, the anxious need to avoid death at all costs.

Such worldly matters no longer troubled us. Our meat was gone, and the desire to return to it, equally so. Our only need was to complete the process we had begun as humans – to merge into what we should always have been, what the fluke of our birth had prevented.

I had, while my body lived, retained a sense of me. Now, far more potently than before I understood the perfection of that which now emerged. I felt no specific emotion, just an overwhelming warmth in our *us*ness, a need to shrug off 'Alan', or 'Laura' and complete our transformation – no; our *reversion*.

In the empty air where our bodies had stood, against the sterile white backdrop of the emerging Mind world, we formed.

It is hard to imagine what Sam must have seen. Badly burnt, standing hunched and blackened and bleeding, we saw the expression fall off his mottled black and red face as his jaw dropped and his lidless eyes stared at the space which we occupied..

Our power swelled. We were new, and we *knew*, understood the potential our mergeform could harness.

Many of the beaked Sentinels were fully through the fold in reality that would soon finish admitting them to their paradise; many more were pushing eagerly against the membrane to join in.

And we forbade it.

We saw the fold in the universe. We grasped it and drew it brutally up and wrenched it stretchily toward us, expanding it in our perception like a rubber sheet over the heads of the massed hordes of Sentinels, although we knew it existed in at least seven dimensions. We drew the sheet to us and we pulled it down so it draped over the myriad Sentinels filling the swirling plains that had once been England's greenglorious countryside, immersing their alien bodies beneath and within a forcewall that they could neither perceive nor conceive.

There were cries from beneath the sheet.

Alien cries, certainly, but cries nonetheless of anguish, of terror, their victory snatched from them when they had been assured of its certainty. We could perceive their forms writhing, sunk into the dense quasi-physical slurry like wasps fallen into honey.

The might of the gateway they had made for themselves had been turned against them and, now, their cries and pleas were as pitiful before us as their hatred of humankind had been merciless against us.

stop!

The voice was Sool's.

He had somehow avoided the fate of his kith and stood aside from the cataclysmically stretched fissure in all universes. He stood there, tall, beaked and graceful, his arms open in a conciliatory gesture but his fear stinking of rotten ponds in summer.

it does not have to be this way, LauraKeeble

His appeal was meaningless, yet we deigned to answer.

Your kind have earnt their destruction through the violation of their eternal duty
Through betrayal of the trust placed with them

Our voice was new even to us; a shockingly alien matrix of fact and data rather than soundwaves in air.

Sool's insectoid eyes remained blank and glinting but his thoughts were filled with fear, with despair, yet with the weak hope that he might reason with that part of us that had been LauraKeeble.

what choice was there for us? Dying came to our realm, when all we had done was serve the universe for all of time. What help for us, LauraKeeble; what justice?

We care nothing for your fate
You have brought it on yourselves

His kind were ours to judge, it was our right and we had no interest in his appeals.

He bent his knees and held out his hands to us.

LauraKeeble, have pity on us. We have nowhere to go back to. Our home, our reality, is no more

You imagine we mean to send your people anywhere at all
We do not

Sool fell onto his knees now, a very human act of attrition for so inhuman a being, as he appealed desperately to us.

Please! A moment!

His thoughts were loud, panicked, like a scream to us.

Mercy! Please, mercy —for our hatchlings! For them at least…
Please!

We cared to hear no more.

We touched his body and his mind and we lit him afire. A blinding flash and a wrenching alien screech concluded Sni Sool Techkatha's existence, his body immolated where he still knelt in his final appeal.

We regretted that he was to be spared the more enduring fate awaiting the rest of his kind, but the deed was done. He had been granted a more merciful death than he deserved.

Power swelled within us and then we sent it out like a hand pushing a toy boat out onto the lake. The density mass engulfing the race of the Sentinels snapped inward and collapsed, tending toward a null state of existence and occupying no spacetime at all.

Shrieking sentinels of many different ages were folded into it and entombed, their bodies crushed but their minds 'alive', whatever that might mean, in the formless void.

Disembodied, condemned to impotent consciousness now and forever in a nothingness between all universes; a place where no-one could ever find them, help them or even be aware of them.

Perhaps some hatchlings or young might have been spared. We were not a force of conscience, so it was not our matter to ponder.

The chaos of the collapsing realms stopped, ending in a single instant.

The aperture the Sentinels had created was no longer even a single point, inverted into nothingness, and without that engine, the pull that had crumpled the emr reduced and the strain on that bridging realm eased.

The damage was not reversed, but the survival of the emr re-asserted some little stability. Now, there was no further bleeding of realm into realm.

The realms would survive but only as they now were, and as such they were unfit for anything living to survive within them.

With a final defiant flash and a crash of thunder the storm flooding the world abruptly ended.

Absolute silence fell.

It was not the world we had known, but at least something of reality had survived. It seemed a hollow victory. The treacherous Sentinels had betrayed the realms they had been sworn to protect, so we alone remained to hold on to that precious duty.

But there was so little left to protect. Perhaps the last living being on this world was the chimera, Sam.

For our parents...

A paradox – this last was not our voice. It was a singular voice; an individual in the space where only our mergeform existed.

For all my wrongs...

A faint sense of a thought, a distant whisper from within us and yet not *us*, not the mergeform.

For my sister...

The ground slammed up beneath my feet.

My feet.

Me.

I frowned, aware of flesh to form such an expression, the weird sensation of expressing myself through the movement of meat. Of flesh.

My flesh.

"I… I don't…"

It was an alien voice, yet familiar.

My voice. The voice of a woman who had died in battle. Laura.

My body had been burnt along with my brother's form, there was nothing physical left of either of us. This made no sense.

Through eyes of meat and liquid I focused on the sight of Sam, staring into the distance somewhere before me.

"Ss…Sam!" I managed to call, finding the constraint of flesh too heavy to control precisely. "What… happened?"

Sam turned sharply.

I stared at him in the silent grey gloom of semi-day and he stared back, his damaged hand clasped in the other, less damaged one, his face dirty but intact. He was his old self still, although his expression as he looked at me suggested that, maybe, I was not.

"Sam?"

"You…" Sam's beautiful, dirty face crumpled into a frown. "You *died*, Laura. I *saw* you, you died!"

I had no words to offer him, because it made no sense to me, either. One moment I had been *we*; an ethereal non-flesh self, and the next… here.

I noticed a black undulating puddle of squid ink hovering in the air, between us but slightly off to the right. It was dark but a little translucent, like a cloud that had got itself lost and dropped down out of the reddened scolded sky above us.

"Is that…" I tried to ask.

Was that what I had been?

"It was thicker," Sam replied. "Before you came back. It was thicker."

I understood, and my eyes of meat and liquid let go of liquid tears. "Shit. He sent me back."

"I don't…"

I turned to the giant. "Oh, Sam. He gave me back my body, set me free so he could take the burden alone."

Sam hesitated for a moment. "Burden?"

A meat and bone hand wiped salt tears from my cheek, seeming to trivialise the depth of meaning in those glistening droplets.

How could I hope to explain the depth of the sacrifice that had just been made?

"We… we understood that stopping the Sentinels just isn't enough, it doesn't change anything. Everyone's still dead if it stays like this, Sam. It's not enough."

Sam took a hesitant step toward me. "I of all people understand that hopeless problem, Laura."

I shook my head.

An odd sensation but the body slowly feeling natural, more like my home again, now. "No," I said. "Not hopeless, just something that demands a terrible price. We have–"

I hesitated, suffering my separation from my brother's essence with a cruel ache of the gut and soul.

"We *had* the means to roll this back, to push our essence into the emr and heal the realms."

Sam took another step, his expression softer than I could ever recall seeing it before. "Then surely that is *good?*"

"The price, Sam, is that our essence would be consumed by the process. We can heal the universe but it will take everything we've got. Literally."

"He can do it alone?"

I shrugged.

I had no idea if my brother's essence would be enough. Perhaps he had stolen a little more of our merged self, given me less than my fifty per cent share when he re-made me.

"It should've been both of us," I said flatly, my gaze returning to the undulating form in the air before me.

"It does not sound like my master to make such a sacrifice, Laura."

"No."

"I think maybe he's trying to make up for everything, Sam. The way you helped me to make up for–"

for you, Laura...

A thought, rippling out from the amorphous essence before us.

so that something of our family lives on...

I frowned, glanced at Sam, saw that he had not heard anything.

The floating pool of squid ink in the air before us suddenly solidified sharply, punching hard into reality like quick setting concrete.

Solid and black, it was an irredeemable ink stain on the satin finish of reality.

Alan was erased from my memory in that moment, and only my dear sweet Peter remained, smiling at me as he so often had before our lives were torn apart.

"Goodbye," I murmured, pressure turning wet within my eyes.

There was a pulse of... sound, or perhaps power? A final, brutal, throbbing undulation tore through the black mass and then it convulsed, the edges cracking and little splinters pinging free, as real and solid as the scarred countryside around us now. Then, the whole thing collapsed in on itself and crumpled down into a dot that emitted a single-point blinding glow of laser-sharp white light.

Sam and I stood in an ocean of silence, waiting for the obscenely tiny remains of my brother to fade.

"Goodbye," I said again, to that little point of light.

What else could I say?

The glow faded, that last ember of my brother slipping down beyond all human perception. Then, even the after-image of the now extinguished point of light faded from my eyes and I had nothing left of him at all.

I felt the weight of Sam's hand on my shoulder. His good hand, I vaguely hoped.

"What happened?" he asked.

I gave a weak shrug. "He's gone, Sam. I don't even know if it worked."

He placed a kind arm over my shoulder and eased me back, away from that spot that was holding me fixated.

"Come along."

We stepped carefully over the ashen physical remains of my original body, and of my brother's only body.

A new body. Shocking. I had a new body, so what, I had to wonder, did that make me? Still human, or another like Sam?

The light was poor, a gloomy twilight now the grey sky had lost its volcanic glow. The rips and rents still hung up there, but black and foreboding, cold and deprived of the power of the emergent reality that had been cast back by my brother's final act. The scarred and flattened wasteland around us was partially obscured in the darkness, and perhaps just as well as Sam guided me carefully away from the shore of the Sentinels' tsunami.

I thought a voice spoke my name. Would have ignored it, except that Sam stiffened and slowed.

We stopped and his arm fell from me as we turned.

"Laura?" the voice appealed again.

I felt a cold glaze seal over me as I turned to face Jennifer Sullivan.

"Jen," I uttered coldly. "How fitting! Only someone as hateful and worthless as *you* would have survived all this."

Jen's painted face was smeared with grime, but there was something more. Under the last of her makeup, under the smudges, Jen was turning *grey*.

"Laur, I'm sorry, I was just so scared and now…"

She was interrupted by a vicious hacking cough that doubled her over.

I hate to admit that a very cruel smile peeled my lips back. "Oh dear, Jen. You do *not* look well. Do you know what's happening to you? Do you know what's *going* to happen to you, now there's no-one to hold back the atrophy for you?"

"Help me?"

"No."

I turned my back on her.

If I'd thought for one second she stood a chance, I'd have cut her down and left her shredded on the ground. But no. As the remnants of my brother's will healed the emr he had helped to break, she was trapped in a universe where she simply could not exist, so she was going to suffer a far uglier, slower death without my merciful hand, and she'd have to suffer it all alone.

Good.

I walked away, aware I was trembling and unsure whether it was my rage, or my grief, or the fear of what awaited me that made me shake so hard.

Behind me, I could hear her whining appeals to Sam.

"Go, Jennifer," I heard him say. "You will get no help here. Make the most of the little time you have left."

Her sobs, her cries, faded behind us as Sam stepped up beside me and we started out onto the barren plains of our dead world.

Sam and I walked in silence, not touching, just contentedly together, side by side.

"How's the hand?"

"Painless," he answered. "And useless."

Out at the horizon, I glimpsed a disturbance. It looked like a sandstorm, seen from a distance. I suspected it was not a sandstorm.

"Your brother's work?" Sam asked. He had seen it, too.

"My brother, eh?" I cast a smile up at him. "Not your *master* anymore."

Sam, for the first time, I think, actually chuckled. "No, Laura. Not my master."

"Huh. Good for you."

He cast his glance away, his expression suddenly hard to read.

"What?" I asked. "You're free."

Sam nodded at that distant disturbance. "Am I?"

We walked for a bit. It just made sense to keep moving in the face of such stillness.

Sam stared out at that horizon, probably to avoid my gaze. "Do you remember our deal?"

"Had enough of me already?"

I was trying to laugh it off, but he really was the only friend I had left at the end of everything.

"I'm serious."

"I know."

It was tough for me. I did owe him his death.

"I may still need you. Sam. Can we... can we wait a little while, see what that cloud out there brings?"

"And then?"

412

I nodded. "My promise stands."

We stopped walking and he looked down at me, a terrible sorrow obvious behind the smile he tried to use to reassure me.

"I understand," he said.

I took his huge hand, the good one not the gory one, and felt his grateful grip, firm but gentle.

We walked on through our mortally wounded world, a half-place that would remain dead for all eternity unless my brother had pulled off his final trick.

Far ahead of us, beginning to fill the horizon, the disturbance now resembled a burgeoning storm-front, a whipped-up mass of dust and debris.

"Perhaps this is a fitting punishment for me," Sam finally said as we trudged through the white sand and ash on a seemingly unending plain. "That I should live on and carry the memory of those I killed."

"Their immortality through your unending suffering?" I let go of his hand and turned to face him. "That's a bit too fucking poetic for my blood, sweetie."

He grinned at me. "Perhaps poetry is all I have left."

"Oh, do leave off, for fuck's sake," I said, grinning back at him.

His grin faded. "Are you curious?" he asked.

"I suppose. Will you and I even exist in a newly reset world, will the change that's coming change us, or just delete us? It's not like either of us really belong to the Earth, or even the Matter realm, any longer."

"I suppose," he answered, "that we don't know much at all."

"No. So, what do we know?"

Sam squinted at the horizon as the first glare of our single sun re-emerged above to pierce the iron vault.

"There's a storm coming in," he said, by way of a non-answer.

"Yeah." I grabbed his hand and gave it a squeeze. "Tell me something I don't know."

~ End ~

ABOUT THE AUTHOR

DSw Shaw is a fictional construct, a nightmare hidden within a cuddly bear, or perhaps it is merely the words, made sentient in this book for you, dear reader.

Find out less at Shaw's website –
https://www.dsw-shaw.co.uk/

www.ingramcontent.com/pod-product-compliance
Lightning Source LLC
Chambersburg PA
CBHW060140260626
47160CB00001B/63